Teague Wars

Emerald X

PHASE 1

Written by Brandon Hoy

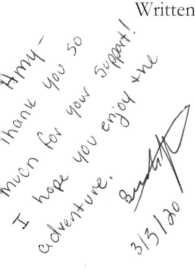

Amy—
Thank you so
much for your support!
I hope you enjoy the
adventure.

Brandon
3/3/20

OWL
PUBLISHING

Owl Publishing, LLC.
150 Parkview Heights Road, Ephrata PA 17522

717-925-7511

www.owlpublishinghouse.com

ISBN: 978-1-949929-37-9

Library of Congress Control Number: In Process

I dedicate this book to my grandmom;

forever my inspiration.

ACKNOWLEDGEMENTS

I want to thank everyone who has ever taken the time to read my material and encouraged me to keep pursuing my dream. Thank you to Krista, Jill, Duane, and especially the A-team at Giuseppe's in Skippack for reading the ever evolving versions of my book. I also want to thank my English teachers, specifically Mrs. Cook and Mrs. Masciantonio, for using their spare time to entertain their student's writing and providing wonderful feedback.

CHAPTER 1

Light sprinkled through the discolored glass overlooking the school grounds. A young man watched as children ran after one another, not a single worry following behind them. Their cries of joy barely cracked the still air of the school hallway as he patiently waited. He knew the rest of Luminar's elementary school students were restlessly squirming in their seats. One class was especially eager as they waited in anticipation to hear a well-known tale told by their local idol. Him.

The man continued observing the fledglings that had barely experienced ten years since their Creation Day. He thought intensely about the story he was preparing to present and his own heritage. His city, Luminar, was one of the five great cities built in his country, Osiren. Osiren had the most land between its borders on their planet, Teague. Teague has four countries total: Osiren, Bancouver, Ventaceny, and EverCrest. Ventaceny bordered Osiren to the left while EverCrest drifted off its east coast with the Marvelous Ocean between them. Bancouver covered their northern tier, experiencing all three suns that floated above Teague. He silently smiled and shook his head, happy he had never to endure the intense heat and extended summer.

His attention shifted to the endless sea of metal cabinets that lined the hallways. He was to wait for the signal before entering his assigned classroom. His fingers drifted into his smooth, brown hair. It had been less than two centuries since the Protectors walked Teague, back when EverCrest was not separated by water, and thus creating the single mass known as Kairos. Only their ancestors had known this world. *It is quite the blessing to have been created in this era.* As all mortals must, the Protectors time had come. Once the power transfer from parent to child was complete, the Protectors' children separated Kairos into the structure in place today. They each governed their selection of land, naming it and ruling as they saw fit. After they passed onto Teague as well, the Era of Silence ensued for the following hundred years. This was a time where the living mourned the loss of their Protectors and their offspring, and focused on the restructuring of their economy. The Era of Beginning became the following century.

And thank the Protectors he had the privilege of existing in a time where the larger matters had been settled.

A creak bounced between the lockers catching his attention and breaking his thoughts. A new source of light penetrated the dull environment before him as a door had fully opened. *Ah, there is my cue.*

"Children . . . children, please, quiet down. We have a very special guest that is honoring us with his appearance today, thus, please give a warm welcome to the heir of our city, Prince Joshua." The teacher moved aside to allow the Prince to receive the class' undivided attention. The kids clapped as the Prince walked to the middle of the room. Handing the teacher his black overcoat with silver linings, he towered over the children as he stood before them. Gazing at the crowd of innocence, he lowered himself to the floor. Once he crossed his legs, he creased his black pants and adjusted his white button up—making sure it was neatly tucked away. The children inched closer to him, copying his crossed-legs. Squirming on the carpet, they stared at the man with glossy eyes.

The Prince overlooked each child with an adoring smile before he began speaking to the sea of youth: "Thank you, my young friends. I have been cordially invited to speak with the young men and women of Mrs. Triage's third grade class. Your teacher thought it'd be a fun idea for someone like me to explain the tale of how our precious land of Osiren came to be. I hope that's acceptable?"

All the children laughed as they nodded and encouraged the Prince to continue. Mrs. Triage chimed in, "They are never this excited to listen to *my* lectures."

The kids laughed once more. Prince Joshua smiled, "I'm sure it is nothing personal, ma'am. Now, this tale has been passed down through generations. A long time ago, Osiren had landscapes only an artist could perfect. The horizon matched the sky with its array of colors as the suns would set for the evening. The world was a beautiful and rich place. The countries were all connected by land. This single continent was known as Kairos. Flowers bloomed, and animals of all different species pranced around carefree. Everyone lived in peace and harmony, side by side, without a worry. We were under the supervision of the Protectors, Kyrudorous and Zorumaka. This glorious era was known as the Prophets' Prophecy."

A hand shot up from the crowd, eagerly trying to attain the Prince's attention. Before the little girl almost wet herself, Joshua allowed her to speak. Bouncing up she asked, "Why was that time called that? Uh, Yo-Your Majesty."

"The Protectors had their own form of military back in their era. These soldiers were known as Prophets."

"Could the Protectors not . . . protect themselves?"

The Prince chuckled, "They were more than capable of fighting any bad men that crossed their paths, but even the most powerful of warriors need an extra hand." The girl relaxed back into her position, still seemingly confused. "Where was I . . . oh yes, this was a time where Kairos flourished; economically, culturally, and spiritually. This lasted until an unknown incident occurred by the citizens—angering our Protectors to no end. In retaliation, they punished us by plaguing the land with a curse. The sky was darkened as the suns vanished. A swirling vortex of mist connected the sky with the ground, touching the center of Pleasant Valley Groove. The cloud flowed across Osiren, corrupting all within its path. With a single touch, flowers wilted, animals scattered and hid, and the trees themselves seemed to cry in agony—"

"Your Highness," Mrs. Triage called, interrupting his story. He paused, turning to the teacher. "I'm sorry, sire, but we have a question." The Prince nodded his head in acceptance as the teacher called to the raised hand. "Yes, Phoenix, please stand."

She pointed her finger to a little boy slowly rising from the back. His bright blond hair shone underneath a few lamps hanging from the ceiling and his eyes widened as everyone turned to face him. He timidly mumbled, "Um, ho-how can the mist . . . well, do all those horrible things?" He played with the bottom of his yellow shirt, twisting it around his fingers.

The Prince smiled, "I'll answer that in a moment, Phoenix."

He noticed Phoenix's face turn bright red as he sat back down into the crowd of children. Phoenix stared at his blue slacks as Prince Joshua proceeded: "So . . . the mist continued to spread its evil across the land. The tale says demons and other dark creatures inhabited the mist. Monsters like none that had ever been seen. They destroyed each village they entered, hiding in the cover of darkness—leaving no survivors. These dark times continued until finally a group of heroic men stood against this mystical force.

"The five of them each held in their possession a beautiful, shining emerald of all different colors. They entered the mist and fought a valiant fight, and in the end, each emerald absorbed a share of the darkness, until it was all hidden beneath their surfaces. The heroes hid them in five separate locations across Kairos. Each warrior became the guardian of their respective emerald. Once the countries had been claimed, Osiren's boundaries encompassed all *five* of these locations! This is how our amazing city of Luminar, along with the cities of Flores, Zannala, Cosarave, and Emerica, were founded: to help guard the objects from ever being removed from their resting place. My great-great grandfather was a guardian and the duty has been passed to each male in the family. As of right now, my father, the King, is the current guardian of the gems. And since I'm the heir to Luminar, I will be the next protector. This is the tale of how the five great cities of Osiren came to be in our nation. Any questions?"

Clapping broke through the silence, followed by a spring of energy as the kids began jumping up and bombarding him. "Have you seen the emerald? What color is ours? Did the King ever see one of these monsters? Who was our founder?"

Immediately, Mrs. Triage came to his rescue: "Children, quiet down! I want to see your hands raised and I shall call on you to speak. Children! Atten—" The ringing of the bell cut her short. On command, the students leapt from the rug and ran to gather their things, already forgetting that their Prince was in the room.

"Oh, time flew fast. That's it for today's lesson! I'll see you tomorrow. Don't forget to study for our exam. Goodness, I almost forgot! Please say happy Creation Day to Phoenix. He is nine years of age! Happy Creation, hun!" She tried to encourage the rest of them to repeat her, but their minds were preoccupied with what they were to do later that evening.

Prince Joshua walked over to Mrs. Triage who bowed before him, graciously thanking him for speaking to her class as the room instantly cleared out. No one had given two thoughts to what she had announced. The two adults stopped talking mid-sentence when they noticed Phoenix was the only student remaining, sitting at his desk scribbling on a piece of paper. The Prince received his last praise and said his farewell before tiptoeing behind Phoenix. Unnoticed, he peered over Phoenix's shoulder. A little boy was positioned in a fetal position in the middle of the drawing with a crowd of kids surrounding him, paying no mind to the young one. The children were colored in darkly, while the child was a light gray.

"Hello, Phoenix."

The boy jumped from his chair. Startled, he spun around to find the Prince peering down at him with an endearing smile. Phoenix flashed a smile back. He began scrambling for his belongings, tossing his picture into a brown woven sack.

"Happy Creation Day, young man! Nine years already?" Prince Joshua glanced down at Phoenix's innocent blue eyes, filled with either fear or admiration. To break the tension, he joked, "You know the bell rang?"

Phoenix timidly glanced at him, "Ye-yeah, I-I just wanted to finish, that's all. I'll head home now. Thanks for the creation wishes."

The Prince could see a red tint appear on his cheeks. "What's the meaning behind your picture?"

"Oh, um, it's nothing, I got to leave. Thanks for the story today, Your Highness, it was nice to meet you." Phoenix hurried toward the door with embarrassment washing over him. The Prince looked outside to see daylight was being swallowed by nightfall. Houses were still visible, but the purplish atmosphere lay right behind its horizon.

"The days are getting shorter. Winter must be near. Would you mind if I escorted you home? It's not safe on the streets to be alone at such a young age."

Phoenix was at a loss for words, his mouth dryer than usual. "Um, yeah, that'd be okay."

The two left school in complete silence. The Prince walked a few feet behind and to the right of Phoenix. The boy practically shook in his dirt-encrusted white shoes. Not a word was spoken until Joshua felt provoked to break the mood.

"Where is your residence?"

"My home is a little down the block, past the lake," answered Phoenix with his voice slowly dying as each word tumbled out. He forgot to mention they were taking a detour, a trip through the shops to make the walk home last as long as possible.

Phoenix traced the giant wall that surrounded Luminar. The cement barrier wrapped around the entire city until it connected with the Luminary Tail Mountains that guarded the city's back side from invasions. The entrance to the city held the market quarters where shops and other stores were located. Phoenix and his mom often ventured down to the shacks and roadside stands that were selling fresh fruit or assorted goods. Farther into the city's center was where Phoenix's home was found. Here there were several complexes that held housing developments and schools: elementary, junior high, and high school. The city Worship House, medical and emergency buildings, and Grand Hall were all stationed in this area. The complex surrounded the palace where Prince Joshua and the King resided. It was a humongous castle protected by a smaller duplicate of the outer wall.

They passed identical houses one by one. Each was made of oak, rundown and rotting due to time and weather. Blooming flowers and strong trees did their best to bring out the beauty of the old town. As the two continued to stroll, citizens gawked at the sight of their idol. They had become the center of attention as they walked through the living quarters, making Phoenix even more unnerved. The Prince waved to his people in hopes that acknowledging his fans would be able to calm his companion.

But, it was to no avail.

It was not until the pair reached Luminar Lake that Phoenix finally felt at ease, gazing at the sparkling waters under the sunset. He smiled, watching the bushes on the island sway in the wind. The Prince interrupted Phoenix's trance by complimenting his unique name, asking how it was chosen.

"My mother says that when she was pregnant she was outside of the city's wall in a nearby jungle. She was in an old, um, place when I was born."

"A temple?"

"Yeah, that's it! She said an amazing flaming bird circled me. The bird flew into the ceiling bursting into flames, and the crumbs fell down on top of me! She knew that's what she wanted to name me right away."

"That's an interesting story. You're extremely lucky. Has your mother mentioned if she saw it's young?"

Phoenix met his gaze. "Why would the bird have a child?"

"Phoenixes are thought to be almost extinct throughout the ages. Legend states the ashes of a phoenix are a sign of a blessed life. When a phoenix's time comes to an end, they show a brilliant display of fire. An offspring is then born from its ashes. If one is to die without a young to emerge, the nearest child is supposedly granted the courage of The Creator." The Prince looked over to see that Phoenix was off in his own world. *I guess not all tales have legitimacy.* He continued to stray behind Phoenix, but closed the gap between them.

"What about your father? Where was he?"

"Mother doesn't mention him, but I don't think she even knows who he is. I'm a gift from Zorumaka and Kyrudorous to her . . . or that's what she always tells me. I live at home with my sister, mother, and this man. He is not my father." He paused. "But I'm told to treat him as such."

"Oh, I'm sorry to hear that." He tilted his head to the side.

Phoenix caught Joshua's frown, fearing he had done something. "My mother talks about you a lot."

"Oh?" His blue eyes practically began sparkling. "You don't say? Positive things, I pray."

Phoenix giggled, "She says you're the best thing to happen to Luminar. She often attends your speeches and announcements." He quickly muttered under his breath, "I'm always with her."

"Well, I am honored to know there are such incredible people supporting me."

Phoenix couldn't put it into words, but he suddenly felt at peace with this heroic figure. A kinship. A comfortable warmth the Prince was emitting. A more intimate experience than the distant feeling of watching the Prince calming a crowd. Something beyond admiration.

"What about your family? Are you married?"

The Prince knew it was inappropriate for any individual to

question royalty, especially on personal matters, but he wasn't a stickler for traditions. "I will never marry; I lost the love of my life and have no young."

Phoenix's face drooped. "Did she take the long sleep?"

"One could say that."

"My grandparents went to sleep about a year ago. My mother said it was time for them to rest and that they won't wake for a while. My sister said they are helping the Protectors. But I know them. They should be waking up within days. Neither of them would miss my Creation Day."

Joshua could only stare down at the boy. He felt the need to comfort him, his hand twitching for Phoenix's shoulder. "Does your family believe in the lore of the land?"

"Well . . . she does—my Mother. She says I will understand, but it doesn't make sense to me. We go to the, um . . . Worship House every so often, but I don't like it there. I get a weird feeling and it's boring." They approached the center city outskirts and to a house on the corner. Phoenix's extra energy in his step signaled their adventure was coming to an end. Phoenix stopped in front of the small brick house with a wooden porch. Joshua spotted a giant oak tree hovering overhead.

Phoenix bowed, "Thank you for bringing me all the way home. I'm sorry if I was a burden."

"Please rise, there's no need. It was my pleasure; now I shall rest easy knowing you're home safe."

The two of them departed as Phoenix hopped up the steps. He jiggled the handle and realized it was not budging. Knocking on his door, he watched Joshua walk away. *I can't believe he did that. We have the best Prince. Mommy was right about him.* His thoughts were lost as soon as the door slammed open, revealing his father figure standing in the door frame. Standing about the same height, Phoenix recoiled the moment he began speaking. Phoenix held his breath as the man began interrogating him.

"Why are you home late? Where have you been?" he demanded as his face began to illuminate with a bright red glow. He didn't care for the answers; he only wanted to have a reason to blow a fuse.

Phoenix brushed him aside, trying to squeeze past him into the house. Pushing on through, he ignored the first few questions and answered the following by shaking his head "yes" and answered every question with "I don't know." He went to his room, allowing the door to close behind him. He waited for the loud bang to echo throughout his four walls before he could relax. Throwing his sack upon his desk, Phoenix was interrupted by a knock. His anxiety began building. *He never follows me in here! This is my safe place.* Before he had a chance to answer, his sister barged inside. She had her long blonde hair gently laying over her shoulders, blue-green eyes, and was wearing a pink play dress with red slippers. The dress was covered in wrinkles with mud caked onto the fabric.

"Hi, Beth," said Phoenix, overcome with joy.

"Hey, buddy, I felt John stomping through the house raging about who-knows-what so I figured you must be home. But, Happy Creation!"

"Thanks." Phoenix gave her a hug, his smile practically glowing.

"Do you want to go down to the lake and do our homework? Jen and Rob are there already! It would be good to get some fresher air." She waved her hand by her nose.

Phoenix gratefully accepted the offer and left as fast as possible. John called after them as they headed toward the lake, but his barks were silenced as the door shut behind them. The smell of water filled his nose as they spotted Beth's friends. Jen was opening a picnic basket while Rob flung a pebble across the lake. It skipped along the water in a delicate movement, making the top ripple with each bounce.

Beth shouted, waving at her friends. She turned to her brother, "Are you hungry, buddy? We have some snacks here to hold us over until supper." Phoenix greedily eyed the goodies, taking off in a dash. Jen and Rob gave their Creation wishes to Phoenix who started munching on the variety of fruits.

The newly aged teens began to play tag while Phoenix politely declined their offers to join. He sat near the basket and watched the last bit of sunlight dance on the lake. His mind began wandering, not thinking about anything, just watching the water ripple. He imagined himself lying on the middle island of the lake, basking in the sunlight. His name echoing in the distance broke his trance. Looking around, he found his mom calling for his sister and him. He hadn't realized how fast the time had passed.

With a sigh of despair, Beth left her friends and ran to meet their mom who already had her arms around Phoenix. The three of them began walking home, hand in hand. "How was work, Mother?" he asked, noticing her dirty scrubs.

"Long, love; plenty of patients visited this evening. How about the two of you?" Her darker blonde hair bounced with each step.

"Learned some things," answered Beth.

"The Prince came in to my class!"

Even in her messy clothes, her face still radiated with happiness. "That's incredible! I heard he was visiting the elementary school, how lucky to have it be you!"

"Surprise Creation present!" laughed Beth.

"That reminds me! After supper tonight, I have a special gift waiting. Make sure you behave!"

The rest of the night went on as routine. The four of them sat down at the table to feast; this time it was specially made to Phoenix's liking. They filled their plates listening to John moan about everything that displeased him—mainly about his job, where he always played sick. Phoenix barely paid attention to his gums flapping, but his sister, per usual, bluntly retorted with a derogatory comment and forcefully left the table. Beth's actions led to more fighting afterward. Phoenix watched as the nightly play unraveled.

Predicting every word that was yelled was a game he had mastered. And took pride in. When the fuss finally quieted down, Phoenix's mom snuck him into the backyard to their family's big oak tree. The cold night air pierced his skin like needles, making him shiver endlessly.

"This has been passed down for generations in our family. The males have the right to it for their 'undying spirit,'" Brenda chuckled as she examined the pitch black hole in the trunk of the tree. "Fortunately for me, I am the only child."

Phoenix watched patiently as his mom probed around the dark cave to find whatever item she was searching for. He was curious to figure out what this big secret entailed. She released a sigh of relief as she finally clutched a metal object, making a clanking sound.

"Now, I want you to close your eyes, and promise not to open them until I say. Hold out your hands." Phoenix, with a mischievous smile, did as he was told and held out his palms. Brenda placed the object in his grasps. He could feel the coldness of the metallic object run through his skin. He flashed a smile holding the mysterious item.

"You may open them now."

His eyes instantly opened to see a katana lying across his palms, but not one he had ever seen before. Not that he had seen many. Out of confusion, he examined every part of the weapon. The hilt of the sword was wrapped in pure white silk, and the cross-guard was a white fang of some creature that protruded to the side, curving slightly toward the end. The blade was made of some kind of white steel; the moonlight glistened upon the shiny metal. On one face of the blade there was a white, dotted figure etched up the side. He traced the drawing, assuming it was a lizard with wings. He gingerly laid a finger upon the tip of the blade, only to pull away immediately. A prick of blood leaked free.

Phoenix was uncontrollably happy. "Thanks, Mom! This is the best thing I've ever gotten!"

Again she chuckled. "Here," she said, handing him a white diamond encrusted case with a belt loop attached. "This is called a sheath. Keep the sword in here at all times to make sure you don't hurt yourself. It can even be worn as a belt." Phoenix eagerly placed the sword back into the sheath. "It's been in our family for ages. This is the White Dragon; apparently one of the three brother swords. There are the White, Blue, and Black Dragons. I'm not too familiar with the legend, but I know the price for these rarities is extremely high." She looked at his eyes filled with wonder. "I'm not convinced the others even exist."

"White Dragon?" He eyed the dots on the blade. "Is . . . is that what this is? A dragon? I thought they were gone forever."

"They lived long before us dear—even before your grandparents. These beasts were held as icons of our ancestor's pasts."

Phoenix stood there holding his new prized possession, his imagination stirring. Brenda peered over her shoulder to see no trace of sunlight left. "Okay, love, it's time for bedtime!"

"Sorry, Mom—I'll go to bed right now." He ran back into the house pressing his new sword against his chest.

Knocking before entering, Brenda went into Phoenix's room an hour later, quietly closing the door behind her. The floor creaked as she made her way to him. The musty smell of ancient wood suffocated the room. With one hand on his bedpost, she spoke with a worn out tone: "So tell me about the Prince, love."

Her tiresome voice made Phoenix glance up. *Another stupid fight must have happened,* he thought.

"He spoke to my grade about Luminar City and the emeralds. I was really nervous, I didn't want to do anything stupid. He walked me home after class. He's a really nice fellow."

"Did he? All the way to our home? I wish I would have known! I would have swept the floor and tidied—"

"It's okay, Mom, it was only to the front door."

"Phew, I was worried. I didn't want to insult him with my

unclean home. I'm happy you had the opportunity to meet him. I knew you would take to him." Her eyes were swollen with a light tint of red surrounding them. Hoping to get her mind off topic, he questioned something the Prince mentioned earlier.

"His family has fallen asleep, too—like Grandma and Pa. They were supposed to wake up today . . . I guess they forgot." She sat next to him, wrapping one arm around his shoulder. She held his body close to hers hoping to bring him comfort.

"Don't take it personally, love, Grandma couldn't remember an important date for her life."

His cheeks raised a bit, but his head tilted slightly forward. She decided a quick change of topic was in need. "What did you do when you left the Prince, sweetie?"

"Well," he began to ponder. "Beth took me to the lake and I had a good time there. Jen and Rob came, too! I'm going to marry Jen one day, Mom, just you watch. Oh, I also looked at the lake. Mommy, do you think I could go see the lake again before I fall asleep?"

"Ha-ha, no, dear it's too late and I hear you have an exam tomorrow. You need a good night's rest. Look at it while you're walking to school."

"Oh . . . alright. Thanks for the present again. It's really nice and it seems really special." Phoenix smiled, gently clutching his sword from under the pillow.

Brenda smiled and rubbed his head. "Well, that's it for tonight. We'll speak again tomorrow. Goodnight, I love you." She got up and extinguished a few candles around the room. As she began exiting, Phoenix asked another question.

"Mommy . . . you know how Grandma and Pa are sleeping?" She clenched her jaw. "Yes, why?"

"The Prince said his wife is sleeping, too. I thought you only went to sleep when you were old?"

Brenda's throat tightened and Phoenix watched as her eyes watered. She leaned forward, kissing him on his forehead. Tucking him in, she replied, "We will talk about this another time. You need to rest up for your exam! I want to see a perfect score!" With another farewell, she exited the room.

As his mother headed toward bed, a few tears busted free, traveling across her skin. Pulling the blankets up over her head, Brenda laid in silence until exhaustion overcame her. *Another day of work, here I come.*

CHAPTER 2

Groups of kids gathered around tables to devour their lunch. Their conversations were easily overheard: one was gossiping about a mentor while another was discussing their problems from home. All the students sat in their unassigned seats just as the day before and as they would tomorrow. Peering over the crowd was the most popular boy. He casually sat atop of his table, legs spread wide, surrounded by peers who were not deemed less than cool. His defined jaw, bulging biceps, and strong voice made him the desire of all women and the source of jealousy among all men. His gaze caught a peer walking in his direction. With no sense of him halting, he hopped to his feet. Standing straight, his broad shoulders and height were enough to strike fear in the toughest of opponents. His friends soon flooded to his side as the fellow went toe to toe.

With incoherent mumbles, the boy spewed derogatory comments. Some about his appearance, a few about his family, and most aimed at his personality. His breath slowly irritated the popular man's nose with the smell of tobacco. Cutting off his hopeless insults, all of the cool kids started chanting, "Phoe-nix, Phoe-nix, Phoe-nix" again and again until his hand rose. With one finger, the room hushed.

Phoenix tightened his fist, placing it by his hip, staring straight into his eyes as he spoke, "You have three seconds. Leave.

Or knock me down."

The lack of fear from Phoenix struck the teenager speechless, but as the count hit two he took his chance. His fist went fast, but not quick enough. With a tilt of Phoenix's head, the strike missed. Quickly retaliating, Phoenix punched the boy square in his jaw. One hit wonder. Cheers erupted throughout the cafeteria. Everyone side-stepped the unconscious fighter to reach Phoenix, hoisting him up in the air. They repeated his name in hurrah until the opponent slowly rose back to his feet.

He simply stared at Phoenix, "Buddy, it's time to wake! We must prepare for class."

Phoenix slowly raised his lids. In a complete state of grogginess, he could barely make out his sister's blonde hair slightly covering her face. He forced himself up, his head as heavy as a thousand bricks. She started speaking, but his brain was having a hard time deciphering fast enough. He clumsily nodded. The moment she left the room, Phoenix laid his head down and almost returned to his slumber.

After the morning's usual struggle, he started his routine. Phoenix left the shower and threw on a clean pair of slacks and a ruby shirt. He brushed his teeth, not once but twice, before waiting for his sister by the door that John always strapped open, allowing fresh air to circulate. He waited silently, careful not to wake up his mother. John went to work at the break of dawn, thankfully. Home was a lot less tense without his presence. He looked up at the clock. Seven forty-five: fifteen more minutes until school began, and forty-five minutes before his mother woke up. As he peered through the front door, he repeatedly glanced over his shoulder for any indication that his sister was ready. Running water, tone-deaf humming, and the sound of tapping suggested the opposite. Finally she made her appearance, wearing a bright yellow sundress. When ready, the two of them left the safety of their home to enter the harshness of school's wake.

"I heard you received a special gift from Mother! That isn't fair," she pushed his shoulder.

"It's a sword! It's really shiny. You don't like fighting or weapons anyway."

"Violence isn't your favorite activity either!" She let out a small laugh. "We must play with it after school. Oh! How was being in the presence of Prince Joshua? I meant to mention it yesterday. He's just wonderful." Her cheeks bloomed. "I wish he would walk *me* home from school one day!"

"He asked me and only me," Phoenix sneered soaking in the envy.

The two continued deeper into their conversation as they approached the divide that led to all three schools. Waiting at the separating paths was a little boy who was rapidly tapping his foot against the dirt while his finger created a beat on his bicep. With each step closer, Phoenix fell behind Beth more and more.

The child's eyes attacked Phoenix like daggers. Easy prey was the only thought. "Nice shirt Pee-nix. I bet your Mother—"

Beth interrupted the bully: "Let me explain this as simple as I can, Greg. If I hear another complaint from my brother about you, I'll *personally* make you learn how to say his name correctly." The boy faltered back, hiding beneath his flaming red, curly hair. Without another word, he ran onto the right path leading to elementary school.

Beth faced Phoenix with her head tilted, letting her glistening hair rest gently on her shoulder. Phoenix always felt relaxed around her, especially when faced with Greg.

"This is where we part ways; come find me when you get home. I can't wait to play with your new toy." She kissed him on the forehead. Phoenix, still suffering from fear, merely received the peck and said goodbye, watching her head down the middle path to junior high.

Following the right path, Phoenix approached his elementary school. The schools were painted the colors of the city. Being the smallest of the three schools, the elementary school was covered in a dull shade of white. Beth's school was entirely ocean blue and the high school was a mixture of the two. Entering those treacherous doors, he aimed straight for his classroom. As he was walking down the corridor, Phoenix watched as all the other children laughed loudly and chased each other, while others huddled in a group watching in disgust. He ignored the whole scene, continuing to his destination. Listening to the advice of his mother and sister, none of those kids were worth his time. When reaching the wooden door to his room, he silently read the sign: "Mrs. Triage's Third Grade Class." With a deep breath, he entered his prison.

In a slight daze, Phoenix endured his normal schedule. The teacher wrote countless numbers on the chalkboard, taught the difference between nouns and verbs, and as Phoenix finally came back to reality, the teacher began the topic of Zorumaka and Kyrudorous, the Protectors. This topic was one of the only things that brought him delight. Talking about the two Protectors that watched over his family sent a fuzzy feeling through him, even if he was unable to grasp the concept.

"Before we begin our Creation lessons, let's review what we have learned. May someone remind the class where the conversation was left?" In her mid-fifties, but with the youth of a spring chicken, Mrs. Triage had a happy go-lucky voice that could soothe rabid animals. Phoenix tried with all his might to make sure she never called upon him, immediately looking out the window as she asked questions.

"Yes, Greg, please stand and tell the class where we ended the lesson?" Her wide smile complimented her aging body. Her brown hair had begun the process of graying and the wrinkles on her face were becoming more defined. With her silver hair in a bun upon her head, she was welcoming her elderly age with grace.

The carrot-topped bully struggled to stand from his desk, using his entire strength to situate himself. His high pitched voice shattered Phoenix's ear drums.

"We talked about . . . how once you take the long sleep, what is to come next."

"Correct," she responded with a haggard voice. Sneering, he sat back down. "To review, our Protectors lived over two centuries ago. Class, may someone tell me how long a century is?"

In unison, half the class shouted, "One hundred years!"

"Indeed it is! When they were around, certain types of magic existed. If we were to live during the Protectors' time, we would all have been born with these incredible abilities. How exciting would that have been? The two belonged to a royal family, like the Prince. Having such high stature in their society, Zorumaka and Kyrudorous were endlessly trained to master these magical abilities." Most of the children listened intently, imagining themselves with the ability to fly or breathe under water, except for Greg, who had started drifting away, jerking his head up-ward every few minutes.

"After maturing into adulthood, they recognized the disease and darkness festering within mankind. Once the Second Teague War came to an end and half the land was in shambles, they combined their powers to change the world. They gathered an army of Prophets, which are . . .?" she gazed over the students and with a quick bang on her desk everyone sparked to life.

"The Prophets are the followers who vowed their lives to help the Protectors succeed. They took an oath of silence and wore silk, metallic, gray robes that covered every inch of their bodies. Their hoods were always on to cast a shadow over their faces. It was said they stayed quiet and hidden to represent the cries of the unfortunate souls who lost their lives to the chaos. Once Zorumaka and Kyrudorous mustered enough strength, they fought the leaders of Teague. To some, this is known as the Third Teague War, while to others, it is the Prophets' Prophecy. But that will not be on the next exam," she chuckled, but no one stirred. Failing to awaken the class, she carefully chose her next target to answer a question. Scanning the crowd of misty eyes, she called Phoenix's name.

"Can you please tell me, once Zorumaka and Kyrudorous

came to be known as the Protectors, what was their plan for those who had passed on?"

Phoenix, fully aware of his surroundings now, stared completely dumbfounded. No response came to mind and no muscle decided to move. He sat there motionless, until the teacher asked him to stand. Forcing himself up, he remained still as a statue.

"Do you know the answer?"

He attempted to articulate a sentence, but nothing came out besides "hums" and "ahs." He scanned the room to find all his classmates blatantly staring at him. Stage fright suddenly clenched his voice box, muting any sound he attempted to make. After a few minutes of humiliation, Greg began a hoard of laughter with the rest of the students following behind. Turning the color of his shirt, he abruptly seated himself, slowly shrinking. Mrs. Triage angrily quieted them down.

"It's okay, honey, that is why we attend school—to learn. The Protectors decided that our lives were too precious to be allowed to evaporate into the abyss. Through the process of reincarnation, all the souls of the gone are implanted into nature. These spirits helped give the environment extra nutrients, which assisted in growing beautiful flowers and gigantic trees. There are rumors that sometimes the souls transformed plants into forest nymphs." She was interrupted by a student asking for a description of a nymph. "Imagine a fairy-type spirit. They take the shape of humans, but are immersed in nature. They are believed to be light green and attached to Teague by roots. However, no one has ever witnessed these mystical figures first-hand to confirm these rumors."

The class again broke into a conversation about the nymphs, aside from Phoenix, who continued to sink in his desk, head down and cheeks burning. A child with dull black hair asked Mrs. Triage about the different kinds of magic their ancestors practiced. Checking the time, she responded, "Quiet down, class, Britney asked a very important question. There were several different types of magic in the old kingdom. There were physical abilities, mind controllers,

necromancers, endurers, and elemental casters." Seeing the blank
expressions staring at her, she realized explanations were necessary.
"The physical manipulators could control atoms and molecules,
bending them to their will. Mind controllers could read someone's
thoughts, make them believe what's not true, and command them to
do an action. Endurers had high tolerances of pain and could
withstand almost all bodily injuries. Some even had the talent to
harden their skin into stone. Necromancers—" Mrs. Triage stopped
as a young girl stood from her seat. "Yes, sweetie?"

"My father told me stories about them! They control the bad
things, like darkness. He said the best Necromancer could summon
dead people. Rolux was a Necromancer! Mother told me that
Zorumaka and Rolux were extremely close when they were children!"

Greg also took a stand with disdain across his face. *He has to
be the center of attention,* sighed Phoenix.

"Well I know all about the elemental wizards. They can
control every element like fire and water. Most of the wars were
caused because they were the strongest!"

"That's not quite true, but we can continue this conversation
tomorrow! Very good discussion, class! It's time for recess and lunch.
Gather your things and I'll meet you on the playground." The class
dispersed from the room and the newly awakened slowly dragged
their butts outside. Once again, Phoenix was the last one remaining,
still the shade of a ripe tomato.

Mrs. Triage made her way to her shy pupil with spirited steps.
Her long dress spun around her as she took a seat next to Phoenix,
who still paid her no mind. She lightly shook his shoulder, only hard
enough for him to focus his attention on her.

Looking down at his beautiful irises she whispered, "Phoenix,
go with the others and play a game." No response. "None of my
students know the answer to all the material. There is no reason to let
that bring your spirits down. Get some fresh air, it'll do you some
good." Phoenix, with a disheartened nod, left with his tail in between
his legs.

A few moments later, she peered outside to see him alone on the swings. The kids were playing ball or hopscotch around him, but he continued swinging. Once the lunch bell rang, the stampede of children made their way to the old worn-out benches. Mrs. Triage searched the mob for a bright red shirt, but came up short handed. Her eyes wandered over the playground to see Phoenix still on the swings with a brown paper bag. Overcome by sadness, she could no longer endure seeing one of her children in this situation. Pulling out a pen, she scribbled onto a pad of paper:

"Group project—Phoenix, Artan, and Michael."

The sound of the class bell echoed throughout the hallway followed by a pool of children pouring into the corridors. Each child filed into their seats one by one as Mrs. Triage handed out their test.

"Alright, class, you have until the dismissal bell rings to finish. If you need any more time we can talk afterward. You may begin now," she said delivering the last paper.

Phoenix waited a few minutes after the bell to begin his departure home. He dragged his feet, bringing up dust with each step. Shielding his eyes against the glaring suns, he looked around his city. His gaze was glued to the outline of the castle. *I wonder what Prince Joshua is doing. Most likely Prince things.* Spotting his sister sitting on their front porch, he ran up and embraced her in a big hug.

Beth whipped out a stick from under her chair. "I found this on the walk home! This will be more than enough against your sword." She swung it in the air causing whooshing sounds to emit from the branch. With a spark of anticipation, Phoenix ran inside to grab his katana.

He entered his room to find John with his grubby paws fondling the White Dragon. John was holding it up against the light coming through the window, watching the rays bounce from its surface. Phoenix couldn't help but be in awe of his shiny new toy. All of a sudden, John plunged the sword into its sheath and faced him. Phoenix's eyes replaced wonder with fear.

Turning instantly livid, John's face scrunched together and an almost tangible smoke burst from his ears. Phoenix shrunk his way out of the room. Before he could make his grand exit, his father figure released a loud growl through his three teeth, making every hair on his head stiffen.

"Where did *this* come from?"

"I-I received it from Mom—a present."

"Not anymore; it's mine now. Should sell for a fine price down at the market."

Phoenix reluctantly watched as John examined it, valuing its worth. Watching John's pupils turn into coins, he struggled with his words. He was not much for confrontation, especially when it came to arguments. Or to John.

"No, it's mine. Beth and I were going to go play with it—"

"One doesn't *play* with weapons, idiot. They are dangerous. Why your mother would trust you with such a thing—"

Stomping drowned his words, which was followed by the appearance of Beth's stern face and her flowing golden dress twirling around her.

"Get your greasy hands off my brother's sword." Before he could react, her hand firmly grasped the sheath and began tugging it toward her.

The two of them began playing an uneven tug-of-war match. "You spoiled little brat," John spewed. "You've been such a waste of coins since the day you've been born."

Beth reddened as she planted her feet firmly on the ground against this three hundred pound man.

"I hate you with everything in me. Mother hates you. Phoenix hates you."

"If I had known your worthless mother was pregnant, I'd have left her the minute we met."

"She only keeps you around for coins. We all wish you would meet the Protectors!" Beth's patience began wearing thin. "Phoenix, help me," she pleaded as John almost captured the weapon. Watching the struggle, he didn't budge.

With one strong pull, the sheath slid from Beth's grasp. She tumbled back, but caught herself and reacted. She struck his toes with a crushing step and cracked his knee with her foot. He bellowed and went down on his knees. The White Dragon slid from his grasp and Beth swept it up without hesitation. With the katana in one hand and Phoenix in the other, she fled the house. The two of them could hear furious barks chasing them from the porch.

Overcome with distress and the rush of rebelliousness, Beth couldn't help but giggle as she led her brother down to the lakeside. Phoenix, gasping for breath, followed Beth and questioned her wide smile. Her contagious laughter finally influenced him as the two of them fell, rolling down the tiny decline only to stop at the edge of the water. Phoenix instantaneously was lost in the ripples shimmering across the lake. The last sun started its descent behind the Luminary Tail Mountains as it did nightly, leaving behind a colorful reflection.

Beth pushed herself up, tossing the White Dragon near Phoenix's feet. "Oh . . . I left my stick at the house . . ." She glanced to the trees on the island in the lake. "I'll head for the center and get a branch! Be ready when I come back." Diving into the water, she reappeared on the island a few minutes later. Drenched, she struggled walking around with her dress clinging to her legs.

Phoenix revealed his sword, watching it glimmer under the sunset. Leaving the sheath on the ground, it took great effort to hold the sword steady. He turned it to the side, inspecting the dragon. Magical was the only word he could use to describe it. When he returned to reality, Beth had crossed back onto land and dropped several sticks before him. She precisely chose one and swung it through the air, trying to get a feel of her weapon.

"Okay!" she announced, placing her left leg back and putting most of her weight on her right one. "Let's go!"

Phoenix copied his sister, almost losing balance. When he was ready, his eyes met Beth's and she leaped. Whooshing sounds flying everywhere, her stick repeatedly attacked his sword. It took most of his strength to turn aside each hit. To strike was an entirely different challenge. Almost lifting his body from the ground, each miss brought him face first against the dirt. But once in a while, when his attempt did make contact, Beth's stick would snap. This one-sided battle went for what seemed like hours until a piercing whistle flew over the battlefield.

Standing in the distance with the orange sky outlining her figure, Brenda stood with hands on her hips. The children ran up to their mother, each gripping her by her waist. She gingerly brushed their hair to comfort them. Licking her thumb, she brushed off some dirt on Phoenix's face.

"Looks like you kids have been busy! Why don't you both tell me about your days on our walk home?"

The happiness lasted until the moment they entered their home. A different menacing, hateful feeling replaced it. A screaming match blossomed between John and Brenda. Beth stayed back with Phoenix, but not for long. She gracefully made her way into the conversation shouting her opinion. In tears, Phoenix ran to his room. Hiding the katana under his pillow, he placed his wooden chair up against the door handle. *Hopefully this will keep them out,* he thought through gasps and sniffles.

He hid under the covers, eavesdropping on the hollering that was taking place outside his room. As his adrenaline began dying down, Phoenix could feel the cuts on his body start to burn and the bruises ache. The darkness in his self-made cave, his safe place, finally overcame him, drowning out the screaming. Sleep overtook his hurt, little body.

The darkness of the night was at its peak when Phoenix woke to a blaring sound coming from beyond his room. Too sleepy to concentrate, he rested his head back on the pillow. He laid on his bed listening to the noise pulsating around him. As he was on the verge of unconsciousness, banging erupted on his door. Confused and alarmed, he made his way to the jiggling handle. His shuffling feet halted as his chair was shoved from its position and his door slammed against the wall. He stumbled back from the abrupt commotion to find his sister staring at him. Her eyes were wide open with fear written all across her face. Her dreadful expression stole the words from his mouth.

The pure shock factor had swallowed both of them. He stared at his sister who struggled to process what was going on. That made two of them. The dead silence was interrupted by regulated siren noises being emitted. Ones he had never heard before—or even knew existed. John entered next, practically appalled.

"We have to go, we can't stay here." He reached for both of theirs hands, dragging them from Phoenix's quarters. Phoenix had only enough time to grab his White Dragon. They hurried into the family room where Brenda stood, skin as pale as cotton. Her lips remained sealed. No explanation or good morning. Phoenix glanced between his family members, still rubbing his eyes. Whatever reason they were awake, his parents didn't seem too excited.

They rushed into their neighborhood where the cold night breeze peeled the warmth from their skin. Finally, Beth was able to work her tongue.

"Mother, I'm scared! What's that noise? What are we doing?"

Brenda merely ignored her, telling her to keep her mouth shut. The harshness in her voice alarmed the children, making them more anxious than before. The four traveled through Luminar listening to the background noise of the siren wailing in the distance. The family joined several more groups, all as sickly looking as Brenda. The entire living quarters traveled down to the Grand Hall. The place held important events and town meetings. It was not usually an open-door policy for every citizen. As Phoenix entered, a large man began corralling his group to the side. Packing them into a tight space, he had trouble peering into the crowd. Panic began ensuing in his body as he flicked between clusters of people who mirrored the same look of sheer terror.

Phoenix felt like he was suffocating being in the midst of a mob. Attempting to pick out faces in the crowd to calm himself, he saw Mrs. Triage with her husband and a few of his classmates scattered around the arena. Mothers held their weeping children as fathers stood against the walls with grim expressions. Babies' whines pierced the air until suddenly, Phoenix heard someone's shouting break through the sound barrier that wrapped around them. Everyone started to look around until a citizen yelled, "Look, the Prince!" Immediately, children quieted down and babies stopped fussing.

The entire city stared up at him, as if he was one of the Protectors. All of his immense fear and suffocation vanished as Phoenix gazed upon the Prince. *Nothing can be bad when he's around.*

The Prince cleared his throat: "Citizens of Luminar, we must remain calm and quiet while I explain the instructions for evacuation. My voice needs to be heard by all." He waited for the murmuring to die down until he continued. "We must travel toward the Luminary Tail Mountains. Luminar has been infiltrated by unknown units. The safe rooms located in the caves of the mountains will keep us all safe. My peoples' safety is my primary concern. I have stationed guards along the path to help execute the procedure smoothly. When I give the signal, we must begin marching." Many of the men bellowed, asking why the King was not present.

Joshua went to address them, but was forced forward from an abrupt explosion. The back wall of the structure collapsed. Through the rubble, everyone could see the soldiers' swords gleaming through the dust and smoke. The Prince struggled to push himself to his feet as he examined the wreckage. Mass hysteria filled the room as the Prince yelled, "Retreat! Go, go, go!"

The citizens started swarming toward the exit, yelling and crying. Phoenix watched as arrows passed him spiraling through the air. Men and women were impaled by the projectiles. Blood shed from his peers' bodies. Adults and children fell. His vision blurred as people brushed against him. His throat closed up as his nose began tingling. Closing his eyes, he began stumbling over his feet. He didn't want to see anymore. It needed to stop. John grabbed Phoenix by the waist and hoisted him over his shoulder.

Screams. Screams echoed across the night, vibrating the very ground they ran upon.

Running blindly, they followed the mob—praying it was the correct direction. As they passed the three way divide to the separate schools, Beth spotted Rob. She stopped, frantically waving her arms. The commotion between them blocked her voice in the chaos. Brenda tugged her, begging her to keep moving, but Beth continued to holler his name. Her mother clutched at her forearm, removing her from her position, but her sight remained on Rob. She watched as he fell to his knees, lying against a body whose back was penetrated by a crimson arrow. A soldier, different from Luminar's guardsmen, caught sight of the scene and ran toward him. She knew his fate, and as she ripped her gaze away, she felt his scream climb up her spine. Her eyes watered.

The four attempted to remain focused, ignoring the scenes in their peripherals. Their escape came to a halt as they reached a dead end. Fallen trees and buildings filled the streets, creating a wall of burning rubble blocking their path. Their first instinct was to change directions, but a single arrow struck their escape route. A dozen soldiers climbed the pile of buildings, taking aim at their game. It was a setup. An ambush. The enemies lined up their bows, and on the count of three, released their bullets into the sky. The crowd hastily retreated as hell rained down upon them. Phoenix began shoving through until he was propelled forward. He turned to find John lying above him. John gasped as he struggled to hold himself up. With his face washed with tears, he whispered, "Stay with Brenda, I-I lo—" With those words, he collapsed upon him. Brenda helped Phoenix to his feet only for him to notice a hoard of arrows outlining John's torso.

The three of them escaped the ambush as the crowd was mowed down behind them. In the chaos, Phoenix lost the grip to his mother's hand. He tried to keep up, but she eventually was swallowed by the pandemonium. He started panicking, calling her name in hopes she would hear it by some chance, or that another person would aide him. He couldn't find her in the stampede of terrified prey.

His vision blurred behind the veil of tears that pooled on his lower lids. The colors around him flowed and mixed, creating a disarray of images that appeared briefly only to be swept away as a citizen scurried past him. The familiar stinging of a Luminar night returned, pricking his skin like a needle to a cloth. Hyperventilating, he began to follow behind another crowd. *The-the Prince said to go to the mountains. Mom was taking us to the mountains.* His stare drifted upward to the looming silhouette.

Phoenix tried focusing on his feet. Left right, left right. The tears no longer treaded the thin line below his eyes, they overflowed, lining his cheeks with his fear. He bounced between clumps of people, hollering for his mother or Beth. As each new cluster brought him closer to the safe houses, he began hearing shrieks in the distance. Not quite words, yet not completely foreign. Indistinguishable cries for help. Looking ahead, more of those men were there. Weapons drawn. People falling.

With a quick twist of his soles, Phoenix shuffled in a different direction. The mountains were no longer a feasible place, but he had to hide. He had to stay somewhere safe for his mother to find him, but where? With a destination in mind, he sprinted away.

Beth held her mother tightly as her eyes raced over those passing by, hoping to find Jen, until she felt her mother let go.

"Where's Phoenix?" Brenda cried. She started hollering his name, tears flooding her vision.

"He's smart—he may have gone ahead already. We have to keep going!"

"No! No! Not without him! He's lost!" She continued to desperately search. "I'll find your brother. You go—get safe. I'll be there soon!" Her mother ran back toward the road-block, toward the danger.

Beth could only watch as she faded away into the distance, trying to hold herself together as her face scrunched. She needed to survive. She had no choice but to muster up strength to keep moving. But she had to find Phoenix. *Where would he go?* Then it came to her—*the lake*! Her face stained with dread, she headed in that direction.

Beth ran toward it at full speed, jumping over each corpse in her path. She was staying focused, even as tears continued to fall. The smell of fresh water filled her nostrils as the lake grew closer. *Only a couple more bodies in the way*, she thought. Leaping over the last pile, she glanced at them. A huge mistake. It was Jen. The family was drenched in blood and almost unrecognizable. She had to retrieve her brother and they both had to live to see tomorrow, but the last of her hope was left with her best friend.

Finally reaching Luminar Lake, she shouted Phoenix's name repetitively. No response. *If not here, then where would he have gone?* Fear struck her as she pictured his bedroom. A bedroom that was now burnt to pieces. Her shoulders sagged as she felt her heart ache. Her stare remained focused on the dark waters, the sounds around her drowned out by an internal scream.

The realization dawned on her. In a crisis such as this, with the bloodshed she had already seen, these bad men were not taking hostages. *John . . . Mother. . . . Phoenix . . . they are all . . .* Her eyes squinted, trying to hold back the hot tears that had already begun dripping from her chin. Beth's fists relaxed, her palms swaying by her side. The world around her had become distant. Her purpose of survival was now in question. *What's the reason . . . the reason to live?*

As she dropped to her knees, she heard shuffling. Not that it mattered. Everyone's gone. She tilted her head to the side as a body began crawling free from underneath a pile of corpses. Her eyebrows rose as a new set of tears washed the rest of the dirt from her cheeks. With a sigh of relief, she hurried over to Phoenix. She wrapped her arms around his small frame, almost passing out from exertion.

"I found you! I-I can't believe I have you," she held him against her chest. "We have to go, and get to the mountains."

"No!" he pleaded breaking free. "Families have already gone

up there an-and I've heard their screams. I could hear them cr-crying out for help . . . and I didn't-didn't . . . My teacher and some of my classmates. Beth, I-I don't know what to do." He fell back into her embrace, soaking her nightgown with tears.

She felt her legs quiver. Her eyes wandered to the mountain silhouette against the moonlight. "We have to . . . We need . . ." Beth's view drifted from the skyline to the lake. She glazed over the water's surface. "The island. Let's get to the island. We'll be safe there."

They began treading water. Swimming with all their might, they dove into the nearest group of bushes. They peered through the shrubbery for what felt like hours, watching as the rest of their city was demolished and their population number dropped. Even the lucky ones who made their way to the Luminary Tail Mountains were entering a slaughter-house. As another family fell, Phoenix noticed a group of soldiers entering the lake's water. He pointed and gasped. Beth felt her entire body tense. *It's over. We're going to die.* She clutched her brother's arm.

As the three soldiers reached land, one of them dropped to the dirt. He fell on his torso, revealing an arrow lodged in his neck. The other two glanced around, finding Prince Joshua with a bow in hand. On instinct, the soldiers surged toward him, waving their swords wildly in the air. The Prince replaced his bow with steel just in time to deflect the first one, knocking him off his feet. The other one came forward, clashing against him. They exchanged a few blows before Joshua parried a strike. The mercenary fell forward, allowing the Prince to slit his nape. The second came for another round. Joshua easily disarmed him, and inserted his sword into his chest cavity.

Sheathing his sword, he approached the children. "Are we alright, children? No need to worry, I'm a good guy." Phoenix lunged for him, grabbing his waist. Beth followed behind.

"Phoenix? Are you two alright? Where are your parents?"

Beth blurted out, "They're gone."

"Your mother? Brenda's dead?"

Beth silently nodded. Phoenix flicked his eyes between the two, breaking into tears. He shoved his face once more in the Prince's black overcoat. Through his muffles he murmured, "Th-the invaders . . . have the safe room." He pulled his face from the cloth. "Everyone's gone, aren't they?"

The Prince felt despair strangle him. He wasn't able to find a response to Phoenix's question, but the answer was in his silence. Beth's heart plummeted into her stomach. Before the Prince could try and comfort them, a projectile clipped his left arm. Phoenix jumped back as Joshua howled in pain. Holding his wound, he spun around to see five soldiers advancing in their direction, the flames of the village as their backdrop.

"Well, if it isn't the mighty Prince," announced the man leading the pack. His white hair was spiked giving him a few extra necessary inches. Both his hair and his gray eyes gave Phoenix an eerie feeling.

"Stay behind me," growled the Prince, placing his hand in front of the siblings.

"No 'hello'? Or 'nice to see you again'? You think after all these years of playing Your Highness manners would have been the first lesson."

"Skull, what do you want? Why are you here? I banned you from this city and excommunicated you from our Worship Houses. I bet you are to blame for this catastrophe." Joshua noticed his armor. "Looking spiffy; how many people did you have to murder to make that?" Skull cracked a smile, placing his hand on the hilt of his sword. Phoenix examined the stranger. He wore gear that appeared to be made of bones. His shoulder pads were human skulls without jaws while his breast plate looked like the head of a bull.

"This is not for revenge, if that is what you are inferring, my sire. I'm a mercenary for hire to whomever fills my pockets with coins. I pray to the Protectors that this will not create some more bad blood. Oh, and this, this was a family of four. And their cow." He unhitched his sword releasing his blade into the air. The four soldiers moved forward as Skull pointed the tip of his weapon at the Prince while licking his lips.

"Just like old times, huh?" he snickered. Skull tilted his head toward his goons: "Stay put or I shall have your heads."

The Prince engaged him in battle. Their swords swung rapidly back and forth. The clashing of their metals electrified the island. Each swing searched for blood. The old wounds from their past encounter resurfaced as the bloodlust between them grew. The Prince slammed his sword downward, forcing Skull to stumble. Joshua gave him no chance to recover as he vigorously swept the weapon along the bone of his armor. He continued to keep his offense strong, allowing no time for Skull to gain the upper hand. As another collision occurred, the two of them fought for power. They stared into each other's eyes, grunting as their swords slowly chiseled away.

Joshua broke their contact and stepped back. In a fluid motion, he swiftly spun his weapon around in an attempt to allow the inertia of his speed to break his opponent's defense. But one of the mercenaries grabbed a hold of his bicep. The man hurled the Prince to the ground. Before the mercenary had a chance to land a blow, the Prince drew a knife from his waist. The dagger was driven through the man's hand. He howled as he released his victim.

Skull stepped back, allowing the other three soldiers to participate in the fight as the Prince rebounded back to his feet. Joshua swiftly kicked away the sword by the first mercenary and shielded his face from a disastrous wound just in time. He blocked and deflected each blow by the three men. He ducked beneath a swing, and raised his sword up the mercenary's trunk. Avoiding another blade, he roundhouse kicked the standing corpse as it bled before him.

Before he had the chance to land, another slab of metal was on course for his head. With a last ditch effort, he covered his face with his bare forearm. The slice penetrated the skin, halting at the bone. He grunted as blood leaked free. He used his free hand to stab the warrior repetitively, inserting the tip of his sword several times before disassembling the warrior's knees from his legs. Adrenaline ached in his veins, propelling him to hack off the extremities of the third mercenary standing. His chest inflated rapidly as he stared at his enemies, until the soldier with the wounded hand body-slammed him. The collision bounced the Prince into the shallow water, forcing him to slosh around like a fish removed from the sea.

Joshua planted one foot forward, pushing himself off his knee. He stared down his enemy with the deformed hand. He readied his sword for impact, but stopped. His eyes grew as he stared out at nothing. He stood there, still as a statue, paralyzed, unable to comprehend what was happening. Then, at once, his body dropped into the water.

Skull strolled up to his victim, reaching for his sword that was wrenched in his victim's back. Blood dripped off the tip into the lake as he wielded it by his side.

"Foolish little Prince." Skull kicked him, flipping him onto his spine. The Prince's eyes were stone cold with his mouth half parted. He was gasping for air, struggling to retain oxygen. "Examining the entire picture has never been your forte. It brings me little pleasure to watch you squirm, so I'll be merciful. Any last words?"

The Prince struggled to tilt his head up, trying to make eye contact with Phoenix. He tried to mouth some words, but his lips only twitched. His face glistened with dismay. Their eyes were deadlocked. Phoenix felt terror constrict his throat. The hero that was to save the day was now lying in a river of his own blood. *No! I can't lose him, too!* The Prince finally got out his final word as Skull implanted the sword betwixt his ribs.

"Phoenix."

His pupils became polished and his body went limp as blood continued to pulsate from his gashes. Phoenix and Beth stood there shaking—unable to move, unable to feel. Phoenix went completely and utterly numb.

Skull chuckled, "His demise was to come now or later. Better it be by the hand of a friend. Though, he did care too much about being sentimental and other's feelings—needed more discipline. Discipline to focus on all that is occurring around him." He turned his attention to the siblings. "Hmm, he sacrificed his life for the two of you insignificant maggots? Pathetic, protecting quivering children instead of preserving his own health. Health that had an ability to lead, command. One that could rally forces against my own!" He scoffed. "Well since *I* have the manners that your royalty lacks, I shall take the boy's life first. Is this going to be executed easily or with difficulty?" Phoenix remained focused on the Prince. "Ah, I see your choice has been decided."

Skull gripped his sword tighter. As he towered over Phoenix, he ripped the White Dragon from Phoenix's grasp. Examining the expensive weapon he asked, "What a pretty little toy you have in your possession. Tell me, does this sword have a name?" He waited for his response as he slid the steel from its sheath. "All valuable weapons have a specifically chosen name. One that reflects the morals and life of the user." He abruptly slammed it shut and tossed it into the lake. "Mine's called Gusher; care to take a guess why?" He laid it against the side of his neck.

Beth darted free from the bushes surrounding her, grabbing a fallen goon's sword, yelling, "Don't you dare lay a wound upon my brother!" She ran over to Skull, wildly swinging the weapon. She tried to cut him head on, but Skull smoothly stepped aside. She stumbled forward, her feet tripping over one another. She dropped the steel by her side as she slid against the dirt. She rolled to her back, only to watch Skull approach her. His sword rose. She swallowed.

Phoenix watched the blade drop, blood splattering. His face was splashed in red. Her body was forcibly thrown toward the Prince. Phoenix helplessly watched as his turn arrived.

"No other scapegoats, boy, it's—"

"Attention my warriors!" boomed an unknown voice. "The King of Luminar is no more!" The voice was harsh and deep—bone chilling. Phoenix shivered as the man finished his sentence. Cheers and applauses came from all the invaders. The destroyed city was in an uproar of huzzahs within a few seconds, filling it with life.

"Troops, evacuate the territory. There is no reason to be present within these walls. The worst fate for all survivors is knowing that their friends and family lie dead as they live on." Skull sneered at the boy. "Besides, the contracts expire immediately. I am no longer in need of your services this point forward."

The loud cheering was quickly silenced as the soldiers up and ran from their positions. Every mercenary hustled away from the city until only dead bodies, Phoenix, and Skull remained.

Skull grumbled, "Lady Luck is on your side this morning. I won't be stealing your youth away today." Sadness emitted from his voice. "I may be a mercenary, but one with some values. Laying waste to a child without pay is against my banner's orders. My real pleasure is having you suffer—for the rest of your pathetic life. You shall remember this day. The day you lost much more than you would have ever believed. To be sure you won't forget . . ." Skull pierced the tip of Phoenix's arm, dragging it down. "This will heal into a pretty little scar and I hope it reminds you of me." He ran away laughing manically off into the distance.

Phoenix looked around at his once beautiful city and once pure lake. All that was left was ashes, smoke, blood, and corpses. He sat, cradling his bloody arm and staring at his two most beloved people in the world lying in his favorite lake—limp and lifeless. He felt the White Dragon being swallowed by the water's depth. A drop of liquid hit his hand, and within a few seconds, a dozen more landed on him. Rain drenched the land. Even the heavens were crying for this tragedy.

He crawled to Beth, wincing each time he pulled himself further. He shook his sister.

"Beth, it's time to wake! This is not the time to take a sleep. Bring me home, we can sleep in our rooms. Please, sis, wake up!" He turned his head toward the Prince. Phoenix placed a hand on him, watching as the raindrops clouded his vision. "Y-you can't be-be sleeping, too, you are the hero. Hero's n-n-never res—" He lost it. He stared up at the cloudy sky illuminated by the flames of the burning villages, crying.

CHAPTER 3

A door creaked open to a quaint home. The wood bounced against its wooden frame as an elderly lady shuffled inside. Her cane stamped the floor in a slow beat. Step, step, thud. Step, step, thud. She scuttled to her dining room table that had seen as many years as its owner. She leaned her third leg beside her as she straightened her purple sundress that loosely draped her body. She gazed across the surface, examining several glasses and two plates that were in need of washing. With one swift brush of her arm, all the dishes fell to the floor. Each plate shattered with an ear piercing sound as the old woman screamed to match its frequency.

"Crystal! Present yourself immediately!" The old, haggard voice barely carried itself to the second floor.

"I'm coming, Grandmother!" answered back a sweet, calm sound. Crystal ran down the steps with her strawberry blonde hair swaying between each bounce. Before announcing her presence, she fixed her pink gown.

"Keep me waiting any longer and I'll be beside the Protectors," she grumbled, slightly trembling. "Tell me, girl, why does *my* china litter *my* floor! They should be washed and placed away in the appropriate cabinets!" She gave Crystal a menacing stare, her voice as creaky as her bones. "Clean up this filth."

Crystal kneeled without a second thought, grabbing a few shards. "I'm sorry, Grandmother, I was preparing for today, I'll—"

"My dear, manners! Only speak when asked to." The slap echoed throughout the room. Crystal's round face reddened, practically glowing. The pieces in her grasp slipped free, smashing on the floor again, breaking into even smaller flakes.

"Be useful and fetch the household a loaf of bread from the market. Be quick about it. Not that your services are required here; you have the cleaning ability of a rabid hound. Maybe the sun's touch will do you some good. Once you return, continue with cleaning this mess. "

Crystal's cheek stung.

"Yes, ma'am, I'll depart immediately. May I have coins?"

Several different types of coin were thrown on to the table. "Perhaps locate a job while you're down there."

Crystal swept the change into a pouch and fled her home. Making her way down the street, she gazed at the boundaries of the city as she strolled along. She always pondered what life was like outside this town. Living in the small, little community of Lanster, not too many exciting events occurred. Lanster had houses, a large market three floors high with stands ranging from a pub to a bookstore, and the inn that visitors came to rest from their travels.

Most adventurers were journeying to the city across Lanster Forest, Emerica. Its name originated from the legendary emerald the Protectors allegedly hid beneath its foundation. Not that this fable was true, but after Luminar was destroyed in search of this mystical fantasy, who could really judge what was real. One of the other great cities, Flores, was raided a few weeks following. No survivors from either city.

Her imagination was running wild as she entered the market. The entrance led straight to the bar, the second most visited place in Lanster. Long tables stretched across the room filled with degenerates that clanked their ale as it sloshed inside the chalices, while children were playing in the toy section beside the stairs in the back. A lone man remained aloof, sitting at the bar wrapped in a white cloak. Hoping to go unnoticed, she tried to sneak her way to the counter, until she realized she held the attention of all the men in the room. Especially the one lad who had eaten one too many pastries.

Uneasiness washed over her as she approached the bartender, gently tapping the counter. She noticed the fellow beside her lift his head, only slightly. She caught a glimpse of his eyes before he abruptly returned to his drink. They were as dark blue as an ocean. An ocean that had swallowed many people beneath its surface. Glancing behind her, she caught sight of the heavy set man staring at her, burning a hole in her dress. The rest of them were gesturing to her, laughing and carrying on.

"Good day, Crystal, how do you fare?"

"Just another day, Michael, I am sure you understand. How's the little one doing?"

"Much better due to the wonderful fruit basket she received. I believe a thank you is in order."

Crystal smiled. "I'm glad to hear it."

"What may I help you with?"

"A loaf of bread please, and that will be all."

"Your grandmother having you run errands again?" She nodded. "My eyes have not laid upon that woman in many years. Barely leaves the house. Three bronze, please." Crystal jingled her pouch as she searched for a silver coin.

"Twelve bronze change. Take care of yourself, dear."

Crystal grabbed her belongings, thanked Michael, and took her leave. As the store's door slid into place behind her, she heard a few chairs scraping across the floor. Fearing the worst, she picked up her pace. She peered over her shoulder frequently, praying she would see nothing, but her prayers were left unheard. Four men trailed behind her, all of them from the market. She felt her heart begin racing. She quickly turned the next possible corner, but was dismayed to find a dead end. Too late to escape, Crystal found herself backed against the farthest wall from the entrance, looking upon the men making their way down the alleyway. The heavyset one spoke first.

"Hand over your possessions or I'll pry 'em out of your pretty little hands."

Crystal gulped, timidly shaking her head. She grasped at her pouch and bread tighter, bringing them to her chest.

"There's nowhere to run, girl, and I don't mind getting my hands a bit dirty." He waddled up to her as she fearfully tucked her shoulders in. He violently slammed her up against the wall, grabbing one of her wrists. She was lifted off the ground like a pebble, dangling in air.

She clawed at his grip. He laughed as she struggled to break free. His comrades also joined in on the chuckle. She began hyperventilating, panicking. Trying to slow down her body, she focused on the enemy in front. Crystal hastily put the soles of her pink sandals against the wall and propelled forward, ramming her torso into his gut. The shock caused him to falter backward, releasing her from his clutches. Landing on her feet, she instantly forced her entire body weight into the man, crashing him into the ground.

Crystal watched as he struggled to get back on his feet as the other three came to his side. Her eyebrows rose as she began to tear. She crouched, protecting her face with her forearms. The intense moment was disrupted as one of the men grunted and the others turned in an uproar. Uncovering her head, she watched as a man draped in white threw one of the fellows at the brick wall. His skull created a crack as it made contact. He slowly slid to the dirt, lying still.

Her hero grabbed another bandit by his neck, tossing him at the chubby fellow. He bounced off, tumbling into the dirt, while the big man slid up against the bricks beside Crystal. The collision shook the whole wall as he laid there in a daze. She started breathing heavily, her pulse racing even faster. She watched as the last of them came from behind and ripped off the stranger's cover. A powerful male was revealed who was not at all happy that his cloak had been taken. Not a speck of dirt or grime was visible on his entirely white outfit.

As Crystal studied him, he kicked the bandit in the stomach. He palmed his face and rammed it into another wall. The cloak floated in the air, but with one quick motion he swept it up before it reached the ground. He started walking toward Crystal, past the two men up against the wall and over the one on the ground. His enormous structure and fierceness terrified her even though he crushed her pursuers.

When he was an arm's length away, he shot out his hand. She cringed, horrified for her life, but when she felt nothing, she looked around. Crystal watched her savior lift up the overweight thug, breaking both his wrists. With each snap, the man wailed. Finished, he flung him over his shoulder like a bag of feathers.

There was a loud boom as the body bounced against the dirt. Her rescuer looked at her almost apathetically.

"I watched them leave a moment behind you. I had a troubling suspicion that these hooligans had ill intentions, so I pursued them. When I reached the entrance to the alleyway, I watched as you knocked the beast on his arse. I hope you're not upset with me for intruding, but I feared the worst." His voice was rough, but sweet. When she glanced into his eyes, Crystal felt nothing. No heroic qualities of light or justice. Just darkness. But even so, his whole aura overcame her, immediately relaxing every inch of her person.

"Yeah, ah, th-thank you, I'm glad you came. You saved my life, I'm so grateful you were here."

"I disagree; if I had not shown, I think you would have done just fine. But my time is limited, and my patience is thin. Pardon me, I shall take my leave. Good day, miss, I hope you make it home safely." He turned around, peering down at his entirely bleached outfit—vest, parachute pants, and boots. Everything crisp and clean, besides his shoes. He licked his thumb, using it to rub the dirt from both his feet.

"Wait! What's your name? Are you a traveler?"

"As I stated before, my time is short. My name is unimportant—know that after today I shall never make your presence again." With those final words, he bounced between the two alleyway walls until he reached the top. Breaching the open space, he dramatically whipped his cape over his shoulders and dashed away.

Crystal watched in amazement. Once her hero was out of sight, she took a deep breath to regain her composure. The excitement left her confused, almost lost. Her adrenaline was pumping as she checked to make sure she was unscathed. Satisfied, Crystal sprinted home. Only when she was safe inside her house with the door separating the world from her did she begin to relax. Her grandmother was still at the dining room table tapping her foot rapidly. The air of the household was much more terrifying than the encounter she had just experienced.

She placed the loaf of bread and coins before her grandmother. Unexpectedly, her grandmother swiftly flung her hand in a quick movement causing a slapping sound to revolve around the room. Crystal stood there in disbelief, holding her tender face. Her eyes widened as she stared down at her elder in pure shock.

"The Protectors were to have me before you returned! You dare to keep me waiting?"

Crystal, still frazzled replied, "But-but I al-almost got mugged!" Tears lined the bottom of her lower lid.

"Excuses? How unladylike! Head to your chambers; keep your face hidden away until morning." Crystal was lost in her Grandmother's madness. "Are you deaf now, too, girl? Leave me!" The old lady went to smack her again, but it was caught to her surprise.

"I'm tired of this, Grandmother. I'll return to my quarters, but this shall be the last time you will see me!" Crystal stole the change off the table while stomping upstairs. She could hear the echoes of her grandmother's voice trailing behind her.

49

The bedroom door slammed behind her as tears stung her eyes. Crystal was too mad to think, but she had too many unanswered questions. *What am I doing? Is this the right decision? She hit me again . . . I'm exhausted of being treated as a possession. Where will I go? What shall I bring? Where am I going to stay?* No responses came to mind, but she proceeded to grab her draw-string bag. Her frustrations made her throw all caution to the wind. She threw the coins in her bag with a bunch of objects and clothing she figured would prove to be important, and then decided to change her clothes. *I need something more comfortable.* She put on blue daisy-dukes and a short-sleeved, purple V-neck blouse that faded to blue toward the bottom. Crystal placed her bag on her back, readying herself for the next step. Quietly opening the window, she hopped through the frame with her fine, straight hair flowing behind her.

She landed awkwardly on her feet, collapsing from the drop. Her knees and elbows were already scraped. Slowly getting up, she began shaking. *I don't know if I'm strong enough for whatever I'm doing.* A screech came flying from her window, one formed from anger rather than compassion. With the disheartening noise coming from her bedroom, she knew it was time. Time to leave and never come back. Regaining control of her emotions, she dashed away. She didn't stop for anyone or anything. Neighbors tried to get her attention, some even attempted to cut off her path, but it was futile. No matter what they shouted to comfort her, Crystal was finished.

She finally slowed down when she reached the outskirts of Lanster. She searched through her bag, praying to the Protectors that it was in there. Her anxiety was released as she retrieved the map of Osiren. Tracing the paper with her finger, she decided to follow the path of all the adventurers who had come through her town and made Emerica her destination. Maybe a little adventure would do her some good.

She knew the only thing separating her from freedom was Lanster Forest. Crystal cautiously walked toward the forest opening. The darkness inside seemed to grow bigger as she drew nearer. *I know*

I have to go through this, but how? I have nothing to keep myself safe. Who knows what evil hides within? The travelers always told stories of dark forests. She shook her head, clearing her mind of the doubts plaguing her. Taking a deep breath, she eyed the entrance. Without another thought, she darted in.

The man landed on top of the city wall, staring down at the city called Emerica. *For being one of the famous legendary five cities, it does not appear to be anything special,* he thought. He could hear the sound of water splashing against the shoreline in the distance. The smell of the sea swarmed his senses. Scanning the area, he located the King's castle toward the back on a high cliff. A twisting road connected the castle to the main part of the city. The entire place seemed disorganized. The man scoffed. Markets were right next to houses and schools were stationed next to hospitals. *How could anyone navigate this mess?* Behind the castle's bluff was the Marvelous Ocean which surrounded its perimeter. The steep drop would be a struggle for any invader to climb, making it a tremendous natural defense.

As he gazed around Emerica, he remembered his mission. Eyes closed, standing upon the wall, he raised his arms. He tipped forward allowing himself to drop. While freefalling, time seemed to slow. *I cannot let this happen again; it shall stay, and the lives of these citizens will remain untouched.* Those thoughts sped through his mind as he landed safely in a conveniently placed pile of hay. Freeing himself, he peered over his outfit. Picking straws of hay from his ruffled, dirty blond hair, he traveled forward. With the citizens fast asleep and the ocean's collapsing waves silenced by the city's walls, the town became extremely ominous. Before letting the uneasiness eat him alive, he searched for shelter.

Crystal stared ahead, doing her best to not avert her eyes. She had to remain focused and not let her imagination manipulate her judgment. The farther she traveled through the woods, the darker her surroundings were becoming. The outlines of trees could barely be identified, turning her hasty run into a cautious jog. The last thing she wanted to do was get close and personal with a piece of nature. The lack of vision was nurturing her fear. She could feel a cold sweat form on her forehead. Wiping it off, she did what she tried so hard not to do: look around. At that instant, she tripped over her own feet.

Tumbling over, she pushed herself right back up. The creepy ticks of the insects startled her more than the darkness. Examining the area, she heard branches cracking and leaves rustling. Things moved in the distance, bouncing and weaving among the obstacles. She backed herself against a tree. Her heart was beating hard and her breathing increased. Just then, a shadowy figure popped up in front of her. On sight it ran forward. Crossing her arms and ducking her head she released an intense scream, shaking the very canopies themselves.

Just like that, it was gone. All the shadows vanished. *Thank the Protectors it was only my eyes playing tricks on me. Okay, okay. I-I need to get out of here now.* She turned to examine the very large plant behind her. Judging by its huge diameter and girth, it was a rather old tree. Placing a hand on it she thought, *this would be a good place to play hide and seek if you ask me.* As her adrenaline died for the second time that day, her head started pounding. With the last of her will, she jetted forward. She was beginning to feel all hope was lost until she saw Emerica's walls through the break of the canopies.

She sprinted free of the forest, hoping to embrace daylight, but was blinded by more night. With her heart still racing, she wiped the sweat from her face. *I guess it took longer to get through there than I realized,* Crystal thought, huffing and puffing. She gleefully examined the outer wall of Emerica, which was a plain cement barrier. Even so, she couldn't believe she was coming this close to the great city. Her eyes frantically searched for the entrance, where she spotted two guardsmen.

"Halt! State your business," demanded the first guardsman.

"I came . . . here . . . to visit," gasped Crystal, searching for air.

"Why is a young lady traveling at this time of night for a visit?" asked the second.

"Where are your parents?"

"My parents? What? I, uh . . . here," Crystal said, digging into her duffel bag. "I have twelve bronze coins that I don't need. Please allow me to enter?" she begged, taunting the guards with the jingling.

The first guard stared at the coins debating, until he opened the door and motioned her to enter. She could hardly believe it; happiness overcame her. She started skipping inside until the guard struck out his hand. Quickly handing over the coins, she continued her grand entrance.

She was astounded by the size of the city. Compared to Lanster, Emerica was an entire country! The variety of buildings, large and small side by side, were astounding. Venturing further, she could already see herself getting lost among all the streets. Lashing her head back and forth admiring the architecture, she was completely unaware of the person standing before her. Colliding into them, she stepped back, almost losing her balance. Crystal looked at the stranger, but could only see their outline.

"Oh, I'm sorry! I did not see you before me. I was not expecting a citizen to be about at such an hour. Shouldn't you be at home?" It was a low gentle voice, clearly a female.

"Um," she giggled awkwardly, not prepared to speak with a stranger about her situation. "I'm an adventurer and my journey has brought me here. My stay in Lanster came to an end. But why are you strolling the streets? That's the King's guards' duties."

The girl chuckled, "I'm on my nightly stroll through the town. The calmness of a sleeping city soothes me. I find solace in the emptiness and lack of people crowding the roads. I may be able to suggest hotels that are still running?"

"I-I, well I don't have any currency on me . . ."

Her smile could be seen through the shadows. "Nothing to worry about; come with me and stay in one of our many guest rooms. Girls have to stick together."

Without worrying about her pride, she curtseyed saying, "I would greatly appreciate that! Thank you! My name's Crystal Thorn."

"They call me Lila."

"Oh, wow! Such a pretty name!"

Lila smiled, "Thank you! Yours deserves such praise as well!"

Joining Lila on her walk, their conversation led to why Crystal had become an adventurer. Crystal explained her home situation and her savior from earlier. The two girls spent plenty of their talk fantasizing about the hero that came to Crystal's rescue. Lila could only imagine what this gentleman would appear like in flesh and blood.

As they continued their stroll, Crystal followed Lila as she turned upon a long, winding path. Crystal explained she couldn't take being under the same roof with her grandmother any longer.

"Why were you residing with your grandmother? What happened to your parents?"

"My . . . You see . . . My parents dedicated most of their lives to the Protectors. Having me around would only . . . distract them from their faith. I've been in my Grandmother's custody since my third year of Creation."

Lila nodded understanding the situation. "Do you place your faith with the Protectors?"

"It's not that I don't . . . I do. Just not to an extreme. Kyrudorous and Zorumaka were heroes long ago; I'm hesitant to believe they still watch over Teague."

"Hmm, I see. What's your age as of now?"

"I'm seventeen years of age."

"Oh my, such a young one to deal with those unfortunate upbringings." The female gave her condolences seeing that the subject was hard for her companion.

As their march continued through the slithering path, Crystal could vaguely see a castle ahead of them.

"Excuse me, Lila, I realized that the conversation circled around me. Incredibly rude. Where did you say you lived?"

"I had not," she chuckled. "Just a little more ways to go."

"The castle is . . . you're not . . . the Princess?"

"Friends call me Lila; my people refer to me as Princess Lilian." She gestured to her home, proud and formidable before them.

"Oh no, Your Highness, my apologies!" she curtsied.

"Please stand, Crystal, you don't have to bow to a friend."

A red coloring bloomed on her cheeks. They crossed through the courtyard to enter the mansion. The Princess showed Crystal to her room. Saying farewell, Crystal showered and freshened up before snuggling under the sheets. Beyond drowsy and worn, she had no problem cuddling with the strange linens. While she was lying in bed, her mind bubbled with fascination that she was in the castle of Emerica. Her. The girl from Lanster who dreamt of the day she would visit this city was now in good graces with the royalty and sleeping inside their castle. The mere idea made her jittery with excitement. She could not wait to explore tomorrow. The allure eventually put her asleep.

CHAPTER 4

She awoke the next morning to birds singing in harmony. *That's nicer than my grandmother's screams.* Crystal dangled her feet over the bed, absorbing her surroundings. The vibrant colors of the room were breathtaking. Red silk lined the mattress, the marble tiles glistened, and the beige walls tied the atmosphere together. She bathed in the stainless steel tub that sparkled, fixed the linen on her bed, and tidied her belongings. When her chores were complete, she opened the twin glass doors and walked onto the balcony. She leaned on an ornate golden railing between two large crème pillars.

Wow, it's beautiful! Her eyes wandered over every inch of the city. Her view was in a perfect position to see the gracefulness of the serene waters and liveliness of the city streets. She looked down as the citizens scurried around looking like ants. The population of any given street was already much larger than her city. Crystal was still unable to process that she was actually here, in the castle. All her life she dreamed of leaving Lanster, but she honestly believed her eyes would never witness anything outside of that jail cell.

As she continued gazing, there was a soft knock on the door. Not accustomed to these types of manners, Crystal quietly answered, "Y-Yes?"

"May I come in, m'lady?" asked a deep voice.

"Yes?" she repeated, almost as a question with an eyebrow curved.

The door opened revealing a guard in leather armor with a bow and arrows attached to his back. The armor seemed sturdy, but looked like it was clumsily put together. The leather was strapped across what she believed to be chainmail underneath. *At least its full body, so they are protected . . . hopefully,* she thought. Upon his entrance, he bowed. *Maybe he has the wrong room?*

"Her Highness has requested your presence in the dining hall when you are ready. I'm here to guide you. When you are prepared, say the word."

Crystal blinked, "Uh, yes, I'm ready to go down. Are you . . . ready?"

Just as confused as she, he gave an awkward smile, "Yes I am m'lady; it's my duty to always be ready."

Embarrassed, she followed behind the guard. As she was led down the hallway, she observed its eccentric appearance: the hall mirrored the elaborate guest room—white marble floors and creamy, brown paint. Gorgeous portraits covered the walls. Each picture depicted the same faces, ones she was unable to recognize. Then at once it clicked: the Protectors. Zorumaka and Kyrudorous lined the halls acting out a multitude of scenes, from having tea to slaying demons. Their faces were slightly altered portrait to portrait, but there was no doubt it was them. Between the paintings, plants flourished, tall and vibrant.

As the guard rounded the end of the hallway, Crystal noticed an ancient looking door. The antiqueness of the wood caught her attention. Rot was beginning to destroy the corners. It was clear that a coat of paint had been used to blend the entrance into its surroundings, but the layer was chipping in more than one location. Beneath the cob webs, she glanced at the knob and peculiarly shaped lock.

"That's an oddly placed door. Excuse me, guard, where does this lead?"

"Why are you inquiring?"

She heard distress cross his voice.

"N-no reason, it seems old compared to the rest of the decorations."

He gave a slight sigh. "No one knows for certain; even Princess Lilian has no knowledge. Only the King himself, though he has never disclosed any information on its use. It's his personal business."

Turning the corner, the hallway opened into a huge lobby. There were three steps leading to a platform with a humongous door on the right. On the opposite side, there were three more steps going into another hallway. A third set of wide stairs lead from this grand door heading to the lower floor. It was all decorated identically to the other rooms except for an ancient chandelier hanging from the ceiling and the red carpet lining the stairs. The chandelier had a medieval feel with its round, wooden circle that held candles in slots carved into the wood. The guard mentioned this was their main entrance and the door on their right was the King's throne room, which was off limits unless service was in session.

The two headed to the lower floor and curved to the left. Behind one of the columns lining the grand stairwell were several more doors. The guard knocked gently upon one. A faint "enter" was heard through the wood. They stepped into the dining hall on command. A long glass table was in the center with twelve red velvet chairs positioned on each side, and one at both ends. Breakfast was placed strategically across the glass, along with lit candles and a bouquet of flowers adorning the middle. Above was another chandelier dangling over the meal, one more eccentric than before, especially since it was bejeweled with an assortment of gems.

Several more paintings and towering statues decorated the walls of the dining hall, all resembling the theme of the Protectors. Crystal had never felt safer in such a religious sanctuary. To the side were the chef's doors leading to and from the kitchen. The King was at the far head of the table with Princess Lillian beside him. The King sat in solitude, barely noticing Crystal's appearance. His long graying beard curled at the end, while the rest of his hair was short and hidden underneath a black cap.

Lila waved to her guest. "Good morning, Crystal!" She was wearing a lovely light green morning gown. Reaching just below her knees, the bottom part was fringed with white cotton. Her short, maroon hair was pulled back into a tight ponytail and her hazel eyes glistened under the candlelight.

Crystal and the guard started walking toward them, but the guard halted. He spun around on his heels and exited the room. She noticed the King had held his hand up, and assumed it meant the guard's duties were done and he was dismissed. As she strolled to the far side of the table, she noticed the wait staff lining the back drop of the room. A glass of water had already been poured and a servant pulled a chair from the table for her, pushing her in when she was comfortable.

"How do you fare today?" smiled Lila.

"I have never had a better night's rest, Your Highness. Thank you for allowing me to stay overnight, your hospitality is immeasurable."

"The pleasure is all mine, and please, Lila will do. This is the least I could do to help a brave adventurer. I'm sure your journey has you quite famished. Help yourself to anything on the table." She motioned her hand to the buffet before them.

Crystal, feeling her stomach gurgle, happily filled her plate with a variety of fruits and pastries. The King violently coughed, startling Crystal and making her drop a roll. She immediately froze, looking at Lila fearfully.

"Oh, Father . . . My apologies," groaned Lila. "Crystal, allow me to introduce my father, King of Emerica."

Crystal jumped from her seat, curtseying, "Your Royal Grace, it is a pleasure to meet you. Please pardon my manners."

The old man's demeanor completely flipped as he gave a hearty chuckle.

"Please ignore the formalities," whispered Lila.

"Sit, sit, my dear. My dearest daughter I'm sure has told you that a guest of the castle and friend of hers has no need to lower thy head." He grinned as Crystal returned to her seat. "The Princess often comes across strangers and brings them to feast. Most peculiar at first, but she has a talent in assisting travelers, despite their cause. She does love a good tale of the outsiders. Her fascination of Teague excites her ever so much. Let us continue with our meal."

The King questioned her journey, asking for details of yesterday's morning to last night's encounter. Crystal retold the story of her mugging, her cause to escape home, and the journey in the forest. She also mentioned her parents once more, this time with more confidence.

"Such events for a lady of your age to be forced through," announced the King as he finished polishing his plate.

"Those woods frighten me to no end, bless the Protectors for guiding you through!" empathized Lila.

"My fear was real . . . I hesitated, but I could no longer withstand my environment."

"As you should," agreed the King. "Did you and the cloaked man share any words? Strange to risk one's life for another without payment in such a situation."

"Well, the moment passed by as soon as it occurred. He said he was pressed for time, cutting our conversation short. I was unable to learn his name."

"What was his appearance? Thug like?"

"He covered himself with a white cape. He remained mostly hidden. He wore all white, without a stain to be seen. He treated me as a lady of worth, but his chivalry was shrouded behind his mysteriousness. The entire scene is hard to explain."

"Sounds like a man I could stand behind."

"Honey, you're starting to drool." The King handed her a

napkin. "Despite his reasoning, luck brought him to your aide. The situation sounds very dire, thank the Protectors he arrived when he did."

Trying to draw the attention away from her mishap, Lila straightened her necklace. She gently caressed the silver pendant that had a green jewel embedded into the center.

"Oh my, that's beautiful, Lila!" exclaimed Crystal.

She basked in the compliment. "This little thing? I hold it most dear to my heart."

"It was her mother's long ago. A family legacy it is, one that has been around since the time of the Prophets. It must not be misplaced." The King finished his stern warning by washing down his breakfast with red wine.

"I am aware, Father, 'tis not as I travel beyond these walls often," she waved her hand to each side of the dining hall.

As their meal was finished, the wait staff rushed to the table. They grabbed ahold of the dirty dishes and leftover food. Within minutes the whole table was cleared and they began setting it for their meal in the afternoon. Crystal noticed how, oddly enough, none of the staff made eye contact with her—with any of those seated, now that she thought about it. *Must be part of their tradition.* The last servant waddled out as the King pushed away from the table, releasing a hefty yawn.

"I'll be retiring to my room for the remainder of this morning. Crystal, I hope you are able to stay and enjoy what we have to offer. I am sure the Princess has duties she must attend to as well."

Lila smirked, tilting her head to the side.

"Thanks for yo—" Crystal was interrupted as a guard pushed through the doors.

"Your Majesty, there's a man in the lobby demanding Your Majesty's attention at once."

"What does he want?" demanded the King.

"Uh, h-he won't tell . . . only to you will he speak."

The King sighed, knowing these sort of intrusions only

caused him an ache. "Bring him in."

The guard left at once returning with the man wearing the white cloak. Crystal practically fainted in her seat. The King, Princess, and Crystal all shared a glance.

"Your Majesty," he bowed. The King allowed him to rise. "My name is Phoenix Reinhard. I have traveled many miles to speak with you," his eyes shifted around the room. "Alone."

"Remove your overcoat, it is disrespectful," barked the King with a rather irritated tone. "We are alone, state your business or leave else wise."

Lila whispered to Crystal, "That man must be the one who saved you." Crystal nodded. "Wow. Even easier on the eyes than expected."

"From where do you hail?"

"I come from nowhere. My home is gone just as yesterday is over. I am now a traveler bound by my oath. I mean no disrespect, Your Majesty, but I hold important information that is for your ears *only*."

"Speak then, child, we are in good company. Stop wasting my time."

Phoenix stared around the room again before continuing, "On my travels, I came across unnerving information that *this* city, Emerica, will soon be under siege. An invasion mimicking the raid on Luminar and Flores twelve years ago."

The announcement had drained the energy from the room. Crystal felt her jaw lower. She leaned forward, hands on her mouth. *The raid on Flores and Luminar? All those men and women murdered . . . How horrible.* She flicked her eyes between the King and the Princess.

The King's eyes narrowed, his forehead tensing. He prompted himself upright in his chair while his fingers tightened on the grips of the arm rests. Lila responded similar to her father, straightening her spine and her doe-eyed stare turned into immense glaring. Though, Crystal thought, the King appeared angry and fearful, while Lila was more . . . frustrated.

"What you speak of, if false, could be considered treason. Where was this information heard?"

"Kyron City. I've spent a large sum of my time there on the streets. My sources informed me that forces have already been stationed within the city, while others wait beyond the wall for a signal. They plan to mount the walls one of these evenings."

The King pondered these words for a few moments, which felt like hours to the audience waiting in silence. His face showed his struggle on how to handle this rift raft. Finally he spoke, "I, the great King of Emerica, am supposed to believe that some street rat heard that my city is going to be infiltrated? Especially from a grimy, back water town like Kyron City? What do you take me for?"

"Your Majesty, please! I speak of only the truth! You *have* to believe in what I say! I wish not the same fate to befall Emerica that Luminar once endured!"

"How dare you come into my castle and question my judgment! This city shall never fall to hired mercenaries. Be gone from my sight at once!" the King hollered at the top of his lungs. He clapped his hands for the guards to come forth.

"Wait, no!" yelled Crystal crossing the hall to Phoenix's side. Disbelief covered his face as he recognized the girl from Lanster. "I be-beg your pardon, Your Majesty, I hate to abruptly intervene in this conversation, but I think . . . he may be telling the truth."

"Why? Saving a person's innocence does not remove them from being a criminal or liar. Why defend a stranger?

"When I was . . . was running through the forest, a figure appeared. One in the shape of a man rushed toward me. When I screamed . . . it-it vanished. I believed it to be my imagination, but now . . . What if there are soldiers in the forest?"

The King looked between both Phoenix and Crystal, contemplating his decision.

"I shall review this information with my council. We shall be called to the Throne Room in approximately three hours to discuss our actions from there—if I decide to believe you. If either of you do not arrive, I'll have my guardsmen prepare for a hunt. A hunt that is in search of no animals."

The King made his exit, leaving behind Lila squirming in her chair. Standing from her seat, she nervously spoke, "Well, if you could pardon my presence, I have some Princess things I must accomplish, as I was kindly reminded. Feel free to explore the city or rest in the guest bedrooms. Take care of yourselves." The wavering in her voice struck Crystal as odd, but she dismissed the thought.

Alone, a few minutes of uncomfortable silence compelled Phoenix to approach his unexpected savior. "Your assistance was much needed. I do not think I could have swayed the King on my own."

"A life for a life; let's think about it as returning the favor," Crystal smiled, her eyes rolling over the man now that her life wasn't being threatened. The vest could barely contain his massive shoulders. Along the seam on the right side, yellow lines stretched up his torso. It was etched into a pattern, but she couldn't identify the picture.

"What would you have done if he sent you away? Or imprisoned you for spewing nonsense of some sort?"

"The matter would be in my hands alone. I would have stood against the adversary at the front gate, even if I were to be the only one. Beyond that though . . ." He clenched his fists. Crystal could see his anger rising.

"Why are you so concerned about this, if-if you don't mind me asking?"

Phoenix looked at her innocent face, immediately staring at her shining blue gems. Just as bright and full of love like Beth's, he thought. Sweet, gentle, would help another no matter the cost . . . No, I can't do this again, I'm not—

"Phoenix, are you alright?"

Refocusing on the conversation, he returned to reality. "Huh? Yes, I'm fine . . . sorry. That's a story for another time."

Crystal whispered "oh," looking down at her pink shoes.

"Though I have a few questions, if you would indulge me. Why Emerica? Lanster seemed to be your home. Unless you attend that bar regularly to chat up the bartender."

"I was not chatting up Michael," she scoffed. "After the incident I no longer felt it was safe to stay. Emerica sounded much more pleasing."

"Which brings you through the Lanster Forest. What exactly do you recall seeing that night?"

"I lost my balance near an old oak tree. As I pulled myself up, I thought I saw . . . *things* bobbing around the bushes and trunks. I believed it was my imagination—I still think it is—I just thought if I spoke up, the King would be gentler."

"Even so, that isn't something I want to leave unchecked. Would you be able to show me where you saw these . . . *things*?"

"I don't want to go back in there . . . I'm scared."

"There's no need to be scared, you can handle yourself and I'll be by your side. No harm will come to you."

She took comfort in these words. "Al-alright I'll show you, but don't you want to be more prepared? What if there are a lot of them?"

"That is the least of my worries." His words held such confidence that Crystal trusted his instinct. "I want as much time to explore before we are summoned to court." They walked through the palace doors into the open air. The wind brushed against their faces as Crystal peered over the side of the bluff. The water aggressively smashed against the rocks. Each time they came together, the tips of the waves slithered farther up the mountainside, almost as if it was reaching for the top. The scent of ocean air wrapped around them as Phoenix traced the long curvy drive into the city.

"The walk to the forest will take us all morning!" exclaimed Crystal. "It'll be an hour to reach the city at least!"

"Climb on," Phoenix knelt down before her. Confused, Crystal wrapped her arms around his neck and her legs around his waist.

"Am I not going to slow you down?" she questioned as he stood erectly.

"Make sure you hold on tight. If you fall, I can guarantee it will hurt."

She held him tighter, pressing herself firmly onto his back. Phoenix sprinted toward their destination. The wind whipped through Crystal's hair as his speed increased significantly. She was at a loss for words. *He . . . this is unbelievable! I'm not slowing him down in the slightest.* Before she knew it, they reached the bottom of the trail. Without hesitation, Phoenix climbed the nearest balcony. From there he hopped onto a table and leapt to the rooftop. He bounced between buildings, losing no stamina between each gap. Most homes were close in proximity, allowing him to merely step between them without much effort. The citizens gawked at the flying man. Reaching the gates, Phoenix descended to the ground by sliding down a pole to another ledge. Dropping from the ledge, the impact made a thud, forcing him to fall to a knee.

Once he regained his balance, he quietly whispered to Crystal, "You can stop strangling me now."

"Sorry," she whimpered, releasing him. Phoenix couldn't tell if she was bright red from wind abrasions or embarrassment.

Leaving Emerica, Phoenix rubbed his neck from the throttling he had just endured. Crossing through the gate, a guardsman shouted after them, "Hey sweetie, leaving requires a toll as well! Better pay up!" He winked as his buddy started chuckling.

Phoenix raised a brow. "What's the meaning of that?"

"I bribed them to gain entrance into the city last night. Don't fret, I'm sure they need it more. It costs plenty of coins to change personalities."

"Go on ahead, I'll rejoin you in a moment."

Crystal merely shrugged and continued toward the tree line. She peered over her shoulder, spying on Phoenix's actions. He was facing the guards, chitchatting. *I wonder what he is up to?* Reaching the edge, she turned, gasped, and toppled backward.

Phoenix reached out his hand, "You're as pale as a ghost."

"Sneaking up on a person like that is awful!" Grabbing Phoenix's hand, she stood and brushed dirt from her shorts. "I had not expected you to be that close."

"I'll make sure you are alerted to my presence next time," Phoenix grinned. "Let's make quick work with this search; let's not give the King another reason to throw me into a dungeon." Crystal checked back on the two guards; one was lying on his back, while the other was against the wall in dismay. *What did he do to them?*

The two darted through the woods, trees passing by in a blur. *Not as bad as the first time; the daylight's making it much easier to see.* She glanced around as she tried to distinguish her surroundings. After a few more yards, the giant oak tree came into view.

"Here, this is where I discovered the shadows. Right around this area."

Phoenix approached the spot, Crystal following behind step by step. Her fear held strong, keeping her at the white heels of her protector. As they got closer, Phoenix's nostrils flared.

"Do you smell that?"

Crystal started sniffing around, "No, I smell nothing."

"It smells like," he inhaled deeply, "smoke."

Circling around the base of the stump, Phoenix stuck his head around to find a camp. Supplies were scattered amongst the site, food and personal items lying on the dirt and benches. A fire was roaring in the middle of the site, black gas dispersing into the air.

Phoenix rubbed his jaw, whispering, "This fire . . . it's fresh?"

"People *were* here when I came through." A smile crossed her face along with a feeling of confidence.

"Who would leave a fire unattended and freshly sparked? Why waste the wood? Unless . . ." His ears perked up, hearing rustling in the bushes.

Crystal slid her hands along the bark. "A good thing I chose not to stick around and investigate. I would have never been able to take—"

"Crystal!" Phoenix yelled as he charged to her.

A whoosh was released from the bushes. Crystal faced him to respond to his cry, but caught sight of an arrow streaming right at her. She stared on in horror as Phoenix swiftly grabbed the projectile in midair—inches from her face. He snapped it between his fingers.

"Take cover! It's an ambush!"

Almost on cue, ten bandits appeared from the bushes and dropped from the branches. The bandits surrounded them as they backed against the trunk of the tree. Phoenix stood next to Crystal, putting his arm in front of her as he shouted, "I will grant you all three seconds. Leave. Or take me down."

Seven of them charged at Phoenix. They wildly swung at him, but Phoenix smoothly glided between each one. He leaned back as another swing came through. He grabbed the goon's hand and twisted it backward. As the others started another barrage of wild swings, Phoenix used the struggling goon as a shield. Each sword sliced up their comrade, leaving his body lifeless. Phoenix threw the man aside, stealing his weapon. Wielding the sword high with his right leg out, he went on the offensive.

Crystal watched, amazed and terrified at the same time. She could not believe this stranger was taking on seven men at once. Watching the fight, she noticed two bowmen in her peripheral. They drew back the string and aimed. She barely made it around the tree before the two shots were fired, piercing the bark where her head was originally. Taking a sigh of relief, she looked back around to see the last bandit charging at her. She dove to the side as the bandit hacked away. She started yelping as she rolled away from each slice. His accuracy improved, but luckily, she kept managing to avoid his swing.

Phoenix was quick on his feet and strayed away from each sword. He shoved his blade in one man's chest, ripped it out, and decapitated him in one motion. As blood from the headless body sprayed, Phoenix retrieved his steel as well. Dual wielding, he went up against another sword catching it in his crosshairs. He kicked him back and swept his leg across the dirt, knocking the bandit to the ground. Another bandit came in a rush, but after a swift deflection Phoenix smashed the hilt against his face.

Crossing over two of his dazed comrades, another man went straight for a stab, but missed the target. The sword wedged itself into the dirt, getting stuck. He struggled to wiggle it free, but Phoenix plummeted his weapon through the back of his head. Walking toward the two goons struggling to stand, he impaled a sword into each of their chests. Another of the squad came toward him, drawing a big gash with red ink. He released his weapons, falling back. The wound caught him by surprise leaving him breathless. Phoenix grasped his chest, watching the final two bandits walk his way.

Crystal rolled her way to the side, escaping another swing. She circled around the oak trying to create some distance between her and her pursuer. Reaching the side with Phoenix, two more arrows spiraled in her direction. She shut her eyes tight, only to reopen them as the gusts of wind brushed pass her. *Thank the Protectors they missed.* She glanced at Phoenix and watched as one of the bandits carved him between his pectorals. Gasping, she placed her hand over her mouth. Feeling something wet, she trembled as she brought her hand into view. The entire palm was covered in a crimson red liquid. Blood seeped from her cheek. Seeing her blood petrified her. She stood there motionless, until the goon brought her back to reality. He ran at her, his eyes searching for skin. She frantically searched the grounds for anything useful until she found a sword in arm's reach.

Phoenix crawled backward, watching as the men lost their patience. One slammed down upon him. Thinking fast, Phoenix caught the blade with the palms of his hands, snapping it in half. The man staggered away astounded by the severity and brute strength. Phoenix hopped to his feet and chucked the fragmented blade at the man's face with great precision. It inserted itself right betwixt the eyes. With only one left who was already traumatized, Phoenix easily strolled up to him and cracked him in the face. Instantly unconscious. He could feel shards of metal in his hands, pricking him every time his heart beat. Which was fast and often. His chest ached, too, but his blind rage was not concerned with his condition. He continuously beat the soldier before him into an unrecognizable mess. He grazed around the camp for Crystal who he found snatching up a sword and barely deflecting a blow.

She's stronger than she believes, he thought. The pain of his gash quickly spread throughout his body. His eyes began pounding as his blood pumped. Through his obscured vision, he watched as she ran toward the bandit. In an attempt, she went for a strike, but he effortlessly evaded. She tumbled over her feet, losing balance and face-planting. She flipped onto her back and tried to reach for her weapon. As her fingertips touched the coolness of the steel, a boot crushed her fingers. She wailed as the weapon was kicked further from her reach.

Phoenix watched as the man stood above the defenseless girl, readying for the final blow. His mind raced back twelve years ago, replaying the scene with Skull and his sister. The sinister armor, her tattered night gown, her scream. He reached for his mouth to wipe away her blood he felt splash on him again. The stress, sadness, and anxiety came rushing back full throttle. His mind went numb.

Crystal watched as the bandit rose his blade overhead. She began crying, knowing this was the end. Death. She was not ready to die. Her life had just started. Not yet. Crying her last words for help, she watched as the sword suddenly halted in midair. He lost its grip, letting it bounce before him. A tip of steel appeared poking through his chest. It twisted, turned, and disappeared. Several times it happened throughout the man's body. As a finale, his entire torso slid diagonally from itself. The spraying of blood paralyzed her and as she phased in and out of consciousness the last thing she saw was Phoenix standing behind him. His eyes were wild, almost completely different. Before she passed out, she witnessed Phoenix thrust his blade into the man's skull.

Calming down, Phoenix returned to his senses. All his muscles eased at once, dropping his sword. His whole body went limp; every emotion hit him like a shovel. A spiral of feelings surged through him, covering his entire self in piercing pain. He observed the deformed mass of meat lying in front of him. His body wavered in disgust. *Who did this . . .?* His eyes trailed to the blood soaked sword. *I? I was the one?*

He lifted Crystal's fainted body. Cradling her, he examined the area in search of the two bowmen or information that could be potentially helpful. Fighting his draining strength, he departed.

The King of Emerica stirred angrily as he sat upon his throne wearing his traditional green cape. With his pride sat upon his head—the most important symbol of royalty, the King's crown—he barked orders at individual guardsmen in the room. His berserk rampage sent dramatic directions: "To each crevice in the pavement to the attics of each bell tower, hunt down that scoundrel. Capture him and Princess Lilian's friend. Dead or alive, beaten or unscathed, bring those—" The King stopped as his Throne Room doors were abruptly slammed aside. Preparing to deal with the maniac barging in, he was flabbergasted to find a bloody mess wobbling forward.

"Aide that poor boy! Retrieve the medic!" He hurried down the flight of stairs that separated him from the peasants of the city. "Assist me in bringing them to the emergency infirmary stat!" Crystal was transferred to a servant as the King hurried ahead, motioning to Phoenix to follow. Servants and workers frantically cleared a path for the parade to march through.

"In the Protectors' names, what trouble did you find? My dear daughter said to roam the city, not get yourselves slaughtered!"

"My Majesty," Phoenix gasped, searching for air. "M-My curiosity won the better of me. I went . . . explore the w-w-woods. She wasn't mistaken . . . soldiers . . . a dozen. I . . . advise—send guards." He aggressively clutched at his wound, groaning in pain.

"Did you not slay all the traitors?"

"N-no, two of them—got away. We were—" Phoenix dropped, bouncing his head against the carpet.

"Phoenix! My lad?" The King shook his shoulders. "Bring him to the medic! He's lost too much blood! Soldiers, rally in the Throne Room, I need all forces in Lanster Forest!"

CHAPTER 5

Phoenix was running. He passed piles of dead bodies emitting a pungent smell. The cries of terror circulated around him. The light from above dimmed until he was submerged in complete darkness. Only blood splatters and illuminated corpses guided him. Running out of breath, he stopped by a small pool of red liquid. The surface was smooth enough to show his reflection. Shiny blond hair covered his forehead with icy eyes staring back at him. His fingers shook as he reached for his bangs. He was a kid again. A weak, worthless, puny child dressed in rags. His face was covered in cuts and bruises. Infections were setting in his wounds.

The sound of drawstrings brought his attention away from the crimson mirror. Fifteen warriors lined up their bows, taking aim. He scrambled to flee from his adversaries, but two bodies appeared before him. Skull walked up to them, kicking one of their sides. Leaning over menacingly, his eyes drilled straight into Phoenix's chest. Once the fear in the boy was tangible, he began laughing manically. Phoenix took a few steps away, only to hear the strings being re-armed.

"Phoenix, my boy . . . as young and naïve as ever. Not a single detail has been altered in the slightest. Years and years have come and gone, maturity has yet to dawn upon you. The amount of pathetic you are sickens me." He took a minute to look over the boy.

"Death was too great of a gift. You watched as *everyone* you cherished rot away in their soaked night-wear. No move was made to assist your sister as she *risked* her own life for yours." His cackle was deeper and darker than before. Skull placed his sword under Phoenix's chin, raising his head and forcing their eyes to meet. "You have earned that scar. It's good to see that you have suffered all these years and will continue for those yet to come."

Skull's words vibrated through him like a chainsaw. Phoenix attempted to ignore his taunts, shifting his gaze between the line of archers and the darkened bodies, when suddenly they began glowing. The shroud of darkness vanished, revealing Beth and Joshua. Their bodies lay there, decaying. He immediately broke, his cheeks burning as they were drenched in tears. He dropped to his knees in defeat and simultaneously, his arm began throbbing. A shooting pain wrapped around his right side. Pulling up his sleeve, he watched as the scar formed on his skin.

"Speechless," smiled Skull. "I'm not going to leave you with just a reminder this time. I want you to ponder how things could have been different. What could have happened, instead of what did. Think about how it was all in your hands . . ." He retrieved an oil can, sprinkling it over the bodies and splashing it on Phoenix. The oil mixed with Phoenix's tears as it soaked into his clothes. An archer joined Skull, handing him a single flaming arrow. Phoenix watched the fire dance in the wind as he gripped his arm tighter.

"Now the boy shall match his name, in honor and fire!" He tossed the arrow on the dead bodies and they were engulfed in flames. The blaze ran toward Phoenix. He had only seconds to scream.

Phoenix broke free from his nightmare. Awake and distressed, his body was covered in a layer of sweat. He took a moment, glancing around the room. Marble floors, wooden walls, cashmere sheets—he was in the castle's guest quarters. His vest hung over a chair that was facing his other possessions on a desk. His clothes were in the worst state he had ever seen. He slid his hand down his face as he examined the maroon splatters and layer of dirt staining his wardrobe.

Gingerly checking his body, his hands slid downward, coming across extreme sensitivity. He flinched as he saw his entire torso wrapped in light red bandages. His eyes drifted to his knuckles finding that his fist had a dressing as well. *What happened?* Struggling to slip his legs from the covers, he sat in silence with his thoughts. The last things he ever wanted to be alone with.

In a haze, he hurriedly threw on his clothing, despite their grungy feel. He wobbled through the corridor like it was his first time walking. He fell against the wall, praying to Zorumaka and Kyrudorous that he was heading in the direction of anybody. After wandering around for twenty minutes, he finally found the doors that had led him to the King on their first meeting. With his eyes squinting in pain, he could barely identify Crystal and the Princess eating breakfast at the far end of the table. Beside them was another person, an older gentleman. He gazed from corner to corner, no one else was in the dining hall. No guards, cooks, servants . . . even the King was absent.

"Phoenix!" Crystal yelled as she abruptly stood, startling Lila. Phoenix lay against the doors, watching her rush to him. She embraced him tightly, forcing him to groan. He allowed the hug to linger a bit before pushing her away with a placid face.

Phoenix tilted his head, raising his palm to the side of her cheek. "You're safe and unharmed. Well, other than this little scratch." He brushed his finger across the bandage.

"Worried about me? Phoenix . . . you've been lying in bed for three days! Profusely sweating, no movement—mumbling nonsense the entire time."

His jaw dropped. "Three days? *Three!* No, no, no . . . The King . . . Has he begun barricading the city? Emerica and its citizens must be prepared for a siege. This will not happen again." Horror struck his spine.

"Several breaches into the city have been attempted, but they were handled accordingly," said Lila, gracefully joining the two of them with the stranger behind her. "'Tis no reason to fret about these frivolous things from this point forward."

"Phoenix, what will you not let happen again?"

"Who's this?"

"My name is Edwin, sir." He held himself with dignity.

"He is my guest, as are you and Crystal."

Phoenix lost his mind. "Princess, permission to speak freely?" She nodded. "This is not an appropriate time to allow strangers into Your Majesty's home."

"He's no stranger—he's an adventurer from Assassin City. He came to explore what one of the great cities has to offer. More than we know about yourself." The comment was bold and underhanded.

Phoenix stared at the man. "Your Highness, I must speak to the King. Where is he? His chambers? Please fetch him, tell him I require his presence."

She paused, almost as if insulted. "Yes, I shall bring him down. Wait here." Her lack of worry left an unpleasant burning sensation on Phoenix's mind. Her eyes, the dull sense of compassion…

Crystal glanced at Edwin, apologizing and asking if he would excuse them. Once he was gone, she repeated her question.

"We may speak about this another time." He searched for the wall for support as he wavered.

"All you ever say is 'this is the wrong time' or another excuse. It's exhausting. Tell me, who are you?" Her own abrasiveness surprised both of them, but she stood her ground placing her hands on her hips. His eyes flared. *The-they look like they did the other day,* she thought stepping back. *But sad, not angry.*

"What need is there for you to understand? To know who I am? My private life is just that—mine. Once this situation is resolved, I'm departing from this city to never return. Why you feel the need to pester me is beyond my knowledge." His face relaxed, regaining his composure. *Control. Stay in control.* He reached for the door.

Crystal sought to go after him, but she had a feeling nothing good would come from pushing the subject farther. As she watched him struggling with the door, she whispered, "My life is in your hands—I wish I knew what those hands have seen . . ."

As he turned to respond, a blood-curdling scream vibrated the entire dining hall. The two shared terrified expressions. In an instance, they searched for the source of the scream to find Lila curled against a pillar. She held her hands firmly to her face, streams of tears escaping.

"What happened? Are you hurt?" questioned Crystal.

Through her sniffles she murmured, "M-m-my father . . . he's dead!"

Phoenix stiffened. It's happening. The onslaught . . . the rumors in Kyron City were true. The mercenaries on the outside and the inside. The guards? He peered around—not a single servant or person of authority.

"He had . . . there was . . . a dagger in his . . . throat!" cried Lila in Crystal's arms. "He was . . . innocent in this!"

"We need to escape, we must exit the castle. They have already won."

"Wha-what? What do you mean?" whimpered Lila through her gasps.

"There's no time; the guards will have us surrounded soon enough. Where's Edwin?"

She hesitated. "He's residing in a guest bedroom."

"My things are up there, too," Crystal blurted out. Phoenix tugged at the girls' arms to get moving. They blindly followed Phoenix as he rushed through the hallways to the guest rooms. He busted through the door, preparing to grapple with any foe waiting for them. Once cleared, he broke open each door in the corridor. Empty. Each room was empty. *She should have never let that man in here!* Returning, Lila stood by the entrance still in misery.

"Your Highness, I understand how you are feeling, but I must ask you a question." She barely acknowledged him. "The legendary emerald; where would the King hide this sacred treasure?" Hearing the word emerald, Crystal perked up her ears.

"Legendary . . . Wh-what . . . What emerald? The ones from the lore? Why are you speaking of nonsense? They are just as you said—legends."

"No, no they're not. Someone *murdered* your father for this legend." Crystal eavesdropped intently until some faint noises caught her attention. She swiftly headed to the balcony.

"My father has never spoken of such a gem!" Lila wiped her cheeks. "There . . . there's this door that was built into the castle long ago, but no one has entered it in this century."

"That's better than nothing; show us the way."

An explosion vibrated the marble tile beneath them. Crystal came running back into the room.

"Hou-houses are burning! They're aflame! Someone's blowing up the town!" This was not a situation for an adventurer like herself. Her legs trembled; terrified was too weak of a word to describe how she felt.

A chill swept through them.

"It's now or never, Lila!"

Her face had gone completely pale. Her ghastly expression made the chill a bit sharper. She hesitated, "Where is Edwin? We must rescue him!"

"He is not in this wing. A hardened veteran like himself will be fine. Let's save our own skins."

Lila remained stationary, no signs of budging. Phoenix curiously looked over her as Crystal took ahold of her arms.

"Lila, please return to reality. We're in danger." A subconscious nod was given before they exited the room. The girls helped Phoenix limp down the hallway, until the group stopped in front of the peculiar door Crystal had spotted earlier.

Phoenix examined the wooden hatch, pulling on the handle.

"Locked. Of course it is. Do you know where the key could be hiding? Did the King have somewhere special he stashed valuables?" Another bomb detonated, causing the entire fortress to tremor. Echoes of men roaring in cheer filled the building.

Lila started to panic, cupping her ears. "I have no knowledge of this, any of this . . ." She went on a rant of self-pity as Crystal just watched her mouth move, not hearing a single word. Her eyes slowly lowered, locking onto her necklace.

"Your necklace! That's it! It has to be the key."

On cue, she grasped her jewelry in shock.

Phoenix watched as her eyes narrowed and her mouth puckered. "The King's heir is the most valuable possession. There would no safer place. May I see it, Princess?" The word left a distasteful flavor in his mouth.

She struggled with the words he said, deciding whether or not to honor his request. Hearing the commotion of their intruders getting closer, she forced her hand to unclip it from the chain.

"Here," she handed it over in defeat.

The necklace was plugged into the slot. Following the suggestions of Lila, he turned it completely to the right and all the way to the left. As he pulled it out, the door produced squeaky clicks and clangs. They waited for a few moments until the door creaked open.

"Hurry and go; they're coming."

The three of them were immediately encompassed by darkness. Only a light glowing brightly from the depths below lit the cavern. Phoenix reached for the walls, feeling moist rocks. Squinting, he could see the steps before him. The circular staircase spiraled around a cylinder of stone that reached the bottom. It was almost an arm's length away from the platform they were standing on. The smell of bat droppings caused them to clench their noses.

"Do we . . . do we really have to go down there? I can barely see my hand in front of me," whimpered Crystal, concentrating on each individual finger.

He gently grasped Crystal's hand. "Stay close, we will be fine." With her temperature rising, the three took their first steps.

They stumbled, their feet searching for the next step. Rushing as fast as possible without tripping, another barrage of yells could be heard throughout the cavern. "They're not far behind!" cried Crystal.

"Look! See there! It's shining!" Phoenix pointed at the light. It illuminated the entire floor of the cave. Reaching the bottom, the three of them were entangled by the illumination. The flood of light was not the same as it would be from the suns. Or even a candle stick. No warmth or calming sensation. Only an icy, chill—one that would put a saint on edge.

Emerica's green emerald was floating in a covert hole chiseled into a stone pillar. They all gasped. *The emerald . . . The emerald from the legends. It's real. All of it's real.* Crystal was beside herself in disbelief.

As they approached the ancient gem, Phoenix felt a horrible darkness being emitted from its surface. Reaching for the emerald, he motioned to the other girls to stop following. The sounds of the soldiers pounded on his eardrums with every second that passed. Phoenix reached for it, putting both hands around the base of the emerald, fitting perfectly in his palm. As he brought it to his chest, he felt his past come alive. Pain and suffering that he had hidden away was now beating against his ribcage.

His lips began trembling as fast as his legs. His body rejected this dark energy. His mind went haywire, making him want to give in. Let go. He suddenly wanted to waste all his training. All his preparation for this journey. His fears, problems, and worries consumed him. Crystal caught his lifeless gaze and snatched the emerald from his possession. Instantaneously, he woke from his trance.

"We need to leave!" yelled Crystal, throwing the emerald into her bag.

"There is a shaft around the corner that will bring us to the coast. Follow me."

Lila ran ahead, the bottoms of her feet slapping against the stone. When they rounded the corner, they found her rolling a boulder to the side. A massive tunnel was carved into the side of the cavern. "The ride is not the most enjoyable, but the scenery is worth the discomfort."

Crystal, without a second thought, quickly hopped in. Her body vanished, but her screams made her seem like she was still beside them.

Phoenix's eyes burrowed into Lila. "No one has been here in centuries?"

She hesitated. "That is correct."

"You have been pretty useful in our escape . . . almost like this hasn't been your first trip."

"I . . . haven't, I was never permitted to. Father's orders."

"Secret exits are usually kept that way."

"My father, *the King*, has told me stories as a child and described its contents like he was reading from a book. Mind who you are speaking to and who rules Emerica."

He crossed his arms, his back straightening. "Heard. Royalty first, Your Highness. The sacred blood line must be saved."

"Uh . . . thank you." She timidly climbed into the shaft, and was gone seconds later.

Phoenix placed his hands on the innards of the escape route. Smooth. He rubbed his hands all around the loop. He couldn't see very far down, not that he could see much of anything. He prepared for the leap of faith as he listened to the guards' feet shuffling against the dirt. With a deep breath, he slipped in feet first.

He slid back and forth as his body hit rough turns. He was forcibly smashed against one of the twists before he slipped forward. A smile cracked through as his eyes focused on his feet. He awaited the next surprise, but the stone started becoming more visible. The exit came in a rush, the light greeting his presence. He squeezed his eyes shut as fresh air replenished itself around him, cooling him with the ocean breeze.

Bracing himself for the landing, the crash knocked him to his knees. He lost his balance, falling forward onto his hands. The soft cushion of sand rushed between his fingers. *The Princess was not lying about the view.* The coast line was laid out before him. Huge cargo ships waded in the water tied to their individual piers. The personal boats mimicked the other ships, but only lost in size. They gently wobbled as the waves splashed against their bases. Bigger waves in the distance rose as high as the blazing suns, only to crash back on themselves. *This is beautiful,* he thought. His skin baked underneath the rays as he stood. The crashing of the water into the cliffs filled his ears.

The peaceful feeling was disturbed as an eerie sense crept through him. He froze, afraid to move until he heard a jingle of metal shake behind him. Hordes of soldiers wielded their swords high and ready. A soldier held Crystal by the back of her hair with her knees burrowing into the sand. Princess Lilian stood beside them, head down with her hands clasped together. In the same row, Edwin proudly held himself—ego bursting. Equipped with unscathed chainmail, his glossy red hair was in a mess, as it was in the dining hall.

Phoenix listened to the chainmail scrape as he stepped forward. The anger in his eyes was almost tangible, as if he was prepared to use it as a weapon. For a second, it was just the two of them on the beach. He searched through the man's fury. *There is a familiarity in his face, something that was not visible before.*

Edwin placed his palm on the hilt of his machete. "Phoenix . . . us on the battlefield, yet again. The years have treated you well. I'm sure you have questions. What's going on here? Or maybe, who I am, beyond the name you have been told." Lila glanced at him.

"I want Crystal released and your blood soaking the sand." He gestured to the Princess. "Why is she not restrained?" He already knew the answer.

"Why keep an ally captive?"

Phoenix's gaze drifted to the royal weasel. "You treasonous scum. Have you lost your pride in Emerica? To place it in the possession of dishonorable mercenaries who care more for the coin than their contractor?" Lila attempted to make eye contact, but continued staring into the distance. "Did you have a part in murdering your father? Your King?"

The silence forged his answer; hitting him like a hammer on a plate of metal.

"My father and citizens were not part of our trade . . ." Her voice trailed off.

"What offer could be as valuable as your citizens that could ease your decision in choosing this lowlife? He was after the emerald and you held the key to its location—"

"She did as she was ordered and will be rewarded handsomely. The emerald was our buyer's objective, but once we learned of your survival—that became mine. Skull never did like leaving matters unfinished. Not a single building or citizen will come between Skull's wish to end Luminar's legacy." Edwin placed his weapon under Crystal's chin. She whimpered, biting back tears.

Phoenix traced them as they fell. They slipped from her face, dripping into the Luminar Lake. The single drop rippled through the reflection of the Prince colliding with Skull. Their swords clashing, metal versus bone. Red clouded his vision as he raised a finger: "Release her!"

"Appears to me you have grown four feet and a backbone. Years of torture can really nurture a boy into a man. That scar of yours was a gift."

Their pursuers from the castle had finally caught up with them; one by one they flew through the air.

"The recognition is not mutual. Mind revealing your identity, and why I should care?"

Edwin removed his gloves. Dropping them to his feet, he fanned his hand out before him. A jagged scar was plastered across his knuckles. "That spoiled brat of a Prince did this damage. The night Luminar burned to the ground, I was present. Cadet to my captain Skull until promoted to captain myself, I witnessed the murder of your Prince."

Flashbacks obscured his thoughts. Phoenix relived that night, remembering the captain vividly. Sweat dripped from his nose as his hate reached new limits.

"Skull. Where is he?"

"What makes you think I'm just going to hand over that information voluntarily?" Through his obstructed vision, Phoenix realized he was now surrounded and all of their weapons were aimed toward him. "Hand me the emerald, and I will release the girl."

His eyes narrowed, but before he had a moment to interject Crystal whispered, "Phoenix."

Lila began to nervously fidget. Watching the scene from the sidelines, she could no longer listen to the banter. Lifting her head to look Phoenix directly in the eyes, she swept up a blizzard of sand, swirling it into Edwin's face. Lila turned to Crystal's captor and tackled him. She struggled with him, trying to keep his arms down. It was a losing battle until Crystal came to her aid.

Adrenaline fueled Phoenix once he saw his chance. He flew at Edwin, thrusting a solid fist to his jaw. The impact disarmed him, dropping his steel at Phoenix's feet. As he retrieved it, he shouted, "Escape! Board a boat!"

Crystal and Lila maneuvered their way out of the crowd of blood seekers.

On cue, the small army charged at their prey. Phoenix valiantly fought off every strike and sweep. He kept his eyes on the archers, evading any arrow coming his way. He swung his sword fast and light, lacerating the soldiers in short range. One by one, they fell with a grunt. Seeing the hopelessness, he began carving his escape route into the mob. With another quick dodge and whip of his sword, five more men fell clearing him a perfect view to the waters.

Crystal ran with every ounce of energy her body possessed. Panting heavily, she slowed to a fast jog when the docks were in reach. Her optimism faltered when a tight grip caught her shoulder, but it was restored once she saw Lila's face. Before either of them could speak, Crystal saw guards pursuing them in the background. They ran up the ship, both helping to prepare it for sailing.

Running backward toward the girls, he parried the final strikes of a few soldiers. With a skilled spin in the air, he dashed toward their getaway vehicle. His sprint didn't last long. Radiating pain shot through him like a bullet. Again and again the pain splashed over his body, bee stings penetrating every inch of his back. But he pushed forward. With his sights on the boats, he could only watch as a few mercenaries climbed onboard.

The women had just enough time to release the sails before a cat and mouse game began. The soldiers chased them around the deck swinging violently, but with zero accuracy. Crystal backed against the edge, facing three goons. She held on to the brim of the boat for support as her knees shook. Not another second passed before each goon decided to take the prize. The trio came straight for her, but she dove to the side. Sliding across the wooden deck she turned to watch Lila forcefully shove them overboard. The men yelled as they plummeted into the water. With a sigh of relief she glanced over to find Phoenix staggering his way across the coast.

Lila left the craft to go to Phoenix's aide. He placed an arm around her neck and put the majority of his weight on her shoulders. Faster than before, but still struggling, they gradually made it to the pier. Lila noticed her clothes had absorbed the blood from his wounds, but this was not the time to worry about her wardrobe.

Phoenix could barely cough his sentence out. "W-why?"

The Princess kept her head forward, "The exchange was supposed to be between the emerald and my freedom. I was to leave the leash of royalty and become an adventurer of my own . . . but my father . . ."

Coming aboard, she watched Crystal yank at the chain connected to the anchor. She heaved it onto the deck, granting the ship the freedom to move. The temporary relief was washed from her soul as the vessel shook. She had just enough time to see Edwin rampaging behind them.

The Princess and Phoenix were ripped apart. Phoenix was tossed to the side like a rag doll, the arrows inserting themselves further as he collided with the floorboards. He tried to keep his head steady, but it was no use. Dizziness setting in, he watched Edwin lift Lila by her neck. Edwin held the Princess above his head as she kicked her feet wildly in the air. All watched in horror as she changed from pale to blue. Edwin placed his other hand on her hair, rotating in opposite directions. He continued twisting until an ear-piercing crack disrupted the entire ocean scenery.

"No!" Crystal screamed falling to her knees. Her body froze, barely able to grasp what she just witnessed.

Phoenix saw the lifeless body being thrown back to shore. The splash echoed through his hollow heart. His vision intensified, blurring his peripherals. Only Edwin remained clear as day. As red bordered his sights, he lifted himself up. Despite the pain, he lunged for the leader of the raid. Crossing his bicep under his chin, he brought him in as snug as possible. He could feel the man choking, watching him try to tear his arm away from his neck. Phoenix used his free hand to rip an arrow from his shoulder. He placed the tip between the leader's eyes, hoping to drive as much fear into him as possible.

"What's Skull's location? Tell me!"

Whether from fear or disobedience, he remained silent.

"This one's for me." Phoenix lowered the arrow to his neck. He pulled his arm away and drew a laceration right along the man's Adam's apple. Blood flowed like a waterfall, turning the deck from a mahogany brown to a burgundy.

With one last gust of energy, he tossed the corpse overboard. He waited for the plop before he began relaxing. The release of his adrenaline allowed the pain to travel through his veins. His body instantly felt like it was hit by a bull. Crystal came to his side, but he lifted his palm.

"Steer . . . steer the boat. I-I just need rest . . ."

She halted in her approach, changing direction to the wheel.

"Lila . . . I'm . . . I'm so sorry. There is so much I could have done, yet I stood aside . . . stood aside and let Lila . . ." Her voice cracked.

"She betrayed her own blood. If he had not done it, I would have . . ." His voice was weak, wavering with every few syllables he spoke.

"Death has been something that I considered foreign. To experience that brutality before my eyes . . ."

He sensed her distress. "Just as is being born, death is part of life. Some experience it earlier than others, but all come to its doorstep."

She stayed quiet, and then, "At least the emerald is ours. Your mission has been successful."

"But I failed Emerica. The lives that fueled the city . . . Chaos. If only—"

"In a small town, not many things are considered traditions. Tales from travelers often mix with our own, thus forgetting the origins of the stories. But one thing that has stayed true, one my father used to say: every success deserves celebration, no matter how little. Who knows which corner despair will be hiding behind . . ."

Phoenix laid upon his side, resting his lids. "Well, your father sounds like an honorable fellow." He allowed the heat to wrap around his body, comforting him. "The emerald is ours . . . Next step, find a place to dock."

Crystal glanced down at him just as a smile grew across his face.

CHAPTER 6

Crystal lay across from Phoenix, allowing the boat to rock her back and forth. The constant motion made her insides twist. She felt as if her stomach was swimming in circles. Curling into a ball, she kept her eyes on Phoenix. His wounds continued to bleed. *They must be on their way to infection. None of them appear to look healthy.* One of the blood stains brought her to his arm where that nasty scar was permanently pressed onto his flesh. She hadn't noticed it before, not until Edwin referred to it several times. The scar was not only covering an incurable wound, but also years of memories. Ones that were hidden far beneath his surface.

Phoenix felt his body draining. He knew blood was still making its way out; it was clear each time he attempted to reposition himself. His body was as stiff as a board and aching as much as it squeaked. He let his eyes rest; no reason to waste energy forcing them open. Once in a while he wanted to glance at his partner, checking in on her condition. She was as green as a fresh forest. Her gagging noises pierced the space between them.

"Zorumaka's curse?"

Crystal leaned on top of the edge, "Ah . . . I suppose—" She hurled, releasing a sickly groan.

"He was not fond of riding the waves either."

"When will we dock? I'm starving . . ." She gently placed her hand over her stomach, as she felt another episode occurring.

Phoenix pushed himself up, scanning the horizon. With a few blinks, his vision was restored and he was able to spot an old, expired port. He winced as he stood on his feet.

"We're arriving to one now. Appears it's been abandoned."

"Thank the Protect—" Crystal let loose over the railing once more.

Phoenix mustered his strength and slowly made his way to the wheel. Steering the boat to the coast, Crystal assisted him with preparation to dock: anchoring the vessel, wrapping the sails, and releasing the bridge. To them, it felt like years since they last walked on land. They cautiously entered the village, but immediately sensed something peculiar. The vacancy sent a chill between them. Its energy was disturbing, making the two of them extremely anxious.

They searched for any type of life. Most buildings were run down, the doors banging against the frames. Trash littered the street along with dust and rubble that had broken from the homes. Most of the windows had been smashed and the remains scattered underneath the scene. Crystal peered into a window that remained intact to see a horrific sight. Plates filled with moldy clumps were set on tables. Flies hovered around the foul dinner plates. Chairs were strewn across the floor, a china cabinet was in shambles, and kitchen appliances were in two. She glanced into a few more rooms finding almost identical situations before calling Phoenix.

"In the midst of dinner, they were attacked, or maybe they fled?"

Phoenix didn't respond.

"This town is completely deserted. I-I wonder what happened here?" asked Crystal.

Phoenix went farther into the ghost town, desperately scouting the area in hopes of someone or something that would raise his spirits. And then suddenly, a glimmer of hope appeared. A small, deteriorating home a few yards away had lights on. *Not much to go on, but better than nothing,* he thought. Gesturing to Crystal to follow, the two of them carefully approached the run-down building. Phoenix led, knowing whoever they were to come across would not be fond of uninvited guests, especially if these were the last of the living population.

The door was lightly pushed and its hinges cried loudly. They tiptoed inside as Crystal whispered, "Is anyone home?"

Silence answered. Phoenix looked back at her, placing one finger upon his lips. Just as he lowered his finger, the door suddenly slammed closed, startling Crystal. Before Phoenix could react, a young boy ran at them holding a broom high above his head.

Taking the strangers by surprise, he whipped his weapon against Phoenix's broad chest. His satisfaction turned into horror as he watched the tip snap in half. The head of his makeshift weapon made a thud against the ground as he began to quiver, slowly retreating. Instant panic engulfed him.

"Please don't fret," Crystal squatted, trying to soothe him. "We're not going to harm you."

He shyly stepped back once more, lowering his eyes. Crystal advanced toward him, but the boy retreated behind a wall, his bare feet clapping with each step. Before Crystal had the chance to pursue him, he reappeared with two males.

"Why are you here?" demanded one with short dark hair. His voice was deep and startling. He stood tall with his arms crossed, bulging through his tattered, black shirt. His face was stern, already prepared for the wrong answer.

Crystal hid behind Phoenix forcing him to speak: "I'm sorry that we trespassed into your home unannounced. We have been stranded at sea and happened to dock in this town. We are lost and wounded. I assumed this was a tavern, not a private residence."

"Stranded in that miserable water?" gasped the other man. He had bright blond hair and was wearing a white t-shirt with gray sweats. "I'm so sorry! Here have a seat," he shuffled over to a table and pulled out two chairs. "My names Brett, Brett Strauser. This is Eric," he said, pointing to the man in ripped blue jeans who gave a grunt as his response. "And he is Alexander." The little boy was right on his heels. He was also wearing tattered clothing; a white shirt and blue slacks. The poor child's skin was smudged with dirt.

"Alex, make some meals for our guests? Warm up some of the leftovers over the fire, maybe the ones from my homemade pasta!" Alexander's orange curls bounced as he nodded. He headed back into the kitchen, examining Phoenix with his brilliant hazel eyes.

"Your hospitality is surprising, but more than welcomed." Brett smiled, waving his arm toward the chairs. They had a seat as Phoenix asked, "Us wanderers have no understanding of where we are in Osiren. What's the name of your home? Do you own maps of Teague? Or Osiren?"

Brett walked to a desk that had not been touched in months, searching through the top cabinet. "This town had a name once, but after all these years it has been forgotten—"

"The ones who know it are either dead or long gone," chimed in Eric.

"Is that why this place is deserted?" asked Crystal in shock.

"Yes, well, they have forgotten and are gone or they're . . . that. Ah, here, I found something." Dust danced off the old parchment as it was taken ahold by Phoenix.

Unfolding the paper, Phoenix leaned back in the chair only to groan as his wounds rubbed against the backboard. Brett saw Phoenix's blood leaking through his torn garments.

"Oh dear! You are incredibly injured!" Brett ran to his side, pulling the map from his hands. He lifted Phoenix to his feet, leading him by his bicep. "You have dried blood all over you! This is no good, no good at all."

Frazzled by the display of kinship, he murmured, "Um, thank you."

Brett brought him to their sink around the corner and immediately stripped his patient of his vest, revealing many bloody sores and gaping holes. Crystal covered her mouth in shock, seeing some of the wounds had tinged purple. Eric's eyes burrowed deep into his bare back, almost with enough intensity to add another injury to the collection.

As the frightening appearance of the battle scars wore off, Crystal gazed at the rest of his torso. *The defining features, the muscular build, his lightly tanned skin, all so . . . Wow.* Realizing her unshaken stare, her cheeks bloomed like roses in the morning. An attempt to divide her attention, she turned back to Eric who was also glaring at Phoenix, most definitely not in the same way.

"Why did everyone leave town? Who's all left?"

Brett wrung out a soaking wet washcloth over the basin. "The smart ones left before they were taken."

"Taken by whom?"

"Well—" Eric spoke before being cut off by a hushed holler.

"I'm sorry! I should have warned you it was going to burn."

"Thanks for the warning."

"As simply as it could possibly be explained," answered Eric sliding a chair between his legs and using the top as an armrest, "There's a group of men who have been raiding this town for years. Usually at night, once visibility is slim. At first, their intentions were unclear. They traveled to town only to scare and torment us, so we believed. That stopped when they began taking victims."

"Why has no one stopped them?" asked Phoenix, grinding his teeth in pain.

"The size of the group always varies, but even if they had lesser numbers, we are no match. Brett's not a fighter and you witnessed how Alex reacts in a situation."

"Why haven't you left town then?" asked Crystal.

"Alright, Phoenix, sit tight and I'll get some of my special medicine that has been passed down through my family." Answering with a sigh, Phoenix sat patiently as Brett exited the room.

"There's nowhere to go. Brett's entire family lives in Ventaceny, but they have been distant since his creation. He had little family here, but . . . He does not have the heart to leave . . . and . . . I could never abandon him. Alexander's an orphan; his parents were both taken. We have been caring for him since we found him on the streets. "

"I was quite curious," pondered Crystal imagining Alex's bright carroty hair compared to Eric's dark black pigment. "Are Brett's and your family's not one of the same?" Eric let out a huge sigh as Alexander came back in with two platefuls of food.

"Crystal, that's enough. Let them keep their privacy."

"We have no secrets to hide," Brett cheerfully whistled, carrying a cream-colored circular container. "Now Phoenix, this *will* hurt—ten times worse. Ready?" Phoenix bit his lip, nodding in defeat.

"In some sense that would be rendered true, but not due to sibling relations. I am his husband. Which is the sole reason why we have been spared the kidnapping. Those bandits only take the straight variety. Jokes on them, they grabbed a few lesbians without knowing it," he shook his head with a forced smile.

"Why does an attraction to the same sex spare you?"

"In the eyes of most, we are inferior. Too weak, too unstable to withstand manual labor. It sounds rather grim, but their poor views and small-mindedness has secured us safety."

Crystal could see Phoenix struggling in her periphery, trying to keep his cries to a minimum. His muscles convulsed as Brett smeared the lotion across the wounds. Receiving her plate from the child, she stared down at the noodles in pure delight.

"Is Alex safe thanks to their bigotry?"

"They believe that he, too, has same-sex relations. Must think it's contagious."

Brought up and raised in a small community, Crystal stumbled for the appropriate words. She had never been exposed to same sex-relationships. Or had known they even existed. Uncomfortable, she shoveled down her meal.

"With that last one, we're done!" Brett handed back the vest and map to Phoenix with a smile. "Hopefully that cream does the trick. This will stop the spread of infection, meaning there will be no need to worry about amputation."

As grateful as Phoenix was, he wasn't quite sure which pain made him suffer more—the lacerations or the medicine. He made his way next to Crystal and, more importantly, his dinner. Eric, again, started his one-sided game of a staring contest. Phoenix unrolled the ancient paper with one hand, while devouring the extra remains with his other.

"Brett, can you show me our location on the map?" Brett stood behind Phoenix, guiding him to their town. A few minutes passed as calculations were made. Alex left the room, clearly bored of the situation, while Brett leaned his weight onto Eric's shoulders. Crystal finished her plate, waiting for Phoenix to start choking on the food he shoveled down his throat.

"The Marvelous Ocean was kind to us. The winds sailed us south along the coast of Osiren from Emerica. The end of our trip landed us in Holick."

Eric snapped his fingers, "Oh yeah! That's the name of this stupid place."

"Holick is not too far from the City of Assassins and fortunately, we will travel through Flores to reach our destination."

Crystal cleared her throat, "Flores? Why does that city bring you excitement? The emerald was already removed years ago."

Brett and Eric both exchanged glances.

"I've been reviewing those events lately," pondered Phoenix. "Something seems odd. There are five great cities and five emeralds, correct?" Crystal agreed. "One was stolen from Luminar and supposedly the next was stolen from Flores. Flores was raided approximately a fortnight after Luminar. Both of these assaults happened back to back. Why wait all these years to continue the pursuit?"

"Is it possible they paused their invasions to hide their identities? Or perhaps they were trying to avoid leaving a trail? If another great city would have fallen, the last two would be on high alert," reasoned Crystal.

"Their army was mostly composed of mercenaries, which would leave no connection to the master behind the plans. I would find it hard to believe the leader would reveal his identity to any of the soldiers in case of their capture. To perform such a high risk movement upon Osiren would take a man with years of military experience."

"What if they were attempting to cover his tracks?"

"If that were to be true, his patience would have been tested. Thinking rationally, his armies would have grown until there was adequate cannon fodder to raid each city at once. I believe *something* halted their advances. Flores's defense could have been composed sufficiently to keep them at bay or even wipe them clean. No matter the reason, there's a slight chance the emerald is safe and secured."

Crystal abruptly rose, "If there is a chance, no matter how tiny, we must get there immediately." Her face brightened, only to dim just as quick. "No one remains in Flores. Their forces were demolished . . . If the emerald is still being protected by the same force . . . are we going to be able to break through it?"

"If it can speak, then it can reason. I'll guide its decision to see us as allies, not enemies."

Crystal felt herself staring at him again. That same power in his voice, the confidence that could rally the most depleted of men . . . How could she not trust such a heroic figure? His words had more strength than the most hardened of metal.

"That's several days' worth of traveling and neither of you are in any kind of condition for such a journey. I suggest you stay the night. Leave bright and early tomorrow, or the following? Oh! I can cook a big breakfast!" Brett lost himself in his excitement. He kept rambling about all the different combinations of meals he could prepare.

Eric sat perfectly still. His immense anger began rising again, only being contained behind his clenched jaw. The tension he emitted was becoming apparent, awarding him curious glances from his guests.

"You're much too hurt anyway! Rest will heal your wounds properly. The two of you could share the guest bedroom! The bed has been vacant since the Mortimer twins were—"

Eric's ticking time bomb exploded, "Whoa, wait a damn second. They *sneak* into our home, say they were *lost* at sea, eat *our* food, accept *our* services, but we gained little, and know less. What's stopping you from murdering my family? Stealing our possessions? Some deformed moral compass?" He slammed his elbows onto the Birchwood, head cocked and eyes starving.

"Eric, my love, manners are everything. Be kind to our guests. This home is more than just yours and I will not stand for your intimidation."

"Then have a seat," he reached for another chair, dragging it beside him. "Who knows if they are not in cohorts with those raiders? I will let nothing threaten the safety of my family. *Nothing.*"

Before Brett could argue, Phoenix spoke to clear the air of discomfort: "We mean no trouble, but what you speak is true. I agree, having strangers in one's home is quite unsettling. All friends start as strangers, though. Crystal, would you begin with Lanster City?"

The two of them explained the experiences they had been through since their first encounter in the alleyway, up to their escape on the boat. Phoenix also explained the emeralds and his mission. He made sure to leave out the Princess, the destruction of the city, and anything else that would lead the two men to believe they were there to cause harm from his tale.

"You broke into the castle and stole the legend from the lore?" stammered Brett slowly, fearing his company.

"No, we had an invitation from the Princess herself!" defended Crystal.

"Then what was the need to escape . . . on a stolen ship?"

"Oh, now I have complete trust in the two of you. There's *no way* you're fugitives," remarked Eric whimsically.

"The ship could be considered stolen to some, but it's not

entirely as it seems. Once we retrieved the emerald—"

"Stop with the lies, those things aren't real; I was told those as a child. They were just bedtime stories to put me asleep. The Protectors, the curse, guardians; all of those things are hogwash to influence innocents into joining their cult."

Brett turned to him with a face of a kicked puppy. "I'm part of that *cult,* Eric. Watch your words."

As the couple began bickering over beliefs, Phoenix motioned to Crystal to hand him her drawstring bag. He caught the weightless sack and ruffled through it until he found his evidence. Revealing it from hiding, the arguing stopped instantaneously. He held it for everyone to look upon in awe.

The gloriousness of the moment was not with them all. Phoenix felt the darkness being emitted from the emerald circulating around his hand. He could feel its tentacles wrap around his forearm. Words hissed into his ears. Whispers were murmured in the background. He checked to see who was speaking, but his company was silent. Snapping from his trance, he chucked the emerald back in the bag.

Crystal noticed his skin flash pale. "Are you feeling ill?" She watched him shake his head as sweat broke from his forehead.

"Is that . . . So it's-it's all true?" Eric lost the defensiveness in his voice.

Brett didn't bother to speak. He joined his hands together, right one in a fist while the other lay over top. He leveled the joining with his mouth, closing his eyes.

Crystal's brow rose in confusion. "What's he doing?"

Phoenix answered, "It's a silent chant; a form of communication with the Protectors."

Eric jumped from his seat, kicking the chair onto its side. He circled around the room in search for more than just his thoughts.

"Even if I were to believe the tale you have just spun, should I be preparing for an Emerican army to march upon Holick? We barely have protection to defend against lowlife thugs let alone an elite group of soldiers."

"No one is going to be arriving from there; they have other situations to handle."

Crystal watched Eric pace, waiting for another bomb to boom until Brett lowered his fist. "Whether or not Eric agrees, the two of you may stay the night. You have free roam of everything we have to offer. Try not to let him get under your skin."

The couple's stares connected, practically exploding. Their emotions and unspoken words battled, electrifying the atmosphere. Eric had full intentions of opposing Brett's demands, but knew one did not simply win in an argument with Brett.

"Fine. Do as you please. Be inside the house by nightfall." He peered through his window to their vacant streets and the last sun setting in the distance. "Which should be soon."

"We are forever grateful and in your debt. If we ever have an opportunity to repay this favor, I'll be sure to make it a priority."

Brett's cheery expression was accentuated next to Eric's sour demeanor.

Phoenix spoke to Crystal: "It seems that fate has placed you at my side. Our time together does not seem to be ending anytime soon, unless . . ."

Crystal felt confused. *A choice? I have yet to think.* "My first journey as an adventurer was to experience the city of Emerica. Now that has come to an end. Being at your side, I'll have the opportunity to explore the rest of Osiren. Who would pass up such an offer?"

A grin cracked through. "Your abilities on the field will need improvement. It would be quite hard to challenge an army if your safety was on my forefront."

"I have never wielded a weapon before . . ."

Phoenix examined the yard through a layer of glass that stretched across the entire wall. "While a sun still shines, we will take advantage of our time. Let's practice in the back to lessen the amount of attention we draw." They exited the Strauser's home.

The couple stepped toward their dust stained window,

watching Phoenix face Crystal, positioning himself several feet away. Eric intensely watched their hand-to-hand combat. As the two began sparring, he heard faint clacks behind him. Alexander had begun clearing the table, but he ignored him. He tried to read Phoenix's lips, reading the advice and tips he was offering. His eyes flicked back and forth following the jabs of the fists, watching them extend and retract in such an elegant manner. He felt his own heart beat racing.

"Do you think they spoke the truth?" asked Brett stepping behind Eric, wrapping his arms around his waist.

"I'm not sure . . . The emerald *looked* real enough. What reasons would they have to lie to us? We have nothing to offer. Or steal."

Crystal braced herself and charged at Phoenix. She prepared herself for the impact, but her wrist was caught in mid-swing. She was shoved back, losing her balance as she toppled over her feet. Crystal's eyes focused on her opponent. *He...he's not even trying.*

"Remember when you learned these kind of things? You used to perform all types of moves in that white robe. You looked so cute in that outfit." Eric's cheeks heated while Brett pulled him in closer.

"I believe that's how we met. A pebble I had thrown bounced off your muzzle."

"The mark is still present to prove it," Brett rubbed his forehead.

Eric peered at the scar. Slowly, going up on his toes, he laid a gentle kiss upon the blemish.

"I love you."

Crystal came at Phoenix again, punching at his fists like sand bags. The task was repetitive. Left right, left right. Attempting to catch him by surprise, she rolled to the left after her last jab and tried to kick his legs out from behind. Almost as if he saw the future, he carelessly hopped above her swipe. She hurried to get up on her feet, but was too slow. In mid-crouch, Phoenix landed and proceeded to palm her forehead. The unexpected strength stunned her, while the blow forced her to stumble back. With one leg out and the other bent at the knee, she tried rebalancing herself. Readying for another barrage of assaults, she filled her lungs with as much air as they could manage.

"I love you, too, Brett," Eric tilted his head, gently kissing him on the cheek. The warmth from each other's bodies wrapped them in a cocoon of intimacy. The romantic moment was disturbed as Alexander came running into the room, glowing with excitement.

"Have those people taken their leave?"

Eric pointed to their windowpane, "They're right there, bud."

His smile quickly formed into a disappointed stare. "That man . . . isn't normal. He broke my broom."

Eric looked at Phoenix on impulse to scold him. He watched his body shift side-to-side, evading swings. "You're right, little man, there is more to him than meets the untrained eye. An oddity I cannot explain. I just can't put my finger . . ."

Brett caught his line of sight, "You will keep your fist clenched and at your side."

Eric tried to laugh to brush the comment aside, but there was no use. Brett stormed away, with him at his heels. Alex stayed behind, watching the martial arts lesson.

Phoenix looked past Crystal into the sky. A bright purplish tinge colored the space overhead. Only the outline of Crystal was visible due to a faint glow emerging from the house. Her back was hunched; heavy breathing filled the air as she steadied herself on the last energy she could muster. He could tell his own moves slowed as the night continued; every body part was now in need of rest. Even the previous wounds began to ache as he twisted his body. *Maybe this should have waited until I was in fighting condition.*

With darkness as an ally, Crystal was invigorated with the thought of landing a single punch tonight. With one more deep breath, she absent-mindedly went for a single quick connect.

Brett sat inside, bundled in old, worn-out wool blankets. The blazing fire kept him warm as he licked his finger, turning the page of his book. All his focus was on the words; nothing could pull him away from his escape. Eric lay on the couch beside him, feet on the arm rest, head covered by a pillow. His snores made Brett struggle to not suffocate him. Alex strained his eyes, still focused on his entertainment. He could barely catch the movements of either fighter, only glimpses here and there.

Clippity-clop. Clippity-clop.

A faint sound of a stampede of hooves made him pick his head up from his palms. He frantically searched around for the source. He saw both his parents in their own world. His heart-beat pounded against his rib cage as he peeked out the front door. Five lights shook in the distance, each getting bigger every moment. He began crying.

"They're here! They're here! Dads!"

Almost as if an earthquake erupted, Brett threw his book aside and Eric bolted from his snooze. Both pairs of eyes filled with fright, matching the size of their son.

"That damn fire needs to be extinguished! Brett take Alex into the safe room! I'll go alert our guests." Eric made his way to his yard as Brett grabbed Alex, leading him to their hidden cubby.

Following the sounds of grunts and thuds against the dirt, he located them. "They're here. The men—the mercenaries—have come back!"

Crystal rolled back from Phoenix, but lost her balance.

"One day this will not be as easy." Crystal grabbed Phoenix's hand, who pulled her up inches away from his chest. The two embraced the moment.

"There is much work to be done until that day, but you're not hopeless."

"The game is over, *now!* We need to hide!" Eric blurted as he clutched Phoenix's shoulder.

The frightening situation finally lay upon them like a blanket. Both of their faces tensed. "Wh-where are we going to hide?"

Eric scanned the area, "I-I don't know, there is nothing but death here. Not that calming if I was to be asked. Brett's already hiding, but it's risky to join him. Upstairs. That's where we'll go."

Shattering echoed from his house as they jogged toward it. *Oh no, please no,* thought Eric as fear impaled his chest. From the instant he had clear view of the living room, the pain increased tenfold. Five soldiers wearing bone-plated armor stood tall and proud. Two of the thugs were holding Brett and Alexander by ropes wrapped around their bodies. The dining room table was cracked in half, chairs were scattered around the room, and the door was smashed up against a wall. The one at the head of the group wore a bone-plated helmet to match, with green hair flowing from underneath.

"Release him!" cried Eric.

"Not until you reveal where you have them hidden!"

"Who's hidden?" demanded Eric, fuming. Behind him, Phoenix readied himself for combat while Crystal shook like a leaf.

"That's them boss. Those are the faces from the warrants!" another goon stated, pointing his finger. He was in an identical uniform as well, but had black hair cut across his face, only revealing one eye.

The leader turned back to his captives. "Caught in the web of your lies. I am not a fan of a person who withholds the truth. Omega, Delta, take these two back to master. Report they were hiding the fugitives and refusing to reveal their location." A man that matched the same height as a tree and another with a tightly-pulled ponytail tossed their captives over their shoulders. The two left the building, hopping onto their armored horses. Brett and Alex screamed for Eric, kicking their legs violently.

"*Release* them!" hollered Eric, running full speed toward his family. The leader gripped him up by his collar and rammed him against the wall, shattering its exterior. His body made a loud gasp as air was released from his lungs. He slid lifelessly to the floor.

Brett continued to call his husband's name. His shouts became more distant as the kidnappers left town. Eventually, his voice was unable to be heard over the gallop of the horses.

Phoenix stepped before Crystal, "Why do you have interest in us?"

"Hefty bounties have been placed upon your heads. Killing the King, burning down Emerica, and capturing the Princess—heavy crimes to commit. Hard ones to accomplish for novice mercenaries."

"We have no involvement with those actions! You are going after the wrong people." Crystal glanced at Eric's unconscious body.

"The Princess was not kidnapped; she had been killed during the raid," defended Phoenix.

"Not one murder, but two: the King and his shining jewel. Even if you are being falsely accused, I travel to where the coins lead me. These crimes will surely secure you a death sentence, if the judge approves. And he will."

Crystal's eyes drifted downward, finding hopelessness in the situation. "You have the wrong people . . ."

Two scrolls of paper were brought into their view.

"Phoenix Reinhard and Crystal Thorn. Do these names match yours?" Neither of them responded. Silence forced him to continue reading the rest of the warrants; listing the same crimes he had mentioned.

"How did you find our location?"

"An Emerican ship docked at the harbor gave us enough reason to visit," he smirked. "Come with us if you wish to be unharmed."

"Crystal . . . run!" whispered Phoenix, and without a second thought, she did. Phoenix slowly stepped before the door, standing straight. His broad shoulders covering the exit, hands at his side, feet firmly on the ground—he knew he had no juice to fight, but he had to try.

"Beta, get the girl. Alpha, take care of Phoenix. I want this finished promptly." The leader stepped back shattering glass under his boots.

Phoenix watched as Beta zipped toward him while pink ponytails waved behind her. He prepared himself for the assault, but it never came. She jumped to the side and allowed Alpha to bring his spear down upon him. He dove to the left and sprung back to his feet in time to dodge again. He glanced at the tip of Alpha's weapon. It wasn't metal or steel, but bone. Hard, human bone. There wasn't any time to be disgusted as Alpha relentlessly continued. He vigorously jabbed back and forth.

Phoenix swept up a leg from the broken table, trying to deflect the continuous attack. But it was futile; after a few successes the Birchwood leg was chopped down and Phoenix was disarmed. Alpha drew his weapon back and came forward, slamming the bone downward. With scarcely anytime to block, he covered his head with his hands and caught the swing. The impact sent a jolt of pain through his limbs. It spread across his unhealed injuries from Emerica, increasing in fierceness as it circulated around them.

Alpha released a hand from his spear and lowered his palm down to his side. Phoenix watched as a separate white bone slid into his palm from his armor. His moment of mesmerism was dashed as the newly formed dagger was inserted through his vest and into his abdomen. Phoenix cried aloud as he felt the object pierce his insides.

The strength from Alpha's spear was lifted from his bloody hands. He rolled away, falling onto his back. Taking a second to breathe and rejuvenate, he surged upward, back onto his feet. The leap failed as he dropped back to his knees. The dagger implanted in his body remained as annoying as a stomachache. With a scrunched face he ripped it free, but the troubling injury turned into a tenderness that spread across his chest. A pulsing ache took control.

Alpha chuckled, "Unlike the skeletons of most, my bones are coated in a toxic chemical. Blood contact triggers the activation of the chemicals, allowing them to stir and awaken. Once removed, it is able to travel freely through the bloodstream. I bring an entirely new meaning to having a bone to pick."

"Protectors' curse you . . ." Phoenix hunched down, holding himself as if that was the cure to stop the spread. *I can feel it throughout my body. Once it reaches my heart . . . I can't . . . even fight it.*

"What . . . what are you?" He held the wound, feeling dizzy and lightheaded.

"These bones are not of my own person. Should I reveal my secret?"

Phoenix squinted, the shapes around him blurring.

"They come from those who have fallen in battle." Alpha watched as Phoenix lay on the floor, convulsing. "The time has come, three . . . two . . . one." The tremors abruptly halted and his body stiffened. His eyes stared blankly at nothing. At everything. Alpha sauntered over to his new victim, sizing up his humorous. "'Tis a shame, that would complete my exquisite collection."

Crystal scampered through the door, running blindly into an open field. She stood in plain sight, contemplating her escape. *Where do I go? Where? Where? I know nothing about this town.* She frantically whipped her head around the yard until she heard steps behind her. She bee-lined for the nearest decaying tree, sliding her back down the bark.

"Come forward, my sweet little flower!" laughed Beta as she struggled to see through the veil of the night. "Where are you?" She lingered on each word, elongating their sounds.

I . . . I have to help-help the others. If I hide, I will be found . . . She searched the ground until she came across a hard object. Popping back into the open, Crystal chucked a brick, aiming straight for Beta's face.

Beta saw the projectile and unraveled a kunai from a heavy, metal chain. The instrument was in the shape of a star, its five points piercing the night. The kunai hung by her side until she whirled it around, then released it. The metal soared in the bricks direction and made direct contact. A loud crack echoed as the object smashed straight through and the brick crumbled in the air. It did not stop there. The collision had no effect on the inertia of her weapon. The kunai continued traveling forward in Crystal's path.

She had only enough time to duck behind the tree. Her panic

increased as she listened to the weapon latch onto the dead wood. Surging with fear, she fled from her position, running back into the darkness.

Beta reeled in her weapon as she watched Crystal stumble in the midst of the field. With a quick round up, she precisely hurled it once more. The kunai slightly missed, slicing right across the fabric of her blouse. Cursing, Beta hurriedly grabbed onto the chain in an attempt to angle the path of its return. Successfully arching it, the kunai made its way back as a boomerang. It struck Crystal, implanting itself into her ribs. Beta listened to the yelp ripple through the air. As she ripped it back toward her, Crystal let loose a tearful scream.

Beta watched as her opponent stood eerily still in the shadows. Round three began just as before, with her projectile missing by a hair, but by shifting the chain once more, it dug into her back on the return. It climbed its way across her shoulder, shredding it as it jumped free from her skin.

Crystal's body shut down beneath her. Eyes streaming with fluid, her face was swarming with tears. She placed a hand on her shoulder, lightly touching the cool wetness seeping from her skin. The startling realization froze her. The blood was hers. Her blood soaked her hand. She could only watch as Beta released the weapon toward her again, but this time she stayed motionless. Her stomach was penetrated. Her mouth dropped, but not a sound was made.

She collapsed as Beta wrapped her chain around her arm. Smiling, she scoffed, "The easiest of coins I will ever receive."

CHAPTER 7

BAM! Phoenix's head slammed against something hard. He dazedly tried regaining his sight, blinking uncontrollably. He glanced around to find a clue that could tell him where he was, but he only discovered two shapes on the other side of him. Coolness lay upon his skin. *Is this metal?* The room shook again, this time allowing light to flow through a window above him. Illuminating the area, the sunshine revealed the hidden figures: Crystal and Eric. He examined his surroundings before the light dispersed. *Metal walls? Rare,* he thought to himself. *The owner must have plenty of coins lying around.*

"Crystal," he whispered. She didn't budge. He pushed himself up, but restraints tugged at his arms. *Chains too?* He inhaled deeply, shouting her name as loudly as he could manage. She remained motionless, but instead Eric started squirming.

"Ugh, my head. Wha-what . . . Where am I? Brett?" Phoenix watched as he, too, tried standing, but was tied down as well. Eric sat for a few minutes, swaying as the room bounced along. "Phoenix . . . is that you? What's going on?"

"We're prisoners at the moment. Beyond that . . ."

Eric stayed silent for a small time. Then all of a sudden, he snapped. His memories came flooding back to him, bringing him to his senses. The tension in their metal confinement electrified.

"You're at fault! You're the reason this is happening. My

family was safe, left alone! We lived happily, guaranteed safety. None of that would have been changed if you didn't dock in town! I knew keeping the likes of you around would only cause problems. Now I'm separated from Brett . . ."

Phoenix listened to Eric's chains rustling as if he was trying to break free. "The warrants must have been written while we were *stranded* at sea. How were we to know the mercenaries terrorizing Holick knew our names?" Again, Phoenix heard his chains, but as if they were settling onto the floor, in defeat. He watched the dark figure lean backward.

"You're still to blame why I'm alone."

Phoenix tried objecting, but Eric no longer wanted to participate in the debate.

Their ears were filled with the constant sound of hooves clapping against the dirt. The rest of the ride stayed quiet between the two. Occasionally Crystal's chains rustled, sparking a slight hope in Phoenix, only to dim each time. He waited for spurts of sunlight to shine through the window, seeing only glimpses of her still body, and Eric's sullen face. Their ride made a few stops with long periods of resting, but no one came to check on their condition. Phoenix's mouth ran dry and his stomach was growling. Eric's body responded with the same sounds of distress.

Eventually the carriage hit a few bumps in the road, signaling that it was coming to a halt. Phoenix's ears perked as he listened to the chatter, noticing Eric also eavesdropping. In a flash of blinding light, the entire space was visible for the first time. Phoenix shielded his eyes and turned his head. Squinting, he could finally see Crystal in broad daylight. She was covered in dried blood and he could count the lacerations on her skin. Her breathing was shallow and weak. The kidnappers climbed onboard, coming for the three of them. They began to unhook Eric's chains from the restraints attached to the wall, only to re-hook them onto a portable, metal ring.

When three of the goons came toward Phoenix and started attaching him to the loop, his spirit ached to resist. But he knew his stamina was low and the odds were not in his favor. With Crystal down and Eric unreliable, he would be fighting alone. All he could do was watch as he was transferred to their ring. Phoenix figured Crystal was next, but instead a pair of them rolled her body onto a blanket. They lifted the sheet up, with her lying in the middle like a hammock. The ringmaster pulled at their chains, motioning them to follow. Using his last piece of strength, he showed his defiance by remaining still. Eric merely nodded, following their direct orders.

His protest didn't last long. The ring holder shouted many insults until one of his friends gripped Phoenix by his shoulders and threw him to the dirt. He grunted as his chest slid against the terrain. He listened to the horses scoffing at him while his chains tugged against his wrists. Slowly rising to his feet, he could feel his skin chafe under his restraints.

Eric stared blankly to the side, paying no attention to the scene. Even as he was pushed forward, his head remained down. A few thugs led them, while the rest followed in the rear. The wanted criminals were being shoved into a rundown building. One that had been abused by time and abandoned by civilization. The windows were stained brown, the paint was either chipped or in the process, and the walls were crumbling from decay.

As they entered, Eric reached for his nose, but the guard restricted his movement. The place was disgusting. Rats scampered around and insects scattered to their homes along the walls. A drop of liquid fell, splashing onto Phoenix's forehead. He prayed to the Protectors that it was water.

While they continued down the hallway, Phoenix felt an itch that increased in intensity every second. Sliding his vest to the side, he noticed a swollen bump. He brushed his finger by it, recoiling from the pain. The area was sensitive and as red as a sunset. *This is where Alpha stabbed me . . . the poison . . . I must have received an antidote or a cure.*

Reaching the end of the corridor, they walked into a large assembly room. Rows of seats were before them, lining up until they reached two tables. Both were rotting away from infestation and had two chairs positioned near them. Beyond that was a giant stage like one would find at a theater. Upon the stage, a podium stood almost as ancient as the rest of the woodwork. Three passages could be found: beside the stage, to their left, and to their right.

The guards whispered amongst themselves. Phoenix could hear their murmuring from behind. One of them mumbled, "She's unconscious and would not know a thing." Another voice commented with, "Why waste time by taking turns? We can all have a go at once."

The bits and pieces he caught were not a lot, but enough to know what they were implying. Phoenix had half a mind to take it upon himself to teach these wild boars some manners, but it would only end with an unfair beating. This time his own. Eric inhaled deeply, signaling he heard what was being said, but remained to himself.

They were brought to the front and their restraints were attached to separate tables. Two of the guards proceeded down the left corridor with Crystal.

"Where are you taking her?" exclaimed Phoenix.

The guard slammed Phoenix's head forward, his jaw bouncing off the grain. "Quiet, maggot. You are not permitted to speak freely in court."

Phoenix straightened his back, but didn't say another word. He stared straightforward, feeling liquid pool in his mouth. As he studied the stage, a man came into view. Wearing a big black trench coat buttoned all the way to his chin, he stepped into center stage. He coughed several times, rubbed his eyes, and stretched. He tapped documents onto the podium. As he prepared to speak, the guardsmen in the room greeted him as they would a royal figure.

He placed his hand in the air, honoring their greeting.

"Phoenix Reinhard, Crystal Thorn, please present yourselves and bow." The announcer's raspy tone filled the void of the hollow building. A long silence passed as Phoenix remained hunched. After a few minutes, a guard made his way to the judge's side and whispered in his ear.

"In the clinic?" whispered the man aloud. The guard nodded and handed him a sheet of paper. He coughed several times again as he read the words before him: "Phoenix Reinhard, remain standing, and Eric Strauser, rise and bow." Eric glared at the man with disgust until a guard elbowed the back of his head. He angrily forced himself onto his feet, snarling a few words under his breath.

"Have the reasons of your capture been released to your ears?" He flicked his eyes between the two. "If you have yet to be informed, I will list your crimes as the rules of court state. Phoenix Reinhard, you have been accused of first-degree murder on two accounts, and mutilation of Emerica. This doubles for the defendant Crystal Thorn as well. Do you understand?" Phoenix stared at him. "Do you have any questions?"

"Where are we? More importantly, who are you?"

"Asked with such impatience." He made a swift hand movement. Instantly, a guard slammed Phoenix onto the table. His head bounced again, making a clunk like before. As he struggled to get up, the man went on: "We are currently at the House of Judgment. All the trash that litters the land tumbles into my room until we assess their crimes. Survivors are transported to the House of Retribution in Assassin City."

"Hired by a force not under any royal ruling?" Eric blurted. The prosecutor shot him a terrible glare and a guard struck, forcing him to falter forward.

"I was not speaking with you. But incidentally, yes. We have created our own form of government that satisfies all parties. The leader will be receiving the coin from the rewards we will collect from selling you fugitives to the officials. Phoenix Reinhard may be seated." A guard sat Phoenix down and the judge turned his attention to Eric.

"Eric Strauser, you have been accused of hiding these convicts and resisting arrest—"

"Bullshit. My neighbors have been disappearing for years by your hands! It was only a matter of time until you came for me."

"You are no use to us. The likes of you would keep us from reaching our goals. Your kind is not needed."

Eric's rage immediately spiraled downward, plunging into sadness and despair. His head tilted forward as the judge continued. His grim expression caught Phoenix by surprise. He almost felt sympathy for him.

"There will be no ruling for the defendant Eric. As stated before, we have no use for your existence. You will be delivered to a work camp and placed under the care of the director in charge."

"Wait I ha—"

"Speaking freely? The impertinence!" The guard struck twice as hard, forcing him to collapse to his knees.

"Please escort these two to their temporary homes. After some other important matters are finished, I will continue with Phoenix and Crystal's evaluation next morning." The short stubby monster exited the stage. He left their presence traveling down the corridor closest to him.

Phoenix and Eric were attached back to the guards' leash. Four of them pulled at the ring, taking them down the corridor to the right. There was a sudden turn in the hallway that revealed six metal cells, three on each side, and a small window at the end. Trickles of light broke through the worn out glass. The men were thrown into their own individual cells and before leaving them alone, the locks were double-checked.

A deadly silence flowed through the hall. Phoenix's mind raced as if it was running a marathon. He had no plan. No idea how to escape. He worriedly strolled around the cell, until he heard Eric rustling in the one beside his. He flashed back to his expression. It was a look that had heard it all before. One of shame and abandonment.

"Eric." There was no reply besides a constant drip that echoed throughout their tiny confinements. "Please, Eric, I beg you to forgive me. I'm sorry for what has happened. I wish I could atone for what I brought down upon your family. If I would have known these series of events would unfold, I would have stayed clear of your path." Still nothing. "This work camp . . . I do not know what they will do to you, but I will liberate us. You, Brett, and Alex—I'll save you all."

Eric still remained silent. Phoenix stared at the bars separating him from Crystal. He only had one last card up his sleeve. "Neither of us can escape on our own. I'm going to need your help. Brett needs your help. Brett's going to be in trouble. He's going to wonder why you haven't rescued him. Eric, please, we need one another if we are going to save him."

A few noises drifted from the cell. "Phoenix, I hate you. And I *hate* that you're right. This idea of atonement . . . is one that I will never be able to grant you. Especially if ill will falls on my family. But, we're in this together. For better or worse."

"Will I be able to rely on you?"

"For now."

"I have an idea."

"I'm all ears," Eric said, huddling against the bars.

A guard strolled down to their confinements, stomping his feet as aggressively as possible.

"You two best be sleepin'," he yelled through the corridor. He waited a few minutes for an answer as he waved his candle back and forth. He turned to leave, but a thud caught his attention.

"What was that?" Again his voice invaded the silent rooms. He walked toward the first cell where Phoenix was being held. He scouted the enclosure letting the warm glow light up the room. He spotted a figure in the corner, motionless. He retracted his light and moved on to Eric's cell.

"Stop! Don't move," Eric growled. The guard halted in his tracks startled by the command. Holding the candle toward the cell, he watched as Eric crawled toward him in a sickly, grotesque way.

"Tell me what's planned for me at this camp."

"I will not disclose information to prisoners—especially to lowlife scum who violate the sacred laws of nature." The phrase struck him deep. "Might as well rest now, there will be no more of that in your future."

"I-If you leave now . . . I'm going to . . . Your judge is going to hear all the explicit things that happened between us."

"What!" exclaimed the guard. "You spout lies!"

"I'll describe how you were being . . . intimate with me," Eric replied. "And you know what they do with lowlife scum that violate those laws."

The guard quivered, "No, no, keep that mouth of yours shut."

"Then you will stand here and tell me all I desire to know."

The guard trembled in his boots as Eric whispered, "Closer." His boots stepped forward as a smirk crossed Eric's face. "Now!"

Phoenix reached around and grappled him through the bars. Placing him into a headlock, he held him tightly until the struggling and resistance ended. He dropped the body, letting it collapse upon itself.

"What . . . What he said . . . I'm—"

"It's nothing. His words and the words of the people of his nature don't faze me. I know what I am, and it's not a single thing he said. Love is a gift from the Creator and Brett's love is all that matters."

Phoenix merely smiled into the darkness as he reached for the guard. *Eric, no one should be treated in such a manner.* He frantically rifled through his pockets, finding a cluster of keys.

"I got . . . all of them," he muttered jingling them in the air.

"Well, guess and check! We need to escape."

Phoenix inserted and twisted about a dozen keys before he finally heard a click. Unlocking his gate, he went and released Eric.

"About time; any longer and I was sure I would have keeled over from starvation." Phoenix stared back, not finding the humor funny. Eric awkwardly coughed, "Alright, next move?"

"We need to locate Crystal. Once we have her, we need to search for the judge—he must have an idea where they took Brett and Alex. I watched him enter the hallway by the stage. Maybe that's where his quarters reside." Phoenix glanced at the empty cells and the unconscious mercenary. "Let's lock him behind bars to keep him from sight. We do not need him to suddenly wake and alarm the others."

"You didn't kill him? He's a loose end!"

"He was unarmed."

"That wouldn't have stopped him from killing us!"

"I am not a monster. I leave murder to the ones who seek it."

"Can't say I agree, but if that will help you rest easy. Toss him in there. But first, let's see if he has anything useful." Eric patted the man down, finding a hard object within his shirt. Ripping it open, he discovered a metal baton. With greedy hands, Eric brought it to Phoenix's attention. "Unarmed?"

Phoenix shrugged. "Grab the candle, too; could prove useful."

Locking the guard behind the gate, the two of them ran into the assembly room. Eric followed Phoenix as he made his way across the room to the opposite hallway where they had carried Crystal earlier. The team stopped at double doors that read "Emergency." Entering the room, the artificial lighting revealed a small poorly stocked pharmaceutical center. Four black curtains were drawn hiding beds behind them; there was a wide sink and a few medical cabinets with red-painted crosses on the walls. In a rush, the curtains were ripped away. On the third strike, they found Crystal lying on the mattress, bandaged from head to toe. Phoenix released a sigh of relief seeing her face again, mostly unharmed. He gently picked her up, holding Crystal tightly to his chest.

"Alright, phase one complete without a hassle." Eric peered through the door.

Phoenix nodded. "Phase two will now commence."

"Uh, I'd like to take back the 'without a hassle' part. Two tangos coming this way." Eric turned to Phoenix. "And they're armed."

Two soldiers opened the door to the infirmary. One went straight for the sink, running the water over his bare hands. Waiting for the water to warm, he noticed a flame shimmering to his side. "Did we leave a candle on our last check-in?"

"It's dark and we're both tired," replied the second man who slid the curtain open to find Crystal tucked neatly beneath her sheets. As he lowered them to her waist, his partner joined his side. He handed him a wet cloth, which he used to scrub her skin. The rag circled her face and traveled the length of her arms. The two men shook with excitement as they reached lower. The blanket barely crossed her feet as the curtains on both sides were torn aside.

The guard with the rag felt a strong grip wrap around his waist that hoisted him up from the mattress. He tumbled along the linoleum, reaching for his sword. As he touched the hilt, a boot collided with his jaw, flinging him to the left. His head cracked against the floor. A flurry of fists pounded away at him until it was lights out.

The other guard did not have a chance to act as he was tackled to the floor. His body was pressed against the tiles, struggling to move under the weight. His face was forced back and forth as hits came from all angles. Blood leaked from his lips as another whack crushed his nose. He lay there still as the other body pushed off him. Barely conscious, he could only witness as the sole of a shoe came down upon him.

Phoenix caught Eric's leg as it went down for the fifth time. "He's beaten. Why continue?"

"I like to be certain our enemies will not come back to haunt us." His leg continued with its course once Phoenix released him.

"There is no reason to kill him. He will not wake while we are still in this building."

"But he is armed," Eric smirked replacing the baton with the sword. "This will be more effective."

Carrying Crystal carefully, they traveled toward the last place they saw the judge. Eric held the candle forward, slowly moving the stick side to side to light the path.

"There appears to be several doors on both sides of the wall," Eric squinted harder. "And one at the end." He moved forward.

"Wait, Eric," Phoenix dropped his voice. "These must be the guards' quarters. Neither of us are in any shape to fight. We need to use the night as an ally to sneak down to the giant door. Avoiding unnecessary conflict has to be our focus. Understand?"

"But I have this!" He waved his sword only to receive disapproval. "You're no fun."

Following behind, Phoenix tiptoed down the hallway in complete silence. They noticed none of the rooms had doors. Thin sheets hung over the entrances as a substitute, blocking the view of the sleeping soldiers.

Eric breathed shallowly. *One noise and we'll be surrounded.* When they reached the end, Eric gingerly pushed it open. A desk was centered in the bedroom, surrounded by stacks of papers. Three tall bookcases filled to the rim with novels were lined up on the right. Behind the table was a glass window with a tall metal cabinet to the side. The moonlight shone through the window onto the sickly man's face. Snoring like a baby, he was wrapped in his sheets.

Phoenix spoke under his breath: "We need to find all documentations that may hold clues to Brett's whereabouts and our bags. I cannot stress enough how silent we need to be." Eric nodded in agreement. Sneaking into the room, Phoenix laid Crystal against the wall.

Phoenix began searching the bookcases from end to end thoroughly. He hoped to find hidden papers and folders stuffed between the hard covers. Anything that would prove useful.

Eric ruffled through the documents on the desk. He pointlessly scrambled around the clutter of papers. In reality, he didn't have the slightest clue what he was in search of. Anything with his family's name on it was going to be equivalent to a chest of gold coins. Each sheet flew into the air scattering across the floor. His hunt came to a halt when he found a folder with his picture clipped to the front. Skimming through the stack of folders, he saw Phoenix and Crystal's papers as well.

"Phoenix, I found the documents!" He covered his mouth in realization. The judge made a couple of grunts, rolling over to the other side. Phoenix stealthily headed toward him, avoiding the noisy hazards now covering the ground. He grabbed the folders, taking a peek inside.

"You're worth quite a bit; overpriced if I were to be asked."

"Good thing no one did. All that is left is our bags," said Phoenix.

"We have one place yet to check," Eric pointed to the metal cabinet.

Phoenix gently unlatched the door. There was muffled rustling, but he didn't seem to notice. Hanging before him was Crystal's bag and his robe. He tenderly pulled them off their hooks, noticing the blood stained hole in his clothing. A glimpse of anger popped onto his face only to vanish. *I don't think this will ever recover,* he sadly thought, caressing it in his hands. In a rush of excitement and adrenaline, he let the door slam behind him. Immediately his eyes widened.

Eric could only watch as the vibrations from the cabinet shook the items on top. A chest fell to the ground, the collision shaking the entire room. The papers flew farther around, adding more noise to the dilemma. The judge jolted upright, his head whiplashing back and forth between the shadows.

"Guards! Intruders!"

Phoenix bolted to the door, throwing Crystal into his arms. Propping her over his shoulder, he watched Eric push the hefty chest toward their exit. His disbelief was put to the side as he left the room to find a crowd of angry beasts waiting for them. He locked stares with the group, almost as if the sight bewildered them. The stupor ended and his comfort zone grew smaller as they raced toward him. He stepped back bumping into Eric who, surprisingly, stepped between them.

"Freeze!" The guards stopped their approach, uncertainty in their eyes. Eric held the judge by the back of his collar, holding his blade underneath his chin. "If one more person takes another step, there will be one less stubby, little man breathing." He tightened his grip on the judge. The whole group stepped down. "Good, good. Now lead me and my friend to the horses that brought us here." No one budged. "No? I could just redecorate your hallways with a new color if that is what you wish. Crimson sound appealing?" Eric rammed his knee into the judge's back making him gasp.

The man had tears streaming across his cheeks. "D-Do as he says! Please stand down! Spare me."

The guards moved to the sides, creating a path. Eric and Phoenix walked between them, wary of their movements. As they smelled the cold night's fresh air, Eric shouted, "Someone retrieve the chest from his quarters!" Obeying, it was brought to his side and loaded onto the metal carriage.

Phoenix laid Crystal alongside the chest, freeing his hands in case of a riot. He walked up to the horses, untying the three of them from their posts. Brushing the white one's mane, he checked to see if Eric still had the crowd under his thumb. He placed his feet into the stirrups and got comfortable on the saddle.

"It is time, Eric, release the victim."

Eric scanned the crowd as he walked backward with his hostage. When his horse was only a few feet away, he stared up at Phoenix. "I'm not a monster, either, I just walk a different path." Before Phoenix had time to object, Eric inflated his lungs to full capacity and roared as he slashed the man's neck. He dropped both the corpse and sword, then saddled up.

That was the cue to escape. The horses began galloping forward as the jail keepers ran after them, swords elevated high above their heads. It was only seconds before the guards and the House of Judgment were left in the dust. When they were out of harm's way, Phoenix scolded his companion.

"We attained what we wanted and had our means to escape; tell me, why did you kill that man?"

"How are you defending him? Who knows how many people he has condemned? How many of those people were from my town?"

"We do not have the power to decide who lives and dies. Their fate is in the hands of the Protectors."

"But he does? The judge, jury, and executioner—he placed that power in his own hands. I would not let him live to see another day and pursue his role as a false God. I will kill the ones he reports to as well. Keep your views of righteousness to yourself."

Phoenix kept quiet. He let the hooves beating against Teague fill the space between him and Eric. He motioned for them to stop. Sliding off the horse, he climbed aboard their carriage. He knew Eric didn't have a destination, but neither did he. No reason why both of them had to be guiding the horses. Especially now that he listened to his nonsense. With Crystal's head resting on his lap, he felt his body jerk as they began moving once more. Eventually the last of his energy deserted him, making the job of keeping his lids open impossible. Allowing them to rest, he fell fast asleep.

CHAPTER 8

Phoenix abruptly shot forward, feeling a different temperature on his skin. The sounds of sizzling and crackling circled around him. Frantic, he jumped to his feet only to plunge his head into a dense smoke. Coughing ensued as he searched for Crystal. She was curled up in a ball encircled by flames and surrounded by charred papers. Trembling overcame him, shaking worse than a starved child. He plowed through the carriage doors, his flesh burning from heated metal. He stumbled out, falling to the ground. Trying to push himself back up, he heard faint footsteps walking in his direction. Lifting his head, his heart froze.

A tall, dark figure made his way toward him. The figure's entire body was aflame with black fire, leaving none of its person visible. An ominous aura swirled around the dark being as it stopped, standing like a statue. Off in the distance, Phoenix heard wood cracking, only to break and fall to the ground. The dark figure's deep sinister voice startled him. The mere sound made his blood run cold and his body shiver relentlessly.

"Phoenix . . ." The voice echoed. "Allow the darkness to consume you. Allow your hatred to show you the light."

He could only blankly stare at the creature. The monster's eyes glowed bright red as it spoke, outshining the inferno around it. Suddenly the icy chill that had stunned him turned into a burning sensation. He began flailing as his body fried. He was reliving all his emotional traumas. Surrounding him, scenes from his past came to life.

His head rolled to the left as he heard his mother's voice rage against John's. Their arguing and shouting pierced his ears. He became anxious, his skin crawling with each word. Before him, the blood of his sister pooled into a puddle. Beth's cry stained his vision as his anxiety was washed away by despair. Phoenix begin cringing, holding his arm. It felt as if a rough object was crossing his arm, a nail scraping along his skin. Peering to the right, Skull had just slid his weapon, the Gusher, into its sheath. His maniacal laugh shook his surroundings.

The suffering, sadness, and despair tied to each memory overcame him in an instant. The intensity of these feelings increased as his whole body was engulfed. The dark creature let out a cynical laugh as the last of Phoenix's body disappeared behind a veil of fire.

"Phoenix! Phoenix!" Crystal yelled, shaking him. "Phoenix!"

Phoenix bolted forward, gasping for air. He slid his hand through his hair and across his face, making sure all was real. He felt the dampness of his clothes as he shifted his body toward Crystal. The doors of their carriage were open allowing a slight breeze to find its way in. *I'm alive. Breathing, no fire—alive.* He tenderly pushed Crystal aside to gain some space. He leaned against the wall, using it to assist him in standing. The duffel bag and documents fell off his lap onto the floor.

Crystal laid her hand upon his arm, noticing his pale skin. "Ar-are you alright?"

Yeah . . . Yeah, I'm fine . . . I need some air." Phoenix staggered outside to find Eric by a stream. He was scrubbing away at his hands, submerging them in water, then repeating. He then removed his shirt to use it as a washcloth. Eric laid the wet cloth by his feet and walked toward them.

Crystal watched as his shirt slid across his torso, revealing his chiseled back. Her jaw dropped as he turned toward his fan club. He was pure muscle. Head to toe, his body was one of a God. The definition and tone was an accomplishment of a man who spent the entirety of his life working toward. His skin was smooth besides the trail from his naval leading down.

Wow, that— he . . . only if . . . Lucky Brett, she thought.

"Why have we stopped? Do you know where we are?" inquired Phoenix.

"Not a clue," grumbled Eric.

"Then why—"

"The horses have been traveling all night; they deserve the rest. Probably should find them a little to eat. Crystal has the map—can you tell us anything?"

"One cannot read a map if they are lost. There is no marker that says 'we are right here,'" remarked Crystal.

As the two started bickering, Phoenix surveyed their surroundings. *Something about this place . . . odd. It feels familiar—I have been here before.* He scanned the sky above the mountains. Walking toward them, he came across what looked like a crumpled wall, one that was scorched heavily. He peaked around the corner to find broken down homes and buildings that had fallen to pieces. The smell of decay filled his nostrils. As he inhaled a whiff of the scent, a tear-inducing tremor blasted through him. The realization hit him harder than any hammer could. His stomach twisted into a knot almost forcing him to his knees. Eric noticed him hunched over and rushed to his side. Crystal followed behind.

"What's wrong? What is it?" worried Crystal.

There was a long silence. He finally answered.

"This . . . This is my city. The once great city of Luminar—my home. Right here. Right here is where it used to stand tall, stand proud."

"This used to be your home? There was only a single survivor, who had vanished." Eric's eye brows rose. "W-was that you?" There was another silence. Phoenix continued gazing at the intersection of the mountains and the morning sky.

"Is it time to tell me all that you have been hiding?" pressed Crystal.

"It may be . . . Follow me"

They entered the battered gate.

"I was the last one. My people were murdered before my own eyes, and I did nothing. Nothing to save them. That guilt has resided in me for all these years. The resentment I harbor . . . To this day I wish I had tried harder and fought back. The lives of others should have been spared, not mine."

Crystal tried comforting him: "Phoenix, that was years ago. You were just a boy."

"That is no excuse. I could have done anything, *anything* to help someone! I witnessed the death of my sister, who was protecting me. All of those lost lives for some damn emerald." Tears swelled around his lower lids. "I dwelled here for days, weeks, may-maybe even a month. I wallowed in self-pity, shedding tears for all my loved ones. All in the matter of a night, I became an orphan, a stranger . . . and a survivor."

He stopped at a path that split into three. He looked at the three buildings the paths led to that once were painted the honored colors of Luminar, but now not a drop could be found beneath the new coat of char. *This place that held my daily torture, one that I would have sworn would have ended my life . . . How I wish I could go back to those classes.* He paused, picturing Beth and him walking to school together, smiling and laughing. A few minutes passed until he proceeded.

"Hysteria corrupted the minds of the citizens like a viral disease when the city was invaded. My parents included. I only managed to grab onto a Creation present, one I had received the night before. A sword my mother had given to me that had been passed through generation after generation. The blade and sheath are rare and extremely valuable. I lost it to Luminar's lake. I eventually retrieved it. Though it wasn't in my possession for long." He clenched his fists. "I was too defenseless to even protect my sword . . . wandering bandits pillaged the village and found me. Demanded I hand it over. It was either my life or my last connection to who I was. I listened to them snicker as I stared at the back of their heads. I could have . . . I could have at least attempted to run." Crystal placed her hand upon his shoulder, but he abruptly shook it away. Eric focused on the remnants of corpses deteriorating beneath their feet. He shivered.

"Not too long afterward, an older adult arrived. A wandering warrior, he called himself. At the time, I had little trust to give freely. He appeared to be past his prime to be a fighter. He wore a black top that revealed his chest through a crisscross of strings and sand colored bottoms. A black cape wrapped around his shoulders. The most peculiar thing was the straw hat he wore."

"Odd getup if you were to ask me."

"Well, no one did," remarked Crystal.

"My legs finally decided to run, but the warrior had me by the back of my collar. I began crying. The man looked at me and threw me on the ground. I've never seen someone look at a child with such . . . disgust. As he left, he told me that once I was finished, find him by the gates before sundown. The rest is kind of blurry. I remember scrubbing my face of ash and dirt. And blood. I soaked in that moment, staring at the reflection. I didn't recognize him. That foreign feeling will always be with me. Before I found the man, I put my sister and the Prince to rest."

Phoenix abruptly stopped again, this time in front of a collapsed building. He looked at the walls that had been bombarded and winced. He pictured Prince Joshua speaking to the crowd of Luminar. When he had placed all his hope into him. *With him as our leader, no harm would ever come to us—what a childish idea.*

"I was told what makes me human had to remain where I was lost to Teague. I was forbidden to feel. Emotions and attachments brought ownership and weakness. Boys like me owned nothing. I was one of many who traveled across the country and abroad. The gaggle of misfortunes were trained in the way of the samurai and martial arts. Tournaments were frequently held where I squared off with the toughest swordsmen to roam Teague. First prize for one of the competitions was the priceless White Dragon armor." Phoenix gestured to his outfit as the three of them climbed over rubble. "My mother's sword was the White Dragon. It was destined for me to win."

"My mentor trained me beyond the limits of mere physical ability. To become a proper gentleman, I studied by the Protectors' Secret Service's chivalry book. I had to be able to blend into any environment, whether it was with royalty or commoners. My mind was tested. To lie and persuade, but to remain silent under any circumstance—"

"Torture?" whimpered Crystal.

He nodded. "My classes included archery, spear handling, and other weaponry courses. Each class was harder and more difficult than the last. Students were not permitted to show any emotion. A mere smile, one tear, and they would have been beaten and placed in punishment, depending on the circumstance." Phoenix's eyes darted around. *After a few decades things start to look different.*

"The final lesson my mentor had planned was mastering the ninja arts. I was trained by the top ninjas of the world. One mistake resulted in consequence. One night included sleeping upon hot coals for getting clipped by a kunai a master threw." Phoenix paused, almost as if he was preparing himself to continue.

"The warrior, my mentor, sent me forth. His last parting words still resonate in my head: 'All that you will ever need is in your disposal. Decide whether it's for revenge or something greater.' I awoke the following morning to find myself alone . . . again. I had to make my own decisions for the first time in years. I was led to Kyron city; it's a wealth of knowledge and rumors."

"Phoenix, all those things . . . that's horrible . . ." Eric's voice drifted away. "Did you ever learn the name of your mentor?"

"He owns no name—at least one he no longer carries with him. Some called him Commander."

"Who-whose Skull? There was a vendetta between the two of

you at Emerica?"

Phoenix stood before a lake, one that had less luster than rust. Their reflections barely shimmered in the murky water. "He's the one . . . the one who murdered my sister and the Prince in cold blood." Phoenix pulled his arm from his robe, revealing his gruesome whip-like line that led from the top of his shoulder down his bicep. "He is at fault for this blemish as well."

"Oh, man, I-I'm not very good—" Eric stopped. He stared at Phoenix whose gaze trailed away.

Phoenix stepped into the lake, treading water. Confused, the other two blindly followed him, despite Crystal making several disgusted faces. They traveled to a small island in the center. Their clothes clung to their bodies as they climbed back onto land. He pushed through overgrown bushes and stepped around vines until he found two disheveled mounds of dirt. Crystal and Eric remained quiet as Phoenix bent down between two sticks hidden beneath untamed grass. The branches were displayed in the center of their piles. *Nothing has grown here since I've been gone. No weeds, no flowers; nothing but grass.* Ages passed before Phoenix rose.

He coughed to break the tension. "There's no reason to linger here any longer. What's dead is gone. May I see the map?"

Crystal stared at Phoenix slightly confused on how he was keeping his calm. "It's in my bag. Hopefully it's not drenched . . ." She searched through her duffel bag. "Here it is!" As she went to hand him it, startling growls vibrated through the bushes.

"Wha-what? What's that?" shrieked Crystal hiding behind Phoenix.

"Eric, prepare yourself."

They braced themselves as two black creatures pounced toward them. One slammed its body into Eric, knocking him down. The other clamped its jaw onto Phoenix's wrist, thrusting its teeth deep into his flesh. Phoenix let out a cry, throwing the animal back. He got a quick glance at it before it lunged again. It stood on four feet, no bigger than a regular dog. Its eyes and coat were a fierce black and it had a long, stringy tail. The creature came at Phoenix again, but with more speed. It hopped into the air, slamming its weight onto him. Phoenix grabbed its neck and slammed it onto the ground. It quickly rebounded and changed targets, striding straight for Crystal. Phoenix slid in front of its path, bashing his foot in its face. The thing yelped, sliding backward.

Eric quickly jumped up only to be welcomed by another attack from the creature. The thing came toward him snapping its jaw. When it was close enough, Eric shot out his hands, pressing its muzzle shut. He lifted the animal, spun, and threw it back toward the bushes. It collided with the other one as they crossed paths. The two of them regrouped, walking around in a circle amongst each other, snarling violently. Their fangs reached below their gums, sharp and ready.

"Around my part of the world, we don't quite have these kinds of beasts. What would you call them?"

"Not the time for sarcasm. They're not finished with us yet."

The creatures started strolling toward them, their raw muscle shifting between paws.

"Well whatever they may be, we need to think of something!" Phoenix and Eric stood before Crystal, waiting for them to strike, when suddenly two objects shot down from the sky, impaling the creatures. They howled as the arrows burned right through their pelts. The group watched in amazement as the creatures fizzled away. Within seconds, only the projectiles remained from the dazzling display.

"What in the name of the Protectors?" Eric whispered checking his surroundings.

"Where did they come from?" Crystal started glancing around.

Phoenix scanned the area. "Quiet, I hear someone approaching."

Almost on cue, three men trudged through the shrubs. Their wardrobes were dirty and blood spattered. They all wore the same, brown raggedy outfit. Two of them were equipped with bows while the one in back had a basket weaved from branches strapped to his shoulder that was holding their supply of ammunition. That man walked to the front of the others, approaching the startled visitors.

He was a short, stout, older gentleman whose face had seen better days. With a large, silver moustache and a few hairs on his head to match, his appeal was rather repulsive, but intimidating nonetheless.

"Rex is what I'm called. These two are Danny and Noel," he pointed at the bow wielders. Danny had reddish hair and a muscular physique—one that rivaled Eric's—while Noel had a skeleton-like body with barely enough skin to cover the entirety of his bones. The dark, brown hair atop his head contrasted with his sickly pale skin.

"We are proud members of the Luminescence Clan, and you're standing on our territory. State your purpose or leave."

"What the hell were those things? Secondly—" Eric stopped as Phoenix placed his hand in front of him.

"In what way are these lands *yours*?"

"Our clan is the remaining remnants of Luminar City." A shock sparked through the group.

"Wait, was there not only a single lone survivor that had disappeared?" asked Crystal.

Phoenix stared at the men in disbelief. He was beyond stunned, frozen by this newfound discovery. As he stared tongue tied, he found himself subconsciously rubbing his wrist.

"He was the one reported to be alive," answered the man. "The other survivors were amongst the citizens that carefully traveled to Luminar's safe zone located in the mountain tops overhead. Bandits had captured our haven, ending many lives that had sought refuge. Courageous men and women brought the bandits' operation to a halt, granting the rest of us safety. Only about two-dozen of us remained. After that night, no one could be certain if the raid had ended. The company had enough rations to last us a fortnight before we were forced to act."

Phoenix's eyes were glued to the dirt beneath his feet. *Survivors? It can't be true. I heard their screams. They all . . . All of them died that night. I'm the only one . . .* His thoughts raced back and forth through his mind as he continuously rubbed away.

"There really are more survivors? That's incredible news," smiled Crystal. "All of Teague will be relieved to hear this! They will be ecstatic!"

Noel noticed Phoenix massaging his wrist.

"But what were those foul creatures?" asked Eric, pointing to the crisp marks around the arrows. Before Rex answered, Noel spoke.

"Man in white, were you bitten by the X-hound?"

Phoenix removed his hand revealing the teeth marks.

"We must bring him to camp immediately before the curse spreads throughout his body," Danny stated calmly without a hint of distress.

"Curse?" yelped Crystal.

"Once he is in stable condition, I shall explain. To treat him, we must depart this instant."

Rex took lead as the rest followed. They walked past Phoenix's burnt down home. He still cringed from the memories of that night. His mother, sister, and even John—he missed them all. His eyes clung to his old tree. It had been crying and mourning for years. The bark was decaying and it had lost its strength to stand tall as it were when he sat beneath it. No one else seemed to sense the despair that suffocated him. The group traveled the mountain trail as if a tragedy never occurred on the very ground they walked upon.

"Please pass the time and skip to the moment I finally hear answers about these beasts," demanded Eric, beginning to fume.

Rex nodded his head to Noel. Noel answered back with the same notion.

"It's not clear on what the creatures are exactly. Or what they're made from. We have encountered four species. We call those the X-hounds since they resemble dogs."

"What are the other species like?"

"There's the X-fowler resembling crows, the X-feline mimicking cats, and then the X-human. They appear humanoid as you and I, but more twisted. The X stands for a variable of the unknown. Each species of creatures are not exactly similar. There are different variations amongst them."

"Other than the fact they're pure evil looking?" chimed in Eric.

"He means," explained Danny, "their appearances differ between each individual. The X-hounds teeth vary in length and shape, ranging from dull to piercing. They may also have a numerous number of tails depending on their rank. We have learned a single tail signifies the leadership of a pack. A few have witnessed a rarity of hounds with double heads."

"Mindless animals. They attack on sight. Before our own eyes we witnessed a pack devour an X-feline. We also have concluded they have an incredible ability to sense fear. It's their source of nourishment."

"What-what's their origin?" asked Phoenix, returning to reality.

"We . . . That has been undetermined," replied Noel. "There are no leads. They appeared from air once the commotion settled in the city."

"That cannot be all you've learned about them! Those arrows in your possession made them sizzle and vanish," argued Eric.

Rex entered the conversation: "The clan was able to capture some of these creatures and test a variety of weapons. One ability all the species share is the strength to regenerate. No matter the blade or metal, a lost limb would be grown by nightfall. On our expeditions, we discovered a certain mineral, Bright Light, that none had ever come across. The Bright Light partook in our experiments and the clan learned it could easily pierce and burn the creatures. In a sense, the monsters have an allergic reaction to the mineral, which completely negates their regeneration at the point of contact. The

Bright Light spreads across their skin and through them internally, setting their innards aflame. The few of us were on a mission to gather more down at the lake, until we encountered the turmoil."

"This Bright Light exists only in Luminary Lake?" Phoenix felt like a stranger in his home.

"'Tis the theory. The mineral gave the lake its glowing appearance, but once the siege occurred, it had become contaminated. Its production slowed to a halt, draining it of its color and appeal. The clan has practically depleted the reservoir. We are in search of another source."

"All that time," murmured Noel solemnly. "As a child I was taught that the tears of Kyrudorous at Rolux's burial made the lake majestic. To think it was a mineral . . ."

"At least there's a weapon in our arsenal that can slay those creatures. That's a good start. Where they originate does not matter. But what's with—" Eric was interrupted as Phoenix fell to his knees in a loud outburst. He gripped his wrist as if he was attempting to cut circulation.

"The curse."

"The curse has spread at an accelerated pace, a speed that has not yet been documented. This is extraordinary!" exclaimed Noel.

"No need to panic; we have arrived," Rex calmly broadcasted.

The campsite was laid out before them surrounded by the safety of mountain walls. Tents were pitched in long rows and columns, each one held stable by wood and stone. Faded red decorated each one. Work-benches were scattered around the campus. Several clan members were using them, most displaying handmade goods. Rex rushed Phoenix through the only entrance to the campsite. They passed several large tents in haste to a specific one stationed in the rear. It covered three times the amount of ground as the rest. An enlarged syringe was painted across the hood of the top. Noel and Danny escorted the other two to an adjacent tent.

Phoenix's eyes were clenched tightly together trying to tolerate the pain. He felt a strong grip on his bicep leading him forward blindly. Dizziness set in, along with nausea. He began stumbling over his feet, slowing them down. The hold on his arm was released only to find himself being lifted off the ground. The wind brushed against his face until a sudden warm and still air replaced it. His body was laid against a stiff board—not that the comfortability mattered to him since he was cringing into a ball. A voice announced they were leaving to fetch the physician.

"Show us your wrist, boy," ordered Rex, leading the nurse to him. Phoenix unsteadily raised his arm until the nurse gently grasped it. He heard some popping noise, but couldn't concentrate on what it potentially could be until he felt a sharp pain. She injected a needle into the wound, forcing a liquid inside his body. Phoenix screamed upon contact.

The nurse removed the needle. "Alrighty, darling," chirped a charming voice. "Stay still and allow the medicine to cleanse your system. The solution does not take long to ease the pain, but it shall be minutes before it has run its course." She heaved a sigh, looking at him struggling, eyelids still sealed.

"Madame Lee, two more guests await for you in the infirmary tents. Tend to their needs if you will. Noel and Danny accompanied them."

"Alrighty, I'll call for the doctor. She will come have a word with you, dear; time goes much faster with a conversation as a distraction." Phoenix heard their feet exit the tent. He sat in silence feeling his body ache, until he heard the sound of the tent door flap as it was pushed aside. He tried opening his lids, but the pain continued to be too much to bear.

"How unlucky, boy," yelled an old, craggy voice, much harsher than the nurse's sweet tone. "Soldiers only meet the claws of these creatures. Most never learn the harsh truth of their bites."

Phoenix cradled himself, barely listening to her babbling.

"See, the curse only lies in those beasts' saliva. Once it is able to enter the bloodstream, it is end game. Rarely is one able to live through this contact without medical assistance."

Oh wonderful, he thought behind his clenched lids.

"What shall I call you, boy?"

Phoenix struggled, "Argh . . . I-it's Ph-Phoenix." The doctor gave him a startling look. Silence filled the void, making him think he had already done something wrong. "Is everything al-alright?"

"Yes . . . all is well. There was a child by that name I had known, a long time ago. From where do you hail?"

Phoenix opened his eyes, but only a blurry vision of the physician was before him.

"If I were to tell the truth, I would become the clan's fool." The blur became clearer and clearer until he was able to fully see the doctor. He forgot to breathe. "Mrs. Triage? From the third grade class?" He sat motionless, his mind stirring in disbelief. He pictured her escorting some of his classmates to the not-so-safe house, and assumed she had perished with the others. But here she stood, twelve years older with silver hair.

"Phoenix? Phoenix Reinhard? It-it can't be. Is this . . . It's really you? Thank the Protectors; I thought you passed along with the rest of your family." Tears brewed as she firmly embraced her former student. He felt drops slide against his cheek. As she helped him to his feet, she spoke despite her flabbergasted demeanor. "I was *beyond* worried about you, my dear. As the night continued and you were never to arrive . . . I prayed to Zorumaka and Kyrudorous all through the dusk for your safety. My, how you have . . . changed. What have you endured?"

Phoenix rested his head upon the wooden board as he began reliving his past with his old teacher.

Crystal and Eric were led to the infirmary. Inside of the tent, rows of wooden tables lined the fabric that enclosed them. A young nurse with locks of ruby hair bounced as she pranced in minutes after them. Her cheery expression instantly brightened up the windowless shelter.

"Hello Noel, Danny; how do you fare this evening?"

Danny stepped forward. "We fare well, Madame Lee." His eyes sparkled as his face took the shade of her hair. "We discovered these trespassers by the lake. Rex has commanded they be treated as one of our own . . ."

Eric felt his blood pressure rising. "This land is owned by *no one*. It's classified as abandoned with a population of zero."

"Even if that may be," replied Noel, trying to defuse the situation, "please perform a thorough examination, along with any ointments or medications they may need. I would like to prevent the spread of illness." He leaned in closer to her. "Search for wounds that resemble bites." She nodded. "We shall wait by the entrance for the procedure to be finished."

Madame Lee's dimples showed prominently. "Alrighty, follow me!"

An hour passed before the two of them left the nurse's care. Both feeling the stings the needles had left behind and the burning sensations from topical creams, they eagerly scrambled for Noel's offer for nourishment. They traveled to a humongous pavilion across campus that matched the size of the medical tent. Entering the makeshift dining hall, a buffet was prepared along the entire backside of the enclosure. Several lunch tables were stationed before the food. The table closest to them was taken by a bunch of rowdy children carrying on and playing with their leftovers. Their high-pitch squeals and laughter was a sight that was displaced in a refuge such as this.

Noel caught Crystal's stare as the kids wasted what was before them. "They have yet to fully understand the importance of what we provide." Her embarrassment showed upon her face. "Do not fret; the hardships we endured throughout the prior years are foreign to them. Food is abundant to them—a renewable resource. It's a better situation to thrive in."

As Eric and Crystal fell in line for the buffet, Danny claimed a table farthest away from the disruptive children. He retrieved napkins and cutlery. The group joined him, lying their bowls before them. Noel held an extra, passing it to Danny once he was settled.

"Now that Phoenix's condition is no longer fatal, there are some questions I would like to be answered," demanded Eric.

Danny glanced around. "If they're not too private, then I shall indulge you. Let us begin with introductions, since you are strangers in *our* home. We know little about you, or the likes that you travel beside. Start talking."

"The name's Eric, she's Crystal, and my sick friend who almost just died is Phoenix. I'm from Holick. They . . . are adventurers."

"What brings you to Luminar? Holick is far for a visit."

Crystal interrupted, "We are here by accident. As Phoenix would say, in due time you will know all that is necessary."

"I like that," said Eric smirking at Danny. "The turn to speak is mine now, correct? What does this curse cause to its host?"

"The curse does one of two actions. Usually, once it spreads through the body, it dissolves all of a person's vital organs. The poison ends up being just as acidic as your stomach fluids."

"From the pain your friend seemed to be in, the poison had begun the process of liquefying. Into acid," mentioned Noel.

"And the other thing that can happen is . . .?" asked Eric, watching Crystal delicately grasp her fork.

"The curse . . . changes you. You become one of their kind—an X-human. It is far and few in between, but it's not an attractive sight."

Eric quieted down as the aroma of a hot meal swarmed around him. Keeping a stern eye on Danny, he began sampling his entrees. Halfway through the meal, Phoenix and the doctor entered the dining hall.

"Phoenix," chorused Eric and Crystal.

"All is well; the curse has been lifted," the doctor smiled, waving her fingers gesturing to her patient.

Without a word, Noel immediately went to fetch more food, while Phoenix sat beside Crystal. His body drooped, feeling weak and almost numb. Struggling to sit properly, he listened as the doctor continued.

"We shall have a clan meeting shortly after your meals are finished. Noel, Danny, please carry the word to the rest of our people and have them meet at the front entrance." With a stern nod, she strode away.

Noel returned with Phoenix's meal as the rest of the crew filled him in on the missing details of the curse. He felt relief that he was not becoming possessed and happily announced the doctor is his teacher who he thought had perished during the raid. Before Danny could question his excitement, the conversation turned to the hot food before him. They had forgotten what a full stomach felt like.

Their guides led them from the tent toward the direction in which they had arrived. Surprisingly, they entered into a crowd of people much larger than they had expected. The clan members gathered around Mrs. Triage, who stood upon a stand. Noel and Danny spotted Rex and went straight to his side. Scanning the many faces in the crowd, Phoenix was unable to recognize any of them. He prayed there would be a familiar face. Even if that face was his bully Greg or better yet—his mother. No one. Just a range of people between young children and middle aged adults. These children were saved from the experience he was burdened with. The murmuring in the crowd died down as Mrs. Triage began speaking.

"Luminescence Clan, I stand at the ready for your attention." She waited for the crowd to quiet down before speaking again. "I recently discovered inspiring news that shall bring joy to your ears!"

A man from the crowd chimed, "We discovered more Bright Light?"

"N-no, we have yet to locate more of the mineral." A sigh of despair bellowed throughout the citizens as a young lady asked a question:

"But . . . but what if those things come back? How are we to protect ourselves?" The crowd broke into chatter, most fearing for their safety. Mrs. Triage attempted to gather everyone's attention, but it was futile. Rex, taking charge, stepped beside the elderly woman.

With his booming voice, he shattered the side conversations and attracted all eyes to him. Silence settled in as she began speaking again.

Phoenix focused on his teacher, trying to concentrate, but his attention kept drifting down to his new scar. An incredible itch clawed at his skin.

"As I mentioned previously, I have an uplifting announcement. Phoenix, would you join me at my side?" Startled, he followed orders and stood beside Rex who stepped back. "This young man," she pointed at Phoenix, "is the legend. He is the *one*, the brave soul that survived that massacre of our village. This, my family, is Phoenix Reinhard."

The entire crowd came together in a collective gasp. Even the younger one's eyes glittered with astonishment. Phoenix watched strangers pointing at him and saying they remember him, while others merely gave a blank expression—a very unhappy expression. The random whispers were drowned away as another man began yelling, "*Why?* Why is he *here?* That boy shames us!" A few men in the audience agreed enthusiastically.

"Running away from the village . . . He did *nothing* to help against the invasion." Taken by surprise, Phoenix faltered. He had no idea how the people before him would react, but hostility never crossed his mind. Taking a second, he regained his composure and straightened his spine.

"How do I disgrace the memory of our glory?" Phoenix felt a rage burning behind his eyes. "I had been the age of *nine*. What about you? How would you defend your pride? The men and women in this crowd ran from the fighting as friends, families, *my family-* were being slaughtered. In which direction did you escape to? The *safe* houses in these mountains. To. Be. Safe. Not assisting those who had fallen behind. None stood against the invasion besides the ghosts who haunt the remains of their home."

The outspoken man faded back into the sea of people, along with his supporters.

"If you all are quite finished interrupting," bellowed Rex, "the reason for bringing this to your attention is because Phoenix offered his assistance in locating more of the mineral. We have *the* legend on our side. If that doesn't boost morale . . ."

Crystal's brows dropped in confusion while Eric scowled at Phoenix from afar.

"We shall be sending three patrol parties to locate the source of the Bright Light; I'll list off the teams." While Mrs. Triage cleared her throat to announce the groups, Phoenix felt a thumping pain throughout his arm. He clutched it, *Damned vaccination. She didn't mention after effects.*

Eric stormed toward Phoenix. "You *promised* me we would find Brett and Alexander! My family is in danger and their wellbeing is *very* time sensitive."

"Yeah," agreed Crystal. "There are other things that need our attention, like finding the remaining emeralds?"

Phoenix's arm began throbbing, pulsing aggressively around his wrist. Before he could respond, Eric continued with his rant.

"Who cares about this damned village? They are nothing to us. The refugees were not in the slightest bit happy to hear about your survival. And I hate Danny. A lot."

He could barely concentrate on the words flowing from Eric's mouth; his hearing was being clouded by a consistent buzz. "I-I understand . . . I truly do . . . but Eric, *this* is my family—what's left. It's my duty to assist in any way I-I ca-can." Crystal's temper was quelled, but Eric's rage still rose. Unable to handle the pain any longer, Phoenix released a loud grunt that turned into a cry of agony. Everyone's attention turned to his outburst as he tumbled to the ground. Mrs. Triage bee-lined to his aid until another person screamed. A scream that froze time.

Confused, the villagers searched frantically for the cause of the terror. Then at once, the entire clan saw a sight that could scare the bravest of warriors. A field of darkness was descending down the mountainsides, flowing into the camp from the direction of the old city. It wasn't until it got closer that they could identify what was coming for them. Crawling down the sides, marching up the path, and flying from above, an entire invasion of X-creatures surged forward. Panic erupted throughout the clan. Rex regained control of himself and began commanding orders, but even his boom box of a voice was blocked by the commotion.

"Wha-what do we do?" yelled Crystal, eyes glued to the horde approaching. The cries of the monsters were becoming clearer and more distinct.

Eric stared at the evil before them. "We fight. We defend these people." He grabbed Phoenix's arm tugging him to his soles. "Come on, get up, if I'm risking my life for your distant relatives then you are as well. Focus on your swings and the pain will vanish." Phoenix slowly started rising as Noel and Danny approached them, arms full.

"Here!" Noel threw a variety of weapons on the ground. "We have only but a small number of soldiers; we need all the assistance you can provide." With that, the two of them rejoined Rex, Mrs. Triage, and a handful of other clan members. Once they entered the circle, Mrs. Triage stared at each of her warriors.

"We fight for our survival and our future. We fight in the name of Luminar!" They all cried in unison. "Protectors, guide thy army to victory."

Eric swept up the spear at his feet. "Crystal, grab the bow. Stay far away." He charged forward.

She did as she was told and scampered toward high ground. As her feet slapped against the dirt she tried to steady her left hand over her right fist, placing it against her forehead. Shouting aloud, she prayed to the Protectors. Reciting the strength charm, she whispered, "Protectors, guide thy army to victory. Bless thy weapons with holiness; shield thy army with His bravery and courage and with Her steadiness and perseverance. If I, or any of us, shall fall in the names of the All-mighty, guide us to the roots of Teague to fertilize the future of morrow."

As Eric reached the fighting grounds, the bloodshed had already begun. Rex and Noel were holding back X-fowlers and Mrs. Triage was handling a pack of X-hounds. Eric spun around Mrs. Triage and pierced the spine of an X-hound. On contact, the dog started dissolving and sizzling away. He studied his spear, noticing a sparkling substance on the tip of the blade. *Bright Light*, he assumed. His research ended abruptly as an X-feline pounced, its paws digging into his shoulders. He was immobilized by fear until an arrow pierced the side of the predator. He glanced up to find Crystal, bow in hand and arrow being drawn.

The demons came in all different forms. The X-fowlers flew high above the ground, some larger than grown men. Their wings varied between two and four, but each one as sharp as a knife. And as deadly. Their beaks were elongated; a few curved at the tip—some up, some down. A large portion of them had two beaks, one positioned right on top of the first. The most frightening variation was the ones with arms connected to the wings. Eric watched as one X-fowler swept up a villager, crushing his skull in midair.

The X-felines were just as terrifying. They had elongated bodies, some reaching six feet long. The fur coats were matted, but small patches of hair stood on end, like a cactus ready to puncture the closest material. The curvature of their body and their gait indicated they had no vertebrae. Flexible, bendable, agile, they could be seen scattered amongst the mob alone and separated from their like-species.

Climbing back to his feet, Eric spun his spear like a windmill, slashing at creatures on both sides of him. An X-fowler swooped down, leaving a claw mark across Eric's back. He watched it fly ahead and swerve around for more, but another arrow clipped one of its wings. The scratch on his back left a stinging sensation. Barely defending himself, he tried to shrug off his injuries. As he sliced through an X-hound's second head, he saw Mrs. Triage coming to his aide, only to be quickly overwhelmed by another pack. Doing a one-eighty with his spear, he caught sight of Crystal who was struggling to pull the string. When she did succeed, only every third shot hit its mark.

Crystal focused primarily on the flying pests. Drawing back the string of the bow took more strength than she realized. Keeping the arrow steady was another struggle. She let about a dozen arrows soar through the air, only a few impaling the targets. Each direct hit would drop the bird from the sky, dissolving its very being as it plunged downward. But with each success, more would replace the fallen. She turned her view back to the others, only to find them in a worse predicament.

Reaching for another arrow, she spotted an X-hound trying to flank Mrs. Triage. The creature was big and burly, barely fitting within its own fur. Its torso was much broader than the fellow monsters, making it much swifter. The tail was whip-like, cracking the air with every twitch. Her hand searched for the next projectile, but when nothing came to her fingers, she desperately turned to find her armory empty. Her mind broke into a panic. Her heart beat pounded in her ears until another two dozen arrows landed beside her.

Phoenix bounced passed Crystal straight for the battlefield. Wielding a rusty yet sparkling broadsword, he jumped in the middle of the fray. In a matter of seconds, he had wiped the surrounding area clean, while defending both Eric and Mrs. Triage. The swing of his sword became continuous and fluid, almost as second nature. He began losing himself in the tediousness of the action.

Fighting alongside him, Eric caught a glimpse of Phoenix's face a few times in between swings. It appeared different. Demonic. The feeling left him startled and afraid.

The mountainside still had a flood of X-creatures swarming into battle. Crystal continued to watch the chaos from afar, but the endless renewal of reinforcements left her team exhausted. The front line was being pushed back. It wasn't until they had fallen to her position did she finally realize the fatal truth of her situation. With her fingers shivering even more, she closed an eye to aim. With a breath, she released her final arrow.

The assault raged longer than the Luminescence Clan was prepared for, until the creatures suddenly retreated. The ecstasy of relief had to be ignored for the moment. Most of the tents on the front line had been destroyed. The mountainside and its base were covered in scorch marks and littered with cracked arrows and fallen clan members. Blood painted the ground around abandoned weapons. All the surviving members regrouped with their heroes in the dining pavilion, ready to lend a hand. Madame Lee hastily treated all the battle wounds. Even Mrs. Triage, despite her own condition, aided her nurse in the recovery of their soldiers.

Danny entered the tent sometime later with an unholy aura. He climbed upon a table, and without announcing himself, he began shouting over the conversations within the tent. Hearing his voice, the talking diminished instantly.

"We have lost . . . many important people in our clan today— to such an unusual, bizarre attack. Husbands, wives, sisters, brothers, friends—all perished in today's battle. This includes one of our beloved clan leaders, R-Rex," Danny choked on the last word. He swallowed hard, holding back his emotions. "A-as his last wish, I'll be stepping into his position as one of the clan leaders. Any objections, speak freely." Not a soul spoke nor did a child cry. *He must hold much respect, just like the Prince,* pondered Phoenix.

"I am hereby announcing myself as one of the clan's leaders along the side of Doctor Triage and Reverend Panelio. As we know The Reverend is away, he will be receiving the heartbreaking news from a messenger." A slight applaud was awarded for this accomplishment.

"With that matter solved, I would like to congratulate *everyone* on their courageous spirits on the battlefield today. I commend all of your bravery. Without your perseverance, our clan would be lost to time. We should be celebrating a victory!" A stronger applause came forth, but still lacked in enthusiasm. Danny stayed silent until it halted. "Henceforth, today will be known as the Battle of the Tails, and all who were lost will be mourned. Rebuilding what has been lost will be my primary concern, but there are other matters that must be discussed. I understand the importance in performing rituals for our fallen, but due to the battle . . . Our reserves of Bright Light has run completely dry. Only several weapons remaining in the arsenal are still coated. I call upon five volunteers to go on a full expedition in search of the mineral."

"Wha-what happens to us if they come back? We will have nothing to defend ourselves!" exclaimed a clan member.

"That matter is out of my hands. Despite being mindless, I have no fear that they will attempt another onslaught this evening. Nevertheless, I refuse to send a scouting group unarmed into the creatures' territory while they are agitated. Who is up to the task of finding a new source that will secure our village safety?" Danny peered over the crowd until a hand rose.

"I am honored, Phoenix. Your participation in the Battle of the Tails will never be forgotten. Who else?" Crystal and Eric glared at one another and with a sigh, raised their own hands. Noel's hand went up, followed by a younger boy in the back. "It has been decided. Any objections? Good. Phoenix, Crystal, Eric, Noel, and Ace, meet me in the armory tent. The rest of the clan, once your injuries have been treated, please report to the ritual grounds." With those final words, Danny stepped off the table, exiting the room.

When he was gone, everyone finished their business and went to their assigned areas. The five volunteers walked to the armory tent where Danny was waiting patiently. He stood beside a table with an array of weapons. Immediately, Ace tried to snatch one, but Noel kept him in his place. Phoenix examined the youth. *He must barely be sixteen . . . If it weren't such dire circumstances, I wouldn't allow him to join us. Such young innocence should be spared.*

"From what we have gathered, we have an idea where more Bright Light may be found. When Rex, Noel, and I were searching, we saw a stream that connected Luminary Lake to Luminar's castle.

We believe more of the mineral resides in an underground lake or water supply. The five of you must travel to the castle and search for the stream. This mission must be without fail. Either return with the Bright Light or do not at all." The volunteers nodded in agreement. "There is a weapon for each one of you laid upon the table behind me. Please select one," Danny declared, moving aside.

Ace gripped a pike, Eric seized the double-edged spear, and Noel took ahold of the bow and arrows. Phoenix received the sword, and Crystal was left with two circular rings. Made of a polished wood, its entire outer layer was covered in steel. On the inside, a curving wooden piece was chiseled into the center connecting one side to the other. Bright Light was sprinkled along the blade of each weapon. Danny disappeared into the tent, returning with a brown vest along with black steel-toed boots. They were handed to Eric.

"As much as I am sure you enjoy your body being seen by all, it would be a positive thing to put up a better defense against these demons. Make them work harder to reach skin, unless that jagged scratch on your back is appealing."

"And you just reminded me why I do not like your company." Eric threw his new gear on. He lost his balance under the weight of his equipment.

Danny turned to Crystal who was dumbfounded. Her puzzled face made it clear she had never come across her weapon before. "Those are a special type of weapon. The legend says these are as old as time itself. They have been called many things such as Chakrams or bladed wheels, but Kyrudorous referred to them as moon blades. These wheels were forged by magic long before the Protectors' lives, but Kyrudorous chose these as her weapon of choice. They are a rarity; only a few exist."

"With such a rich past and value, are they safe in my care? What if they were to be damaged or worse? The responsibility is too much."

"The weapon chooses the one who wields them. Probably a spell the creators casted upon the steel, giving them a mind of their own, but nevertheless none have been chosen from this clan. Therefore they remain here, unused and gathering dust." Danny faced the group. "Do what is necessary to retrieve Bright Light. Our camp will be in your debt, Phoenix."

"I refuse to fail."

"Take these tubes to collect the samples. Make sure to rest up before you begin the travel, today's war has made us all suffer. Depart at dawn. Stay vigilant; little is known about these creatures beyond their physical features. Who knows where they reside or what makes them act. Prepare yourself for whatever may come." With that, Danny saluted the group and marched away. Ace anxiously shifted his feet while Phoenix hooked the sword to his belt.

"As the suns begin upon their courses in the morning, we shall as well. Let us meet here and we will move forward from there," announced Noel, his voice wavering as he spoke to his team. "Ace, run along and do not add this night to your list of sleepless ones. As for the three of you, I'll show you to your quarters for the evening."

CHAPTER 9

The morning light flowed over the mourning campsite. Phoenix swept his legs from underneath his covers, his body embracing the briskness in the air. Covering his bare back with his vest, he stared at his reflection in a mirror. He glazed over himself, a person forged from hate and pain. His eyes flicked between the scar on his arm and the new one on his opposite wrist. The two small, jagged lines that now marked his skin had become more of a nuisance than his last one. Whatever Mrs. Triage inserted into him had the marks constantly throbbing. Breaking his stare, he picked up his weapon and exited his tent.

Crystal bellowed a yawn as she reached her hands into the air. Rubbing her eyes, she felt the warmth of the fresh sunlight slipping through her wooden cabin. Stepping free of her sheets, she turned to fix her bed. Properly placing her pillow, she slid off the gown she had borrowed and began changing into her outfit. As the blouse crossed her nose, she relived the battle from the day prior. She watched herself unable to save her friends in the heat of the moment. They were swarmed and surrounded, while she just helplessly let arrows slip through her grasp.

Collecting her hair, she tightened it into a ponytail. Using string, she tied a little bow at the top of her hair. *I would have been more useful to Phoenix if I were to have just stayed with the rest of the clan.* She picked up her Chakrams, gently holding each one by the connector in the middle. She twirled them around. *No. This is where I belong. I may have been drawn into this situation, but now . . . I have someone to protect. Phoenix, and Eric and his family. My grandmother thought I was good for nothing and weak, but I am stronger now than I have ever been. And there are others who count on me . . . and care for me.*

A gentle knock rapped against the door followed by a muffled voice, "Oh sunshine, dear, it's time to wake."

She opened the door to find Eric's forced grin. "I'm all set!"

"Glad to hear, you are the last to arrive."

She looked beyond his shoulders to find the rest of the volunteers standing behind him, weapons in hand. Phoenix smiled, "Good morning, hope you rested well." She returned the gesture.

Phoenix turned to Noel as the other two entered their circle, "Are you ready to lead?"

"I-I ah, yes. I shall do my best. Should we move out then?" Ace ran ahead to the road that led into the remains of the old city. The rest followed him at their own pace.

As they headed down the trail, they all fell in line. Noel was in front with Ace at his side, while Phoenix, Crystal, and Eric strayed behind. Phoenix stayed quiet, the other two noticing his unusual behavior.

"I still don't understand. Why did you volunteer to help them, again? You are supposed to be helping my family! And to collect those emeralds."

"Eric, please, let it go."

Phoenix kept walking in silence, gathering his thoughts. "These . . . these are my people, the last of my family. The danger they are in is dire. Hiding in fear, suffering from poverty; you were a witness to yesterday's slaughter. I have been alone, dreading my mistakes for years. But now, I'm not all alone. This is a way of correcting my wrong doings." To his surprise, his hand fell into the grasp of a more delicate touch.

"Phoenix, you have us now. We can be your family. We're never to leave your side."

"Well, not until we rescue my *real* family that is . . ."

Crystal punched Eric's side. He faltered a bit, but regained his poise as she and Phoenix locked eyes. When they met, she saw his lower lid brimming.

The stare was broken and he released her hand. He tilted his head to the side and quickened his pace to catch up to Noel. *This is not the time or the place; I cannot let these feelings distract me.*

Crystal watched the back of his head. She looked down. *Is what I said wrong? Am I being too insensitive?* She felt an arm cross her shoulders.

"Don't look glum, dear, I think you are finally connecting with him."

She glanced at Eric. "How can you be sure? Each time we speak, I feel as if we grow further apart."

"Trust me, since I met the two of you, I could see the bond as if it were tangible. It's rather sickening. When we were locked away at the House of Judgment and you were unconscious in the infirmary, saving you was his utmost concern. I believe you breached his faux cold exterior."

A smile grew. "If the feelings we share are one of the same, why not just be honest? I'm being kept at a distance."

"That's the point. Remember his trip down memory lane? His teachings included him being alone; I was taught the same. It's basics 101. Try to sympathize with what he has been through."

"I suppose you are correct."

"Of course I am! When am I ever not? Besides, if the hero fell in love the moment he met his fair maiden, he would not be able to keep a cool composure. Relationships are not my strongest quality, but thanks to Brett, I have learned a bit . . ."

Crystal wrapped her arm around his waist. "We *will* get them back soon. Phoenix will have a plan." Eric nodded, receiving her hug in gratitude.

The five of them reached the perimeter of the lake. Phoenix examined its sad condition. He thought back to the way the suns laid across the still water, while his sister and he would relax beside the edge. *Those were better times.* Noel located the stream that Danny had mentioned. The runoff water was just as tainted as its home.

Ace traced the stream, running beside it at full speed. The others were left in his dust, no one feeling the need to match his energy.

"Ace! Stay with us!" Noel yelled after him, but he was too far gone.

"Has this stream always existed?" asked Crystal.

"I was never aware . . . I cannot believe another lake resides beneath the castle."

"I don't quite remember it as a child either," pondered Noel. "But we must join Ace before he hurts himself. If he were to be ambushed, no matter his motivation, he would not survive unscathed."

As they hustled along, Noel came to Phoenix's side with a disgruntled expression.

"I'm doing my best to remember you, but I cannot seem to place you in my memories. Your age must match my own. Our paths must have crossed on several occasions."

"I don't recall your enrollment in my classes. Maybe you knew my sister, Bethany?"

As soon as the name left his lips, Noel's face became a blush pink and grew a wide smile. "Bethany's beauty matched Kyrudorous herself! We had spent much time together in class. My feelings of affection for her were—" He peered at Phoenix, whose brows burrowed. "Now I understand your familiarity . . ."

The awkward tension between the two didn't last. Soon after, they were reminiscing about the past. The two boys spent time admiring the Prince, talking about the night that changed their lives, and Noel brought up Bethany with every opportunity. Phoenix even threw in some derogatory comments toward Greg, but would add, "Protectors guide him." Crystal and Eric stayed behind, watching them relive what was left of their childhood.

The team followed the stream around the entire city. Phoenix recognized the ruined streets he was raised on. He occasionally made a comment to Noel about how he played by this building or how often John would visit this residency. After an almost complete circle around Ancient Luminar, Ace came into view. The stream led right into the walls of the castle.

Phoenix stared at the eroded walls and broken dreams. A structure with extreme amount of power and potential now lived on in memories. In one night, all that culture was blown to the heavens, alongside the smoke from the flames. The King and Prince Joshua lived here once. Happily. Alive.

"Have you ever entered the castle, Phoenix?" inquired Eric chuckling. "Being the home of a king, I would hope it has seen a better time than it does now."

Phoenix ignored the comment. "The castle is relatively intact from its glory days. How are we supposed to enter? Walk through the main entrance?"

Noel glanced around. "The exterior may not reflect the appearance of its interior. Time is of the essence and adventuring through crumbled stairwells and blocked hallways is not sensitive to our situation. These walls must have a weak point. They have been remaining tall for twelve years with no maintenance; their strength had to diminish. Feel for an unstable anomaly." The team began placing their hands onto the cement, feeling for weakness. Ace ran around the corner without a word. Before Noel could react, he returned.

"A section of a wall has already crumbled! Let's finish this job quickly and become heroes!" He showed them around to the broken defense revealing a pile of rubble blocking a hole. They began heaving debris to the side, removing it to gain access. Clearing part of the entrance, they piled themselves through one by one.

Their manmade entrance led them straight down into the catacombs. The temperature decreased significantly, causing Crystal to shiver violently. The smell of dirt overwhelmed them. They found it difficult to survey their surroundings with the only light source coming from behind. Venturing onward, they traveled deeper underground. Dropping down a few ledges, they found their way into an enclosed cave. In the center of tiny cliffs and hills was another lake. Its shining brilliance lit up the entire area with a green radiance. Astonished, none of them were able to speak. *This is where Luminary Lake came from. Incredible,* thought Phoenix. *It's just as beautiful as its offspring, but something is off . . .*

"Look at all the Bright Light in the lake! It's like a million lightning bugs huddled together!" exclaimed Ace.

Crystal stood by Phoenix still shaking uncontrollably. *Such a sight to see!* She thought to herself as she studied the lake, looking at the luminesce water. Though it was a beautiful sight, she felt an eeriness she could not explain. It seemed as peaceful as the one from before.

"I feel uneasy. The lake lacks a calming sensation."

Eric spoke to Luminar's residents: "Why does it have a green tint?"

"There is no answer here," remarked Noel. "The other lake never gave such an impression."

Ace jetted toward the water, "I'll explore!"

"No wait! Stop!" yelled Noel chasing him.

Phoenix was statue still, examining their discovery. Why does it have that tone? Noel is correct; there was nothing like that in the original lake. Where did this malevolence originate? As he watched the two running, his arm began pulsing significantly harder than all morning. Clutching his wrist, he let out an injured wail. All eyes turned to him, but as he picked up his head, the sight before him forced the pain from his mind. In the center of the reservoir, a giant, black vine began rising from the depths. Its fingers spread wide as it stretched toward the cavern ceiling. The main branch made a loop, almost like it could hold something, cradle it.

"The emerald was held down here! It resided all those centuries on that vine!" He pointed toward the plant, his friends' eyes following his finger.

Almost on cue, black balls began spewing from the plant. Some of the orbs plunged into the water, while others remained clung to their host. Each one started morphing. Some of the basic shapes looked like different types of animals. Noel and Ace were too late when they realized what was occurring before them. Filled with fear and horror, they turned to escape. But the X-creatures were too fast, surrounding them in an instant. X-hounds, X-felines, and X-fowlers went in for the kill. Noel lashed out his bow and rapidly shot arrows at the demons, while Ace spun his pike like a fan.

"No! Phoenix, we need to save them!" yelped Crystal, making her way to the scene.

Eric was already in route and zoomed right past her. With the tip of his spear facing forward he impaled several of the creatures like a kabob.

Phoenix whipped his sword from its sheath and slashed through a dozen X-creatures with a single swing. Hacking and slashing, his onslaught didn't halt until he reached Noel's side. As they regrouped, an X-feline pounced on Phoenix's back. Its claws dug deep into his skin as he flat-lined forward smashing his chest into the dirt. He struggled to knock it off, but it remained tightly attached.

Eric slid one side of his double-edged spear through the feline's jaw, evaporating it on contact. He heaved Phoenix to his feet by his underarms as three X-fowlers came swooping down. Hesitating, he watched as all three dropped from the air.

"Three birds with one arrow," cheered Noel. "I'll clear the air of these winged bastards. Cover me and take care of the rest!"

Crystal stayed back, intimidated by the commotion she was witnessing. Her anxiety skyrocketed. She grasped her moon blades tighter, trying to calm herself down, but it was too late. The X-hounds smelled her scent and were scampering straight for her. Their claws struck down hard as she tried blocking with her rings. She covered her face and chest, listening to their dreaded howls and demented barks. *I can't let them down; I must stay strong. Focus. Phoenix can trust me.* The mutts moved to her backside, getting ready to flank her. A gang of seven crowded around, making her suddenly claustrophobic. Tears forming, she grasped her wooden weapons and struck. She deflected their pounces and tried to ward off their claws.

She fell to her side as one X-hound dove for her. Just missing the collision, she rose back up with a flick of her wrist and sliced through its stomach. It quickly boiled down and dispersed. Watching her first victim dissolve, a surge of new-found courage blossomed in her chest. She turned to face the next enemy coming toward her and hacked away. With the twirl of a ballerina, Crystal spun in a circle and repeatedly waved her rings around. She felt like she was at a recital rather than a battle.

Ace made his way out of the pit and continued moving toward the lake. He was bombarded with creature after creature, barely fending them away. His jab and roll technique kept him alive. His determination stayed strong until an X-fowler slammed itself against him, clutching at his pike. It attempted to fly away with its prize, but Ace held his grip. He struggled with the bird back and forth until an X-hound flew through the air into the tug of war. It forced the bird away, but the hound's weight shattered the spear in half. With all his might, Ace threw the creature off him. He was overcome by despair when he saw his broken pike laid out across the ground. He grabbed the steel end, preparing to move forward, until he watched the sea of darkness multiply around him. He took a deep breath.

Phoenix and Eric destroyed each creature as they came toward them, while Noel blasted wooden bullets into the dank air. Eric's full attention was on twisting the spear back and forth, fighting off the offense. Demons crept behind him, silent as a dog whistle. A creature tested its luck, clawing his back, barely making a scratch. Feeling a push on his vest, Eric slammed the spear over his head. With accuracy, the tip traveled through the demon and penetrated the ground. Eric then did a backflip aside his implanted spear. Landing, he stomped on a demon's head, ripped his spear free, and swept the steel around him, killing a dozen easily. He released a sigh of relief as he patted his vest: *Thank the Protectors for Danny giving me this lifesaver.*

Phoenix uncontrollably slashed back and forth. Even in the midst of battle, his concentration was focused primarily on Crystal. He wanted to make sure she remained unharmed. Blood dripped from a few cuts from a pouncing cat and a dog's claw. He watched Eric do a backflip, and wipe out most of the enemies in the area. As Phoenix forced his sword down on a creature, an ear-crackling scream filled the cavern. The warriors halted in their tracks, searching for the source of the cry. As if a spotlight beamed down, they all found Ace being mauled by an X-hound. Noel swiftly shot the hound clean off him, but Ace remained motionless. No directions needed to be verbalized to know what had to be done next.

The four fought their way to Ace's location, regrouping around his mangled body. Blood pumped from his throat. His face was mangled, almost unrecognizable. The males continued to protect Ace while Crystal ripped the sleeves from her blouse, tying them around his wound and applying pressure. With a free hand, she checked his vitals.

"His heart beat is slow and his pulse is almost non-existent, but he's alive!" Phoenix hurriedly finished the last X-feline and came to her aid.

"In his condition, he will not be for long. The creatures have retreated, but it'll be only a matter of minutes before they spawn and strike again."

Noel examined Ace. "He is infected, too. We need to take him to camp immediately! If he isn't treated soon . . . Phoenix, Crystal, collect some Bright Light. Eric, help me lift him!"

Phoenix and Crystal started treading water, test tubes ready. Phoenix looked up at the vine as they got closer. A strong radiation of dark energy was pulsing from it. *Just like the emerald,* he thought. *Wait, if the emerald's gone, shouldn't the darkness be lifted with it?*

"Crystal, remain here. I want to examine the weed closer."

As she watched him swim toward the sad excuse for nature,

she began to notice something growing. A clump of dark matter was increasing in size. *Another X-demon?* The mass shook and shifted, growing alarmingly larger.

Within seconds, the figure was fully formed, hunching over to avoid hitting its head on the ceiling. Standing on two feet, it had four arms and a long spiked tail. The creature surveyed the battlefield, roaring a petrifying cry that shook the entire cavern. Phoenix and Crystal stared upon the monster, astonished and terrified.

The others could only watch as the monstrosity grew, reaching the top of the cavern. It easily reached heights higher than most castles. The scene captivated them, keeping them from noticing the movements on Eric's back. Ace's skin started squirming. His pale tone swirled into a pitch black. His pupils dilated, iris's glowing red. His body started shifting and he wriggled free of Eric's arms. Ace bounced away, landing in a squat. Before they had time to react, he tackled Eric, forcing him to face plant. Noel spun around in time to evade Ace's fist.

"What's happening? He should be dead, not an acrobat!"

"The curse . . . did the rare . . . It changed him. He's an X-human. He's one of them now." Noel's emotions went haywire; his guilt manifested into physical sickness as he looked upon the young lost youth. His stomach knotted.

"The cure is to rid his body of the taint."

Eric watched as Ace prepared to attack. "We can't kill him, he's a boy! Is there no other way?"

Noel reached for an arrow and took aim. "There's only, but one cure . . . Bright Light." Noel released his projectile and the shot flew past Eric at top speed.

Ace casually moved aside of the arrow, missing by a hair. He flew toward his victims, in a strange contorted dash. His back was arched and to the side, while his arms hung by his sides. With all his strength, he choke slammed both of them to the ground. Noel's arrows scattered among the dirt. Ace lifted Noel and Eric off the ground with his devilish claws still locked onto their throats. They grasped at Ace's wrists, but it was no use; the grip was too tight.

The giant monster swung his tail, bashing into Phoenix's side, bouncing him across the water like a pebble. Crystal had enough time to duck before it swept her clean out of the water. She dove underwater and swam toward the beast. When she reached the monster's feet, Crystal retrieved her circular rings and cut a long, deep gash across a leg. She could feel its scream rippling through the water. The monster forcefully kicked her straight into the open air. She gasped for breath as she was propelled into the shoreline. The creature roared once more as it started to tread toward land.

Phoenix aggressively swam in front of it, blocking the path. The monster shot down one of its arms and plucked Phoenix from the water. His arms were crushed against his sides as its single claw practically wrapped around his entire structure. He squirmed to get loose, until he realized the monster was bringing him closer and closer to his mouth.

Crystal, horrified, sprung back into action. She looked down at her weapons and thought fast. *I hope this works.* Closing her eyes, she did a swirl and on the third spin, she released her grip on her rings. They gyrated at the enemy and chiseled at two of the monster's hands. It continued on its path until it sliced through both appendages. The rings zoomed past and smoothly glided back to Crystal. She frantically went to snatch them before they missed her, but they seemed to find *her* hands.

As it howled from the pain, the palm that held Phoenix plummeted into the water as he struggled to escape the dead grip. He finally slipped free when the claw was engulfed. The splash washed him ashore, next to Crystal. Getting up, Phoenix lost balance and toppled over his feet. Crystal went to help him, but was stunned by the sight before her. The beast's spiked tail had dropped from above onto Phoenix, plowing him into the coast.

Eric attempted to squeeze off Ace's grip, but it was futile. He started losing consciousness, the grip suffocating him. He glanced at Noel, seeing him struggle to breathe as well and his skin color turning blue. *This can't be it; Brett still needs me.* Releasing Ace's wrist, Eric urgently searched for his spear. The touch of metal never felt this good. He whipped it free from his holster, implanting it in the center of Ace's chest.

Ace violently tossed the two of them away, sliding back from the impact. He fell to one knee holding the wound. Noel recovered, searching for his arrows, while Eric swiftly breathed in a few breaths. Ace removed his hand, revealing steam floating from the stab. Eric's focus jumped from Noel to Ace, and he decided to take the opportunity. Before he had a chance to move, his idea was welcomed with a fist to the face. Eric removed his hand from his muzzle to find Ace coming back, thrusting fist after fist.

Eric smoothly dodged the wild swings. Ace tried to sweep him off his feet, but Eric hopped and slammed the edge of the spear against his shoulder. More steam rose as Ace grunted in pain. Eric went after him, swiping his double-edged spear up and down his abdomen. He quickly spun, cutting one final laceration straight across Ace's pectorals. The collision knocked him onto his back. Eric cautiously walked up to him as he squirmed like a fish removed from water. Staring at his red eyes, all he could see was the bright pupils of a boy. He swallowed hard, biting his lip.

Lifting his spear, the job was finished as he pierced his heart. Ace cried as his body began to disintegrate. *Those cries . . . sound just like a child's*, Eric thought to himself. The black coat from the boy began to sizzle away, revealing his body again. But much to Eric's dismay, Ace's human form began dissolving, skin melting from the muscle as it dripped off his skeleton. In seconds, nothing remained. Ace was gone. He watched as the last puff of steam faded away. Noel gathered the last of his arrows as he heard Crystal scream.

Crystal watched as the monster trudged closer. His tail slid back into the water revealing Phoenix's body. He lay there, limp and lifeless. Her heart skipped a beat while her eyes widened. The beast grew closer every second, but Crystal was too scared to react. It shot down one of its hands and gripped her up. Eric rushed to save her,

EMERALD X

but was accidently thrown aside by the monster's tail. Crystal screamed as the grip grew tighter.

Noel watched as he climbed on top of a high cliff. He scanned his arrows. *Damn, they're all broken except . . .* He equipped his last arrow and put it in position. He carefully aimed his shot, yelling, "This better work!" He let the arrow loose. It whizzed through the air, soaring right by the monster and making direct contact with the vine. The arrow burrowed into the vine, burning a hole through it. As the projectile fell into the water, the vine remained standing.

Despair crossed his face as he watched Crystal be crushed in its claw. Noel started nervously backing away until a loud, sizzling noise emerged from the lake. Light burst through the plant's surface, sending beams in every direction. Then, within seconds, a flash of brightness followed by a rumbling boom erupted. Noel went blind as a mystical force knocked him from his feet. He landed on his back, slamming his head against the rock.

Crystal opened her eyes, first allowing them to adjust to the settling darkness. Her body felt lifeless, wading back and forth. She picked her head up, checking her surroundings. She was floating in the middle of the lake. The demon had vanished. No trace of it insight. Even the vine had disappeared. As she began swimming toward shore, she noticed a pure glow emanating around her. *The green coating has been lifted. The lake . . . has been cleansed.*

As she stepped onto dry land, Eric had just picked himself off the ground. He brushed dirt from his vest as Crystal wrapped her arms around him from behind. His apprehension turned to endearment as he held her back. "How do you fare? Are you hurt? That monster swatted me away before I could come to your aid."

"I'm alive, but have you seen Phoenix? That *thing* crushed him!" She raced forward, finding Phoenix in a newly formed crater.

Eric checked his vital signs and tenderly felt for broken or displaced bones.

"His breathing is shallow, but still present. He also has a faint pulse, which is wonderful news." Half of Eric's face rose. "A few of his ribs seem to be broken, and he's going to have a fit when he sees his outfit. I've never witnessed cloth turn white to completely muddy."

Crystal watched as Noel came jogging to them, holding the back of his head. As he joined them, she asked, "Noel, what happened? How did you save us?"

"This should be discussed at camp with the leaders. Phoenix requires medical attention stat. Eric, we have to create a makeshift gurney to safely carry him home. A single mistake and he could lose the use of his legs permanently." As the men gathered supplies, Crystal went in search of her weapons and to gather the mineral they were sent to retrieve.

Danny and Mrs. Triage were sharpening weapons when they heard a commotion gathering outside their tent. They joined the crowd welcoming their brave volunteers entering the campsite. All the hurrahs turned to horrified gasps as their eyes lay upon Phoenix. Mrs. Triage immediately called for Madame Lee and rushed them into the medical pavilion. The ladies carefully transferred Phoenix from the makeshift carrier to the bed. The others were taken to the same infirmary tent from before.

The three of them paced back and forth waiting for news on Phoenix's condition. Hours passed without new information. Crystal sat in tears, worrying herself to death. Eric stayed beside her, trying to provide as much hope as he could manage. Noel was leaning by the entrance, watching the first sun slowly hide behind the mountains. The men tried to hide their feelings, but they were ready to match Crystal's tears. The worst scenarios played in their minds repetitively. Several more hours passed until Mrs. Triage and Madame Lee came to them. Crystal stared hard with worried eyes as the doctor began speaking.

"Any longer for his arrival and this conversation would have quite a different tone. The three of you accomplished a magnificent task, transferring him here without any contradictions. Three of his ribs are indeed broken. There is a gash on his leg that may be infected, and he most likely will be suffering from a slight concussion."

Madame Lee added, "We also assume that his femur has a hairline fracture and he will retain head trauma. His neck will be very sore for the upcoming weeks."

"We bandaged him to the best of our abilities, but we are not well equipped. He should rest for a while; his body requires time to recover. We gave him medical herbs that will allow him to sleep and not suffer from his concussion."

"I'm happy to hear he will survive, but we must be on our way. Too much time has been spent in this place while lives depend on us."

"Eric! Phoenix almost died! If he does not heal properly, we won't have a chance at saving anyone."

"But he's *not* dead. That's the news we were anticipating."

Danny stormed into their conversation, "By the Protectors' names, the hell happened to your team?"

"As clear as day, a few complications crossed our paths," spit Eric gesturing to the medical staff.

"*Two* nights have gone without a word." Shock set upon the group. "The conclusion was either desertion or death . . . I prayed for the latter."

"Tw-two days?" Crystal repeated him, hoping she misheard him.

Danny's eyes traveled between each face realizing their astonishment.

"Follow me to the multipurpose tent. I want a detailed explanation of what has occurred since your departure." He paused. "Where is Ace?"

"I . . . will tell you all that has happened," replied Noel.

"Tending to Phoenix requires my attention. I shall stay back for his health," announced Mrs. Triage retreating to her tent, Madame Lee following behind.

Sitting at a table with a dozen papers scattered across the surface, Noel finished explaining the past 48 hours.

"That sweet child . . . He was an impatient one. He deserved to greet the Protectors in a more graceful manner. I'll prepare another ceremony honoring his sacrifice. What am I to tell his mother and father?" He sighed. "And there is no recollection of the missing time?"

"The explosion must have knocked us unconscious," responded Noel.

"And what of the Bright Light?"

"I was able to fill a few vials," Crystal remarked, displaying them to Danny.

"We know very little of this . . . abomination we faced. If I were to create an explanation, I'd say the threat is no more. The dark essence the emerald holds was absorbed by the surrounding area—this being the vine. The year of creation of the emeralds and when they were officially hidden is undocumented. Therefore, residing upon that vine for an undetermined amount of years, an extraordinary amount of its energy had seeped into its resting place. Once the emerald was removed, there was no longer a force that kept the darkness in control, thus releasing demons," explained Noel.

"The vine has thrived in a pool of its own self-annihilation. Shouldn't it have already disintegrated?" asked Eric.

"Maybe it depends on the purity of the form. The mineral is extracted from the water and sprinkled directly onto the metal of our weapons."

"Remember the eerily green glow it held? It is possible the power that was collected either diluted or negated the effects of the mineral."

"Phoenix and I saved the emerald from Emerica . . . which will result in these demons roaming the city streets?" asked Crystal.

"If my theory stands correct, then that would be what is happening. When my arrow penetrated the source, the darkness was eradicated. The explosion could have erased the X-creatures in the area or possibly, since there was no longer a link to their power source, they may have dissolved on their own."

"Luminar can now rebuild and reach its former glory!" exclaimed Danny.

"If the X-creatures are infesting Emerica, would they spread to other cities or towns? Like Lanster?"

Noel thought for a minute. "They may have to remain close to their origin point."

"Our mission was to collect the remaining emeralds . . . What is going to be the future of those cities? Zannala, Flores, and Cosarave will be overwhelmed by these demons. Those citizens don't deserve that fate," Eric slammed his fist against the table.

"The weapons that aided you in the fight are yours to keep. Phoenix must have lost his sword in the catacombs. Please help yourselves to our armory. As well, take the Bright Light that was collected. We will extract it from the tubes and give you the results. If the area is indeed safe, we are no longer in need of this defense. And if that were to change, we know where to collect more." Danny turned to Crystal. "From what I hear, those rings have finally made a decision. Someone was bound to be chosen; I wonder why you?" Feeling slightly insulted, Crystal smiled un-amused.

"Unless there are any more questions, Noel and I should spread the wealth of knowledge and speak with Ace's family. On this table are the things you came here with, and other information to help along the way. A team was dispatched to nourish your mounts and repair the carriage attached to them. For Phoenix's safety and your own health, please feel welcome to stay as long as needed." He motioned for Noel to follow.

"Time to form a plan, Crissy," said Eric, laying the documents they had secured from the court upon the table. He skimmed through them. "Hm, we know the accusations against our names. High bounties have been waged for our capture." He studied another sheet, while Crystal held her duffel bag on her lap. Eric's eyes widened. "Brett and Alex . . . were sent to the same city as the rest of

Holick's population: the City of Assassins."

"Those mercenaries . . . They must be working with Skull? Which means they are with him?"

"I suppose," Eric whispered paying no attention to her speculation. He continued reading. "It does not state their fate. They have no accusations listed, meaning they may very well be alive." Eric grinned ear to ear. He rummaged through the remaining documents and retrieved the map. "The City of Assassins is directly south-east from Luminar; Cosarave City is down south, Zannala is north-west, and Flores is on our course to Assassin City."

"I know Phoenix would like to find Skull." Crystal peered at the map. "If we make our destination Assassin City, we are most likely passing two villages before we reach Flores. If this is true, we will be able to resupply."

"Appears to me we have formulated our first plan. Hit Flores hard, reach the City of Assassins, rescue my family, and kill Skull," he sighed. "Knowing our destination gives me a sense of relief. Hopefully there are little more surprises." Eric leaned back in the chair glancing at Crystal. *What did I get myself into?*

They remained with the Luminescence Clan for a few days as prescribed by the doctor herself. Eric and Crystal soaked in the hospitality that their heroicness granted them. They dropped by the armory tent and picked up two blades for Phoenix, hoping they would suite him. They spent a good portion of their time caring for Phoenix, but had the opportunity to explore the ruins of Luminar and meet the villagers. They often found themselves with Mrs. Triage or Noel. Danny had much to focus on and Madam Lee had a countless supply of people who needed her attention.

The two of them attended Ace's ceremony. Depending on the beliefs of the family or city, the rituals consisted of different routines. Luminar believed the soul met with the Protectors and was cast into Teague to help in its growth. However, this required the cremation of his body, which had deteriorated in the catacombs. Instead, close relatives and friends recalled stories since his creation and chanted safe passage charms, praying to the Protectors that he found peace by their side, all while Danny burned logs. The entire ceremony soothed the souls of the living who were forced to continue without their loved ones.

CHAPTER 10

On the morning of their departure, Eric and Crystal left their quarters to find Noel standing beside their horses, who were neighing and ready to run.

"We retrieved your horses and brought them up the mountain. Phoenix is comfortably set up in the carriage. When you decide it is time, we will send you off." Without hesitation, they gathered their things. They silently agreed they could no longer spend more time there. Walking into the town's square, they found the entire clan gathered waiting for them enthusiastically. Crystal placed their belongings beside Phoenix, including her duffel bag and paperwork. Eric kept the map and approached Danny, who stood before the crowd with Mrs. Triage at his side.

Danny stepped forward, speaking in an uplifting tone: "Rex, I, and the rest of the Luminescence Clan owe you our deepest gratitude. I can proudly say you have family here with us. Thanks to Phoenix, Crystal, and you, we can sleep at ease and rebuild our city. Our home. We shall resurrect Luminar right from its own fossils and use its graveyard as the foundation. If trouble ever finds you, as I know it will, do not hesitate. No matter the reason, send word by pigeon. We will find you once again."

"These kind words do not fall on deaf ears. Thanks to your hospitality and resources we are back to full health. If Phoenix were conscious, he would preach something along the lines of family and how he cannot wait for Luminar to stand proud once more. He would also be jealous of all the time we had frolicking around the area. If it's not a bother, I'm taking this vest. If ever a need arises, trust me when I say I won't forget your name," Eric stuck his hand out and Danny firmly grasped it.

Beginning their departure down the road, they watched as the entire clan waved goodbye to their new friends. The horses carried them farther away from the village, bumping them back and forth on the dirt path. Crystal held the map to make sure Eric stayed on course.

"I suppose Belinda will be our first stop?"

"It's a small city, but they will have the supplies we need."

Time passed and Eric started feeling uneasy as the silence became deafening. "This quest we are on . . . We will be together months from now still. Let us pass some time with good ole fashioned conversation, shall we?"

"I've dabbled in such a foreign concept. What do you have in mind?"

"I don't know. We—none of us know much about one another. Besides the obvious of my family having been kidnapped and we are in search of religious artifacts."

"Where to begin," Crystal giggled.

"I'll start. I'm an open book. I was born and raised in Holick. I grew up in a normal comfortable lifestyle. My dad . . . was never in my picture. It was just my mother, my siblings, and me. Around the age of eight, which was about, hm, fifteen years ago, I began my career of supporting those around me. Your turn."

"I was under the impression you were an only child? What happened to your siblings?"

"Hcy, hcy, hey, you can't skip that easily."

Crystal sighed. "I was born in Kyron city, but soon after I became an orphan. I went to go live with my grandmother in Lanster."

"The one in which you ran away?"

167

"The same."

"A drastic decision. Family is extremely important. Especially at your age."

"The father position in my life is filled," she said, grazing his arm. "She . . . It was far from a healthy household." Crystal paused, glancing to the side.

"D-do you want to stop? The topic can be changed . . ."

"No, it's good to speak of this and clear my spirit. I was treated as a servant. I performed all that was required of me—from scrubbing the tiles to helping her bathe, but nothing mattered. I would only ever be beneath her. Forever. I suppose I never experienced a *real* childhood. From when I could remember, fun was never allowed, especially if that fun was not in a proper environment for a young lady. I was sheltered from almost everything." She stopped to see if Eric was still paying attention to her. "That's why . . . Brett and you took me a minute to digest."

"She does not sound like she was aging with grace."

"Yeah . . . Speaking of Brett, how did you meet him? He's a genuinely nice fellow."

"Yeah, I agree," Eric blushed, grinning from ear to ear. "Luck was on my side when we met. I believe I was thirteen when our paths crossed; well, more like he crossed the path of my rock. The mark is still on his forehead if you look closely."

"Who just throws rocks?"

Eric shrugged, "I was accepted to this prestigious knight academy located a little beyond Holick's borders. It was an opportunity I had always dreamed of having. Brett always seemed to find himself there, probably inspecting our little armors, making sure they were up to his standards. But from that day forward we were inseparable. He always tried to sneak around and scare me. He thought it was hilarious watching me jump from my skin . . . The affection I felt toward him had been hibernating until I returned home a year and months later—arrived in Holick to those damned bastards kidnapping my people." Eric stared hard at the map, clearly pausing to restrain his anger.

Seeing his pained expression put Crystal in shock. This macho man, tough man, on the verge of crying? Impossible.

Then, there it was. Tears. A fountain of tears.

"Eric, I'm sorry, if it's too difficult . . .'"

Through his muffles, he tried speaking clearly. "Befo-before I-I started at the academy and when I began working, a sickness spread through the city—claiming my mother. I was left to raise my brother and sister alone. On. My. Own." He pulled on the reigns, causing the horses to slow to a trot until they completely halted. Concentrating on the road was too much.

"Protectors . . . I loved them so much. I worked so hard to provide for them. I almost passed on the academy. They meant the world to me. When I came home, Brett spent all his time at my mother's house. H-he cared for them, too. We became a family. Do you know how long I solely carried the burden of raising them?"

Crystal could only gaze at him as he released his pent-up emotions. Placing her palm on his shoulder, Eric continued. "One night . . . One cursed night . . . Derrick came home late for whatever frivolous reason—and they *followed* him. They barged through the door, attempting to take us all. My sister was able to escape in the commotion, but we were in the middle of dinner. I guess I should be thankful—they assumed Brett and I were a couple even though we had not officially spoken about our label. Being gay was equivalent to being a necromancer to those men." He paused. Breathing heavily for a few minutes, he sniffled through tears and slapped the reigns. As the horses started galloping, he continued his story. "Outnumbered and useless . . . I watched as they took him— snatched my brother from my arms. That did not end the harassment. Within the next day, those mercenaries targeted Brett's family that *did* live in the city with him. That story does not end any prettier. Brett moved in and I continued watching over my sister cautiously with a vigilant eye. Until another night where I was a stupid, selfish prick." Tears flooded his vision. He stopped their ride again, until his fit subsided.

Crystal leaned in, giving him a hug. "What? Did they kidnap your sister as well?"

He shook his head, wiping his tears away. "That night, Brett and I had been on a date. You know, trying to enjoy ourselves for once. Time slipped through our fingers. Slightly intoxicated, no concept of time was in mind. But it was way past dusk and I had to get my sister from friends on the other side of town. Once she was with us, we headed home. Brett and I were in such high spirits, and that's more contagious than a virus. We began horse-playing, goofing around in the alleyways. But . . . before I knew it, they were back again. The gang was *pissed off* to see the three of us that happy. His head was smashed into the ground. Picked him up and continuously beat him against a wall. Few others ganged together and struck me. Crushed my jaw, broke my arm. Wreaked havoc on my entire body." Another long silence. "They killed her. They killed my sister and took her life."

Crystal scrambled for the appropriate words, but there wasn't a remedy for such emotions that had been fermenting for years. A twisting, gut-wrenching feeling began rising in her, imagining those mercenaries taking a little girl's life. All she could do was hold him; hold him as tightly as possible. She told him how sorry she was several times and that he truly did all he could.

As he fought the rest of the waterworks, an uncomfortable quiet sat between them for the rest of the ride. Crystal was feeling guilty and Eric had never felt weaker and more vulnerable in the entirety of his life. Eventually, Eric felt his eyelids getting heavy, forcing an immediate rest for the evening. They fell asleep inside a tent Danny had given them.

Phoenix turned his head toward the black abyss surrounding him. He listened intently to the conversation being held upfront. Lying there, his chest got as heavy as the intensity in the air. The things he heard could have never been fabricated, even for an infinite amount of coin. He tried shifting his body, but the pain in his torso was too much to bear. He quietly lay still, following his comrades' lead and dozing into the night.

The next few days consisted of small conversations between Eric and Crystal, checking on Phoenix now and again, and sleeping. Neither of them were ready for another deep talk that could easily swallow them whole. As the first sun reached high overhead, they finally arrived at Belinda. Both of their stomachs rumbled violently as they descended from their mounts. Crystal's first concern was Phoenix, who remained fast asleep.

"Now that we are here, what is our first objective?" asked Crystal.

"A delicious meal. Neither of us is of use without fuel. Afterward, we should gather enough supplies that will last us from here to the next town. A few days' worth."

Clutching her duffel bag, Crystal asked, "What should I do with the emerald? Bringing this into town along with our warrants will only cause an issue."

"Hide them with Phoenix. Place the emerald under his arms, just in case."

They entered the town with an adventurous mindset and excitement in their steps. Neither of them had been far from home, making the quick stop a cultural experience on its own. The place was a small but industrious town. A surprisingly large number of buildings were located within the city, ranging from restaurants to jail cells to headquarters for local businesses. As they traveled farther into town, the villagers greeted them with open arms. By the time they reached a local diner, all the citizens in the village knew about their guests. *News travels fast in such a small place,* thought Crystal, looking up at Mama's Delight's sign. The restaurant was almost empty besides a few patrons. The hostess was able to quickly seat them and with a huge smile, the waitress gave them each a menu.

"Hmm, this all looks good!" exclaimed Crystal.

"It all sounds good; the food has yet to be seen."

Crystal stuck out her tongue, and continued reading. The waitress came back with two glasses of water, asking politely for their orders. Crystal ordered a very healthy lunch, while Eric ordered a hefty slab of meat. With Phoenix in mind, Crystal also ordered a meal for the road.

"Once we finish here, we will be parting ways."

"Phoenix needs to eat first; he must be starving. Then I'll see to my errands."

"Fine, whatever works. I will go to the market and purchase what's necessary and possibly find nourishment for our horses. Find someone who is capable of sewing our outfits back to their better days. Especially Phoenix's suit. He's going to have a mental breakdown seeing the variety of colors on his vest." Eric laughed as he watched the waitress bring them their entrees. They eagerly began devouring their dishes.

Phoenix rolled over on his bed, picking himself up without flinching from pain. In fact, he felt brand new. Walking to the carriage door, he gave a big yawn and stretched, placing the tips of his fingers against the ceiling. *Feels like I haven't moved in ages.* He opened the door, faltering back in fear. His eyes widened to the awful sight of a dozen bodies scattered before him. Coming to the side of the first corpse, he examined it. She was dead. A stab wound right through her neck. *Her face is familiar; I must know her.* Phoenix ran to the next closest body who was face down. This time, fresh blood still dripped from the person's skull. He gingerly rotated the body to see their face, only to gasp in horror. *Mrs. Triage!*

"Who did this?" he cried.

Nausea ensued. He checked the remaining corpses. One by one, he spoke their names: Rex, Noel, Alexander, Danny, Brett, Ace. The smell had become suddenly overwhelming. Returning to the first corpse, his eyes locked on to her flashy necklace. *Princess Lilian.* Phoenix fell to his knees, sweating heavily, his eyes reddening. He stayed still as a portrait. Eerie laughter filled the void, crawling into his ears and lingering around him.

Fueled by anger, he sped toward the merriment. *The laughter must be the one who is responsible.* Passing even more corpses, he attempted to avoid locking sight on them. The chance he would find them familiar was too great. Traveling into the village, he was surrounded by buildings. Burning buildings that were filling the air with smoke. *Why does this always happen? Why would someone do this?* His thoughts circled his mind until he came to the source. Turning the corner of a flaming structure, he found three figures.

Eric was lying on the ground, his arms twisted in odd shapes. Crystal was raised in the air with hands around her throat. The one holding her was hidden by a slight shadow, making him unrecognizable. She squealed as her skin color changed different shades.

"Release her!" screamed Phoenix as he ran toward them. *Not a time to keep my cool, she's in trouble—she needs my help.* The figure holding Crystal slowly turned around in reaction to Phoenix's yell. As his face became more and more visible, Phoenix's pace slowed down to an immediate halt.

"It's . . . it's . . ."

"Me." whispered the same deep, sinister voice from before screeching in his ears.

The doppelganger turned back to Crystal, retrieving his sword from the dirt. Her eyes watered as he drove the tip of the blade through her abdomen. He slid his sword through her like butter. Her body was dropped as her murderer stepped to Eric. His boots nailed him in the face. His show continued by implanting the sword through his skull. The thrust created a tremendous crack that caused a building in the background to crumble. Leaving the sword in place, he faced the original Phoenix and took a few steps forward, chuckling the entire time.

"That's not me. You. Are. Not. Me! I would never hurt these people!" Tears streamed down his face. He wasn't sure what was making his stomach most uneasy; the fact that he watched his companions fall before him or that he was the one who did it.

"Are you sure?" questioned the voice. His clone's mouth was moving, but the voice seemed to come from somewhere else. "Your heart is *filled* with darkness. Allow it to consume you. Be who you were meant to be." The voice whispered the last few words and dispersed to only reappear beside him. It placed its long hand on Phoenix's shoulder. Its coldness surged through his body, sending shivers across his skin. Out of the corner of his eye he could see black flames dance around the demon's hand. "Are those tears?"

"No! I would never kill an innocent! I've seen the damage and pain that it causes first hand. I'll never travel that path!"

"What is it that you consider innocent?"

"I-I don't—"

"All those soldiers back at Emerica—"

"They were mercenaries!"

"Trying to make a living to support their families. Had they known what they signed up for, would they still do it? Are they not innocent?"

"Stop questioning my morals. I slay the ones that kill."

His sinister laugh erupted. "If someone were to slay you, would they become the hero?" He didn't respond. "People are quick to judge what's right and wrong, but it's all matter of opinion. Your death toll increases with every place you visit. Leaving a trail of blood behind, killing is your passion. Something that makes you *thrive*. Have you seen your hands lately?"

Phoenix lowered his eyes to find his hands stained in blood. The longer he stared, the more blood he could see drip from his fingers. "You cannot control your fate, Phoenix; you have already begun the journey."

Phoenix blinked. Suddenly, his point of view changed. He could see another version of himself again, staring down at his palms, while a large menacing cloud hovered behind him with a fiery hand on his shoulder. Irrational. He was becoming irrational. Stepping back, his foot caused a splash that soaked his leg. Turning, he found himself feet from his comrades' lifeless bodies. He quickly glanced around at the blood splatters. Following the trail, his eyes found their way to the blade that he grasped firmly. Immersed in their blood. He began to quiver, losing grip on the weapon covered in hatred. It bounced against the ground, causing the world to vibrate. He fell to his knees, crying over Crystal's body. The creepy figure loomed over his shoulder, whispering in his ear:

"Accept this fate—it shall not change. You will destroy the world as we know it. Phoenix, you are the legend who will bring the new age to life!"

Eric polished his plate and dessert, while Crystal remained patiently on her meal. Waiting for Crystal, he glanced around the diner when something caught his eye. A young man was sitting at a booth reading a newspaper. Eric squinted, examining the article on the front with the headline "WANTED." Straining his eyes to read the tiny font, he saw a picture of each of them with their names written as the description. He abruptly stood, startling his companion.

"What in the Protectors' names, Eric?"

"Shush! Our names are omens!" He threw coins upon the table top to cover the payment and grabbed ahold of her arm. He forced her outside as she held onto Phoenix's meal. Before she had an opportunity to protest, Eric interrupted.

Grabbing a newspaper from the nearest stand, he shoved the front story in her face. "Our reputation is becoming quite known."

"What do you mean?"

"Our smug grins are now in black and white."

She scanned the page, her jaw slightly lowering with an apprehensive expression. "This is no good. The entirety of Belinda will know of our presence if we don't leave town. If one person learns the truth, all will know."

"I agree, but we have yet to finish the task we came to

complete. See that Phoenix eats his meal and continue with the clothes shopping. When I'm finished, I will meet you at the horses." The two of them separated in haste.

Crystal hurriedly jogged back. She unhitched the carriage door, allowing sunshine to pour through. The brightness cleared the darkness, bringing life to the haul. The happiness vanished when she found Phoenix shifting back in forth in his bed, drowning in his own sweat. She rushed to his side, trying to wake him. Shouting his name and aggressively shaking him, he at last opened his eyes, which were wide and wired. At first he stared at her, almost through her. He lunged forward for a comforting embrace, placing one hand on the back of her head and another around her waist.

"Is something the matter? A night terror?"

"Crystal . . ." he breathed tiredly. He tried to finish, but exhaustion overcame him and he collapsed in her arms.

"Phoenix! Stay awake!" *The medication must be having an adverse effect; he may still have the concussion.* She lifted him from under his arms and dragged him into the sunlight. She propped him against a tree, allowing the shade to cover some of his face. She left in search of liquid, returning minutes later with a handful of pond water. The splash brought him back to life, confused and disoriented.

"Crystal!" he shouted. "My dream, I must—"

"Nope, eating comes first. It's been days since your body has had a decent meal. Once it's finished, I'll listen."

Phoenix's horrid stare slowly changed as he happily accepted the sandwich without an argument. His mouth watered as he brought the food to his lips. With just a few bites, it was entirely gone. Once he finally found the words to confess his dreams that haunted him, much more flowed without a filter. *No more secrets . . . I need help.* He explained the dream he had in Emerica, the one when they first arrived at Luminar, and the experience he had just encountered.

He explained each nightmare held death and destruction. He became engulfed by a mystical darkness. He wept in her arms for what seemed like hours. Though he felt relieved, he was beside himself. The one thing he swore was to never reveal his inner feelings. He had done more than just that. Realization set forth as he stared into her eyes.

"Where do these dreams come from?" she spoke quietly, consoling him.

"They happen at random, far and few in between. But this last . . . tops them all."

"There seems to be reoccurring themes in each of these surreal experiences. It's possible that these are more than just night terrors. Visions perhaps?" She felt as if she was a fully-fledged psychiatrist. *Call me Dr. Thorn.*

Phoenix gazed at Crystal's flushed cheeks and her strawberry hair tied into a ponytail. He remained locked onto her face, until she glanced at him and their eyes met. His emotions were calmed by her serene presence. The strong connection he had felt came to light.

"It seems . . . that I'm there. As if it's reality, but I have no control of my actions. None of this makes sense and I don't wish to understand them, but to think that I may succumb—" he paused. "The prophecy it preached stated I will be the change in Teague. A change that does more damage than healing. What if this is a forecast of my future?"

"Phoenix, remember when we met? Back in the alleyway as drunken fools were harassing me, I was rescued. Rescued by a stranger that asked of nothing in return. Never have you done a deed that betrayed your beliefs. With a clear mind, remain on the side of what is believed to be good. Stand with your decisions that are held to be true and that future will not come to fruition." Crystal lovingly held him, witnessing the worry tormenting his face disappear.

A trance captivated the two of them as they stared at one another. Slowly, they inched closer until the warmth of their breath lay upon each other's skin. He gently placed his hand along her docile face, stroking her cheek with his thumb. The instant their lips met, the town around them vanished. A tingling sensation exploded between them, stimulating their senses. She felt the warmth of his body lying against hers, and the comfort and protection he offered. He dwelled in her compassion and sincerity. Their lips remained locked; perfectly in place. She pulled him in tighter, wishing there was a way their bodies could become closer. The moment was magical, but abruptly ended.

Realizing his actions, Phoenix retreated. His head dropped, and then slightly turned the opposite direction. Crystal, her heart beating in her ears, moved back, turning the shade of a rose. The heartfelt moment was interrupted as Eric appeared with bags.

Eric observed their ripped and tattered clothing and the filth that still clung to its threads. "Why am I not surprised? More than an hour has passed! My tasks have been—" he stopped mid-sentence, breathing in the tension. With their flushed skin and the ability to process simple math, his conclusion formed.

Phoenix could watch as Eric struggled to react. Even a fool could recognize what occurred between them. His scrunched brows relaxed as an elated smile grew. As he listened to him speak, the tone and pitch of his voice said more than his nonverbal expressions.

"I see that I have interrupted a moment. Then I'm glad I purchased a few things before . . . this happened." He reached into the bags, revealing cheap pieces of fabric. "Here are clothes to cover yourselves—or not—while we bring our outfits to be cleaned." Both of them took their new outfits and went to respective hiding spots. They came back dressed and refreshed. Giving their original ones to Eric, he responded, "Right, feel free to return to your original activities." He dropped the bags, practically escaping from his position.

Feeling guilty, Crystal began to unpack the supplies. Stocking their carriage required less time than expected with two sets of hands, leaving them with nothing to do in their awkward silence, both wanting to speak, but neither managing to form words. Phoenix was brushing his horse's mane as Eric returned.

Phoenix examined his empty hands. "Where's my vest?"

"Relax, princess. I was thinking as I roamed the town's

streets, 'does another rough night on the road please me?' The answer was *hell no*. I spoke to the concierge at a small hotel across the way. That is where your vest is hiding."

"You're the one who read the newspaper," warned Crystal. "We are wanted criminals with a reputation that will reach the ears of all the townies. This is a terrible idea."

"Calm down, Crissy. A pseudonym was given and a generous tip to leave us be was left as well."

"None of this will go well . . ."

"Optimism is a beautiful thing. Let us practice."

Phoenix spoke, "The risk is high, but we do deserve rest. I doubt the carriage will be vandalized, but let's keep the emerald at our sides." He turned to Eric. "Hide our horses, too."

Crystal sighed, "Fine."

"Happy to have your approval, Phoenix. Glad to hear we have accepted this plan once you say so." Eric's attitude lingered toward Crystal, leering at her.

Phoenix felt the dagger at his throat, too.

Once their carriage and steeds were hidden behind a small settlement of trees, the three of them journeyed with their duffel bags in hand to their beds for the night.

CHAPTER 11

The hotel was a one-star dump in desperate need of cleaning. Phoenix swiped a finger across a table and a layer of dust coated the tip. Crystal could hear scampering across the floor and instantly squirmed in her skin. The idea of a warm, not dirt floor, kept them motivated to stay the night. They separated into their assigned bedrooms, men in one and Crystal in her own, and each of them sprawled underneath the sheets. Phoenix hung the emerald's duffel bag on his bed post by his pillow.

Big difference between this and Teague's floor, Eric thought as sleep fell upon him.

The night was silent. Only the occasional breeze knocked against their windows. A terrifying scream broke Phoenix's serene sleep. Crystal's cry was ringing in his ears. He frantically leapt from his covers. Both of his comrades were missing, along with her bag. He busted out of the room and ran down a long, dimly lit hallway. The walls stretched for miles. He could only see the ongoing carpet on his horizon that never ceased to exist. His heart rammed his chest, the collision booming in his ears. Another scream echoed around him. A rougher voice: Eric's. A door came into view and with all his might, Phoenix crashed into the woodwork.

An intense light caused his pupils to narrow. He stepped onto a floating platform as pieces of wood crashed around his feet.

Following the trail of chips, he found stairs before him leading to an altar. The room was suddenly soaked in darkness except for lit torches scattered up the stairs and around the altar. Phoenix peeked over the edge of the platform and saw nothing. Not a bottom. No foundation holding the stairs steady. Nothing. *How the hell are these things levitating?*

Phoenix slowly approached the steps. He put his foot upon the first one and applied pressure. *Seems sturdy enough.* Cautiously trying to find his way between torches, he searched for each level before stepping higher. Reaching the top, he found Crystal and Eric bound by rope to a pillar. At the bottom of the post was fire, gradually consuming the wood. Neither of them moved as a dense smog surrounded them. He could barely see their chests rising. He cried their names, but neither responded. The silence of crackling fire filled the void, until *that* voice resonated around the chamber.

"This is your future, Phoenix; *accept* the inevitable. Nothing can be changed about what is to come."

"I am not these visions! I will save humanity, not destroy it!"

"Your mind says such frivolous sentiments, but your heart screams differently. It *desires* to watch flames dance. Watch them burn. Watch them destroy. It yearns to hear the melody of the innocent cry and to drink the blood of the slaughtered. You want others to suffer, just as *you* have."

"No one deserves such a fate. No one deserves to die . . ."

"If you care as much as you say, why remain cold and aloof? Afraid they will discover the truth? If you were as noble as you believed, then you would dismiss these visions being witnessed. To believe one is pure is a breeding ground for chaos. Pureness has only yet to be corrupted." Phoenix remained silent. "A demon lingers deep inside that growls to be released. Look around, Phoenix, you will succumb to this image once we rule." On cue, the entire altar's perimeter was revealed. People dangled by ropes strapped to their necks. With lacerations on different parts of their bodies, blood slowly dripped. Phoenix watched as the red drops fell below him.

Following their descent, he was horrified to see them splash into a pool of the same. The five emeralds rose from the depths of the bloody collection, surrounding him with an assortment of colors.

"These are your weapons of mass destruction; the tools that will grant ultimate power."

Phoenix watched as the emeralds floated around him. Sheer terror paralyzed him, stiffening his muscles. *I have never trained for such events. The emeralds are too much for me, I'm not strong enough to handle any of this. The emeralds will be captured; the world will be their playground.* His fear grew with each passing second. Each of the colors rotated around his body, mesmerizing him. He finally snapped free of the trance.

"Stay *out* of my head. This is not Teague's future! I'll fight against it; the three of us will stop this chaotic revolution before it begins."

The creature became angry and roared a blood-curdling screech. "How dare you defy me? You little bastard, I am the reason you breathe! Your body and mind are mine!" Black flames shot from thin air, inflicting intense bursts of heat upon his chest. His shirt combusted on impact and knocked him flat against the platform. The five emeralds hovered above him, aimlessly in a line. They positioned themselves one behind the other. The one at the rear strengthened its brightness, shooting a beam into the next one, which increased its level of light. When the reaction hit the front emerald in the column, a mass of energy started to accumulate.

As each jewel sent its signal, he helplessly watched the display. He was in no position to fight back. He tried to think rationally. *The demon is hiding somewhere in the dark, I'll never be able to fight him. Running away is not an option. Could I jump?* Peering over the edge, he recoiled. *This is his world. This nightmare is his paradise. There has to be a solution somewhere—*

The growing ball of energy was unleashed and a beam flew directly at Phoenix. In an attempt to escape, his face was saved from the devastation, but his torso received the full impact. He produced a sound he never imagined he could make.

Phoenix lashed out of his bed bellowing the same noise from his dream, waking up the others in dazed confusion. Eric frantically turned the lights on as Crystal barged into the room. The two of them stared, speechless. Tattered shirt, burnt skin, a stream of blood leaking from his abdomen—the whole scene left them flabbergasted.

"What . . . Ar-are you . . ." Eric fumbled for words.

"It happened again; death, fire, blood . . . *Him*. He was there—he would not release me. He wants me, but he's angry. The emeralds are the tools that will destroy Teague." His panting interrupted his sentences.

Eric, finally coming to his senses, ripped away Phoenix's sweat-stained shirt. There was a gash across his stomach and his shoulder was charred.

"We need to get you to the infirmary *fast*. Crystal, stay and clean up a bit, would ya?" Eric delicately wrapped the already-ruined sheets around the wound, applying pressure. He threw Phoenix's arm around his shoulder, helping him down to the medic.

Still lost in the commotion, Crystal could only drift her gaze around the room. He was in our sights, how could this have occurred? To be physically hurt by a dream? Is it even possible? He said the emerald was the key to the destruction. Is the emerald the reason behind these nightmares? She snatched her bag off of Phoenix's bed post. In the carriage we kept the emerald by his side for safe keeping, and at Luminar City he was holding it in his possession.

With a passionate hatred, she chucked her bag across the room to the farthest corner. *If this is to be blamed, then it's not welcomed. Storage; it will stay in storage with our other useless crap.* She looked back at the red-stained sheets. Her adrenaline was diminishing, allowing waves of emotion to be released.

Eric noisily entered the room, waking her in the process. In a state of grogginess, she attempted to pretend she had been awake the entire time. "Where is he? How is his health?"

"He's . . . doing well. They patched him with some medication and bandages. They rubbed burn ointment onto his shoulder. The medics in white don't have a clue how he received these injuries. The burn confused them more than the cut; the hotel does not even own a fireplace. The one doc mentioned mental illness. They suggested there is a possibility this is his own doing . . ."

"No, no I refuse to believe these are self-inflicted."

"Crissy, with a past like his . . ."

"One could say the same about yo—yesterday, he confided his dreams to me, how there is a connection between them. There is something that you should be aware of . . ."

Crystal and Eric sat onto the bed, avoiding the still damp cloth. She told him about their chat by the tree before he had returned with the clothes. She explained the dreams in entirety and mentioned her theory of the emerald being the cause.

"Noel had said there is an energy beneath the emerald surface. I suppose it *is* possible it could engulf Phoenix the way it changed the vine under Luminar castle. But is it likely for it to have amassed that much power to break those boundaries? I may not be a scientist, but dreams and physical harm are not usually said in the same phrase."

"It's a theory, but you do not stand with the medics about their accusation . . . Do you?"

"I'm not positive about anything, Crystal. I agree though, the cursed object should be kept at bay for now. If it's proven true, I would hate to fall from a cliff in a dream and wake to broken legs." Eric glanced at the sunrise. "No matter what's happening, the moment Phoenix returns, it's time to leave. If they decide these are intended injuries, guess who is responsible to pay the dry cleaning bills? That red will not wash from the cloth for just a few bronze coins," he fussed, gathering up their belongings. "Meet us outside in ten minutes. Where is the jewel? I'll hide it away." With the tainted emerald in hand, Eric left the room with a quiet click of the handle.

She crossed back to her room, picking a shirt from the floor. She paused. "Ten minutes? I'm taking advantage of what is already purchased." She smiled to herself, strolling toward the bathroom.

Eric quickly dressed himself. A medic brought Phoenix back in a wheelchair. He waited for the medic to leave. "Yes, I understand it is still dark, but we are considerably poor and cannot pay for the bills you just brought onto us. We have already spent most of what was in that chest we stole from the House of Judgment. Unless you want to turn in Crystal for the reward money . . ." Eric helped Phoenix into his pristine vest. "All nice and white; just how you like it," Eric said in the most upbeat voice possible, but the fake cheeriness failed to uplift the mood.

Phoenix merely looked at him while he put a leg into its socket. "Thanks, Eric."

"For what?"

"You . . . you only joined us to save your family—" Eric cut in, pointing out the reason they were taken was his fault in the first place. "Even so, you've been a big help since then. I'm glad you decided to join us, and I apologize about tonight."

"All is good, don't thank me. I'm beginning to sort of, in a way, enjoy your company. Just a little bit. But, why apologize? This was not your doing," he gestured to his wounds. "Not unless this *was* your doing . . ."

Phoenix's disdain scrunched his brows as the night air trickled over their skin. He hastily responded, "I may be having some issues, but I'm mentally stable. I would never be able to cause myself such pain—the amount of blood that was lost . . ." He observed Eric's reaction. "You believe me?" Eric smiled with a nod, but Phoenix saw through it. The two of them waited outside the hotel entrance for Crystal, who was clearly tempting Eric's patience.

Crystal washed and combed her rustic pink locks. She put on her worn attire. She examined herself in the mirror, eyeing up the rips in her blouse. *This was my favorite shirt,* she frowned. Once satisfied, Crystal doubled checked her possessions and slammed the door behind her.

Reaching the sight of the boys, both remarked on her arrival. Phoenix murmured, "You look . . . great." Eric complained, "I thought I said ten minutes?"

Crystal giggled, "It's been awhile since we had running water, I did not want to waste the opportunity." She sniffed the air. "Maybe you should have done the same." Eric merely snarled, throwing his hands above him.

Crystal walked to the man of the hour and Eric saw that a sappy conversation was about to unfold, and with intuitive instincts, hid inside the carriage. He returned minutes later as the two of them let go of each other's embrace. They mounted their horses.

"To our next stop, Kyron City!" exclaimed Crystal between the two boys.

"That's where this all started," sighed Phoenix. "Feels like I'm traveling down memory lane."

CHAPTER 12

Belinda was left behind in the dust. Crystal watched the scenery as they galloped along while Phoenix quietly spoke to Eric about Kyron, reminiscing about his time spent there and about the rumors Eric had heard. Most of the days went by without a whisper, unless a sudden conversation sparked. After four days of traveling, Crystal broke the silence.

"Phoenix, have you ever thought about your plans after this is through?"

He glanced at her with a blank stare, while Eric answered, "I know me, Brett, and Alex are packing up and moving far from Holick. Maybe we will live in a nice and quiet village like Belinda. Well, once my face is no longer enlarged and printed in every newspaper. And my tab disappears. What about you, Crystal?"

"I will never live with my grandmother again, that's definite. My dream home of Emerica is destroyed. Not much thought has been given about my future. I may travel to Cosarave—it's less dangerous and different from a small community."

"Cosarave is on our list of citics we have to visit and prevent its annihilation. What seems safe about that?"

"I mean *after* this is all done, it should be a nice place."

"Oh yeah, I would be eager to be neighbors with crumbling buildings and piles of rotting corpses; perfect place to build a life.

Cannot forget the wildlife. The roaming X-creatures will make perfect additions to your yard."

"I believe the question was aimed at me. I think . . . once I'm through with this errand, I'll head back to Luminar. Hopefully help fix what's been lost and reclaim its title as one of the five great cities."

Crystal smiled, "Maybe we will come help you. I'm not in a hurry to leave."

"I-I don't see why I couldn't lend a hand. I'd like that. You two have grown on me . . . like ticks." Eric whispered under his breath, keeping a steady stare on the road.

Crystal retired to the carriage for a rest while the two men rode in silence. After a few hours, Eric noticed buildings arrive on the horizon. He quickly showed Phoenix who shouted for Crystal's attention. They watched, waiting until the sign appeared welcoming them to Kyron City.

Nearing the perimeter of the city, the smell of despair and hopelessness swarmed the carriage. Phoenix took a glimpse around; *Nothing has changed since I'd been here last.* The buildings' walls were dingy, homelessness plagued the streets, and theft was alive and well in every shop. He heard Eric murmur under his breath that he would not be returning for a visit, ever. They tied their horses tightly to a tree.

"We need to retrieve more supplies for our journey to Flores. I'm familiar with this city already. I will be the one who goes shopping. Crystal, you can accompany me, but Eric, I would like you to stay back and keep a close watch on this," Phoenix patted the side of their mobile cabin. "It would be a terrible fate to return and find it nowhere in sight. It's too vital to our situation to allow scum to swipe it from under our noses."

"Give *me* the babysitting job. If I have to stay by myself, it better be worth it," he smirked.

Phoenix dismissed his comment. "Hand me your spear, I will sharpen our weapons while we are in town."

"How am I expected to defend myself? I'm sure these thieves

have sharp metal objects that I would like to keep at a safe distance…"

"What do you mean 'it better be worth it'?"

Eric gathered their equipment, handing them to Phoenix. "What does it sound like, sweetheart? Once you are back from your romantic walk through town square, I want the two of you to be on cloud nine." He gave a sly wink and stepped away before she had a chance to swing.

Crystal's face began burning up. "I swear to the Protectors—I hate you." He chuckled to himself as Phoenix tugged on her arm, trying to refocus her attention.

Diffusing the situation, the two of them traveled into town. Feeling completely exposed, Crystal crossed her arms tightly while staying close to Phoenix's side. If the rumors about this city were even slightly true, this was not a place for a lady like herself. It wasn't a place for any human, really. Though that is how Kyron City began—on lies and rumors.

After visiting several convenience stores and avoiding contact with the citizens, Crystal spotted a slightly less-ransacked gift shop. She joyfully trotted toward it as the sound of glass shattering filled the store. Without a word, she ran to the scene and peered through a window. Unable to see through the dusty slab, she rushed inside, spotting a man in front of a cashier.

The robber had short purple hair that was generously gelled, imitating a faux hawk. His eyes were a dark, majestic brown which complimented his tan skin. Goggles rested on his forehead and a red bandana with diamonds lining the bottom hung loosely around his neck. The rest of his attire consisted of a beige jacket, white undershirt, black elastic pants, and black boots. He was leisurely leaning forward on the counter, his right leg out straight and left one bent at the knee, holding a rusty dagger, pointing the tip at the clerk's neck. Shards of some of the cashier's merchandise lay on the counter and at his feet.

"If you don't return my coins to their rightful owner, there will be serious consequences," ordered the robber, leaning closer while keeping his back straight. "We don't want that, or do we?" The clerk shook his head 'no.' "Agreed. Then on with my coins." The clerk reached into the cash register as Crystal and Phoenix made their entrance.

"Step away from him!" yelled Crystal ripping her rings from Phoenix's grip.

The robber carelessly glanced at his audience. He rolled his eyes, "Go away, this doesn't concern you, little girl."

Phoenix tried to stop Crystal, but she darted toward him. She was ready to swing, but the robber chucked the dagger at her. Out of fear, she stood there frozen, but the projectile missed by a mile.

She started gloating, "You couldn't even—" her sentence fell short as she was hurled to the ground by a falling net, entangling her on the floor. She struggled to free herself, but it was futile. Phoenix scanned the room, noting the robber's demeanor. *He purposely missed; he was aiming to release the net on the ceiling.* Phoenix made his way toward the strange man, pulling out one sword.

"Seriously? I just want my coins! I was ripped off—*I'm* the victim!"

The clerk argued, "The price was ten bronze coins, and that's what I received."

The robber slammed his fist on the counter, "I gave you a *silver* coin! If I don't get those five bronze coins back I'm going to completely saw your head from its post! And smile while doing it." The robber retrieved another dagger from his jacket, just as damaged as the previous. He held it right against the clerk's neck, pressing against his Adam's apple. Phoenix reached into his pocket, tossing five bronze coins onto the counter.

"This is a rough town as it is; the clerk doesn't need this problem. Take the coins and leave." Phoenix shredded the net before sheathing his blade. The robber collected his earnings, closely watching Phoenix. His eyes brightened in awe when he came to a realization.

"I recognize your mugs! You are those wanted criminals. What were the names? It was bird-like . . . Raven? Falcon? No—It's Phoenix! Phoenix Reinhard and Crystal Thorn! You have large bounties on your heads."

The clerk's eyes sharpened, "No! More thieves? Protectors get me *out* of this city!" He hollered running out of the store.

The robber, without looking, threw the dagger at the register commanding the drawer to open. Phoenix helped Crystal to her feet while examining the man. "Cause problems with us and this will be the last time you breathe. I suggest you be on your way." Crystal tried to appear threatening, but practically tripped over the ripped net.

The robber waltzed over to the register, collecting his earnings. "Oh, feisty; I like it. I'm not going to start with the people who killed Emerica's King, but . . . here you are. Two big time idols. Murdering the princess and burning down Emerica? Those are huge feats many criminals would love to do." He started counting his coins.

"We are not dirty criminals as yourself!" exclaimed Crystal.

The robber laughed, "You flatter me, sweetie, but you can call me Wolf. Lone Wolf for a little more of a title." He walked over to Phoenix, handing him back his coins. "Why are the two of you here? Sure, Kyron City is a beautiful and romantic vacation hotspot, but you must know that dangers lurk around every corner."

"We didn't come here for a good time; we only had to make a stop." Crystal spat as snarky as possible.

"Such attitude, I like it." Wolf winked at her.

Phoenix stepped betwixt them. "You have what you want. Make your exit. We have more important things to accomplish than deal with vigilantes."

Crystal was the first to leave, followed by Phoenix. From behind, they could hear Wolf yelling:

"Don't leave yet! There are some great stores we can profit from together!"

Finally back on task, Phoenix and Crystal continued on their way to find the blacksmith. A block away, the two of them reached her. Phoenix gave her all their weapons and without hesitating, asked the lady to make sure they could pierce steel. Not shocked by the brutality of the question, she responded, "I've seen enough death to be worried about you folks."

While they waited, Phoenix pulled out twelve bronze coins. "Remember these?"

Crystal observed them. "Am I supposed to?"

"These are the coins you bribed that guard with back at Emerica. When we went out to search for the thugs in the forest, I persuaded them to pass these along into my possession. I forgot to return them until now."

Crystal smiled, thinking back to the guard up against the wall. "I can't believe you got them back! I'm surprised you kept them all this time." She paused. "Didn't you just give these same coins to that thief?"

"Ah, ye-yeah about that . . . I had the intention of repaying you in full." While smiling, Crystal gave him a big hug. He gently placed his arms around her, letting their bodies come together as a classic puzzle piece. He laid his head on top of hers, and they stood still as time continued around them. The blacksmith politely telling them their items were finished—and to get a room—eventually ruined the moment.

"We never are able to have a moment alone," Crystal blushed.

"One day, I'm going to forget your face isn't naturally red," laughed Phoenix.

With all their shopping done, they headed back to Eric. Once he was in sight, they were taken by surprise. A stranger was sitting on top, kicking his legs back and forth. Their first thought was Eric, but they found him on the ground like a little puppy barking at their guest. It wasn't until they got closer that they recognized the distinct pigment of hair.

"What's going on here?" asked Phoenix.

"This *thing* came by and hopped onto our ride, saying he knows me. He also says he's friends with you. I wouldn't have believed him, but you have a tendency to make friends in odd places."

Wolf jumped to the ground with a thud. Completely ignoring Eric, he waltzed up to Phoenix. "I prefer criminal instead, thank you very much."

"How can we help you now?" asked Crystal crossing her arms.

"I missed you as well." His expression was practically emotionless.

Phoenix gripped him by his jacket, his face as stern as ever. "Answer the question. There is no time to deal with common thugs."

"Getting a bit touchy, aren't we? We are moving too fast—we have only just met."

"What. Do. You. Want?"

"All business I see. You're not as fun as I was led to believe. But you should rethink your approach when speaking with me. I remembered something after we separated. Some information that might *actually* interest you."

Phoenix's patience was being tested. Pulling his steel out, he laid the tip against Wolf's abdomen. "Talk."

"You're not going to hurt me."

The blade was pressed against his white tee, causing it to darken. "Okay, okay! There's a rumor about a rare sword passing through here. The story behind the sword is that it was stolen from a child in Luminar. That would be you, I presume?"

Phoenix lowered his blade, blatantly gaping at him. "Ho-how did you . . .?"

Wolf smirked, "Phoenix, you are aware of how Kyron functions. Information is spread through these streets like a bad disease. I have also heard word of a clan back at the ruins of Luminar? Oh! And the Doc from the Brotherhood is reported to be deceased? That's huge news."

"Phoenix, is it the White Dragon sword?" asked Crystal, hiding behind Eric.

He didn't respond at first. "Possibly . . . Where would I go to find this sword?"

"I don't know everything. My best guess is that we have to hit the central base of intelligence in Kyron," Wolf pointed over top the buildings to the tallest of them all. "That's where *the* mastermind thief lives."

"What makes him special?" asked Eric.

"Nothing. Besides him being *the* richest person in Osiren. He has enough security to prove it."

"Is it hard to have a meeting with this man?" asked Phoenix.

"He will never allow an audience of such stature in his domain. Especially asking for an expensive item for no cost."

"Would it be difficult to access the building in other means?"

"For the average citizen, it would prove to be quite the challenge."

"What's that supposed to mean?" accused Crystal, giving him a dirty look.

"Meaning, I will be able to get us through without a problem. But only a single guest may accompany me. What do you say? Is that sword worth the trouble?"

Phoenix looked around at Crystal and Eric. She spoke, "We just met this man. Robbing a poor clerk. Can he be trusted?"

"Not a chance," the man laughed.

Crystal saw the longing on Phoenix's face. *What an opportunity . . . This may be the closest he's ever been.* "Go for it. This is your family sword. Don't let this opportunity slip away."

"We will wait here until you return I suppose. But don't get hurt! I won't be there to rescue you from harm's way." Eric examined their *guest.* "No word in an hour and I'm coming in full force."

Phoenix thought for a minute. He grabbed the base of his other sword. "Lead the way—but I'll be watching every step."

Lone Wolf nodded and spun on his soles. Walking toward

the building he called, "I would not bother bringing your weapons. It will only draw attention and cause trouble. In here, that's the last thing we want."

The two of them walked in a line, Phoenix following behind. The trust between them was scarce and Phoenix was more than aware of the kind of person this Lone Wolf was. He had dealt with his type on more than one occasion and they all desire one thing: profit. The chances of him actually having his sword were slim, but this is the closest he had been to his weapon in twelve years. No matter how low the odds, he could not pass on this chance, nor live his life on "what if's." This weapon was more than an object of war. It had meaning. It held value. It had the connection to his family which he desperately needed. The chance to wield it once again was worth more than his own life.

The marching ended as they reached a brick wall that fenced in the perimeter. Wolf walked to the gate and placed his hand upon the rough exterior. Phoenix searched for the end of the wall with his eyes, but none was found. *Must wrap around the entire place.* Wolf slowly slid his hand against the stones. His mysterious movements stopped upon a specific rock. Counting aloud, he hit the stone five times. He aggressively pushed the rock inward. They waited a few minutes until a concealed door revealed itself.

Phoenix cocked his head. "Interesting. How were you aware of this hidden entrance?"

"I heard some information here and there. Be sure to follow as I do and stay quiet."

Silently, the pair traveled through the door, entering into a courtyard. Large henchmen were clustered throughout the area. All of the goons were burly with none shorter than six feet. The herd of steroid-fueled gorillas was too focused on their tasks of manual labor to notice any commotion in their surroundings. Motioning Phoenix to follow, they ran toward the towering building. It had to be the largest structure in all of Kyron.

Reaching the side of the monument, Wolf whispered, "The main entrance would be the graceful way to enter, but in what good story does that happen? There is a small ventilation shaft right . . . around . . . here." He kicked the metal grate.

Phoenix eyed the tiny crawl space. "How are we to fit?"

"Not comfortably. Once I remove the lid, I will head in first. Trail in afterward, but make sure you replace the vent. These are not the brightest bulbs on the chandelier, but even one of these flicking, testosterone fueled garbage piles will notice a misplaced grate."

"Besides for a good tale, why are we not to walk through the entrance?"

"He has tight security. Cameras are positioned at each corner. Nobody has broken in before—until now. And this is more exciting." He checked both ways and pulled out a dagger from an inside pocket. He squeezed the tip between the top of the grate and the wall, prying off the cover. When it popped off, he slid in smoothly on all fours.

Phoenix struggled to follow behind, squeezing himself into the tight space feet first. He even had more trouble replacing the cover. He tried to match the pace of Wolf, but his awkward squirming was not as graceful as Wolf's army crawl. In the duct, there were screens every few feet showing them what was held below. Phoenix took a deep breath each time he came across one of the openings to help calm himself down. The tight space and uncomfortable position had him ready to lose his mind.

At last, Wolf found something of interest in one of the rooms below. He unhinged the screen from its position and knocked it onto the floor. Wolf dove to the ground while Phoenix followed behind gently lowering himself. Phoenix watched as Wolf made his way to an expensive, fancy high-tech security system that left him mesmerized. The flashing lights and sounds were overwhelming and the massive keyboard and several monitors were much for him to experience at once. In all his years, he had never seen something this technologically advanced.

"This must have cost a fortune! Guard dogs alone cost more than three gold coins; this had to cost him several hundreds."

Wolf started playing on the control panel while responding, "Technology is too rare a privilege. All things developed that require electricity cost plenty of coins. Anything taking more man and brain power than usual cost at least ten gold. Platinum coins would be the only currency with enough value to purchase any of this. The two of us shall never see enough coins in our lives combined to purchase such luxuries. I have doubts either of us will ever lay eyes upon a platinum and all its worth."

Phoenix watched as random numbers and codes scrolled onto the screen only to disappear seconds later. None of what was happening before him made sense. The inventions of scientists boggled his mind, which made him grateful he had an intelligent companion. After another handful of code sequences appeared, the words "Access Granted" in green, flashing letters shot across the main monitor.

"Access has been granted to what?"

"To those security measures I mentioned previously. There's a fan at the end of the duct that is now disabled. Thus allowing us the ability to sneak through without being pureed. I also disabled all cameras that would have captured us trying to enter the vault. I even was able to bypass the security of the alarm, muting it. Which is a pat on my back, because I was even unaware that could be done."

"Strange nobody has ever broken into this place before, but yet you sure seem to know exactly what needs to be completed."

He looked at Phoenix, "As I stated before, it's Kyron City. All knows all."

"There's something you're not telling me," Phoenix got in his face. "Start talking."

"Phoenix, this is not the time for a rumble. I'd like to, oh, I don't know, leave this place alive."

Phoenix sighed realizing the wisdom in his words. Even if he refused to admit it, he was in the middle of a mess that brawn had no solution for. Wolf's skills were necessary, which made his health very important.

"Noted, what's next?" Creating space between them, Wolf pointed back at the duct. He hopped on top of Phoenix's shoulders to reach and pulled himself back into the crawl space. Phoenix, distressed, climbed in after him.

Scurrying along the path, Phoenix spotted the fan at the end of the duct. *If that wasn't turned off, we would have been worse than Swiss cheese*, he thought. The two of them carefully maneuvered around the blades to reach the end. They bashed through another screen. Once they landed, Phoenix checked his surroundings. A giant, metal vault sat in the center of the room. Another keyboard resembling the control panels from before was attached to the wall beside it.

"I'm assuming another code is required," he turned to Wolf. "And I'm sure you are well aware of the fact?"

"I wouldn't dare come unprepared," he remarked, making his way over, ego clearly glowing.

Wolf started talking to himself, while Phoenix looked around the room. He must have another reason to be here; he knows more than he's revealed. I bet it's the coins behind the vault, but is it stealing if he's taking from a thief? His thoughts were interrupted by loud footsteps. His eyes widened as a powerful arm grabbed him by the waist and a hand covered his mouth. He yelled, but his scream was muffled.

Wolf stopped when he heard steady clapping. He turned around to find Phoenix bound by an oversized animal, and two other men beside them. The other large male was practically identical to the first. They each had blond crew cuts with entirely dark attires. A tight, spandex tee tucked into cargo pants with huge boots on their feet. All black. And they were the color of paste.

The third man was between them. Averagely built with olive skin, he wore a purple and black pinstriped suit. The stripes matched his hair—black with purple streaks. It was gelled and smoothed to the right. The gentleman stopped his applause. "To think that one such as yourself would believe stealing from the master would be this easy? There is much to learn, Talon."

Talon? Who's Talon?

Wolf rolled his eyes. "Nice to see you are well . . . brother."

"I disowned our relation. The name's Mr. Z."

Brother? They are brothers?

Talon glazed over the bodyguards, "I see dumb and dumber remain at your side as loyal pets. Can't find better help these days, huh?"

Mr. Z was about to speak, but the guard holding Phoenix yelped. He released Phoenix's mouth, revealing blood dripping from his index finger. Phoenix jerked his head backward bashing it into the lackey's nose. He squirmed free of his grip and jabbed him in the face. The buffoon stumbled back, falling into the other who tried to catch him.

As they struggled to get stable, Mr. Z turned to Phoenix. "Talon, I had not realized that you were traveling with company such as Phoenix Reinhard?"

"That makes it appear we are friends. And we're not." Phoenix stared at the so-called "Lone Wolf."

"What's that mean for you?" asked Talon.

"If he's here, I can safely assume he wants his dearest sword back?"

"Was a biography written about my life?"

"Good deductive reasoning. That is indeed why we have come and unless you have nothing better to say, we would like to get back to our search." Talon stared down his brother.

"To save you the trouble, it's no longer on the premises. I had it transferred to the City of Assassins the other day." Phoenix felt despair strike his gut.

"If that is true, then we shall take our leave. Let's go, Phoenix."

"Not quite. He is worth money, making him valuable. But you . . . you're becoming a burden. I think it's time to rid the taint from my family line."

Phoenix stepped forward. "Over my dead body."

"I'll receive my coins whether you are delivered alive or dead. That is your choice."

Talon studied the room. The facts and observations swarmed his head: *shaft, cables, rusty, brother, velocity of the initial force.* He absorbed his surroundings, becoming one with them, and proceeded to take action. He swiftly retrieved a dagger and chucked it at a cord suspending the ventilation shaft in the air.

Mr. Z began laughing, "You are becoming more and more worthless every time—" The moment the dagger made contact, the cord snapped, releasing the duct from the ceiling. It shot down with extreme force, slamming against Mr. Z. The impact knocked him from his feet and against the far wall. His goons retaliated.

"Phoenix, tend to them! The safe is almost cracked . . ."

"Does it matter? My sword is no longer here," his voice raged as something inside him sparked. "The sole reason we are here is because you are a rotten criminal helping yourself to his savings!" The two henchmen started stampeding toward Phoenix.

"I plan on swiping gold, but that's not it."

Time for arguing was finished. The henchmen lunged for Phoenix, but he skillfully slid from their grasps. He grabbed one man's head, kneeing him in his face. He reached over to the small of his back, gripping his pants and spun him around twice, releasing on the third spin. The guard's body hit the wall, leaving a dent. The other goon elbowed Phoenix in the back of the head, knocking him off balance. He then body slammed him. His entire weight plummeted Phoenix onto the floor. He tried to roll him off, but it was futile.

Struggling, Phoenix groaned, "Talon, hurry up! I can't handle, *ugh,* the weight." He felt his lungs trying to inflate only to absorb nothing.

"Hold them for a bit longer."

Phoenix could feel the pain of the pressure spreading through his body. His eyes flared. He forced himself off the ground slowly, lifting the lackey with him. Suddenly a burst of energy surged throughout him and he brushed the man aside. He slid his fingers around his neck and chucked him as far as possible. The henchman slid across the tile, past his partner who started running toward Phoenix yet again.

He attempted to grapple him, but Phoenix plowed his fist straight into his abdomen. The energy of the punch caused the man to freeze and cough blood. Fist after fist, Phoenix impaled the man's stomach. He swiftly roundhouse kicked him, his jaw colliding with the floor. Phoenix kicked the body away from him as the other came charging.

Talon was at the keyboard, still murmuring aloud while listening to the fight behind him: "If I just place that number here, and then change this to that . . . That's it!" He exclaimed as one of the apes bashed against the vault, leaving another imprint. Stunned, Talon hit the key to open the door. Air hissed through the seams as it gradually separated. Phoenix approached Talon with anger in his eyes, but he was too preoccupied with his success. Talon slipped through when the space was wide enough.

He frantically scanned the room. From wall to wall, shelves were brimming with coins: bronze, silver, gold, and even platinum. Amongst the mountains of money, random documents and bags sat upon and in between. *All holding valuable merchandise,* thought Talon. He rummaged through a few of the sacks before Phoenix grabbed him by the back of his jacket.

"Why do you prefer the hands on method always? If you cannot tell I am busy . . ."

"Answers. Now."

"What do you want to know? These coins are not my reason for coming . . ."

"You have been *lying* to me this entire time. Now to discover this master thief is your brother? Sibling rivalry?"

Talon struggled free from Phoenix's grip. "My life story is

mine alone. I came here for something of personal value, and yes, I've been here before. Attempted to get what's mine, but his pets always stopped me. That's why I brought you along, to handle those beasts. But none of that matters, my treasures are not here . . ."

"That's correct," stated Mr. Z limping into the vault. "After the third attempt, I realized the object of your determination. I had it accompany his sword on its travels to the City of Assassins."

"Bastard! I cannot believe I once considered us family."

"No need to worry yourself about that ever again. I'll give you a choice. A, you can leave safely, empty-handed. Or B, my alarm will be triggered and waves of my men will pulverize you where you stand."

Phoenix nudged Talon, "We should leave. Neither of our objects still resides here. There is no need to fight our way out."

Talon tore apart his brother with his stare, "I wish . . . we never left. I'll make you pay for all you have done. Be sure of that."

"I'll be waiting for that day," Mr. Z laughed pointing at the exit. "Now if you would, please use the door this time."

CHAPTER 13

Eric and Crystal sat by the horses watching clouds float by as they heard the crunching of rubble beneath the soles of boots. They both leapt to their feet, ready to brawl any scum that threatened them. Fortunately, it was only Phoenix and Wolf stumbling their way. Both of their shoulders relaxed, even though the tension with Wolf was still present. Crystal examined Phoenix. The eagerness in her face vanished.

"Where's your sword? Didn't we just clean that outfit? Can't you watch a battle from afar at least once?"

"You sound like his mother. Keep this act going and you may start wrinkling," chuckled Eric nudging her.

Phoenix shot a menacing glance at Wolf. "Blame Talon for the mess, and for why I'm unequipped."

"Was I supposed to know my brother had this planned?"

"Talon?" questioned Eric. "Who in the Protectors' names is Talon?"

Talon's hand shot into the air. "How was I to know they had been moved?"

Phoenix was about to argue until Eric spoke over them, "Either way, it's no longer here. Did you at least learn of where it is?"

"The package should have arrived at the City of Assassins by now," answered Talon.

"Convenient. Saves us time hence that is our destination anyway. Let's leave this rat filled town," hurried Eric, leaving the group and mounting his horse. "I've wanted to leave as we arrived."

"Is that where we are headed to next? Or are there other destinations between then?" Wolf strolled to their carriage.

"We plan on stopping at Flores first then . . ." Crystal stopped, realizing whom she was speaking with. "Wait, what? Who said you may accompany us?"

"That offer was not made by me," stated Phoenix glaring at him. "What makes you think I'd allow you to join my team after what just happened? You have proven you are not one to trust and barely worth calling an ally."

"No one on this *team* possesses the intelligence that I do. Or the skills. My intellect is immeasurable. I will easily become an asset on your journey."

"Right, and I'm a descendant of Zorumaka, able to level cities with fire. That sounds like a bunch of hogwash," called Eric. Phoenix listened to them banter. Before he had a chance to speak, Talon cut the conversation short. "Crystal, may we have a minute?"

In disbelief, she turned to Phoenix who nodded his head. Throwing her hands in the air, she joined Eric.

"I would like to speak with you, alone."

"We're alone. Go ahead."

"I-I'm sorry . . . that I didn't reveal my true identity."

The apology shocked him. "Why hide it? Are you a fugitive?"

"Names can kill. They have power. More power than you and I can control. Which makes them a dangerous weapon. Hence my code name—Lone Wolf."

"Power? Power for whom?"

"Anyone. My brother, the Brotherhood . . . Whoever is collecting money."

"The Brotherhood? You've mentioned them before. Who are they?"

"Huh? What? Never heard of them?" He shook his head.

"It's a band of deadly thieves—wait, hold on, this is off topic. I just wanted you to be aware that there was a reason behind my deception. Does this not reflect the reason behind your name?"

"My name is my name: Phoenix. Same goes for Crystal and Eric."

Talon glanced at him, eyes wide. Almost like he had a complete change in personality, he reached out his palm. "It's my pleasure to meet you, Phoenix Reinhard. My name is Talon Zaccaro."

Without a word, Phoenix firmly grasped his hand. Observing his new member, he announced loud enough for the eavesdroppers up front to hear, "You may join us until we reach the city. On arrival, we separate. Agreed?"

"Understood," nodded Talon, grinning.

Phoenix watched as Crystal motioned for him to hurry. "I plan on staying in the carriage for this portion of the ride. I don't fully trust him."

"Why allow him to come along?" asked Eric.

"There is . . . a mysteriousness. He will prove useful, but I would be foolish to leave my back exposed."

In the carriage, the quietest of creaks echoed. Talon barely locked eye contact with Phoenix, who had no intentions of making conversation either. Crystal and Eric played games to keep themselves entertained. Three days of little stopping passed before Talon became stir crazy. The horses were slowed down to a halt. They were tied tightly to the nearest tree, while Talon jetted away.

"Sundown the ride leaves with or without you," Eric shouted after him. Crystal and Phoenix decided to spar a bit, while Eric climbed up the nearest tree to take a nap on the branches.

Phoenix positioned himself facing her. "Sparring is the most basic form of combat and there will come a time when there is no weapon in sight. Let us practice some techniques and we will move on to weapons."

Eric watched the two of them start throwing fists at one

another. Crystal barely dodged his swings, until one almost made contact. Luckily, Phoenix stopped his fist inches from her nose. It continued the same way, except for when Phoenix spiced the show up with roundhouse kicks or when he accidentally connected. Eric thought back to when he first witnessed them train. Brett was in his arms. He started drifting away to the memory.

Eric suddenly woke up as he almost fell from his tree. He scanned his surroundings; the sky was orange. *Nighttime is approaching,* he thought. Crystal and Phoenix were still training, but she was breathing heavier now. They held their weapons high, ready for the next round. Dark marks covered her body. *Phoenix isn't taking this session lightly.* He checked the carriage in search of Talon, but he was nowhere in sight. Bored, Eric decided to be nosey and find what he was up to.

A mile or so from their location, Eric finally found him. He was standing amidst trees and a giant boulder. Talon's arms crossed his chest with a dagger in each hand. His eyes were closed, almost as if he was meditating. As Eric stepped closer, he moved. Talon back flipped onto the boulder, landing in a perfect squat. He released both daggers into the canopies of each tree diagonal from him. The daggers flew into the leaves, suddenly releasing more daggers from the branches, three from each side. He quickly curled into a ball on the boulder as the six daggers shot right past him, crisscrossing in the space above his head. They all landed on the opposite side of view from Eric.

Eric was astounded. *If Talon had remained standing, he would have been shredded apart. I wonder what the point of this exercise is.* He circled the scene to peer around the boulder. The daggers released from the trees hit a bull's-eye in six different spots. Amazed and dumbfounded, Eric returned to his friends, hoping he was able to stay hidden.

The two battle partners were still staying strong despite their energy rapidly disappearing. Crystal fell to her knees, exhausted and breathless. Placing his sword into his sheath, Phoenix helped her stand. She clumsily fell into his arms. They stood there, arms wrapped around each other. Eric walked behind them, coughing violently. Crystal sighed in response.

"Did I interrupt again?" asked Eric, looking at them with a puppy-dog face.

"No, Eric," she whispered walking away. "You never interrupt anything."

Eric happily patted Phoenix on the back as he headed toward the horses. Phoenix looked into the distance, seeing Talon making his way to them. When the four of them were settled, Eric prepared the horses for travel and began the trip to Flores once more. Phoenix decided he wanted time alone with Crystal, much to Eric's dismay. Crystal traded seats with Talon, placing him on a horse beside his new friend. Most of the ride consisted of Eric and Talon spitting insult after insult, and arguing about frivolous problems.

"This is the outcome of placing sarcastic, stubborn people together." Phoenix and Crystal listened to each conversation and the remarks that were made. The creativity of their retorts kept their attention, but none of it truly caught their interest.

"The side of a barn would be a hard target for you to hit. Everything that happens is just an accident!"

"Coming from a true accident himself, that doesn't hold much value. Besides, my ability was observed just the other evening. You were a witness to my talent. The targets were hit perfectly as I am sure you recall."

Caught by surprise, Eric choked on his reply. "Tha-that's right, you best look forward."

"Much better view than your ugly mug only a mother could tolerate!"

"Jealousy is an endearing quality for children, Talon. Don't be distraught your face doesn't match this defined jaw and most wondrous features."

"My mind only has enough energy to focus on how badly I lust you."

207

"As long as my marriage is known, lust until your heart's content."

"Speak a little louder since your head's shoved far into where the sun don't shine. Makes it difficult to hear one's own thoughts."

"What are you referring to?" asked Eric suspiciously.

"I catch the way your eyes find their way to Phoenix; the Forgotten Language is harder to decipher. It's sly, unnoticeable, almost seemingly an accident—to a person of ignorance. Your jealousy of Crystal is as noticeable as your ego."

Eric, his mouth half agape, became quiet. The galloping of the hooves filled the void where his words should have gone. The beating pounded in his ears as if his heart was searching for a way to escape. To hide. His mouth opened to speak, but he only exhaled.

Maybe that was not as tactful as I thought to believe. Talon pondered whether to console him or allow him to mope, but decided on the latter. It was already said, why apologize?

"Only . . . only you see that ri-right? No one else?"

"No one else."

"This stays between us. I love Brett. I love him with all my heart . . ."

The enormous tension traveled back to the cargo hold where the eavesdroppers felt uncomfortable, knowing that this conversation was not to be heard by them specifically.

"We mustn't reveal that we heard this. The team needs to stay united," cautioned Phoenix.

"How will you handle being around him with what was just learned?"

Phoenix didn't reply. He had no answer. He drifted away from her gaze, staring at the wooden gate. Guilt ate at him from the inside, making him flush with embarrassment. The rest of the ride to Flores continued on just like that, awkward silence between them all.

CHAPTER 14

Talon, on the verge of another breakdown, took interest in the road before them. He observed the path, soaking in the colors around him from the environment: *dirt road, blue skies, uneven grass lengths.* He peered at Eric from his perimeter. *One hand on harness, eyelids hung lazily over his view. Yawning, forcing his head to stay upright. Tapping his free foot impatiently, waiting for something new. Tired, needs to rest.* His examination continued until a town approached on the horizon. Excitement rose between the two of them as they closed the distance to Flores. Eric quickly yelled back to the others announcing their arrival. When the buildings were close enough to describe, the two boys could see the destruction left behind.

The entire city lay in ruins. Every single structure was destroyed. They had crumbled to the ground years ago, moss festering upon the remains. Piles of rubble from collisions were scattered amongst overgrown weeds. Decaying logs were strewn across the ground. And the smell. The smell was the worst. The stench of death suffocated all that it encompassed. Eric settled the horses at the demolished entrance gate.

"'Tis a shame," mumbled Talon. "Before this was considered one of the five great cities, there was no wealth circulating within this town. After the Protectors deemed it with such a title, they funneled coin into the streets. With such an increase, King Hammond built an enormous and exquisite wall surrounding his city."

"I don't see any sight of a barrier that had been built besides this small pile of rubbish," responded Eric, kicking a mound of rocks.

A few pieces bounced against Talon's feet and he picked up the clump of cement. "It was encrusted with diamonds. Grave robbers and thieves seemed to have picked the land clean."

"Thanks for the history lesson, professor."

"Enough." Phoenix glanced between them, his skin flushing as the dialogue from before played in his ears. "Grab your weapons—anything could be lying in wait."

As Crystal attached her hoops onto her belt, sparkling caught her eye. "Talon, your weapons haven't been sprinkled with Bright Light."

"That sparkly glitter on the steel of your weapons?"

She nodded. "That's the sole offense we have against the X-creatures."

"The monsters we spoke about that had you trembling with fear?"

"If you were there, you would understand."

"Looks like you all will have to protect me," joked Talon, retrieving two daggers.

"I'd rather see you undergo transformation and become one of those beasts," hissed Eric.

Phoenix sharply spoke before Talon could respond. "That's *enough*; on the field is not a time for an argument. We heard enough of them during the ride . . ." They all froze. "Ne-never mind. Crystal! I heard Danny passed the samples we collected along to our possession?" Desperately wanting to escape this group, she went in search for their rewards from Luminar. She returned moments later with a singular tube.

Phoenix took a hold of it, asking for Talon's daggers. "These specific daggers are the only two that will be treated with Bright Light. Do *not* throw them carelessly, understood?" As he responded, the mineral was sprinkled onto metal, coating it with their magic. The now damp items began to shimmer and shine.

"What would we do if, theoretically, these daggers go missing?"

Eric grumbled.

Capping the vial, Phoenix passed it into Talon's possession. "Now that your safety is back in your own hands, let us get down to business. From the readings about this city, I gather the castle is toward the back past the villages. Its natural defense was the dense forest, but now . . . it's more of a swamp."

"Flores was recorded to have been mutilated two weeks after Luminar was destroyed. Just as Luminar, this city's population dropped to a complete zero with *no* survivors. No one in Osiren could bear entering the gates after its destruction. The ones brave enough never returned to tell the tale. Rumors say the place is cursed."

Crystal felt a shiver crawl up her spine. Feeling the eeriness, Phoenix told Talon to knock it off.

The four of them traveled through the remains of the lovely city, examining the scenery. Talon remarked time had not been merciful to the place. He thrived off the history that surrounded them. Every brick, every blade of grass had a story and he felt like he was traveling into the past. They passed one particularly disheveled building. Walking by, he witnessed its destruction. *Crumbled, scattered. Blown up.* He peered closer. *Scuff marks. From explosion? Possibly.* Amongst the rubble, Talon caught sight of shattered bones. Most were cracked, while some remained fossilized at the scene. *Wreckage trapped villagers. Marks from attempted escape? Angle too out of range. Came from outside—helpers. Survival? Discoloration of wall. Time? Rain? Blood.*

He paused, inhaling deeply. Almost like rewinding time, he was able to watch the entire scene from start to finish. Mercenaries bombarded the building from within, causing the entire side to crumble, trapping innocent bystanders running for their lives. As they begged for help, other villagers tried to claw their way to them, digging their nails into the cement pieces. But the mercenaries did what they were paid to do: slaughter them.

Talon broke from his rewind, snapping back to reality. He caught up to the group, much to Eric's disappointment. He continued to explain the chaos that occurred, but Phoenix had enough of the reminders.

"Talon, stop. I've *experienced* this first hand. I don't need explanations. Or to revisit." He turned to him, showing more despair than anger. "These people deserved more than this. Being here is wrong. This entire place should be resurrected as remembrance of the fallen, not as a symbol of destruction."

"I-I did not . . ."

"I still don't understand why someone would do this. How much power could these emeralds really possess?" asked Eric. "Are they planning on releasing the curse again?"

Phoenix glanced at him, only to turn back to their path. "It doesn't matter. We cannot let whoever is against us collect the remaining ones and cause this damage to Cosarave and Zannala."

Continuing into the remains of the city, the group came across a body. One that was . . . fresh. The skin was stretched over the bones and bugs had made its orifices their homes, but it was less than a month old. The color of the skin was pale from the lack of fresh oxygen and blood, but the overall pigment was darker. The body lay there contorted, with limbs in positions not normally possible. Whoever or whatever did this had claws. The body was raked aggressively from every angle.

The thick, silent aura around them was disturbed as a loud crack pierced the atmosphere. Phoenix took stance in front of the team, facing the direction of the noise. One hand gripped his hilt tightly, while the other hovered in front of the group.

"This is supposed to be an empty town?" whispered Crystal.

"Dead things should remain dead," shouted Talon chucking a dagger toward the nearest pile. It made a tiny *bing* and rebounded back to them.

"What did Phoenix tell you?" yelled Eric.

In that split second, a black shadow sprung through the air, snatching the dagger from its recoil. The thing landed on two feet, tossing the weapon back at them. Talon let his knife slide across the dying dirt, eyeing up the monstrosity that stood before them. Slowly retrieving it, he gave a sly look toward Eric's smug face.

"This isn't like any of the X-creatures we faced at Luminar…Wh-what are you?" questioned Crystal.

The creature stood about six feet on two legs. Four limbs hung low stemming from its abdomen. A long mane erupted from its skull, flowing all the way down its back. Menacingly hunched over, its long thick tail swung, sweeping up dirt with every rotation. With a dog snout, rabbit ears, and sharp claws on each paw, this abomination was terrifying. Staying completely motionless, it was devouring them with its sunken eyes.

The creature hesitated before howling. The vicious sound traveled through them, piercing their stomachs with anxiety. The tone, on the other hand, did not match its expression. It was friendly, lighthearted. As it died down, Phoenix took a step forward, but the creature hopped back. Motioning its head toward the right, it scampered away in that direction.

Crystal looked at Phoenix, "I think . . . it's friendly . . . and wants us to follow. What should we do?"

"Friendly?" argued Eric. "That thing was not made for friendly."

"He tossed my dagger back to me, basically rearming me," Talon analyzed the situation. "His coat was covered in blood. One of its claws was chipped and the way it limped—it has been in a few scuffles recently. Which could explain the rotting flesh we found. Or possibly why no one leaves Flores."

"That poor thing couldn't have been here all alone this whole time? Must be really lonely," Crystal said, oddly worried about its existence.

"I would assume they are impotent. Not that it would matter since we haven't come across a similar creature. If it were violent, it would have attacked on sight. And that body would have been picked clean. I think Crystal may be correct."

Phoenix thought for a minute. "It's clear that it's some form of X-creature. If that stands true, the emerald would no longer be here. We have to find out what it knows. Be cautious; this could be a trap."

They chased after the abomination's trail, passing clusters of bones. Death littered the city. Torn fabrics were still among the remains of the departed. Once they caught up to the X-creature at a dome shaped building, it ran into the broken structure. The place was almost as wide as the entire perimeter of Flores. Phoenix caught a glimpse of the Forgotten Language above the entrance. *Was this the castle? Or maybe a worship house for the Protectors?* The interior was as broken as the rest of the city. The group was in a singular square room with nothing but shattered glass. Anything the place had held was either stolen by looters or disintegrated.

Waiting for them to take notice, the abomination sat in the corner of the room, its stare glowing in the dark. Sensing they became aware of its presence, he quickly hopped through a gigantic hole in the floor. It was not a structural design, but more of an accident—or maybe on purpose. Eric and Crystal both began to protest, arguing these types of stories do not end well, but they followed their fearless leader nonetheless. Jumping into the depths of the unknown, their feet pounded against the moist dirt as they made contact. Torches immediately lit up across the room, brightening their surroundings.

"An underground basement?" Eric checked the corners. "There's nothing but dirt and decaying plants. Why the hell did that mutant lead us here?"

"Wait . . . Where . . . where did it go?" Crystal searched the small, enclosed space.

Phoenix stepped forward only to be pushed back by a mysterious force. He slowly rose from the ground as a huge light flashed in the middle of the room. It illuminated all four corners.

When the light finally dimmed, it began morphing. It turned into the glowing figure of a man. He was wearing bright blue armor and a helmet that had wings sprouting on both sides. The man spoke in a deep, mystical voice.

"I am the spiritual protector of the city of Flores and thy emerald. I am called Hammond. Why do thou trespass?"

"Spiritual protector, as in a phantom?" Crystal whimpered, placing herself behind Phoenix.

"Hammond? *The* Hammond of Flores? You were the first king of this city," Talon blurted, more intrigued than scared.

"Correct," announced the spirit. "I was once the king eons ago. The very first."

Talon stewed in his excitement as Eric spoke: "Why are you still around? Shouldn't you be . . . dead?"

"My soul was split before leaving Teague. One half combining with the emerald to remain vigilant in its safe-keeping. I trusted my sons nevertheless."

"Hammond of Flores . . . Wow . . . I have many questions for you. You fought alongside the Protectors? You experienced—"

"Enough!" The booming voice vibrated the walls. "Why is it that you stand before me?"

The voice quieted the group. Phoenix slowly looked between them before speaking: "The four of us have come here to do only what you have done for centuries. We want to extract the emerald and keep it safe."

Hammond's eyes lit up. "Removing the jewel from its resting place and my protection?"

"The people—the ones from before—will make another appearance. They will not stop before it's in their grasp. They will take what they failed to last time."

"Yes, I recall their visit. Not many journey this far, but I remember their presence. Misguided are their views with a leader that was born not one of the same, but regarded as such. Their goal was not accomplished. I will stop them once more."

Eric barked, "They have armies, uh, Your Highness."

"Why shall I trust outsiders, none of which were born of my blood or village?" asked Hammond.

"You are an all-powerful spirit and legend. Do you not possess the capability to interpret if our intentions are pure?" questioned Talon.

The spirit remained still, his face emotionless. "Each of you is troubled by a horrible past. The pain scars your faces. Dangerous futures are present for everyone in this room." He turned to Crystal. "Madam, you have the blood of the ancients, ones with whom I share kinship. How nice it feels to sense such a bond to my presence. I even see you carry on your person the moon blades. One of your elder's most cherished weapons." He gestured to her metal rings on her hip.

His gaze traveled to Eric, who avoided eye contact. "The obstacles that lie in your future are heartfelt and heavy. Remember the ones you lost and gained as you journey on."

Talon stood firmly as the focus turned to him. "As intelligent and tongue-in-cheek as you are, the past haunts you. Running from your problems create more in the end. There is no coincidence that you are traveling with these others."

Last but not least, he spoke to Phoenix: "I have no words to describe what experiences you have undergone, and less to explain what shall be accomplished by your hands. My words are not needed to understand this. Remember what defines a person is not what they have done or will do. It's *why* they do it. The strongest metal is forged in the hottest fire."

Hammond regained his composure as he processed what he experienced through each of their perspectives. "I believe that your words stand true. Even with my blessing, you may not proceed without passing three trials that have been placed to safeguard my treasure. Before I go, the presence mentioned earlier—the ones I shall never forget—have never removed themselves from my residence. With that, the first trial will begin . . ." He instantly vanished, leaving the room just as dark as before.

Each of them gazed at one another. Talon's stare stayed locked onto Crystal. "Cupcake, what did he mean 'blood of the ancients' and a 'bond to his presence'?"

"None of that meant anything to me . . ."

"More importantly, did you hear the last bit?" loudly whispered Eric. "He said he could feel the intruders still. Does that mean they are here?"

"I have not noticed any movement since we arrived," answered Talon.

"Maybe he's confusing it with that X-creature. There is that fresh corpse," Phoenix pointed out.

Before anyone could respond, five iridescent blue orbs formed in the middle of the room. Each one shone vibrantly with a mixture of hues. Creating a horizontal line in front of them, each sphere grew to form a translucent man. The men appeared to be average citizens. The spirit's voice boomed overhead.

"Each man has a riddle; each riddle must be answered to proceed."

"These men . . ." whispered Talon. "They are wearing the insignia of Flores." On the top right of their shoulders, a small diamond shape was pinned to their clothing. Each diamond had a wing on both sides, similar to Hammond's helmet.

"They are supposed to represent a diamond shard in honor of the Protectors' donation and their expensive wall that was built. The wings are for how Flores flew into battle at a moment's notice and soared to victory. At first the pin was made of real shards, only for the King and family. But once the pride for their city hit all the citizens they made forgeries in honor of their greatness."

"Again with the history lesson," sighed Eric.

Talon ignored him. "The way the pins are shimmering means they are the originals." He took a minute looking between the spirits. "They are brothers, or close family members . . . these are Hammond's sons. He made his sons protect the emerald along with him . . ."

Crystal gasped, "He doomed his own family to life of servitude?"

"We are not here to judge his actions. Without doing so, there's a chance the mercenaries would have gotten the emerald on the first try." Phoenix bit his lip. "Let's focus on these riddles."

"Riddles are child's play! Sir, all the way to the left," called Eric pointing at the spirit. "Speak your phrase!"

The spirit hovered forward. "I have oceans without water, cities with no people, and mountains with no elevations. What am I?"

Eric gawked at him. "Oceans with no water? Um . . . a board game?"

The spirit shot a beam of light that traveled through Eric. "Incorrect. Three chances remaining."

"What in Teague was that?"

"What do you mean by three chances left?" asked Crystal, counting the spirits lined up.

Hammond spoke: "Each of you may answer any of the four questions throughout this trial, but once you answer incorrectly, you are silenced until the entire trial is completed."

"And the beam was for?" angrily asked Eric

"It eliminates the chance of you answering."

"Which means only us three can continue to guess," stated Phoenix glancing at the others.

"I can do this," said Talon stepping forward. "An ocean with no water? Cities with no men? Hm . . ." He stood thinking, until he snapped his fingers. "A map? Sounds right."

The spirit nodded. Turning back into a bubble, it flung away from them into the back wall, leaving a blue stain where it made contact.

"Nice job," applauded Phoenix, patting him on the back. "Who's next?"

The next spirit stepped forward, and recited its riddle. "I have the strength to heal and power to end. I am both life and destruction. I once was the symbol of protection, but now the terror of death. What am I?"

Talon thought for a few minutes, "Give me a hard one. You are—"

"You don't get to go twice in a row! The answer is—" Eric spoke, but nothing was said. He aggressively tried to pronounce words, but it was useless.

"Anyway, the answer is necromancers. They had the ability to restore people to full health. Which was largely forgotten the moment they truly understood the massiveness of their talents. That's when they learned how to bring people back from the dead. Such a terrible fortune."

The spirit also transformed back into an orb and followed the same path as its predecessor. It left a mark right above the other one. The third moved forward.

"I appear once my opposite leaves. She is day and I am night. I watch over Teague with a million others. Kyrudorous was fond of my mysterious ways. What am I?

Talon went to answer, but Crystal spoke first: "May I have a chance to answer?" she asked earnestly. "You're . . . the moon!"

The spirit repeated the process of its brothers, splattering against the far wall. "Nice one, Cupcake, how'd you know?"

"Well, back at Luminar, Danny said these were called the moon blades. Since these were Kyrudorous's favorite weapon . . . makes sense?"

The next spirit spoke: "I am the beginning. My essence is the foundation to life. Now I remain as a failed deity. The sibling of mine had done more than I ever shall. Who am I?"

Crystal mumbled, "The Protector Zorumaka?"

A jet of energy zoomed through her. "Incorrect, two chances remaining."

"The mentioning of a sibling and deities . . ."

"Neither of the Protectors existed at the dawn of time," responded Talon. "Which means the correct answer is the Creator?"

The spirit repeated the process of the others, splashing against the wall as an orb. "Odd, not once have I ever come across texts mentioning a sibling of the Creator?" He continued pondering as the last spirit hovered into position.

"I possess the strength to move mountains, but the restraint to not. I made the greatest sacrifice that has been mistranslated through the years. My name will live far beyond my own being, carrying hope and courage to generations. Who am I?"

"Care to answer, Phoenix?" asked Talon.

"Perhaps the riddles should be left for you to solve."

Talon shrugged. "The names that which you speak . . . only the Protectors have survived the centuries. Out of the two, one was an elemental caster. Kyrudorous could twist the mind as if it was a toy and her brother held the ability to shatter Kairos. He split the mass of land, creating the separate country of EverCrest. My hesitation is on his sacrifice that's been altered. The answer is Zorumaka." The spirit followed suit. Now that all the spirits had been answered, the room became black once more, besides the blue splatters on the wall that continued to emit energy.

"Th-this . . . I can talk? Sweet Protectors, thank you!" exclaimed Eric.

"I enjoyed the quiet," laughed Phoenix.

Talon chuckled, "Now I'm sure you are happy that I came along. I knew I would become a necessary tool."

"Don't get a big ego now," spat Eric. "Still have time to make a mistake."

"The only mistake I made is when I chose not to kill you when I had the opportunity."

"Powerful threat for a scrawny man—can you back that up with those little daggers?"

The spiritual protector appeared in front of them, illuminating the room with his energy. Standing in front of the group, he loudly announced, "Congratulations, you have passed the first test. If you would follow me, I'll lead you to the next trial." Hammond transformed into an orb and shot through the middle of all his son's spots. Immediately the blue spots on the wall began connecting, stretching blue shimmering lights to each other. Once they were all in contact, the insides of the outline flashed and dispersed, leaving an exit into the next room.

The four of them cautiously walked through the hole. When Phoenix stepped into the new room, torches engulfed in flames along the walls. The light revealed a door on the opposite side, but there was nothing in between. His heart began racing as he looked in the vast abyss. Pupils dilating, the flames on the torches danced around the room, taunting him. As the rest traveled through, their feet on the ground crackled in his ears. Backing against the wall, he let the others step forward.

"A lot of repeating patterns. Blue orbs, darkness, and torches along the walls?" remarked Talon. "It's already becoming a bit tiresome."

"How are we supposed to cross?" questioned Crystal.

"Fly?" answered Eric, looking over the edge.

"Phoenix, do you—Phoenix? What's wrong?" She rushed over to him, watching his chest pump rapidly. Eric heard the worry in her voice and looked over. She touched Phoenix's shoulder, but he jerked away. "Phoenix? Can you hear me? What's happening?"

Listening to her speak, he fought against his will to make eye contact with her. Once he did, his body instantaneously relaxed. Seeing Eric join her side, he could have practically wept. Pushing off the wall, he grabbed onto both of them. "I thought you guys . . . I thought I was too late . . . I'm glad both of you are okay."

While they tried to console him, Talon shouted, "Almighty Hammond, what is the next trial?" He listened to his voice echo around the chasm. Almost like a trigger, a platform floated up, latching onto the ground they stood upon. He examined the magical land. "It appears pretty sturdy."

"Will you be okay to continue?" asked Eric with genuine care in his tone.

"What happened? What did you just experience?"

Phoenix regained his composure and nodded to his friends. Trying to avoid the questions, he moved past them and was the first to step onto the new platform. He walked toward the middle, stamping his feet against the dirt. Announcing it was safe, Crystal and Eric attempted to cross onto the hovering stone, but an invisible force kept them at bay.

"What the hell? Are we not as good as Phoenix to cross?" yelled Eric. He realized what he said, and responded, "Actually don't answer that . . . I hate this magic garbage. Should have gotten lost in history."

Hammond's voice again boomed overhead, "The second trial is as follows: one person may be on the platform at a time until they finish their challenge. Each of you must fight one of my creations to have the next platform rise from the depth."

"Your creation?" asked Phoenix.

As soon as Phoenix finished his sentence, a gust of dark mist swirled up from the depths of the room, revealing the same creature from before. It's long flowing mane waved around as it sharpened each of its claws.

"This is my creation, Lycanoid. When my soul parted, I was granted the ability to manipulate the emerald and all its power. I created the strongest guardian from its strength. I released my pack when the first invasion occurred and the emerald was disturbed from its slumber. Waves of energy were emitted, absorbing all matters of life force. Enough power was obtained to allow one of my children to live without the home of the emerald, the very one that led the way here. One shall be defeated by each to finish this trial."

"You manipulated powers that only the Creator should possess!" shouted Talon, marinating in an acute rage. "You are no purer than the curse the Protectors casted down on Teague. You are the darkness."

The monster reacted violently to Talon's remarks, snorting and growling wildly. It shot its deadly gaze at Phoenix. It crouched, placing two of its paws on the ground. Letting out a snarl, the abomination zoomed forward, stretching out its claws. Phoenix unsheathed both of his swords and stood there, waiting. When the two of them were in striking distance, the creature flung his claws, but Phoenix skillfully deflected each strike. It went into a frenzy, swiping without mercy. All four paws were clawing relentlessly.

Phoenix was able to block each strike. He slid back, quickly flipping his swords. He bluntly jabbed the end of each weapon against its chest. It created the distance he needed, but the creature showed no sign of harm. It attempted to grip Phoenix, but he whipped his swords around, slicing off two arms. The abomination released a roar and snatched away one of Phoenix's blades. Examining the weapon, the werewolf crushed it within its grasp. The metallic shards bounced around its hind legs.

Phoenix, astonished, jumped onto the creature, shoving his sword through its chest. The force of Phoenix's body weight made it fall to the ground. On top, Phoenix began shifting his sword, watching the steam from the minerals float into the air. The sizzling grew louder as it tried to get up, but all attempts failed. It swiped one last claw at Phoenix's face, making direct contact, but suddenly stopped struggling. Its eyes went dim and at once, the beast vaporized into black dust particles. Phoenix got up, feeling the blood collect around his chin.

"He broke my sword," he said looking down. "And it scuffed my clothes!"

"The X-wolf also left a nice little paw print across your mug," pointed out Eric.

"X-wolf?" questioned Crystal. "It fits. I suppose demonic beast is not in question?"

"We should test for rabies once we reach a clinic," chimed in Talon. "If you wish to not have scars, I suggest we clean those up. Oh, and we shouldn't honor this such obscure mash of nature by giving it a pet name . . . But my vote's for X-beast."

Phoenix smiled, completely ignoring the pain. Another

platform rose, connecting to the previous one. Phoenix tried to advance, but he was stopped. Noticing this, the rest of them came to his side. Crystal ripped some of her shirt and applied pressure to Phoenix's face. Talon asked who was going next. Eric glanced at the others and bravely stepped forward.

"What a hero," remarked Talon crossing his arms. "Don't let the X-beast give you rabies—if they have not already been acquired."

Eric took his stance, spear at his side, ready to rumble. He watched as another whirlwind of darkness spiraled onto the platform, releasing the second creature. This time, it had no patience. The creature came after him, shoving each claw in his direction. Eric smacked away each strike with his spear, keeping his distance as much as possible. Seeing the hopelessness, the creature jumped high into the air and crushed Eric beneath him. He tried to stay standing, but the weight was too much too hold. He was slowly lowered to his knees. The werewolf continuously swiped at his vest.

Quickly thinking, he fell to the ground and rolled out of the way fast enough to escape the pressure. He spun his spear, throwing it in a desperate attempt. The X-beast caught it in midair, tossing it aside. Before it realized the situation, Eric's foot came crashing forward. He kicked the creature square in the muzzle, knocking the X-beast off balance. It stumbled backward, falling over the ledge of the platform. Seconds later, Eric watched the black particles dance before him, followed by the next platform.

Talon ran onto the third one before Crystal had time to object. The next X-beast appeared as Talon whipped out his two magical daggers from his vest. While his metal clashed against the creature's claws, Phoenix had an uneasy feeling in the pit of his stomach. Examining his surroundings, he turned to the others.

"Do you feel like we are being watched?"

"Hammond sees all."

Crystal spoke, "No . . . No one else is here."

"You're being paranoid; who visits an abandon city?" responded Eric, watching the fight.

Phoenix shrugged off the feeling, but remember Hammond's words. The mercenaries . . . there's not really a chance they could be here, could they?

Talon was swiftly dodging each attempt by the X-beast. He glanced at his surroundings, and saw his chance. He flung one of his daggers toward the creature, attaching its tail to the ground. The beast struggled to free itself, howling in frustration. While it was distracted, Talon swiped his dagger across the abomination's throat, leaving a long laceration. He continued to nonchalantly spin with his weapon drawn while the monster evaporated into small bits.

As the last platform arrived, finally connecting them to the doorway, Crystal took a deep breath. "My turn now . . ."

Phoenix smiled at her, watching her walk toward the last piece of land. The moment her foot stepped onto the platform, the last creature appeared from the mist.

Crystal forcefully made the first move, flinging one of her rings at the creature. It circulated around the X-beast, cutting it on all sides, only to gently glide back into her hands. It roared in pain as its skin burned away. Crystal ran up toward it, releasing both rings. Each of them circled the beast on several orbits, slicing it repeatedly.

Once the barrage ended and before it had a chance to recover, Crystal spun her arm rapidly, letting the ring free on the third rotation. It spun right into the creature, rotating furiously, penetrating its fur deeper with every cycle. The demon clutched onto the weapon with all four paws, attempting to immobilize it. Bellowing a roar from deep within its chest, the thing hauled the chakram to the side. It took a few steps, only to fall forward. The vaporization process happened instantly, the monster disappearing before it reached the ground. Crystal's panicked expression changed to joy as she retrieved her weapon. She merely smiled at the others as Phoenix wrapped her in his arms.

"That was beyond brilliant! I knew you had it in you."

Eric hollered over Phoenix's shoulder, "Can we get back to the last trial, please? Have the lovey-dovey moment later."

Talon rolled his eyes as he approached the next entrance. "Hammond, present the last challenge. I think we shall prove worthy."

The spiritual voice bounced between the walls, "The next challenge is to merely pass through the remaining entrance and enter the resting chamber."

"That's all? I've been preparing for this moment my entire life," snickered Eric waltzing up to the open space. He tried to pass through, but his face slammed against an invisible barrier. "Another wall? *Really?* An entire lifetime stuck in this place and all you could come up with are force fields?"

"The last trial is the simplest, but yet the most challenging. The chosen must be the lightest of all."

Eric peered over to Crystal. "I'm sure you weigh the least. Go ahead."

"That's . . . that's not what he meant, Eric," said Phoenix.

Hammond spoke again: "Only a person with purest of hearts may enter through thy barrier."

"Knowledge, strength, and purity . . . they were the skills and morals your trial tested," noted Talon, questioning the spirit. There was no reply. He looked at Eric, placing his hands against the air. "Might as well stop trying; there is no way in Teague you will be allowed through."

"Try yourself, hot shot!"

"I am not attempting; I know I will be denied access. I am the furthest from being pure," laughed Talon.

"Well, we know the ones that will be able to proceed."

The couple glanced at one another and stepped forward. Crystal cautiously attempted to cross through, closing her eyes. Feeling nothing pressing against her, she reopened them to find herself on the other side. No one was surprised, but she still glowed in her purity. "I almost did not believe I would make it through! Glad my heart's a good one!"

"Or maybe you're just too innocent."

Crystal stepped backward, giving Phoenix space. Waiting for his arrival, she watched his chest rise as he made his way through. But his bold aura dispersed as he smacked against the magic. All eyes laid upon him in extreme disbelief.

Phoenix, flabbergasted, caught the stare of his peers. "Crystal, you're on your own for this one." Disappointed, she turned around, heading farther into the room.

I . . . was not able to enter. What does that mean? Are my dreams coming true? Am I actually losing my path . . .?

Hammond stood before her, glowing brighter than ever. "Congratulations, Crystal Thorn, you have passed all three trials. It has been shown this woman standing before me is honorable and of moral intentions. I shall bring forth the emerald of Flores. " A swirling white light spun around the spirit, forming a miniature tornado. As the whirlwind died down, Crystal was finally able to see it. A radiant, pink emerald floated upon a diamond-encrusted pedestal.

Speechless from the beautiful sight, she gently grasped the emerald with both hands. Immediately, a spiritual wave burst from the jewel. The magical barrier keeping the others out imploded on itself, creating a small fizzle before dissolving. While the others quickly gathered around her admiring their prize, her hands went numb. The coldness of this evil manifestation traveled along her skin, searching for something. An entrance. A way in to corrupt her— destroy her. The dark tendrils drilled into her bones, making her body ache; toes to teeth. The trance was interrupted once Phoenix tried to make contact with it. Crystal snapped free and pulled the emerald close to her breasts.

"We agreed they are not to be near you," she muttered.

Phoenix went to object, but a powerful explosion shook the entire structure. They covered their eyes and once they were able to see, they found Eric pulling his spear from the pedestal.

"We're *not* having another Luminar experience again. That one big monstrosity was terrifying enough to last a lifetime."

"I was not present, but I will take your word for value." Talon shook his head, imagining the X-beast three times larger. "Flores makes this two emeralds? Which leaves two more cities, since our opponents have Luminar's. I assume, though, we will make them our destination after our business in City of Assassins is finished."

"I agree, but we need to leave . . . There are more people here than just us."

"Phoenix, stop with that ominous talk; the only other things are ghosts," Eric grumbled, giving him a glare.

"Fine. Either way, we are departing."

Talon spoke, "You are not wrong. We have been followed since we arrived, breathing and footsteps could be heard in the distance."

"Why didn't you mention this earlier?"

"It was not of concern. I mean . . . now it is."

They all took a moment to digest the information. In a silent agreement, they decided a hasty retreat was in order. The four of them traveled back the way they came until they heard rustling in the strength chamber. With a dead stop, Phoenix examined his surroundings. He unsheathed his sword, pointing the tip toward the danger laying in the darkness. Startled, Eric and Crystal both prepared as they watched Talon arm himself.

"Come forth, we know you're here!"

Phoenix listened for a response, but footsteps greeted his command instead. Two people stepped out of the shadows, a man and woman. The man was shirtless excluding the silver chains wrapping around his body. Scars were etched across his entire chest. His black hair was spiked up in the front, but long enough on the sides to cover his ears. Hiding his darker skin tone were light brown baggy pants that were patched with discolored pieces of cloth. Standing upon the ground without shoes, he practically hid behind the female's presence.

She demanded an entirely different atmosphere around her person. Strict, strong, ruthless. Her hair was tied into a tight ponytail, not a single strand out of place. Her pristine, black skin radiated under her purple halter-top that barely covered her abdomen. Wearing the same style of pants as her friend, her bottoms were much darker and without any repairs. Pointed shoes covered her feet as she firmly stared down the group.

The woman spoke: "Thank you for assisting us through those treacherous trials. We have been waiting for someone to be able to complete the remaining one." The man stayed behind her, watching the scene from afar. "Since the little game is finished, we would appreciate if you were to ever so kindly hand the emerald to us. We would not want this to get ugly."

"Too late for that," remarked Talon under his breath.

The man lashed out, giving Talon a deadly snarl. "Do not disrespect my lady!"

"Whoa, calm down there, sir," uttered Eric.

"Keep your dog on his leash; we don't need more disease," smirked Talon, peering at Eric.

The woman raised her arm motioning him to settle. "Remain in control." She turned back to them. "We want the emerald. Do not put up a fight that you shall not win."

"We fought beasts before; what makes you different?" teased Eric, but Talon tapped him on his shoulder, pointing forward. Dozens of men and women marched behind them. All of the soldiers were identical. With the women leading, they marched inside the room, blocking their path.

"Gauri, what is our course of action?" asked the man. "They are awaiting your command."

"This is your final warning. Now or never," demanded Gauri, staring Phoenix straight in his eyes.

Phoenix took a deep breath. "Run!" Without a word, the tiny militia approached to greet them. Each of the warriors began attacking as soon as they were in arms reach. Talon evaded each strike, while Crystal used her rings to ward them away. Eric went to behead one of the men, but Phoenix grabbed the spear in mid-swing.

"These fighters are defenseless, basically cannon fodder. Don't you dare think about striking them down."

"What should we do then?"

He thought fast, and bluntly knocked each one of them back with the hilt of his sword. "Keep your blades down, strike with a blunt end!"

Crystal examined her rings for a side without a blade, but failed. She hurriedly hooked them to her waist as one of the men made a dash for her. She slid from his path, tripping him by accident. He toppled into a few others, causing a pathway to appear. She instantly quickened her pace to the exit, hoping the others followed behind her.

Talon noticed first and followed her lead. He hopped onto one of the warrior's head, and started treading the mob of people. Phoenix watched as he smashed his hilt against a few more skulls. He called to Eric to join as he escaped toward the exit. Eric was trying to slam people away as bluntly as possible, but they started to grab onto the base of the spear. He wildly whipped the spear around, making the passengers fly across the room—most falling to their demise. When he heard his name, he began making his leave.

They carefully made their way out of the obstacle course they had conquered. Helping each other climb up through the hole, they escaped from the temple. Ignoring all that was around them, their surroundings passed in a blur. As they reached their steeds, they mounted them in haste. Eric whipped the horses in a sprint. The team had their necks angled to watch the little army chasing them.

Phoenix watched from the back of the carriage. The warriors hollered after them, until a dark streak jetted into the crowd. Their hurrahs changed to screams. The X-beast devoured the unworthy. As they were carried further away, the cult of warriors grew smaller in size. He could still see some being flipped into the air. As they were clear from his sight, a final piercing cry shattered the sky. A small, faint fog drifted upward, dispersing amongst the clouds. Several miles away, Eric settled the horses for them to regroup.

"Phoenix, please enlighten us on who our surprise guests were and why they looked identical?"

"During my travels, I have never come across people like them. Maybe they are a cult?"

"Their skin tone is common for residents of the country Bancouver, but their clothing resembles the civilians of Zannala . . . especially with their mannerism. The men were obedient while women held the leashes," quietly thought Talon.

"A pure heart was why they have been waiting. Are they a group from the original army that attempted to take the emerald?" pondered Crystal.

"From the raid twelve years ago? Waiting in such a desolate place, would any of them have survived this long?" argued Phoenix.

"It would at least explain their appearance . . ."

"Stay focused, Eric, this is serious." Crystal barked at him. He merely shrugged away her comment.

"The coincidence of their arrival and ours on the same eve are low. There must be a base of operations not too far from here. On the bright side, we have another emerald and are a step closer to saving Teague," chuckled Talon.

"Do we have a plan from here on?" inquired Crystal.

"I—"

"First, that emerald needs to remain far from all of us. No more panic attacks waking me from my slumber," Eric motioned to Crystal's hands. She completely forgot it was in her possession. She left to hide it along with the other.

"We most definitely are heading to The City of Assassins, as previously discussed. There is unfinished business that we all must resolve in that city. Once our tasks are complete, we will travel to Cosarave. Zannala will be our final destination."

"I suppose I was not heard; those raiders most likely *belong* to Zannala."

"Why attack their sister cities? That's treason."

"There could be any number of reasons, like being hired

mercenaries," reasoned Eric.

"Power and strength corrupt the most intelligent of men," replied Talon. "Who knows what Zannala's Queen has planned? She rarely joins or partakes in annual Osiren meetings. Her withdrawn nature has been under speculation for many years."

"Not only are we fighting paid rats, but now we are to battle against an entire city?"

"Zannala, in comparison, is relatively poor to Emerica and Luminar. Full scale battles, historically, have been avoided since their title was granted."

"Explains the small faction stationed at Flores."

"Hmm, if these speculations are proven to be true," thought Phoenix, "Zannala must be our last destination. There is not a reason to rush if the emerald is already in possession."

Changing the topic with a worrisome voice, Talon asked, "Phoenix, have you ever pondered the course of action that will be taken once the emeralds have been gathered? Keeping these nasty, dangerous relics from our enemies is a decent foundation of a plan, but they have been sought after for who knows how long. Those groups will persevere and track your every movement."

"I-I never actually considered how to handle the situation. Back during training, I had no faith in my survival, let alone laying my eyes upon a single emerald. There is still time to find a solution, but as of now, I have none."

Crystal joined the gang as they finished their conversation. As the last sun started setting, the team began to set up camp. They instantly fell asleep once their bodies relaxed.

Bright and early in the morning, they packed their luggage and hit the trail. With Crystal and Talon residing in the carriage, Eric and Phoenix played games and chitchatted to pass the time. About twenty miles had been travelled when Eric made a comment that caught Phoenix's attention.

"'Between Crystal and I'? What are you inferring?"

"I have been a witness to the time that's spent together;

there's no lying to me."

"She's a friend. No more, no less."

"You say? I see differently, as does the rest of Osiren."

"Enough, Eric. Speak your mind."

"The connection between the two of you is vibrant and visible. The way your eyes travel her skin, how her smile grows when you speak—if those are not signs, then romance is dead. Face it; your heart is not completely stone. Slowly, but surely, it is being chiseled away."

Phoenix stuttered, "Okay . . . and if this be true, why does this involve a third party? My personal business is mine alone."

"An answer is all I wanted and that's what I received. Don't allow your intimate feelings to interfere with our mission . . . ." Eric grew solemn, remaining quiet for some time.

CHAPTER 15

Before long, they spotted the city on the horizon. A guard stopped their approach outside the city's perimeter, demanding that the horses remain behind due to size limitation. No one understood the reasoning behind the restriction, but they followed the directions. No need to attract attention before they even entered the place. With weapons equipped and Crystal's bag swaying across her back, they entered Assassin City and understood why less traffic was ideal. The streets were narrow and crowded; a horse-drawn carriage had no hopes of traveling through. Buildings were touching, people bumped shoulders, and no nature was in sight. The four of them formed a circle once they discovered a patch of clear space to spread. Talon spoke.

"I have data that needs to be collected to locate my treasure. A popularity game. Who knows who, who owns what. I will also track the whereabouts of your sword."

Phoenix nodded, as Eric went next. "I will also be gathering information on the sentencing of the convicts that were captured and relocated here. Hopefully my husband and son are still here—and safe."

Crystal added, "I would like to send a message to my grandmother. She has been in my thoughts the past few evenings. With all that has occurred—X-beasts, monsters, mercenaries—it would be nice to hear how her health fairs."

Phoenix rolled his head to the side, giving her a questioning look.

She shrugged, "It's odd how dire situations gives one time to reflect. Until then, I will stick with Phoenix."

"Right, we shall part ways then." Phoenix glanced around their surroundings. "In three days, report back to this location by noon. No excuses."

"How will we remember this spot specifically? It's not as if this is a huge, crowded city or anything." Eric noticed Talon gave him the "shut up" stare and answered with a shrug of his shoulders.

"That tree will be our indicator; I doubt there is more than one," Phoenix pointed at the cherry blossom about a yard away. "All in agreement? Three days from now at noon we regroup." They all agreed. "Stay safe."

Talon dashed into the distance, while Eric calmly turned and paced away. His head rolled around his neck as if he was sightseeing.

"We are searching for that mercenary; Skull is his name? Where should we start?"

"Investigating the Thieves Guild will give us the best leads. We can speak with the police department and check their records for documentation?"

"Are you asking or telling me?" giggled Crystal.

Phoenix smiled, "I am telling you. The Thieves Guild first, but a warning . . . be wary. Unlike Kyron City, this place is literally filled with underhanded rodents."

The two of them wandered around the city aimlessly, walking in circles. Eventually, Crystal asked a local resident for directions to the guild. She explained in detail how to reach the building, ending the sentence with, "It's an eyesore—you'll know it when you see it." Thanking the woman, they followed the trail exactly as it was explained. Both were in awe as they came across the building. Standing higher than all else and shining brighter than the suns, the Thieves Guild covered several lots of land. Colored in dull white with stained glass windows every few feet, Phoenix was shocked they were able to accumulate enough wealth to afford such accommodations.

"It's as if they are not even trying to hide! What are the police doing?"

"Something is amiss; these men must not be troubled by the authorities at all."

Entering, their amazement continued. Without a touch, the doors parted to their presence, allowing them passage. The entire lobby was beautifully decorated. The floor had a cream colored carpet with black furniture to contrast. The walls were as white as the carpet. A desk was stationed in the center of the room with stairs on both sides. A young lady sat in a chair, pen in hand, smiling at her guests.

Crystal's jaw was still touching the floor as Phoenix approached the lady who had a surprisingly angelic voice.

"Hello! My name is Janice. Welcome to the Thieves Guild, how may I help today?"

"Being a thief pays incredibly well in this city," Phoenix noted.

"Yes it does! Being a *Personal Item Collector*, as they are preferred to be known as, is a proud profession in the City of Assassins."

"This is a shockingly expensive building that houses a bunch of criminals. How do the police not end this entire operation?"

"In this city, guardsmen and police have no authority. In the early beginnings they once had control over the citizens and the streets. But soon enough, more and more Personal Item Collectors arrived and overpowered them tremendously. Without hope of reinforcements, the police allowed the thieves to stay without them interfering under certain agreements."

"Which were?"

"None of the thieves come near them, their families, or homes. Each collector who settled in the city had to pay each officer a fixed amount of coin to remain."

"I wonder what the police station looks like," pondered Crystal.

"Now is there a matter I may assist with?" Janice bubbled with hospitality.

"Yes, I'm searching for someone—an ex-mercenary. Would you be able to help?"

"Is there any more information you can provide?"

"He was a captain in the raid on Luminar. There is a possibility he may be retired and goes by Skull?"

The upbeat, optimism in her voice vanished with her smile. Janice clearly lost her thoughts for a second, searching for a phrase in her guide of hospitality. The cheeriness returned just as quickly as it disappeared. "The room to your left holds records of residents in this city and where they reside, including all high officials. Feel free to rummage through them."

Thanking the now startled receptionist, they headed to the room, keeping an eye on her. *She wasn't kidding,* thought Phoenix. The entire room was brimming with filing cabinets stuffed with papers. Most of them were overflowing.

"Crystal, start on that side and I'll begin here. Look for a male with a first, last, or alias name that reads Skull." On cue, they began to search through the mountains of information.

Eric was walking around the streets examining his new environment, from the people to the buildings. *Where would they be?* He had the question on repeat, hoping he would magically create an answer. Running low on ideas, he figured following a patrol group of guards would bring him to a lead. He stalked them from afar as the group brought him to an enormous building, which they referred to as the "King's Suite." *It may as well hold a king; it's the size of a palace!* Eric gathered its purpose was one in the same as a city hall. He examined the architecture, nonchalantly strolling to the entrance. *The whole place must be made from an expensive stone,* he determined, catching its sparkle under the rays of the daylight. Reaching the last step, two large men stepped into his way.

"Only authorized personnel may enter. From that outfit, I can tell you are no guardsman and you sure as hell are not our Union Leader. Please leave the premise." The cold, intimidating bodyguards repeated the first line a dozen times before Eric understood he was not accessing the King's Suite. Like a dog with its tail between its legs, he walked away from the structure as lost as he was before.

After wandering through the streets, he decided to treat himself to a bite to eat and locate a sleeping arrangement. He attempted to talk to the citizens, but he was shunned. None of them would give him the time of day. After hassling a poor fellow, he pointed Eric in the direction of the nearest restaurant. On his way to his meal, he began harboring an eerie feeling. He glanced over his shoulder several times. *Well isn't that ironic?* He stopped and completely turned around, but he only found a guardsman patrolling along.

Eric was in and out. He didn't feel safe staying in a place for too long, especially when he still had that unwavering shadow following him. Slowing down, he turned into an alleyway in hopes to lead the pursuer with him. Peering around the corner, he found his stalker approaching. *It was a guard after all.* Eric reached the far end, waiting behind another turn. Listening to the footsteps approach, he charged at him. Grabbing him by the neck, Eric held him against the wall.

"Why are you following me? Who are you?" interrogated Eric, rocking him around. The helmet clanked several times. "Shouldn't you be more productive with your time, possibly saving cats from buildings?" He dropped him, waiting for him to catch his breath.

The guardsman recovered and reached his full height. He made direct eye contact with Eric, helmet to eye. Eric was unable to move, almost as if he lost control of his body. Something was not right, but he had no clue what it was. The moment remained intense, thrilling anxiety circulated around them. Eric's shoulders tensed and his fists squeezed the air from his palm. The guard's shoulders dropped and within a second, he grabbed onto Eric. Arms wrapped tightly around his waist. Beyond stupefied, Eric forcefully broke them apart. The guardsman stepped away and removed his covering. Eric's mouth parted in disbelief.

"Brett."

Eric's lips immediately found his husband's, throwing his arms around Brett's neck. The unbreakable strength of holding his lover again was invigorating, reuniting him with a warmth he had almost forgotten. He forgot how it felt with him in his arms. He embraced him for as long as he could bear the heat from the metal armor.

"Why were you following me? Lack of communication has never been a problem before!"

"I had to be certain you were real, and not just my imagination. I could not afford to make that mistake. The repercussions would have been horrendous."

The difference in him was not just in his physical features, but his voice as well. It was cold . . . unfriendly. The sweetness was drained from his words. His docile face no longer had that compassionate charm. Brett and Phoenix's face now shared the same expression: loss, pain, helplessness, and regret. Even the blond in his hair lost its shine. *Just as dark as his heart is by now.*

"What happened to you, my love?" The last word rolled off his tongue, leaving nostalgia and heat to swarm his body.

"When we reached this forsaken city, Alex and I were split— taken from my arms. I became a guard to the Union Leader and he was thrown into the library as an assistant. They awaited orders for our future placement, but I'm sure we have been lost to this chaos. The academy, prisons, and rules changed me. I hate who I have become, but who I was has been lost. If I chose not to conform to their regulations, I would never have had this opportunity to stare into your eyes again." His lips quivered. "That's all I ever wanted since I was taken from home. I knew you would rescue me, like always." He picked up his head to catch the evening sky begin its transition. "We shall speak more tomorrow; I need to be present for the nightly routine check. Meet me outside the library around three. The excitement in Alexander's face will be a treasure to hold dear."

Before Eric could say more, Brett kissed him a final time. He hurried away toward the King's Suite without another word. Watching him disappear around the corner, Eric slowly mumbled the words, "I love you . . ." He stood and stared until his lids hung heavy, drowsiness casting its spell. His feet finally shuffled forward to find a motel for the night.

Phoenix and Crystal finished searching through the mounds of documents several hours later. Crystal joined Phoenix and showed him three files, each having the name Skull on the sheets with an address, but no picture. In return, he showed Crystal the fruits of his labor.

"Five total people use the name Skull. Odd to believe it would be this common. What do you want to do next?"

"It would require too much time to search each house," he shuffled through them. "Some of these houses are on opposite sides of the city. We need more information, and I think Janice might be the woman who has it."

Janice's jolly face greeted them as her guests returned.

"Thank you for allowing us the privilege to search through the files."

"My pleasure; our knowledge is yours."

"May I borrow these files and return them later?"

"As you wish. We do have policies in place: the files must be returned two days after from which they were borrowed."

Phoenix nodded to Crystal, and she slid them into her duffel bag. "Is there any other way you could help? Possibly show the pictures of some of these men?" he inquired, not sure what to expect.

Again, a flash of disgust crossed her face. She sneered, "We do not help others hunt down our own."

"If I remember correctly you just said your knowledge is

ours."

The friendliness had entirely drained from her face. "I suggest venturing to the police station. They would be more than happy to assist, but as for us, we are closed. The inn down the street has lovely mattresses. Enjoy your night."

Escorting them out of the guild, Janice shut down the doors, locking them behind her. "This question may be since I was raised in Lanster, but does she have a problem?" wondered Crystal.

"There was definitely something odd. She's hiding a few secrets, but employed by assassins, that's bound to come with the territory. I suppose it is none of our concern. Let us find the inn she recommended. I don't need your feet dragging us down." He playfully nudged her as he walked past.

She smiled.

CHAPTER 16

All three suns rose early the following morning, but Eric had already been out of bed for hours. The excitement of his family being reunited kept him energized. He sat on his bed meditating, focusing on his life as a whole. Taking a peek at the clock every so often, he hopped up as it struck noon. Suddenly exhausted, he looked around the small, bug-infested room. *I can't believe I slept here; thank the Protectors I wasn't bitten . . . Did I just thank the Protectors?* He smirked, his cheeks blushing. *They deserve the gratitude. They are the reason I'm here.* Seeing another bug scuttled away on the wall, he exited the room, repulsed. He headed to the main desk and asked the clerk for directions to the library.

Phoenix and Crystal both left their beds an hour earlier. Setting out before noon, they agreed to head to the police station, which was only two blocks away. As they reached the perimeter of the station, they came across a boy and girl dragging their feet in the dirt. The female had beautiful red hair that reached the small of her back, but it appeared as if she had outgrown her clothing. Neither her sweater nor pants covered the entirety of her limbs. The boy, on the other hand, had clothes that fit, but not a single article was intact. Stained or ripped, his jean vest and cargo pants appeared old and worn. Trying to ignore the underprivileged youths searching for gold coins, they tried to keep forward and remain on course.

Phoenix was unfazed by the appearance of the police station, but Crystal was in disbelief. The door was unhinged and creaking, the windows were all mostly shattered, and the sign was falling apart. Despair poisoned the air as they stepped into the rundown workshop. Crystal barely noticed two men playing cards on a coffee table through the dim lighting. There was a third officer asleep at his desk, drool leaking from his bottom lip. Not a single officer made it seem like they noticed their presence. They were too involved in the game.

The man started obnoxiously snoring as they approached him. Crystal began coughing loudly, but it was no use. The officer finished a snore when Phoenix slammed his fist onto the counter. He immediately jumped and whipped his head around murmuring phrases. When he finally focused, he wiped away his drool and said flatly: "Welcome to the police station. Leave."

"That's no way to speak to someone," scolded Crystal.

"My apologies, miss; please leave." The officer watched as her brows burrowed, but as he crossed to Phoenix's stern scowl his attitude changed immediately. "What may I assist you with?"

"I was wondering if you could help us locate someone in the city."

While Phoenix explained their situation to the apathetic man, Crystal examined the room. She happily spotted a large contraption attached to the wall with a dusty sign reading, "Voice Finder." She unhitched a corded object and dialed her grandmother's home, but there was silence. She repeated the same steps continuously until one of the men playing cards told her it hasn't worked in years.

"If you wish to send a message, we can have a mail pigeon carry it. They barely travel Osiren anymore. Whom do you wish to contact?"

"My grandmother in Lanster."

The policeman disappeared into the back room only to return a few minutes later with a blue and green colored pigeon resting on his wrist. The other officer handed Crystal a piece of paper and a pencil.

"This one is specifically taught the course to Lanster. When you finish your letter, I'll attach the parchment to her leg. Make sure the name of the person who it's intended for is written on the outside. I'd say it should take no longer than a full day."

"How can you tell the difference between the birds?"

"Each pigeon is color-coded for their own cities. Luminar is a bright blue and Emerica is a dark shade of green."

Crystal sat next to their game and began writing her letter. *They are not to have a need for the green one anymore.*

Phoenix finished telling the officer his situation and the man began to argue: "Searching for these criminals violates our treaty and I will not place my family at risk."

"No one will know you assisted in this search; it will stay between us. Besides if we were to locate this man, there would be no worry about him spreading rumors." Phoenix unhitched his sword, both as enforcement to his statement and as a threat. The man rethought, and started searching the applicants.

"We photograph all citizens who settle in our city, besides the unfortunate and forgotten along the streets. Only three of those men are photographed. The other two either bribed us or escaped our cameras. Either way, here you are." He moved backward to allow Phoenix to observe the photographs. He closely examined each picture, not missing a detail.

"None of them are the Skull I'm in search of."

"Well then, sir, I cannot help any further. I suggest you travel to the addresses of the remaining houses. Perhaps speak with the librarian a few blocks over. She sees all kinds come through her doors. Whatever happens next does *not* involve us. A tip for next time: let sleeping dogs lie. Ever hear of the phrase?"

Phoenix ignored the man's comment and stood by Crystal, who was placing the finishing touches to her letter. She ended it with "Sincerely, your granddaughter." She gently rolled up the note and handed it to the officer. He pulled out a piece of string, wrapping it around the parchment and the pigeon's leg. Tying it into a knot, the officer released it through an open window.

"It should return tomorrow at some point throughout the day. The birds are out of shape—I guarantee she'll stop somewhere to rest. Come check back in with us."

"Thank you, it would be nice to hear from her."

"Sir, is there a possibility you would be able to do us one small favor?" asked Phoenix.

"Depends on the favor."

"I need these returned to the Thieves Guild," Phoenix lifted three of the five profiles. After a minute of thought, the officer accepted them.

Eric roamed around the perimeter of the library, anxiously waiting. Every guard that came close caused him to smile and his heart to race, only to watch the guard walk right past him. After several more false encounters, he stopped his search and sat down on the nearest bench, defeated. *He must have forgotten*, Eric thought to himself. *Hopefully. Hopefully he forgot. Nothing bad happened to him. Maybe they saw us together? No, think positive, Eric.* He broke from his thoughts as a thud dropped beside him. He turned to find a guard staring back at him. The guard jerked his head and stood once more. Eric waited for several feet to separate them before he followed.

Reaching the corner of the alleyway, he was ambushed by a strong grip. Brett pinned him to the bricks, kissing him passionately. They held each other with no space in between. Brett went to let go, but Eric held on even tighter. Tears fell across his cheeks.

"Why the tears, my love?"

"I never believed . . . Phoenix actually brought me here. To rescue you and bring you home. I thought my last memory of you would have been that moment before I went unconscious. I love you, Brett. I would be lost if I were to ever live without your smile." Eric was pulled closer, their foreheads gently clashing.

"I'm here . . . I'm with you now and forever," sobbed Brett.

"Will you leave with us? Grab your possessions and Alex, and leave with Phoenix and I?"

"That's all I've dreamt since my arrival."

Brett felt another peck against his cheek. The tears rolled down his face and across his lips. He latched onto Eric once more, embracing his touch for as long as possible.

"Let me fetch my luggage. Head inside and request assistance from the librarian. Alexander will be sent to help, but be sure to act as a stranger would. No emotions. No familiarity. They mustn't be aware of your relationship; he is still a criminal on lock down. Tell him to guide you to the fiction section; it'll be the nearest bookshelf to the door. When possible, escape. We will regroup here."

Eric's eyes remained locked on Brett as his face vanished behind his city-mandated mask. Staring at the back of the helmet, he waited for Brett to calmly walk back onto the main road. It had to appear as a coincidence they both used this shortcut and not that they were back there together. When it felt appropriate, he revealed himself and headed straight through the library doors.

The condition of the library was terrible. The carpet was ripped from the floor almost as if an animal came in digging for treasure. The couches in the sitting area had not been cleaned in years. The fabric was worn and ripped on the cushions and armrests. All the woodwork in the entire building was rotting and had not seen any upkeep since it's opening. But despite the state of its appearance, not one shelf was without literature. The spines of the written works lined case after case in mint condition.

Eric strolled through the water-damaged flooring to a lady who was clearly not enjoying her life's work. Assuming she was the librarian, he did exactly as instructed and she moved away from her counter in search of her servant. As he waited, Phoenix and Crystal opened the smudged glass doors.

"Eric!" exclaimed Crystal. "How is your search coming along?"

"The success of my mission cannot be measured in words. All is finally perfect. We will be needing to clear space in the carriage for two more passengers; I know there will be no issues with that."

The realization dawned on them as they both grinned.

Crystal blurted, "Where are they? I want to see them!"

"Shh! Please refrain from say anything else," warned Eric. "Brett is preparing his possessions and Alex will be here momentarily."

On his last word, the librarian came around the corner with her assistant. There were definite changes in Alex. From the boy they remembered to man before them, it was clear as day. Cuts and bruises painted his body like a canvas. Bags hung under his eyes like weights. His orange curls had even lost the bounce to his step. *Those experiences will haunt him forever.* Facing his father, his misery vanished. His hazel eyes shined brighter than they had in months. Speechless, he made his way straight toward Eric, arms open.

Eric ached to grab him and pull him toward his chest, but this was not the time. He raised a hand as an offer for a shake. Alex's face returned to a normal state of defeated as he grasped his father's cold greeting. The librarian's eyebrows rose.

Catching their onlooker's glance, he realized his part needed to be played. "Thank you for helping me, sir. Would you please escort me to the fiction section? There's this new title that has been released and I would love to browse your selection." Seeing Alex's puzzled expression, Eric winked.

He started awkwardly walking toward the bookcases, "If you would, follow me . . ."

The other two watched them hide behind the bookcase, pretending to search the shelves. The librarian stared at them, tapping her foot. *She knows something is amiss.* Thinking fast, Phoenix twisted his torso, his elbow colliding with a pile of books. As the tower tumbled downward and each hardcover crashed against the floor, the diversion was made clear. Eric grabbed ahold of Alex and escaped.

"I'm sorry, I had not realized they were there!"

The librarian knelt down to gather them, "No worries, sir, it was merely an accident. My assistant knows better than to leave a stack that tall. Is there anything I may help you with today?"

"We are in search of someone. We have visited the Thieves Guild and the police station. I was to hope you would be able to lend us some assistance in our investigation?"

She paused. "I'm terribly sorry, but how is a library going to be any help?" Phoenix felt blown back by the question. How were books going to aid him?

"Almost all the citizens must come through here. I'm sure you have overheard gossip from all walks of life while stocking your shelves. There might be a small possibility you may have information that you've heard about our man?" Crystal insisted, sweeter than sugar.

The librarian checked her surroundings and whispered, "If it's a criminal you are in search for, we made a pact to keep their identities safe. What is the name?"

Phoenix answered, "A retired criminal who goes by the name Skull. Five total reside in the city, but we eliminated three. We have two addresses and need to know which is correct."

"Are there any photographs?" Phoenix shook his head. "Well, let me have them." She examined the profiles. "It is most definitely not the one across town. That is my nephew's address and he never does anything wrong. His family is locally renowned for helping others in need. Why his alias is Skull I will never know. This one . . . I know very little. If this man and the one I'm thinking of are one of the same, he is apparently a hermit. Never leaves that house of his. Tons of rumors spread about this gentleman. I heard the other day he still runs a criminal business. Though I doubt this gentleman could harm a fly."

"We have our only lead," Crystal stated.

"How would we go about finding him?"

"Pass the King's Suite through the courtyard, make a right, and head down Rave's Road. You should spot his house . . . It is hard to miss."

"I've heard that a lot lately . . ."

Phoenix thanked the librarian and asked if she could take the other profiles back. She happily accepted. They left the building to find Eric and Alex around the corner.

"Thank the Protectors, I will never have to serve that witch again!" announced Alex, practically jumping out of his skin.

Eric wrapped an arm around his shoulder, pulling him against his thigh. He turned to Phoenix.

"I have time to spare before meeting with Brett; where are you headed? I'll accompany you."

"We need to locate the King's Suite."

"Convenient, I found myself there yesterday. It is only down the road; follow me!" Both Phoenix and Crystal saw the change in Eric's personality. It was as different as glass and metal.

CHAPTER 17

Talon hopped rooftop to rooftop through the chilly night breeze. Every so often, he took a moment to examine the sights around him. He wanted to master the cities layout to the point of drawing it on a map with his eyes closed. Collecting intelligence was his primary concern. No information was considered useless. *Dirty. People everywhere. Gallant Street. Library. No trees. Rats. Beggars. Criminals stealing. No one paying attention. Treaty keeps them free.* He dropped to the ground, landing firmly. Picking up his head, the Thieves Guild stood proudly before him. He peered through the windows, searching for signs of movement. Sensing no threat, he retrieved a dagger and jammed it into the lock. Physically sliding the doors apart, he tiptoed inside. He scanned the white walls and carpeted floor.

Quieter than a whisper, Talon crept upstairs. Reaching the top, he found four separate rooms, two on each side. A fifth was between the two stairwells. Each door had a pinned sign that read "Sleeping Quarters." He glanced at the one beside him: "Office." He picked several locks on the door before he could pry it open.

His movement caused lights to flash on. As his eyes adjusted, the outline of several safes could be identified around the room. *Filing cabinets. Desk. Back of chair. Turned around. Cliché. Wait for it.* Seconds later, it did just that, revealing a woman with a red bob-cut, her arms folded across her chest.

"Very original," he said, dragging the words out. "No one has done that before."

With a smile, she tilted her head. "I knew you were coming, Talon, but what you desire is not here."

"Again with your artistic ability! Where do you come up with these lines?" The woman's air of hospitality dispersed as her smile turned into a glare. He chuckled, "If not here, then where can I find them?"

"They are secure at the King's Suite. Wind of your arrival has spread with your items. No one has ever broken into the Suite and survived."

"Suppose I'll be the first then; there is a first for everything. It has been a pleasure, truly, but I'm to take my leave. There is work to be done on your whole 'I'm an evil assassin's assistant' appearance for next time." He disappeared before she could respond.

Sirens blared behind him, but he continued jumping between buildings. *Assassins. Mercenaries. Cult members. I will be found. Vigilant. Remain calm.* Talon finally reached the top of a building across from the King's Suite. He'd seen pictures of the palace in books and newspapers, making it easy to locate. Knowing the guardsmen slept here during the night, he decided on resting himself. He found a nice hiding spot he took comfort in, prepared traps just in case, and dozed away.

He awoke the next morning to a large commotion. Hundreds of voices swarmed his rooftop. Ignoring the sparkling building across the way, he examined the scene. *Large crowd. Wild hand waving. Angry gestures. Protesting? Rallying? Wooden stage. Man in black. Noose. Public demonstration. Enforcing strength or inducing fear? No one gets punished here.* In the corner of his eye, Talon spotted Phoenix and the crew entering the wild mob. *Play it safe. Remain watching,* he decided, tracking his friends.

Eric proudly marched the rest of the group into the town square. An enormous crowd swiftly overwhelmed him. He grabbed

Alex's hand and allowed Phoenix to take the lead instead.

"What's happening, Phoenix?" worried Crystal, watching as the guards herded the citizens inward.

"Is it an announcement?"

"It's a public execution," confirmed Alex, hiding behind his father.

"Public? I thought they were against the law?" asked Eric.

"Laws do not exist in this city. These are very rare. This only happens when someone commits a crime that hasn't been seen in a long time, or if it's the first of its nature to have been committed."

Phoenix watched the guardsmen surround the people like sheep. No one was permitted to leave. He even caught sight of the librarian and Janice among the crowd. He continued to overlook the heads around them until he felt Crystal leave his side. He turned to see her speaking with a guard. The guard disclosed three soldiers were being hung. One of the captives was on death row for a past crime, and the other two for new ones.

"Let's not watch this, Phoenix, I don't want to see this," begged Crystal, tugging at his hand. The four of them squirmed through the mob, hoping to escape, until a voice echoed from above freezing them still. They looked to find a man on stage, surrounded by two guards and the executioner.

"This reminds me of our time in court," whispered Eric.

A stout little man stepped onto center stage.

"That's Anklo. He's not a good man," Alex whimpered, holding onto Eric.

"Attention citizens of Assassin City, here today we have three traitors that went against the unofficial rules of this glorious utopia. The first one is charged with murdering small children. This has been the first ever charge, and I would have hoped nothing like this would ever occur, but yet, here we stand. For your crimes, Edward Schwas, you are hereby sentenced to death by the power of our leader." The man slowly turned to him, placing his hand on Edward's right shoulder. With a swift jab of his sword, it sunk straight into the man's chest, appearing on the other side. The body went limp immediately. The two guards disposed of the corpse and returned to their original positions.

"I suppose we should be okay with this? He murdered children . . ." reasoned Eric.

"This can't be as bad as we believe; they at least killed that dangerous murderer!" added Crystal. Phoenix and Alex remained silent as the man started announcing the next victim.

"Next, this man is being charged for two past committed crimes. I thought all would have listened and obeyed the laws, thanks to the bloody massacre from before. He is being charged with treason and obscure actions. The first offense, treason, is due to him being caught packing his bags with plans of escape and for stealing money from the royal safe . . ."

A sudden chill shot through Eric's body. A cold sweat formed on the back of his neck, his heartbeat quickened, and his pupils dilated. His clammy hands made Alex uncomfortable, but Eric's grip became tighter every time he tried to pull away.

"The second offense, obscure actions, is for being seen in public with another male behind the Library. It has been stated that he gave the other man a signal to follow. There was a witness to his actions." An air of terror surrounded the team, all of their attention focused onto Eric. His fear was confirmed. He felt like he was suffocating, someone slowly wrapping ice-cold fingers around his neck. The grip steadily strengthening, tears fell from his face.

"Please bring Brett Strauser on stage." A guard led Brett next to the announcer. His hands were tied behind his back with a black cloth covering his head. The announcer stepped toward the criminal, noose in his left hand and a fist in his right. The man towered over Brett as he was shoved to his knees, casting a large shadow upon him.

Blood boiling, Teague became hazy. Eric pushed Alex aside and jetted through the entire crowd. His instincts were on high alert, but he ignored the shouts from Phoenix. With steaming hot tears staining his cheeks, he swerved around each citizen, even knocking some to the ground. The noose was being carefully placed around its victim when Eric mindlessly climbed onto stage. He bluntly body-slammed the announcer and slit the noose in half with his spear.

Gasps and cries erupted throughout the crowd. They began shouting questions, "Who is he? Where did he come from?" Phoenix told Crystal to watch Alex, and he, too, made his way on stage. He joined Eric's side and turned his view to the crowd, whose questioning stares began turning into angry rage. He stepped back, glancing at Anklo, who was being helped to his feet by the executioner.

Eric had only one focus. Slipping the cover over his head, Brett's pale face was revealed. His eyes were swollen and glistening.

The demand for reinforcements was made as Eric freed his husband's hands. The guards around the stage joined the fray, surrounding the fugitives. The announcer whipped his sword from his sheath, pointing it toward the in-subordinates. With Brett being safe-guarded in the middle, Phoenix and Eric took stance on opposite sides. Anklo stared down the rebels and shouted at his men to slaughter them.

Eric stabbed guard after guard before they had a chance to swing. Blood dripped from his steel each time he slid it free from their abdomen. He continuously twirled his spear, marking his territory. No one was allowed to pass him. One guard ducked under his swing and grappled onto his arms. Struggling to free himself before more came, armor scraped his skin. With nothing but pure fear and aggression fueling him, he decided to use his head for once. With a quick wham, his skull bounced off the helmet. Blood broke from his forehead as his arms were released. The guard held onto his helmet trying to stop the ringing as the spear was inserted into his chest.

Phoenix slaughtered the men that came within feet of him. He kept his side of enemies at bay, laying waste to the guardsmen until he noticed civilians from the crowd crawling onstage. They charged at him, barehanded. Fists flying, he ducked and weaved between their swings. Between the guard and the common man, he skillfully flurried his weapon, only striking the armored fighters. He flipped his sword around and bashed the hilt against the citizens' skulls. Being knocked out cold, their unconscious bodies littered the stage beside the dying soldiers.

More men and women lined up to brawl. They were becoming outnumbered fast and Eric's adrenaline rush was fading. His swings became sluggish, barely defending himself, let alone Brett. The stinging on his forehead turned into a massive headache. With no inclination of the lineup ending, Phoenix cut down another dozen guards before commanding Eric to take his chance to escape. Eric finished several more armor-less warriors before taking ahold of Brett's hand. The two of them dropped from the stage, taking refuge in the mob.

Phoenix tried attracting attention to himself, but a few guards began to chase after the two. Pushing the forces away that stood before him, he hurried to stop the men. Luckily, they halted in their tracks as a rusty dagger penetrated the wood at their feet. Talon appeared in their path, landing as elegantly as a dancer. Already prepared with four daggers ready, he shot them forward, killing eight men.

"Talon! Where have you been hiding?" Phoenix huffed, deflecting a blow.

"You know," he said, kicking a guard in the face. "Here and there."

Talon replaced Eric, targeting who remained. Tossing his daggers left and right, he kept an eye on any warrior that tried to leave the stage, wounding their legs and striking them down.

Crystal followed Eric's trail, dragging Alex by his arm. Leaving the vicinity of the arena, people scattered from the streets as the two pairs ran through the narrow openings. Making random turns, they finally caught up to the men in front of a burnt down office building, which had an electrical sign falling off its hinges, barely lighting up the words "The Habitat."

"Eric! Brett! Are . . .?" She breathed heavily. "I was so . . . so worried about you!"

Alex raced to his dads, giving them a big hug. Brett leaned in, kissing Eric. "I will never be able to express my gratitude for saving me, my love. In the barracks is when they suddenly restrained me. I was told I was being watched as I joined your side on the bench." Alex backed away, giving them space. They continued to hold each other, fear pumping hard. "I thought . . . there would be no chance in being saved this time. Especially by you again. Oh, Eric, thank the Protectors for you . . . I love you so damn much."

"There! The traitors from the court!" shouted a guardsman. Three more men appeared next to him, swords and spears drawn. Eric readied himself and struck first. He ducked beneath one blade and retaliated with an uppercut. Whirling his spear around his back, he used the extra force to impale the soldier. Avoiding two more strikes, he stabbed the second man in the chest, throwing him at the third. Eric carved into his victim while he laid on his backside.

Intimidated and scared, the fourth guard backed away slowly. He dropped his weapon and with terror written across his face, he spun around and headed in the opposite direction. Eric chucked his spear, making a direct hit, dead center in his back. Falling face forward, he drowned in a puddle of his own making.

They cheered, running to greet their savior, aside from Brett, who stared at him. A strange vibe came across the group. Eric walked up to him, arms wide open, worried that his actions had appalled him. Happily, Brett came forward, falling into his arms once more. He landed perfectly into his chest, throwing all his weight into the hug. The spark of happiness turned to horror.

Eric was holding him—all of him. He wasn't standing. Eric looked at his husband in shock when he came across an arrow lodged into his back. Blood was streaming from the penetration, turning his shirt into a bloody rag. His face began to droop, while his arms dangled at his sides.

"Criminals are never to make me appear a fool at my own ceremony," barked Anklo, waddling around the corner of The Habitat. "His death would be sooner or later. Better it be by my own hands. The three of you will be following him, since you assisted in his escape." The announcer stood there with a grin and a bow.

Eric stared at the lifeless body, laying Brett on the ground. Eric's eyes remained steady. His breathing got heavy, his eyes glossy, and his pulse rapidly increased. He slowly lifted his head to the man, locking their stares. Crystal could see he was trying to hold back his tears, his emotions. But slowly drops snuck free.

"I'll tear you limb from limb."

Anklo gave him a smug expression, loading his bow again.

Eric darted toward him with lightning speed, standing before him before he had a chance to draw his string. Gripping the bow with both hands, he ripped the weapon in half and tossed the pieces to the side. He snatched the arrow from Anklo's grasp. He drew a line down the center of Anklo's face. Ignoring his screams, he plucked the eyesight from the man. First the left. Then the right. The announcer began begging, pleading to release him.

"Pray to the Protectors, you won't find mercy with me." Eric stepped back and slit the man's neck. His body collapsed to the dirt. Eric left the arrow implanted in the man's crimson covered face.

Crystal was by Brett's side, doing her best to keep him breathing. As Eric approached, she stepped away. Eric propped Brett against his chest, holding him for dear life. His tears mixed with Brett's upon his face, as Eric stroked his hair. He was slowly losing his mind.

"It will be okay," whispered Eric. "You will be fine. I'll save you. I'll care for you. That's how this works, remember?"

Brett slowly shook his head. He placed his hand on the side of Eric's face. He licked his lips, attempting to speak, but nothing came out. Eric stared at him helplessly. Staring into his eyes, he could see the end. He quietly whispered in his wavering voice, "I love you . . . I love you to death and beyond. Forever and always, you will have my heart. An-and I will never forget you, Brett." He slid his fingers against the mark on Brett's forehead. He squinted his eyes while his lips began to quiver. "It's funny . . . when I first met you, I gave you this scar, and now it looks like you'll be leaving one on me . . . I failed our family; I failed you. I failed."

Eric went to say more, but his heart skipped a beat. He felt it. Brett's hand slowly lowered from his face, collapsing onto his own chest. His eyes became still, his breathing became shallow. Nonexistent. With no energy left, he mouthed, "I love you, Eric . . . Strauser."

The two of them were motionless. The last of Eric's breath escaped his lungs, leaving him utterly weak. And hollow. He remained focused on his husband's irises. Alex began making his way toward them, but Crystal kept him from the scene. There was nothing they could have done. Alex did not quite understand what was happening, but the mood reached him. He began to uncontrollably break. He hid his feelings into Crystal's shirt while she tried to comfort him. There was no use. She could only rub his back while she let her emotions overcome her as well.

Eventually Talon stumbled upon the crime scene with Phoenix close behind. Neither of them knew how to react. They both remained silent in respect. Talon tilted his head down, gently resting it upon the knuckles of his left hand, which lay over the fist. Bits of noise were heard, but he stayed quiet.

Phoenix kept his sights on the death before him. He knew the pain Eric was feeling; watching ones family die before you is more than any person should bear . . . The pain and memories came back to him in a rush, flooding his mind. But he kept them restrained. He refused to show sadness. This was Eric's moment, not his.

Many minutes crawled by without anyone making a move. Phoenix decided to take the first step as he placed his hand on Eric's shoulder. He was violently brushed off, forcing him to keep his distance. Eric slid his hand across Brett's face, forcing his lids down.

He rose to his feet, still holding his loved one cradled in his arms. With his head down, he crept along, dragging his feet away from The Habitat. The crew strayed behind, watching from afar. He led them out of the city. He stopped at the nearest patch of greenery. Laying him against the bark of a tree, he began digging.

He furiously struck the ground, scraping the dirt away. Realizing his course of action, the other men attempted to assist. Weapons out, they made their way to the site, but they were halted. Sharp edge of the spear keeping them at bay, Eric forced them back. He kept repeating, "My-my problem, my responsibility, my heart . . ."

About an hour later, he finished the grave. It was roughly six-feet deep and five-feet wide. He looked down at Brett, stroking his hair one final time. With a last kiss upon his cheek, another teardrop splashed against his skin. He began saying his last goodbyes, finishing with, "Please never forget me while you stand with the Protectors." Eric carefully placed the now cold body into its final resting place. Losing his stamina and the heart to see him anymore, he started covering Brett with a dirt blanket. Three dumps and he lost it. Eric finally broke.

He fell to his knees, tears pouring. Everyone heard the air crackling-cry and rushed to his side, besides Phoenix who stayed aloof. Crystal bent over, latching onto his body and listening to the words he tried to form. Talon called to Phoenix, and together they finished covering the corpse. Before Eric finally could leave, he planted his spear above the grave. He kneeled at his weapon, fist in palm, mumbling a few words. Back on his feet, he eyed the shimmering tip of the metal. With a sudden movement, he slit his wrist on the blade.

Everyone watched as a trail of blood followed Eric to the carriage that was tied nearby. Still bleeding, he slammed the doors shut behind him. A burst of cold air swallowed the entire landscape, making Crystal shiver. Before they could question his actions, Talon spoke.

"It's a warrior's prayer. Depending on one's beliefs, it's used for safe passage of the soul to Teague, or as a statement that the warrior has conquered this area. It's written that the Protectors performed this prayer often." He gazed at the blade. "This was his way of saying 'I love you' a final time."

CHAPTER 18

The uncertainty of the situation grew as they continued to share their own moment of silence. As a group, they stared at one another. No one made a sound. Occasionally, the wind would scrape across the surface of Teague, giving life to the lifeless. Muffled sobs could be heard from the back of the carriage.

Crystal felt broken. Lost. Distraught. The reality of her situation had finally been brought into light. She clutched her Chakrams tightly. She had watched her friend's soul depart from his body. Losing Rex and the Princess were different. She had felt no emotional connections and they were in a war. There is no war without casualties. Brett was a husband, father, friend . . . stolen from his home and passed into slavery. A common citizen, not a warrior. But this . . . The injustice happened in front of them, and there was nothing that could have been done. None of them were trained medical professionals who could have even attempted to save Brett. Even with vengeance of his killer, there was no resurrection. He was now one with the Protectors, helping Teague survive.

Her nausea did not come only from this realization; it could have been her who was buried. She could have been the one with an arrow in her back. Dead. If Anklo had decided she was better suited . . . The rules of the game have changed. In fact, it was no longer a game. She was involved in a life or death folklore that was read to children before bed. She was up against an evil warlord with little experience with weapons, let alone killing. Murdering. X-creatures were demonic creations; she had no problem burning them from existence. But another soldier? A person with a family? How was she to protect herself from this fate . . . or help the others from it as well?

Alex remained separate from his companions. He sat by Eric's spear, sitting upon the freshly shoveled dirt. The darkness that loomed overhead clouded his vision with despair. To lose his birth parents and now another person that he called family . . . Maybe he was the curse? This was entirely his fault. He was bringing this bad luck with him. He laid his head along the shaft of the weapon, tears darkening the ground beneath him.

Both jaded from their pasts, Talon and Phoenix remained numb. Though they could separate themselves from their emotions, this was never part of the plan. They failed. They failed Eric. They failed Alexander.

Phoenix thought back to the jail cells, where he pleaded for Eric's help and in return he would rescue his family. Death to him was as big a part of living as breathing, but to have failed an oath to a friend in the most devastating of ways . . . He was no longer a young boy who could blame the failure on his inexperience. He was a warrior—a warrior who failed to protect.

"Let's . . . leave him be. He needs some time alone to recover," assured Phoenix. "We would all become a bother to him, I'm sure." He walked to Alex who was still in tears. An odd ache came across his chest. *This boy . . . No child deserves this.* He knelt beside him, placing his hand upon his hair. "Do not think you are alone; we are here for you. Cry for as long as you need, but for not a single second think this is any fault of yours." They locked eyes, pausing the crying for the moment. "There are still tasks that have yet to be accomplished in the city and the librarian's assistant having gone missing will be well spread by now." He stood, turning to Crystal. "Keep him company?"

"I will not leave his side," she whispered, her heart still heavy.

"There should be a letter waiting for me at the police station soon."

"I will make that our final stop. Try to comfort our young friend here." She nodded in agreement, holding onto him once Phoenix led him over.

Phoenix nodded at Talon, and the two men left the sullen atmosphere. A decent distance away, Talon commented, "Glad Alexander's staying far from the city. You do not have a way with children, especially ones who have just lost a father."

Keeping his head forward, Phoenix chose not to respond.

"Do not give me that. Eric and his son are hurting, rightfully so. That stoic grimace will not jump start the healing process. Death and loneliness may be common themes in the lives we live, but not all are equipped to handle such difficult matters."

Phoenix sighed. "I will send my condolences when we return."

"I suppose that's a start."

"Have you learned the location of our possessions yet?"

"I have, but they are locked up tight in the King's Suite. It will not be in our best interest to make an appearance there. I have no doubt the city is frantic and on high alert after the stunt Eric pulled. And the Thieves Guild is still hunting me."

"The Guild? What have you done?"

"Besides breaking and entering, let's say not all wounds are healed by time."

"Understood."

"What about yourself? Has the world renowned Skull been found?"

"I'm confident he resides on Rave's Road. Town square is nearby."

"We should head straight to his home then. The King's Suite will wait."

With a powerful leap, the two of them energetically jumped between walls. Clinging onto window ledges and protruding bricks, they climbed their way to the rooftops. Traveling above the city, they watched as guards and policemen scurried among the streets. Once they reached the King's Suite, they took a moment to examine the area. The crowd of people had been replaced with an army of angry soldiers. Important looking men stood shoulder to shoulder as they watched a few guardsmen carry a body toward them. Phoenix and Talon safely assumed it was Anklo's carcass.

They began their acrobatic stunts again, crossing a dozen more rooftops before they reached a small sign reading Rave's Road. Only a few structures were built along the path and even less nature was growing here than in the rest of the city. The road appeared utterly deserted. They inspected the rundown homes.

"Skull has not been doing too well for himself," jested Talon.

Phoenix's thoughts raced laps around his head. His eyes inched across each building, determining which could be Skull's base. *It's the one in the back; it has to be it.* The sudden rush of finding his motivation for all these years surged through him. *Almost time. More than a decade later, and I will finally have my revenge.*

"Phoenix . . . Phoenix! Stop daydreaming, which is it?"

He stepped forward, making his way to the home. "The last one," he decided, pointing at the house at the end. "We're going to use the front door."

"Yes—barge right in. I'm sure he has it *completely* unprotected with no alarms or traps."

"I want him to be aware of my arrival. I want him to know I'll handle anything he can throw at me."

Shocked and intrigued by Phoenix's response, Talon eagerly followed him to the door. His tone was stern and aggressive. Talon could sense a transition occurring within Phoenix.

Without a moment's hesitation, Phoenix plowed through the door, creating a disruptive crack and boom that echoed. Taking a deep breath, he bravely stomped into the building. He was surprised to find it looking like an ordinary home. Feeling incredibly uncomfortable, he searched through the house, hoping to find anything relating to his prey.

He entered the kitchen. The chairs were neatly pushed in and the counters were spotless. Next he visited the living room, only to find nothing. Phoenix even peered into the bathroom to see a tower of towels sitting by a basket. *This doesn't look like the home of a murderer. Did I misjudge this place?*

"I have a strong inkling that you have the wrong address. This looks like an elderly man's residence," Talon glanced back at the door. "He will most likely charge us to for that."

He didn't acknowledge Talon's joke. Spotting a staircase, Phoenix flew up the steps. He walked into a hallway with a few doors on either side. Slowly making his way to the first one, he placed his ear against the wood. He heard heavy breathing and a hushed conversation. Unhitching his sword, a surge of power washed over him. Breaking down the door, it revealed two women sitting on a bed with fearful expressions. They shrieked and ran into an adjacent room. Utterly embarrassed, he hurried back into the hallway.

"You will have to pay for that door, too. And those girls' therapy."

"This is the house—it has to be. It has to be."

Discouraged, he started bashing every door into pieces. Talon tried to stop his rampage, but he went deaf. It halted only when one entrance held another set of stairs, leading to the attic. Creeping his way up the staircase, he picked up on a few voices. Reaching the apex, he could see a conversation occurring between two men, one of which was hidden behind a chair. They were facing a window, the daylight illuminating one gentleman's hair. Short, green hair. *He was in Holick! One of the men who attacked us!*

The chair spun slowly around, revealing an older gentleman. Disgruntled, he shouted at his companion, "Gamma, round up the rest of your squad. We have a pest to exterminate." Gamma's head snapped in their direction. He leapt through the window shattering glass across the floor.

Talon entered the room remarking, "Make that two pests, my fine gent."

The older man laid back in his seat, swallowed by a black and white robe, appearing to be the size of a child. His cheekbones showed prominently through his receding skin and his irises were dull. White long hair lay down his back, matching the length of his graying beard. The old man slowly rose from his chair, examining Phoenix, head to toe.

"What brings you to my humble home? Did I steal your belongings? Murder your family?"

"The years have been kind to me, as a previous lackey of yours once said. But to think you would forget my face, Skull?" His body temperature began rising.

"That name has not been spoken in many years . . . There is a familiarity surrounding you boy; did I sell you into slavery?"

Phoenix felt a knot form in his throat. His vision narrowed, the periphery turning red. He dramatically dropped his cloak from his shoulders to the floor. Crossing his arm, he revealed his scar. A minute passed as Skull pondered his memories, then a mischievous smirk cracked through his face.

"Ah! The bastard. If I were to bet that our paths were to cross again, it would have been a pity on my pockets and me. I figured scavengers would have killed that spineless little twerp. Yet, here we stand. Puberty has indeed been kind."

"Too bad age reached you before I did. I'm assuming it hasn't been a graceful process?"

"Now, now, my child, don't allow appearances to deceive you. I have more spunk than you can imagine. And as the phrase states, wisdom comes with age."

He lifted his arms, letting his baggy sleeves droop. Two swords slipped from the depths of his robe and he skillfully caught their hilts. "I'll be sure to end your misery this time."

Skull charged toward Phoenix and aggressively bashed his swords against his. With only enough time to block, Phoenix slid back from the impact. The two of them went at each other, swinging their weapons wildly. Skull brought both swords upon Phoenix's defense to gain the upper hand, but it was futile. Phoenix hopped to the side and retaliated fast, cutting off a strip of his robe. Skull tried for another heavy hit. Their repetitive clangs against metal bounced around the room. Talon watched from afar, choosing not to get involved, slightly for his own safety, but primarily due to Phoenix's vendetta. With his unpredictable emotions, he didn't want to be the next one in his cross hairs.

After another attempt at decapitating Phoenix, Skull was deflected and shoved aside. Phoenix saw his opportunity. Swinging his sword along Skull's arm, the tip of his blade created a jagged incision across the skin.

"Feel the pain I felt all these years." Hearing his howl of agony, Phoenix found a new source of strength and courage. He cut Skull's weapons from his palms, kicking them away. He held the blade at his throat.

Skull could see the anger in Phoenix's eyes as he snarled, "Any last words before I slaughter you like you did my family?" He pushed the edge closer.

Skull smiled. "Attack!"

On command, five warriors came through the already broken window. Alpha, Beta, Gamma, Delta, and Omega made an intimidating formation as they posed around the scattered shards. Immediately Beta threw her kunai with chain around Phoenix, wrapping it around his body. With an abrupt tug, Phoenix was forced away, falling against the wood. Shards of glass pierced his skin. Talon hurried to his rescue.

"Damn, these villains are the definition of cliché. Is it hard to be original?"

After collecting her chain, she helped Skull back on to his feet. Gamma came to his aide and with one arm around his neck, the two of them began making their way out of the room. Phoenix's blood boiled at the sight of his prey escaping. With only him in his sights, he jetted after him. His pursuit was interrupted by Alpha blocking his route. He struck Phoenix with a bone, knocking him to his knees. Whipping the femur around, he boasted, "Should be just as quick and painful as before."

Phoenix slowly raised his head, locking onto Alpha. With an intense focus, he roundhouse kicked him. Spinning back on to his feet, he lodged the sword into the gang member's chest. He grabbed ahold of the hilt, and aggressively tore it free. Before he could repeat, his weapon was entangled in Beta's chain. She ripped the steel from his hands. Weaponless, he created distance between them. The others began making their way toward the fight, but a dagger caught them both between the shoulder blades.

"Hey, baldy, pick on someone your own size. Like a tree or a mountain I suppose . . ."

Omega slammed his fists against the floorboards, causing the entire room to shake. Losing his balance, Talon toppled onto his back. Delta twirled his hands, chanting a few chosen words that summoned a red, shining disk out of thin air. Delta grabbed the circle on both sides and spun it like a steering wheel. It gently hovered as it rotated by his waist, until it released a beam of energy. Talon back-flipped out of the way, just in time to avoid being singed. An array of shots was launched from this mysterious object, but he smoothly dodged each one.

"What the hell kind of magic do you call that?"

"Your death."

"Straight to the point."

With another escape from a blast, Talon saw in his periphery a giant hammer flying in his direction. Barely any breathing room, he leaned back far enough to let it swing by.

"Now, where in the Protectors' names were you hiding that monstrosity?"

Omega flung around his oversized hammer like a tree branch. Being attacked by both fronts, Talon had to be fast on his feet. Maneuvering around each strike, he studied his opponents. After another beam was sent forth from his disk, Delta released the disk toward him. Talon aimed a dagger directly at the weapon, but it disintegrated on contact. The beam hit his shoulder, knocking him on his back again. The pain scattered throughout his shoulder and pectoral muscles.

No time to be in pain. The rotating object was gliding over the floor like a saw, aiming to separate Talon's torso from his legs. He rolled to the side, only to be welcomed by a swing from Omega's hammer. Catching part of his knee, the cracking sound intensified Talon's senses. He let loose a distressing yelp.

Phoenix went back and forth with Alpha, while simultaneously evading Beta. His knuckles began to bleed as he made contact with his armor. Bruised and swollen, the feeling in his hands became numb. With each strike and dodge, his rage intensified. *Skull will not escape me again. Even if I have to burn this city down, I will have his head separated from his body. I. Want. His. Blood.*

Skull's demise was his only motivator. Seeing a clear shot to Alpha's jaw, he propelled his fist forward only to be caught by Beta's chain. The kunai wrapped around him several more times before latching on to his right forearm. He recoiled from the impact and Alpha took advantage of the situation. He marked Phoenix's chest with a huge, incapacitating "X."

Phoenix could see the blood seep through his vest, soaking it with his tainted fluid. Moving his clothing aside, he noticed a purple tint outlining the wound. *The poison; I'm poisoned again.* He saw Alpha smile, knowing that his secret weapon would be flowing through his veins once more. Phoenix started fading in and out of consciousness. His sight became hazy, his vision becoming red. Then suddenly there was a moment of clarity. Almost like in third person, he watched himself free his forearm and dislodge the metal from his skin. As his mind disconnected, he couldn't feel anymore.

Alpha and Beta witnessed the change in his eyes. Then, just like that, a beast was released. Phoenix watched as his body retrieved his sword, despite a kunai impaling his chest. The man continuously struck Alpha. Each swing held more ferocity than the last. With a final blow, Alpha's weapon broke in two from the stress of deflecting the onslaughts. Astonished, he attempted to search for another, but the mindless body before him had no intentions of allowing that to occur. Phoenix found his free hand latching onto Alpha's throat, strangling him. Lifting him off his feet, his once bleeding knuckles were now turning blue-ish white.

Beta tried to help, but her chain was diced in midair. The kunai continued on its course, flying through a window. Phoenix could feel his fingers digging deeper into Alpha's jugular, clamping tighter, waiting for the color to drain from his skin. Beta recklessly sprinted to aid him, but impaled herself into the tip of a blade. She cried out. Her groans increased as she struggled to retreat, revealing more of the weapon with every inch. She tried to cover the wound, but the blood spilled between her fingers.

With the last of his life, Alpha watched Beta fall to her knees. Still struggling for air, he squirmed within Phoenix's grasp. Phoenix squeezed one more time and without hesitating, bashed Alpha's skull against the floor. On impact, the wood caved inward, causing the surrounding five feet to collapse. Regaining control of his autopilot, Phoenix fled as the henchmen were swallowed, buried underneath the rubble.

Talon barely dodged several more hits before he could formulate a plan. His knee was throbbing in unison with his shoulder. His gait was staggered, limping every time he placed pressure on his right foot. The wounds were almost unbearable. He knew he was losing feeling in his leg; bending it put him in extreme pain. *They balance each other. Delta fast. Omega slow. One blast per 45.2 seconds. Disk backup. No. Second strike. Speed with speed.*

"What's wrong, little man? Too afraid?" heckled Omega, swinging his hammer around once more. "Or are you suddenly unable to walk?"

Hammer after disk sent. Distraction from retaliation. Can't harm Delta, Omega decoy. Can't harm Omega, Delta recharged. "Good at cracking jokes, I see."

"I'm better at cracking skulls." The blunt object was wound

up and released. Talon escaped by a hair, only to roll into another beam from the disk.

"Are you even trying to fight? This is getting tiresome . . ." whispered Delta, giggling to himself.

"Waste of our time!"

The two went through with another routine of their dance. A beam was released, followed by the saw. Able to avoid the first two, Talon was clocked upside the head by the hammer. Dazed and confused, he stumbled back to his feet trying to focus. *Disk released, several seconds later. Forcing me back. Ranged fighter. Enough time to avoid. Hammer dropped after disk misses. Slow to recover. Still time before recharge. Vulnerable. Both vulnerable.*

"I'm not . . . not wasting time. I'm just prolonging it."

"Your death will be here soon, I assure you."

"No, you misunderstand. I'm evaluating your fighting." He quickly dodged. "Delta, each shot of energy is followed by your magical disk-saw thingy. The blast is powerful—too powerful. It needs to recharge. My ogre friend here is to distract me from fighting you in close proximity. He, though, moves very slowly, and since his weapon of choice is extremely heavy, he is unable to swing repetitively. He needs to wind up, regaining his stamina. This creates just enough time between the windows to cut your throats." The two of them stopped mid-movement, stunned. "Don't believe me?"

Delta was enraged with Talon's cockiness and inquisitiveness. He shot another beam and let loose his disk. Talon dove out of the projected energy's path and flipped over the saw. He then ducked in time to evade the hammer. Both of his enemies now vulnerable, he let loose two daggers striking both of his targets. They became infuriated and began blindly attacking. *Tension building. Lost sight. Teamwork gone. Game over.* Repeating the same steps, Talon knew it was finished.

Time all around him stood still as he stepped aside of Delta's blast. Moving past the flying disk once more, he retrieved three daggers. With only a few seconds to spare, he released each one—

directly pegging Delta up his torso. Twisting his body, he watched the blunt weapon ride the air toward him. Placing his feet strategically on the flat side of the hammer, he used the inertia of Omega's thrust to propel through the room. With two daggers in hand, he slammed up against Delta and cradled his legs around his waist. The impact knocked him on his back and during their fall, Talon embedded the tips of his weapons into each side of Delta's neck. Freeing himself from the howling mess, he watched as the disk returned, slicing through his legs.

Talon landed perfectly on his feet, but the injury in his knee caused him to lurch forward. The abrupt movement worked in his favor, slightly leaning out of Omega's swing. He turned to see Omega spinning his weapon around his head, preparing for the final blow. *Trying to prove me wrong, I suppose.* Talon stepped back toward the amputee victim who was attempting to make his way to the battle. With a lucky escape, the swing missed its target, but hit another one instead. It elegantly swatted Delta off the floor and into the air.

"One hit wonder," whispered Talon watching as Delta bounced against the destroyed attic leaving a splatter with each contact.

With only Omega left, he turned back to his opponent. The stare down was interrupted as Talon tumbled to the ground. The pain intensified, vibrating throughout his body. Omega watched him falter and lunged at the opportunity. Unable to stand, Talon prepared for the incoming assault. Before they had a chance to duel, the entire level began to shake. Omega lost his balance, stumbling over his own feet. Talon searched for the cause to find a giant crater in the floor. He then caught a glimpse of Phoenix diving through the window.

Phoenix zipped down the street. He was blinded by revenge, seething with animosity. He traced the dirt beneath his feet, looking for anything that would lead him to Skull. *Blood . . . blood; he's bleeding. Where is the blood?* It was as if his mind was caught in the center of a tornado and his thoughts were whipping by him, too fast to focus on them. His last day in Luminar appeared more than once. His mother's last words. His sister's heroic act. The Prince's dull eyes. His memories became hazy as his lust to find Skull increased. Only his face—Skull's face—stayed plastered on his brain from when he ran away from the massacre laughing at the chaos. The menacing sound vibrated his eardrums as his nose started tingling. Stimulating his senses, he recognized the smell. *Blood. Fresh blood.*

Following his nose, he found himself at an abandoned shack a few streets away. He shattered the front door, barrel rolling into the room. The place was barren. No furniture or appliances. It was only decorated by cobwebs and rat droppings. A few sounds found their way to his ears. He recognized the voice, immediately refueling his drive.

"This . . . this I *never* expected. The child—man's strength is . . . unbelievable. Matching me in skill . . . The rumors of his survival were just that—rumors! Next time we face, he'll remember why he feared me."

"There is no *next time,* Skull. You won't be walking away from me again!"

The response froze time as the runaways' eyes turned to a corner in the room. Phoenix suddenly stepped into their line of sight, his stare locked onto them as if he had seen them through the wall.

"Gamma, kill him!" Gamma did as commanded and took up arms. He ran straight at Phoenix with the intent to fulfill his order.

Phoenix remained motionless, facing down the enemy as he came closer. Without hesitation, he parried the strike. He flicked his sword, disarming Gamma. As the weapon collided with the dust, Phoenix went on the offense with an onslaught of strikes. After a flurry of jabs, Gamma's body went limp as he clutched at the punctures in his abdomen. He grasped the ledges of Gamma's armor, carelessly throwing him to the side. In one last act of defiance, Gamma struggled to stand, supporting himself with the wall besides him. Phoenix landed a devastating blow against his jaw.

CHAPTER 19

Skull trembled as he witnessed the little boy he once spared carve death into his underling. Survival had become a must, but before he could get his legs to run, a strong grip took ahold of his forearm. In retaliation and in a last ditch effort, Skull flashed a hidden knife from his robe, thrusting it into Phoenix's ribcage.

Absorbing the pain, Phoenix returned the gesture by plummeting his sword into Skull. After hearing an audible gasp, he withdrew his blade and created space between them. He listened to the groaning of the man before him. Watching as the small blade was held high, he motioned for Skull to come.

Sparks flashed as their metal collided, piercing the dank, dilapidated home with each clash. A few slits cut their skin, but neither was able to land a fatal strike. Phoenix's adrenaline kept the pain dim, allowing him to shrug away the stinging and effects of the poison. Skull matched his pace, but his stamina finally began to diminish.

Fleeing to Gamma's side, Skull swapped their weapons. Inhaling, he tried to steady the sword before approaching Phoenix for the next round. He whipped his blade in several directions, which all missed. He lunged forward, using his free hand to grab Phoenix's hilt while he lodged his weapon into his shoulder. The deviousness vanished from his snarl as he noticed Phoenix didn't flinch. Appalled, he ripped it free and swung again—except it was caught in mid-swing. Phoenix's palm was engulfed in blood as he clamped tighter onto the metal. The flood reached his forearm, dripping from his elbow.

In that moment, Skull realized this was no duel. He was being toyed with. His hold on Phoenix's arm was broken and he was disarmed instantly.

"I want the same pain I harbored for years to torment you! I'm going to engrave my anger and regrets into your skin. When I drive my sword through your forehead, I want to hear you scream. Loud."

Skull's mouth went dry. He couldn't speak. There was nothing more to say.

"I'll enjoy *every* second of this." Phoenix raised his sword to eye level. "Pity. I thought when this moment happened I would have had to fight harder for it."

An extreme deafening yell tore apart the very fabric of the city. He retracted his blade, and devoured his reward through his eyes. But, he felt nothing. His mind stayed stagnant. No excitement, no joy. Just emptiness.

Phoenix wandered the streets, splattered with blood. He stumbled around drunk off his desires. Hours passed before Talon came across the sloppy mess. Concerned about his health, Talon asked several standard questions. Phoenix's lifeless gaze answered them all. His attempt to speak was only a few mumbled words before he lost consciousness.

CHAPTER 20

Crystal and Alex laid under the shade of a nearby tree. She held him close, one arm wrapped around his shoulder, lovingly rubbing his shirt. She had never been in this situation before—not that many people have—making comforting him rather difficult. They kept their attention to the sky, watching the clouds drift by endlessly. Alex was quietly weeping in her arms, but whenever he tried to speak, his throat closed. The long moment of silence was interrupted after Crystal pointed at a cloud shaped like a flower.

"Crystal . . . what happens now?"

She looked down at him. "What do you mean?"

"I've been away from home for so long . . . my dad . . . I don't remember the last time I smiled. What's next?"

"You still have Eric, sweetie."

"It won't be the same . . . He won't be the same. My fathers . . . were everything to each other. I loved him, too, but Eric's life revolved around him. It's like . . . his souls gone now, too."

Crystal blinked several times as she struggled to speak. "Alex . . . Eric is strong. He will be able to—"

"No! I want—I want it to go back to how it was! I want to go home! My *real* home! I want to go to school. I want my family. *Real* family. And friends. I want Brett and Eric to be happy. I want their happiness to make me feel safe." Gasps and snivels interrupted his words. "Ever since I left . . . I . . . I haven't felt anything similar. Teague has been so, so cold." She held him tighter, at a loss for words. She could feel the tears against her skin.

The tension dispersed the moment walking road kill came into view. Talon limped in a quick pace, cradling Phoenix in his arms. He shouted her name with all the energy he could muster.

"What happened?" cried Crystal meeting halfway.

"No idea! One minute we were fighting, and the next, he jumped through a window. I eventually found him wobbling through the street like a drunken fool."

Her eyes traveled to Talon. "What's your excuse?"

"I was left behind to finish enjoying my tea party with a wizard and ogre. Ones straight from a fantasy tale."

"And where did all this blood come from?"

"Mostly from himself. Good chance some belongs to Skull."

"The bleeding needs to stop." Crystal ripped open the carriage doors, flashing light onto Eric. He didn't budge. She rummaged through their belongings, retrieving their casual wear they had purchased in Belinda. She shredded each pair of clothing to wrap around Phoenix's wounds. Applying pressure, she poured some water on to a piece of cloth to clean the dried blood.

Crystal glanced at Talon, "We are going to need medicinal supplies from the city. His wounds mustn't get infected."

"He's already infected. The poison must have circulated from Alpha by now."

"Alpha? If so, he should be dead already."

"He may have built up immunity against it."

"Even still, we best clean these wounds thoroughly."

"I honestly have no understanding on why he chooses to wear white. He is a walking target for blood and dirt. Next shopping spree, he is getting a new wardrobe."

"Talon . . . you're hurt, too," Crystal noted, watching him limp. "Rest is in order."

"I'll be fine, I have to walk it off."

"None of that nonsense; I'll care for you."

He smiled. "Thanks, cupcake."

Crystal carefully laid Phoenix on a bed of clothes. Leaving Alex behind to watch Phoenix, the two of them traveled back into the city. They bought the items they needed as fast as possible. After several arguments, the duo split up. Crystal made her way back to their patient while Talon remained in the city. He watched the final sun slowly set behind several tarnished buildings. Taking the chance to rest his drained spirit, he slept upon the rooftop across from the King's Suite. His traps from the night before were still in position which provided a sense of security. Too tired to hold his eyelids open, exhaustion swallowed him whole.

"Psst. Wake up. Mr. Zaccaro. Wake up."

Lifting his heavy lids, Talon could barely identify the blurred visions in front of him. His entire body ached, head to toe. Blinking a few times, the shapes began forming into clear objects. *There are two . . . no, three people around me. Tingling in arm. Injection site.* His head dropped to his side bringing a man with a needle into his vision. *Needle. Green liquid. Drugs. Drowsy vision. I'm being sedated. Who are these people?*

"Mr. Zaccaro, I need you to reply when I speak. If you can hear me, nod."

Talon barely heard the sound rumbling around him. He could only make out the word "nod," and he did as asked. The three men began bickering, everything sounding like mumbles. Talon could feel himself becoming heavier, making blinking become a difficult task. The man who drugged him stood. He motioned Talon to follow, but none of his limbs moved. The motion was given again, but Talon didn't try. Suddenly, a blow to his right side pulsated through him. Before he knew it, he was thrown over two of the strangers' shoulders, and dragged down the side of the building.

The scenes around him went by in a blur as he was manhandled inside a large structure. *Didn't travel far . . . must be the King's Suite.* He couldn't see much of the scenery or who was passing by him. The only thing on his mind was his objective. *I'm . . . in the building. Good . . . good start.* Even his thoughts were scattered. His senses didn't return until he felt an oddly cold breeze cross his skin. *Cold air . . . Basement. I'm underground.*

With the ability to walk returning to him, Talon stayed in line with his captors. The one who drugged him was sporting an overgrown beard. On his right forearm was an unsightly tattoo. Two black bands circled around his wrists, separated by a few inches of bare skin. Talon instantly noticed the other two men had the same ink in the same location. *They are part of the same club. Must be thieves. Working with that secretary. Wonder how much I'm worth.*

They entered a room cluttered with random objects and computers. *Not as high tech as my brother's place.* A picture of Phoenix on a nearby desk caught his attention. Scattered around the photo were more mug shots of their team. "WANTED" was clearly printed in red lettering at the top of each.

"Oh Protectors, we are receiving a reputation. We are wanted for crimes in a criminally-ran society. Irony describing irony. I have never seen a truer example." He was ignored by his company.

The next room they entered was empty. He was shoved forward as he heard the door behind him click shut. His three guides made their way in front of him with their arms crossed, doing their best to express an intimidating manner. Before Talon could speak, a door on the opposite side opened. Another trio of men joined their group. The man in charge was wearing a fine suit, but the others were in rugged clothing. On their forearms was the same tattoo—except they had two more bands further up their arms.

The nicely dressed man's presence sent Talon an entirely new definition of horror. A brace was tightly strapped around his neck. A jagged scar ran from under his right eye into his well-groomed facial hair lining his features. Stepping into the middle of the floor, all attention turned to him.

"Mr. Zaccaro —"

"Call me Talon."

"Or should I call you the Lone Wolf?" A cold sweat formed

on the back of Talon's neck. "That caught your attention."

"Why bring me here?"

"There are oh-so many reasons. The coin for turning you in is always nice, or maybe because all the thieves in the city are in search of you?" His voice was smooth, but chilled.

"Okay, means you are not affiliated with my break-in. I suppose you are your own sector. Or cult. Better question: how do you know me?"

"We know you are from Bancouver, you and your brother. We have the relic you're searching for," he stated, pointing his attention to one of his henchmen. He revealed a duffel bag, playing with it in his hand. "And the famous White Dragon sword in my other associate's hands." The other man unstrapped the diamond-encrusted case from his back. "You may choose one."

Phoenix's sword?! "I don't quite understand. This doesn't add up."

"We have our own motives."

"Well . . . What is stopping me from taking both?" On cue the gang members puffed up their chests.

The man chuckled. "You are. I know that brain of yours can calculate several scenarios in seconds. Tell me how you would escape." No response. "To reinforce this, try to undermine me and I will have every available force in this city sent to track you. Choose one, and be on your way."

Talon gulped, "What will happen to the one I don't choose?"

"It will be shipped away, possibly pawned off. Make your choice now."

He took a long hard look at his enemies and the prizes. His brain went silent. He was outsmarted.

CHAPTER 21

Phoenix woke from his coma while Talon was gone. He discussed with Crystal the events that had occurred. Talon finally returned to them, overhearing Phoenix explaining his emotions.

"I was overtaken by a force, like another person rose up; a new burst of power . . . This has happened before, but I know not what triggers them . . . Most of my memories are a blur."

"I've witnessed this change; back in Lanster forest. You went berserk. Something changed about you—inside you. Something bad." Before Phoenix responded, they noticed Talon entering the vicinity. They both eagerly greeted him as Crystal wrapped her arms around him.

"You've been gone for over a day, Talon, where in the Protectors' names have you been?"

"I'm sorry for leaving your side during the battle—"

"My errands took longer than I thought, and do not fret. That big oaf was a piece of cake and the other one didn't *stand* a chance." He chuckled. "What happened with Skull? That wasn't all your blood stained on your vest?"

Phoenix's eyes slowly drifted over his outfit, seeing his clothes ruined. Before he could get upset, Talon stopped him.

"I thought ahead and grabbed this stain remover from a local mart. Your outfit will be fine."

"How did your search fare?" inquired Crystal, noticing a bag in his hands.

"While on the hunt for my beloved relic, I was drugged and kidnapped. During that escapade, I learned that our faces are scattered throughout the city. The news from Emerica must have finally traveled. We should steer clear of the city. Forever. We are wanted criminals."

"Wait a second, kidnapped? What?" questioned Crystal.

"Well, that was not the most important thing I mentioned."

"I cannot leave yet; I have to learn if my pigeon has returned!"

"Our treasures are still at the King's Suite as well."

"Calm down, you two, I stopped by the police station." Talon retrieved her note from his bag. Handing it to her, she tenderly accepted the letter. "And Phoenix . . . I was not to forget about you." He gently slid a large white object from his bag. The diamonds enshrined on the case began gleaming under the sunlight. "Presenting, your incredibly priceless sword." The blade was delicately handed to its rightful owner.

Phoenix held the White Dragon in his hand. His emotions swelled against his chest. *It has been more than a decade since I've held you. My family heirloom; still as perfect as I remember.* He separated the sheath from the sword slowly, allowing himself to be washed in ecstasy.

His feelings getting the better of him, he latched onto Talon. "I cannot believe I have it again! You actually located it!" He fully freed the dragon, admiring the carving that remained intact. "Were you able to find the item you have been in search of?"

"I'd rather not discuss it. It's no longer here; that I am sure of. Let's leave this terrible city. Nothing is left except for despair and memories. And those memories will bring more despair."

Phoenix turned to Crystal to share in the excitement, but it was subsided. His enthusiasm dwindled as his heart sank. Her eyes were filled with tears, while her body trembled underneath her. The parchment fell to the dirt as a few whimpers were released. Phoenix embraced her as she fell into him. Talon picked up the note and decided to read aloud:

Dear granddaughter,

This may come as a great sadness to you, but Lanster no longer exists—only as distant memories and as a location on a map will Lanster live on. Once Emerica was destroyed, the raiders burnt down the entire Lanster forest. They demolished the city, killing all who resided there; leaving nothing beside corpses. There were no survivors and all the buildings are in piles of rubble. I am a mere traveler who came here to visit. I did manage to find one adolescent boy who went by the name of Michael. He was being crushed under a pile of wood. I did my best to remove the rubbish, but I was not in time. He died several minutes later from what I assume was crushed organs and possibly smoke inhalation. My heart broke watching that youth die. I'm sorry I have to be the one to tell you this. I wish there could have been another way to receive the news. Your grandmother lives on with the Protectors, and I bet she would tell you she loves you with all her heart. I'm extremely sorry for your loss.

Sincerely,

Maxwell Neilson

The mood of the group was ominous as Talon raddled off the writer's name. Phoenix continued to hold Crystal who seemed to be lost in thought. Her eyes drifted over his shoulder as she wrapped her arms around his waist. *She's gone. My home's gone.* Numbness engulfed her chest.

No one felt the need to remain in the City of Assassins anymore. They had overstayed their welcome and now, being wanted for more crimes, a safe distance away would do nothing but good for them. Besides, the group was too weak to get themselves in another ordeal; Eric was an emotional wreck, along with Crystal; Phoenix was recovering from his confrontation, and Talon was badly beat and still feeling the effects of being scdated.

Talon began loading their belongings into the storage space in the back. Phoenix stepped away from Crystal to consult the map. The men made the unanimous decision to drive to the second to last great city on their list. Cosarave was their next destination and knowing the weather conditions, Talon made a mental note to gather some heavily insulated clothing. With Eric out of commission, Talon mounted the middle horse with Crystal and Phoenix beside him. Alex rode along with Crystal, his arms wrapped tightly around her waist.

No words were exchanged between the passengers. What was there to say at this point? They were happy to watch the city vanish into the horizon. Only the quiet cries of Crystal and sporadic neighs of their steeds filled the time. A few days had gone before the crew crossed another village. Talon slowed down the ride in hopes of bringing everyone back into reality.

Alex was the first to sprint onto the dried patches of grass. The rest of them followed, immediately beginning to shiver, feeling the cooler air surrounding them. Talon and Crystal agreed to search the village in hopes of finding supplies and their exact location. As they began to move toward town, Phoenix decided it was time for a visit to the cargo hold.

Taking a deep breath before opening the pit, he braced himself. A gust of misery trickled through the opened doors as he spotted a small figure in the far corner. One leg lay straight while the other was bent against his chest. His arm rested upon his knee with his hand covering his face. The sunlight brightening the room didn't force him to move. *I don't know how to handle these situations.*

"Eric, we stopped at a village. Come and stretch, or roam around. I think some fresh air will help." Eric didn't budge. Phoenix merely sighed and walked away, leaving the doors wide open.

Alex eventually came across some other children that had ventured to see the strangers. He quickly made friends with the townies and started a game of tag. Phoenix watched from afar, seeing Alex's wide smile appear. *To be young again. Not having a single worry.* He began experiencing the same ache he felt a few days before. Watching Alex smile and laugh practically brought a tear to his eyes. He felt warm, warmer than he had in years. He decided Alex's best interests were his as well, as he watched a fight occur with a little boy pushing a girl against the ground.

There was a burst of laughter from the children as they gathered around the scene. The boy continued hollering in the girl's face, who was terrified. Alex made his way to the situation, practically pushing the boy away and toppling him over. All eyes turned to him as the bully was helped back to his feet. A few words were exchanged before abrupt shoves pushed Alex onto his backside. The scene brought Phoenix into shock and a state of unconsciousness. They all gathered around the outsider, yelling, taunting, chanting. The bully stood above him, staring at the poor child between his legs.

Phoenix's body froze, stirring with fear and anxiety.

The bombardment of children's insults was let loose as random voices were overhead.

"You're an outsider! Why are you even here?"

"We stopped for a break . . ."

"Where are your parents, weirdo?"

"My dads are—"

"Two dads? What a freak! You can't have two fathers!"

"Which one's your mommy?"

"I bet they're weirder than you."

Alex crawled backward, picking himself up. He kept his vision down toward his sneakers. He trembled, unable to speak. He began to step back until he bumped into someone. His fear was replaced and confidence restored, finding Eric at his side.

"This must be one of *them*. Your son's a freak of nature and you're as bad—"

Eric, without a single thought, gripped the child's shirt and threw him several feet away. Making a thud as he skidded against the dead ground, the bully began wailing. The others watched in horror, and the moment they remembered how to walk they sped back toward the safety of the village.

Picking the boy off the ground by his collar, Eric burned a hole through him with his eyes. "Never *ever* dare make my son feel like he doesn't belong. Do you *understand* me? Huh? Do you!"

Phoenix broke from his trance, racing to them. He grabbed

Eric's forearm and wrapped one arm around his neck.

"Eric Strauser, drop him or I'll break your neck."

He merely scrunched his face in disgust, but dropped the kid from his grasp. The boy slowly crawled to safety, staring at the crazy man. It wasn't until he was at a safe distance did he finally get on his feet and hightail it away.

Phoenix released him who fiercely stared him down. Something in Eric was not right and he had every intention of finding out what that was.

"How dare you threaten a child?"

"Where were you?" he spat. "My son's being harassed and you watch from afar?"

Phoenix choked on his words, but before he could fabricate a lie, Eric snapped. "Don't touch me again or it will be the *last* thing you do. I do as I please, when I please. I will not be disrespected." As his last few words surged forward, a demonic aura surrounded him. Eric's body erupted with anger and darkness that suddenly engulfed his torso. He watched as almost tangible tentacles of a black mist swirled around him. In utter shock, Phoenix was unable to respond. Eric passed by him, clipping his shoulder.

Crystal and Talon visited several quaint stores in search of food and warmer clothing. In their visit, Crystal passed several mirrors. By the fifth one, she examined her outfit. Tracing the line that separated the purple from blue and playing with her loose sleeves, these pieces of cloth described her as a person. Despite how minuscule, she was brought to harder times. Times, though more light-hearted than now, that held her as prisoner of her home. She outlined her face with her palm. Bags hung under her eyes accompanied by light scratches that would permanently scar her once innocent face. She jingled the coins in her bag.

Meeting up with Talon, she struck him speechless. Crystal had replaced her old blouse with a white long-sleeved top and a vibrant purple vest covering her shoulders. The shorts were exchanged for black stretch pants and sensible magenta boots. The attire was complete with black fingerless gloves. Talon, on the other hand, purchased four heavy jackets for the men.

"Well, *hello* there, cupcake." She smiled, giving a look of disapproval. He traced her disgust to the coats folded over his arms. "They're not meant to be fancy, just practical."

Reaching the final store, the two of them found a big commotion forming. Before they had a chance to even question what was happening, a few villagers noticed them. All at once, the entire mob came rushing toward them. Surrounded, they could only watch as hands went flying and random accusations were casted. Without being able to defend themselves, they were practically evicted from the village. All the citizens stood as a wall near the entrance, making sure no one decided to turn around.

The group reunited and Talon remarked, "To be removed from a city this fast? I have yet to pilferage or steal . . ."

"Did our crimes reach their ears as well? I thought our names would remain a secret at least while we were in town."

"No . . . our identities remain anonymous. It's Eric . . . He almost struck a child."

"Where's Alex? How does he fare?"

"He's safe. He's with his father."

Crystal nodded. "That's unusual . . . Not like his character."

"I'm surprised he left his corner . . ."

"What I witnessed today . . . He's not himself. I saw . . . I—I don't know exactly *what* I saw."

"How so? A back-bone was grown?"

"Talon, this is serious! Try to explain what happened."

"A darkness flowed from his body, like a mist or a powerful odor. It covered him in a blanket of it . . . Almost as if it was suffocating him. I really can't explain beyond that, but he had to be compelled by another force to perform such an action like . . . like that." Phoenix shook his head. His attention switched to Talon when suddenly a light sparked.

"Talon, I believed our partnership ended once we reached Assassin City?"

"I've grown attached to the way you freak and lose yourself."

Phoenix shrugged, retorting, "And I have grown to enjoy the way your mouth never shuts. You're more than welcome to stay."

Talon smiled. "I appreciate the offer, dare I ever turn down a berserker."

Preparing to leave, Phoenix noticed the wardrobe change. "Crystal . . . that new shirt. It's white. Like snow . . . Pretty . . . you look . . ."

Crystal chuckled, listening to this heroic figure stumbling with his words. Embarrassed, Phoenix fled the situation as she shouted behind him, "Thank you!"

CHAPTER 22

Coasting across Teague, Crystal listened to her stead neigh in unison with the others as she turned toward Talon. "Since you are now staying until this mess is cleaned, I would feel more comfortable if we learned more about who we were traveling with."

"Ask away, cupcake, I'm as open as a creationist's arms to new followers." He continued before she could respond. "What do you yearn to hear? I was born, raised, abandoned, became a thief, and here I am. Happy as could be."

"Give more detail between those events. My childhood is known, as well as Eric's. Let's hear yours?"

"That's his business. Do not pry into his personal life."

"It is only as private as the fun we have in our quarters. This should be a fun tale until we reach the city. What exactly do you inquire of my younger years?"

"Where were you raised?" she asked eagerly.

"I was not born of this country, Osiren. My brother and I come from the northern country."

"Bancouver?"

"Precisely."

"From the time I spent in Kyron, I learned Bancouver was taken by three tyrants. These tyrants forbade migrating, no?"

"Correct. Next question?"

"Why leave Bancouver? Why Osiren?" questioned Crystal.

"This . . . this was the story you were searching to hear. Twenty-three years after my creation is when trouble began brewing. A cry for change called to me. A rebellion against the current King was being rallied, and I eagerly signed on. I underwent strict tests before officially joining. The leaders wanted to see if their recruits were qualified and met criteria and what not. After a few dozen physical and mental exams, they realized I was naturally gifted." He smirked, his ego glowing.

"A person of your ability would prove useful in a mutiny."

"One could almost say they used me."

"As most organizations will do, but continue."

"The big heads learned about the gifts I possessed and I received my code name. Recruits were awarded a unique name of their own; a safety measure to protect our identities. Our creation names linked us to our friends and family. If an enemy could find this information, the people closest to that soldier would be at risk . . . The Lone Wolf. The title chosen for me. And I stayed true to the name. I was told I'd never cooperate with another unit or teammate. In fact, I never had a companion throughout the rest of my training. Even on missions I was solo—which I preferred. On the eve of the assault that would shift the power of the country out of the King's hands, I was requested to work with five other agents. My dossier had been read, re-read, studied—they knew what I was capable of performing. Yet, they were strangers to me. Didn't learn anything beyond their code names. During the mission, the team separated to accomplish their assigned tasks and all went as planned. But after the siege, we discovered a mistake we made; there was a casualty. The six agents returned as five. We lost a man and his whereabouts are a mystery." His voice dwindled with the last few words.

"No way! *You* were part of the Fist in the conspiracy that helped the dictators gain the throne?" Crystal was bouncing on her seat, literally and figuratively.

"Those *dictators* were pure of hearts before the riches. The power, fortune, fame must have warped their way of thinking. Though I was a witness to their transformation, I was blinded, but . . . once they condemned their most loyal agent to death . . . my life was endangered. I gathered my family and together we fled. My parents . . . did not survive the journey."

Phoenix commented, "Mr. Z has quite a huge fortune for a runaway from another country. Many barely have coins to spare."

"Our inheritance. My family name has a long line of wealth. There were also rewards for being in the Fist—a pretty hefty sum. I shared it with my family. When we lost our parents, my broth—Mr. Z stole both our shares. That was the beginning of his egotistical madness. Assuming I know where these questions are headed . . . Let me see . . . Our travels together have been several months correct? Since the night of the raid . . . roughly five years has passed."

"You're twenty-eight?"

"And I'm still as handsome as ever. Age has only been a friend."

Laughter filled the space between them, lightening the mood. The adults continued to chat the rest of the journey to Cosarave. Crystal pestered Talon about his trip to Osiren and begged him to describe the culture in Bancouver. He spent most of the conversation focusing on himself and explaining the number of mates he had every night. Crystal merely giggled at his vulgar yet amusing stories.

She listened to the banter as everyone awaited their turn to talk. Her gaze drifted over both of their eyes. And smiles. A ball of warmth started swirling in her chest as a slight grin appeared. *We have spent much time with one another. We're a family now. To think . . . all of this started over a loaf of bread.*

The jolly spirits were interrupted as they approached an unusual phenomenon. An extensively long barricade was built, blocking their path. Plenty of guards were situated upon the blockade and along the front side. Several weapons were strapped to their waists, a range between daggers to whips. Before anyone dismounted, bows were drawn and aimed at the trespassers.

"Only personnel with approved permission may enter to reach Cosarave City."

"What in the name of the Protectors is this?" protested Talon, keeping an eye on the archers.

"Protection from unauthorized outside terrors that have intentions of causing a disturbance in the city."

"The blockade is rather far from the city," stated Crystal.

"We were positioned a calculated distance from our border. If a force would try and break through, a warning would be able to reach the King before the enemy invaded."

"That sounds . . . utterly idiotic. Unless there are horses hidden behind your poorly built gate house, that guard has a far distance to sprint with the fear of terrorists chasing after him."

Phoenix placed his hand on Talon's shoulder to shut him down. He stepped forward declaring, "The name is Phoenix Reinhard. I prove no threat to this city. My only wish is to assist in defending its people against an army that will soon be marching to this location. Protecting Cosarave is my only intention."

The guard's eyebrows rose as he heard his name. He called to a few of his buddies, and they huddled together. A few silent whispers escaped their circle revealing nothing. Once the three of them made a decision, their weapons were drawn.

"Phoenix Reinhard is a wanted criminal across Osiren. For many different accounts of criminal activity, it is hard to believe that goodwill brings you here. Each city that has been visited by your cult, corruption sets forth and destroys their way of life. I'm in charge of this barricade and if I did not have to attend to my duties, I would bring you into custody. Five minutes to leave or I will be forced to make an arrest under the law and guidance of Cosarave."

Crystal fled back to the safety of their carriage. Talon, though, scoffed. "You're allowing us to flee? No hidden agenda? We are nationally renowned criminals; bringing us to justice should be more important than your wall."

Crystal whispered, "This is completely unnecessary."

The guard's mug turned into a look of disgust. "As of this moment we are hired as gatekeepers. Arresting you is not in our job description."

"Mercenaries. Hired arms trying to make quick coin. It is a pleasure to see Cosarave is employing the work of good, honest men."

"Leave. Now."

"Talon, enough," cautioned Phoenix.

As the three horses began cantering away, Crystal angrily grumbled, "The emerald needs to be under our watch before those people steal it. Who knows if troops have not already infiltrated their defense like in Emerica?"

"Starting another brawl and adding another item to our list of felonies will do more harm than good. Avoiding this conflict is annoying, but necessary. Even if it's a risky and dangerous decision . . . We have no choice, but to leave the city be. Zannala will have to move up on our priorities."

"We must remain careful. Remember back at Flores? Those people were dressed in common clothing from Zannala. If that's more than just a coincidence, we need to be cautious. That small army has sent word with our success and reached them by now. They will be awaiting our arrival."

"We will have to prepare for anything."

"They better have troops ready to greet us, otherwise the emerald is as good as ours."

Crystal looked at their damaged bodies, examining their conditions. No amount of rest will cure us of all our ailments. We're still hurting. If there really are forces waiting for us, I just hope we can escape and survive.

CHAPTER 23

Many days passed as they traveled north. An approaching doom appeared in front of them as a sea of sand flew through the air. The ground's life continually worsened as they headed toward the city. Eventually its death was so apparent, not a sign of nature could be found and the horizon was nothing beside a blanket of tan. Going a bit farther, the horses began crying in pain as the hot terrain had found its way into their hooves.

"It is safe to assume their defense is sand."

"Zannala's surrounded by sand . . . a full complete circle." Talon descended from his horse. "We will have to release our faithful companions. It will only worsen as we journey forward and it would be cruel to force them along. They deserve a rest after carrying our weight cross-country. The sand and heat will practically kill them. Our carriage would look like a dune in no time."

"What are we to do with them? Just release them?" worried Crystal.

"The only danger they would find themselves in is from hunters. Most will adapt."

Phoenix looked at him. "It's good you are always right."

A heavy gust of wind rushed by them, picking up loose sand. As it whipped by, the particles scraped against their skin and scratched at their clothing. The suns' heat became immensely stronger underneath the barrage of rocks, toasting them. With their vision blinded, they trudged through the storm to the back of their carriage. Rushing inside to escape, the group found Alex leaning against his father. Eric was still in the same position intently staring at the wall, except this time his arm laid around Alex's neck with his hand limp against his chest.

"Eric, the pity party's finished. We have to walk," barked Talon.

"If we leave anything behind . . . it will be left for scavengers. Finding this again . . . is an almost impossible task. But I have no clue how far the city is." Phoenix squinted through the wall of sand floating with the wind. "It could be a far walk . . . Bring only what's necessary."

With every bag packed to the fullest, bursting with items, they set out to Zannala. The horses were released, completely removing their reins and saddle. At first, they remained still. The team tried shooing them away, but they refused to budge. Deciding to move forward, their steeds tried to follow, but the conditions kept them at bay. As the sand blocked their view, the horses disappeared behind the storm.

Crystal kept their recovered emeralds in her duffel bag and far away from Phoenix. Talon instructed them to use scraps of cloth to keep their faces covered. He also warned that any bare skin should be hidden. Phoenix put on his cloak with his hood down low over his eyes. Talon lifted his bandana over his mouth and lowered his goggles. Crystal tied ripped parchments across her face like a veil, and Eric and Alex wore the heavy jackets. Bearing the wilderness, they traveled through the treacherous landscape, watching the sand swirl, dancing to the rhythm of nature.

Trudging along, their spirits were revived when they finally came across signs of civilization. Huge wooden walls stood before them, worn down and scuffed. Entering the lost city in the sand, Crystal and Alex dropped to their knees. Exhausted and aching, they took a few minutes to watch the civilians go about their lives. Oddly enough, not a single child was spotted among them.

Crystal was surprised to see all the citizens' skins were a darker pigment and they were barefoot. Before Flores, she had never seen someone who was drastically different than her. And to wear nothing on their feet, when they stood all day in sunbaked soil? Her mind was blown.

Beige was a popular color between both genders. The men had pants that were noticeably cut above the knees and wore no shirts, while the women's attire consisted of harem pants and strapless bras. The women also adorned their faces with a colorful piece of cloth covering from their nose to jaw. Only the women's face protectors had vibrant colors.

The structure of each building was simple: built with clumped sand and supported with wood. Some small shops and huts were inside dunes. The houses appeared old. And decrepit. A giant palace was stationed in the central part of the city. Made primarily of their unlimited resource, the castle was made of three towers connected together by catwalks. Each tower was topped by circular domes that shone underneath the suns' rays, causing Talon to point out the possibility of it being made from metal. As they admired the scenery, no one noticed a young female standing before them. She coughed gently, trying to assert her presence.

The woman, wearing a purple veil with red marks along the edges, smiled as all eyes came upon her. "Hello, welcome to Zannala, city of the sand and home of the scorpions. My name's Sydney and I'm here to guide you throughout our precious home."

"You are our . . . We have an assigned tour guide?" asked Crystal. She nodded politely.

"I-uh, what? Scorpions? Why would you advertise that?" Talon stared at her questioningly.

"We are proud of our inhabitants that coexist in the city with us. Our founder, Althea, brought them to a high esteem, as her pet was a scorpion and helped fight along the Protectors in the Third Teague War, creating the new era of the Prophet's Prophecy."

"Would you say the people of this city were religious?" Phoenix watched her carefully.

"We have worship houses located at each entrance. Zorumaka and Kyrudorous are the deities that the Creator should have been."

"We want a hotel," spat Eric.

"Ah, an excellent request!" she chirped with a cheery voice. "I shall lead all of you to our most luxurious establishment if you'd like? It can be quite costly—"

"Don't care. Take us now."

The snappy response caught her off guard. Her grin faltered a bit. "If you would follow me . . ." Her voice deflated.

As she led them down Eastern Street, she began explaining the city as most guides would. Eastern Street was one of the four main streets. It divided the city into four quarters. The northwestern quarter was primarily the lower class. The Less Quad was made up of refugees fleeing from the countries Bancouver and Ventaceny, along with citizens who could not afford to live in High Quad. The majority of the population was male and female runaways from other countries. The High Quad, the northeastern section, housed only the wealthiest residents. Mostly women; the only men that resided there were guards, servants, husbands, or men who had relocated from within Osiren. The Coin Quad, the southwestern part, and the Med Quad, southeastern part, were where most of the stores and buildings resided.

Each of the Quads were positioned specifically: the High Quad welcomed all movers from other cities in Osiren to join them, while the Med Quad was there to heal any abrasions from the sandstorms. On the opposite side, the Less Quad was where all cross-county visitors would stay. The Coin Quad was close by, mainly for all the Less Quadrians to have easy travel to their jobs.

Being on the wealthiest street in the city, the group was able to witness the highly architectural homes and buildings. Most of the homes looked exactly the same, without any variations between them. Even the rich houses were beginning to wear down from being surrounded by their own defense. They continued to walk down Eastern Street until Sydney stopped their travel in front of one of the tallest places in Zannala.

Bringing them inside, Sydney left them and a lady at the front desk took her position. With her orange veil, she received payment for two rooms: honeymoon and group-size suites. The honeymoon suite was accommodated with a single bed, couch, bathroom, closet, and small kitchen supplies. The group-size one was identical, besides two extra beds and was more spacious. Unloading their belongings like pack mules, Eric took his chance. He grabbed Alex and brought him into the honeymoon suite, slamming the door behind him.

"Eric must still be taking Brett's death really hard . . . He seems to be more over protective of Alex now," mentioned Crystal, placing her duffel bag under the bed.

Talon and Phoenix both nodded in agreement as they unpacked. With his skin itching, Talon exploded with feelings. "Phoenix, I don't like this. No city has a welcome center. Especially one of the poorest cities in Osiren. They knew we were coming."

"I completely agree, but we're exhausted. That adventure through the sand has left us weak."

"For certain, this hotel was not suggested as a coincidence." He began pacing around the room. "I will return shortly; I would like to scan the city. Not knowing my surroundings will drive me to insanity."

"Before you go, I noticed we have only passed women. And they wear different color facemasks. Why is that?"

"Cupcake, you have such an inquisitive mind. When in a foreign place, it is best not to sound ignorant. Those masks are called murans, sometimes referred to as muranos depending on your origin. It is derived directly from the Forgotten Language, roughly meaning "purpose in life." The color represents a woman's place in Zannala society. The clerk downstairs is wearing orange, which translates to the working class in their culture. Sydney's muran, which was purple, represents royalty. The red marks . . . baffle me." He stood at the frame of the door, seemingly alarmed by his observation. "Native men are not often found throughout the day since they are required to work. After all, the city of the sand is a matriarchal society." Before he made his exit, he paused again. "Joking aside, remain vigilant. No woman wearing a purple muran would escort us travelers through the city. Keep an eye on the shadows of the room while I'm gone."

As the door shut behind him, Phoenix came from behind, wrapping his arms around Crystal. He tightened his grip around her waist, nuzzling his face into her neck. She smiled.

"What's the occasion?"

"There has been no time for just us," whispered Phoenix, still holding her close against him.

Her warm smile radiated through him, forcing him to copy her grin. She spun around to face him, their eyes immediately finding each other's. She leaned in for his romantic touch. Their lips met, sliding into place. The sensation sent them soaring, feeling weightless. Reuniting their lips again and again, she felt the world around her was distant. None of the bad things happening actually existed, as if they were scenes from a poorly produced play. Phoenix loved holding her, keeping her close to his chest. She always felt protected, safe. *His hugs are so reassuring,* she thought. There was a knock and they parted. It was Sydney making sure they were feeling at home.

"All is well. Not much time has passed since we parted ways earlier . . . Take the evening to relax, we will manage fine." Phoenix's tone was as sharp as his blade.

"Talon made a good move . . . Shall we go for a stroll?" suggested Crystal.

Leaving Sydney behind at the hotel and double-checking their locks, the two of them went for a walk along North Street. Crystal slowly noticed more men appear on the streets, bringing life to the city. Many people from other countries were roaming around as well. She easily spotted them by their fashion sense—*nothing beige on them*! Witnessing the mixture of cultures from three different countries was an experience words could not describe.

As they traveled under the relentless suns, Crystal spoke: "I feel for Eric; he's suffering. Suffering alone . . ."

"Lost loved ones are the hurdles of life. There are different ways we handle the pain. His . . . his is to be in solitude."

"But he has his son."

"Who he is afraid to lose . . . This . . . I am to blame. All of it. I should have been faster . . . stronger. If we never docked in Holick . . . What if I had stayed with him as they ran, instead of on stage? Brett would still be breathing."

Crystal was stunned, listening to a hardened veteran take fault for events not in his control. "All those are just speculations. No one can tell what the future would have in store if we changed our actions. If the stage were abandoned, the guards and patriotic citizens would have been in pursuit. We would have been banished before Talon found the White Dragon or I learned the fate of my grandmother."

"At least there would be six of us. And a happier Eric. My sword does not equal a life." Phoenix stopped walking, turning slightly to Crystal. "I was referring to more than what happened at Assassin City. Our first meeting . . . If I had been able to defeat Alpha—all of them. That family should have never been involved. I ruined their lives. Especially Alexander's. He has lost all that he loved; to be taken in by wonderful parents . . . only to be kidnapped, enslaved, and forced to witness yet another father's murder. That night in Luminar should have produced a different survivor."

"Whoa, Phoenix, you have accomplished *so* much."

"Thanks to my failures, Emerica was lost and your hometown destroyed." His voice trembled as he clenched his shaking hands.

Crystal let her hand fly, merely tapping his cheek. Startled, he looked down at her. "What happened to Lanster has nothing to do with us. Listen to the words I have to say." She waited as he tilted his head up. "Without you, I would have been beaten back in that alleyway. Possibly killed . . . or raped. Without *you,* I would have become another casualty in Emerica. Our enemies would have collected all the emeralds and caused enough chaos I could never fathom."

"But Brett—"

"His death is heartbreaking. Terrifying. But he is a casualty of this race for the emeralds. A casualty, like the citizens of Luminar, Flores, and Emerica. Time could only tell when Skull's scrooges decided to finally kidnap them. Or kill them? It was *fate* our ship stopped in Holick. We helped Eric escape that cage he was trapped in, surrounded and tormented by his own memories. Talon, even— we saved him, too. That feeling must have crossed your mind as well. A family was brought to him after years of isolation. Phoenix, your strength and courage and wisdom has far exceeded your scope of view, touching more people of Teague than you will ever understand." His face grew soft, listening to the words that flowed through her mouth. "I think . . . there is a need to celebrate every victory, no matter how small. Who knows when there will be another?"

Crystal stayed quiet watching as he perked up from his despair. "The wisdom you possess leaves me astonished and beyond words."

She blushed. The mood was set; this was her time. She had to know. "I hate to pry, but how did you feel . . ." She suddenly began fumbling for her next sentence. "How do you feel about . . . us?"

"What? What about *us*?"

"The connection between us. It feels . . . right. When we kiss, and when you hold me—I never want anything else."

"I'm just . . . I'm friendly. Friendly, that's all."

"Then why have you not yet locked lips with Talon? Or Eric? We both know a *friendly* kiss is definitely on his list."

"Where is this going?"

"When I'm thought of, what feelings and thoughts do you associate with the image? It has been . . . almost a year, and yet you still remain closed from the team. Your emotions and state of mind are still kept hidden underneath. I am tired of being left in the dark."

"Crystal, you're just my friend. A companion. A comrade that I could not have done this without."

"Lying has never been your strength. Too afraid to open the

path to your heart? Afraid to allow me close?"

"The act of another person becoming close is dangerous. My thoughts would be divided between survival and my goals. I would become vulnerable, weak. You . . . would be my weakness. We are nothing more than friends. That's final."

Crystal saw a flash in his eyes, a flare of rage, but this time she was not fazed. Tears started flowing as she sobbed, "To be known as the weakest human in all of Teague would be an honor with you. More of an honor than being a bitter, lonesome monster with no one to love." Crystal stomped away back toward the hotel.

He attempted to chase her, but Talon appeared in his path. Before Phoenix had a chance to explain, Talon raised his hand: "Not my business. Not getting involved. I have urgent news."

His mind too rattled to think straight, he mumbled, "Continue."

"My investigation brought me to the public library in the Coin Quad on Zannala's traditions. We have some bad problems." He enunciated bad, prolonging its sound. "Remember those red stripes on Sydney's muran? Yeah, well, they represent servitude."

"Her job is to escort strangers. That could possible make her a servant."

"No-no, you're not connecting the dots. Her primary color is purple, which symbolizes royalty. Put those two together and what do we have? Do not say magenta. Together, let us say the answer. She is a *servant* of royalty. A woman with her status would not be seen outside of the castle working the streets. She had to have orders to leave. In search of someone. In search of us."

"Does that mean the King is behind this treason?"

"There is no King—at least one with any political position. The Queen sits upon the throne. It's a possibility, but perhaps they are trying to capture us for the reward? Collectively, we would bring in a large sum of wealth to these streets. Either way, I have *no* desire to meet her."

Phoenix's brain pulled itself together and collected his

thoughts. Vitalizing his body, he focused on Talon's stern face. "When the suns rise, we will be gone. We cannot leave until we retrieve the emerald. Less Quad will be the best move; we should blend in smoothly."

"Is waiting that long smart?"

"It's starting to get late," Phoenix glanced at the clear sky. Stars glimmered faintly far above the sunset that was three quarters past the horizon. "And we are still exhausted. On the run, we would be as good as dead."

"As much as I would like to implore that we retreat now, I'll remain by your side. But Eric needs to be physically dragged him from his slump. If we are to be refugees within a day, he needs to be back on par." Phoenix unwillingly agreed.

"Sir," whispered a high pitch voice. "Emerald X has entered Zannala city. The four of them are traveling with a little boy, who has no records in our database. They are residing at Eastern Quad Hotel."

No response was given. The woman started becoming uneasy until a low grumble echoed throughout the room. "Unexpected, their arrival and the boy, but he may be of use."

"What are my orders, my King?"

"Bring a halt to all troop movement. Recall them. Soldiers stay within city boundaries."

"Yes, Your Majesty!"

"Sydney, we are to discuss the *details* on how to execute the plan for tomorrow. Every single word that I speak needs to be repeated to Gauri. No exceptions. If it does not go as planned, the Protectors will have the privilege of meeting you early."
She inhaled deeply and listened intently.

CHAPTER 24

The following morning arrived and the three of them were awake and prepared to start the day bright and early. Crystal avoided Phoenix at all cost, pretending he never existed. Phoenix did the same, slowly becoming disgruntled. Crystal spent the most amount of time in the shower. While she was still bathing, Talon reminded Phoenix of what needed to be done.

"What am I supposed to do? What should I even say?"

"Comfort him; bring him back to a normal, fighting state. If we are ambushed, he'll be dead first."

"My charisma fails me in these situations and emotions are not my specialty. Are you able to take my place?"

"He and I have not created a bond to withstand the intensity of this situation. It would end with me insulting him more than the latter. If you're nervous, bring Crystal."

"She refuses to acknowledge me . . ."

Talon was about to question the tension, but realized it was none of his concern. "Muster that courage and go already!" He started leading him to the door.

As he pushed him out, a hotel maid came through wearing an orange veil. "Pardon my intrusion, is there a Mr. Zaccaro in this suite?"

Alarmed, Talon stared at her. "That would be I."

"A letter has arrived for you in the mail room."

"It has been barely a day since our arrival, who possibly knows where I am residing?"

"The subject was named 'relic'?"

He raised his eyebrows. "They must have the wrong person . . . but I'll have a look. Phoenix, when I return, you better *not* be here!"

Phoenix sighed, casually approaching the honeymoon suite. After three knocks, there was a faint "enter." Phoenix opened the door to find Eric lying on his bed and Alex doodling on a piece of paper.

"What are you drawing, buddy?"

Alex shielded it from his view. "Nothing important."

Phoenix merely shrugged. "Would it be okay to continue drawing with Crystal in the other room? I need a few minutes with your father, alone."

Alex gathered his things. He left the room with the door quietly clicking shut.

Phoenix sat beside Eric, who continued gazing at the ceiling. "I think it's been long enough; we should talk."

"About?"

"Nothing. Everything?"

Eric stayed silent.

"Maybe a walk through the Quads and the fresh air of Zannala will help." Eric again stayed silent, but dragged himself off his bed. Making a snarky remark about how polluted the air is with sand, he left the room. Phoenix took a deep breath, following behind him.

Walking along North Street once more, he strayed away from Eric. Phoenix was at a complete loss on how to handle the situation. Armies? Mercenaries? Demons? Easy to handle; simply a blade to the throat. But fragile states of friends and their emotions? That was uncharted territory. *What do I say? Should I ask him about his feelings?* He kept thinking the same thoughts repeatedly until Eric beat him to the punch.

"Without Brett . . . I'm lost. I have no one but Alex now. Who will eventually leave me, too. There is no longer a home to return to. I've never felt this alone . . . so distant. I know you've lost more than I ever will, and this sounds like a whine session, but this is a first for me. When I lost my family . . . it was painful, but Brett was my best friend, brother, therapist . . . lover. All I can think about is keeping Alex safe in fear of losing him too soon."

"That's why I stay away from feelings. No one gets into my heart."

Eric barked, "That's a pitiful line. Crystal burrowed her way through to your heart. Just because you won't admit it does not make it any less true."

How in the Protectors' names am I having the same conversation on the same street?

"No, she did not."

"What is the purpose of lying to yourself?"

"This conversation is *not* about me!" he shouted, snapping at him.

"Then what's it about, Phoenix?" Eric's voice increased in anger.

"You and your issues!" Phoenix felt the pressure of Eric's energy again. The dark, demonic aura came forth, intoxicating him. This time though, Phoenix felt the same mist flow from his own person. The two energies seemed to be searching for one another and the minute they combined, Eric's pupils dilated.

"The only issue I deal with is that nothing goes my way!"

"What do you want?"

"I want Brett! I want a normal life. I want my family." Eric's anger continued to soar.

Phoenix sensed the aggression. "That is not all."

"I want . . . I want . . ."

"What is it?"

"You. Phoenix, I want you. Irresistible is the only word to describe you. Strong, smart, and gorgeous. That rugged, hard exterior and the mysterious man beneath it. Even when on the hunt to find Brett, I thought about you. Every time I saw you with Crystal it destroyed me to no end. You're just another thing that's out of my reach." They stopped abruptly. Phoenix blatantly gawked at Eric, unable to speak.

"I . . . I overheard your feelings for me. Back on our way to Flores. Why did it take this long to talk about it?"

"If I kept it to myself, it would remain a secret and not be real. Our friendship is important. I would not want to lose that or have my feelings interfere with the mission. I dreamt of only a single moment with you . . ."

Eric slowly went in, leaning forward. Phoenix was too in shock to move. Eric placed one hand on Phoenix's waist and the other behind his head. At first, Phoenix resisted, but the temptation was too strong. They passionately made contact, skin on skin, lip to lip. Coming to his senses, Phoenix pulled away. No words would be able to describe what just occurred. He took a few steps back. Their connection split as each of their own darkness's receded.

The walk back was more awkwardly silent than the first. Phoenix trailed behind Eric by several feet. He had no interest in catching up, and Eric didn't necessarily want him to. As they reached the hotel an ominous feeling sparked between them. Something was amiss. Fear seeped into their stomachs as they entered the lobby only to be appalled by the sight. The entire interior was a wreck and in pieces. The windows were shattered, the doors broken, and items scattered across the floor. Without communicating, they booked it to their rooms.

Oh no, Crystal.

Alex better be there.

All their supplies were damaged and carelessly tossed around. Not a single piece of furniture remained intact. Even the bathroom was turned upside down. Phoenix rummaged through his things, praying to the Protectors to find a clue. Crossing into Eric's room, he found his clue. Daggers stuck out of the wall in a perfect line, with blood splatters decorating the background. *They got them. Talon was right. They're gone.*

Flipping his mattress in rage, Eric spotted a crumbled paper on the floor. He flattened it out and instantly recognized the drawing. The one Alex created earlier. Alex wouldn't show it to him, so he took a moment to examine it. A poorly drawn boy was in the middle. The boy was holding the hands of two men. The one on the right was coming out of a tree. His torso formed into a tree trunk. The male on the left was surrounded by black fire. He slowly folded the paper and hid it in his pocket. He turned around to Phoenix's wide eyes.

Before he had the chance to speak, Eric shouted, "Don't say it! Don't you dare—"

"He—they're not here. They've been taken."

They raced out of the hotel looking for witnesses. Male, female—anyone that could have given them an idea of who took their friends and where. But the streets were empty. They visited building after building, busting down each of their doors. It was in vain—everything was deserted. The entire High Quad had a population of zero.

"This is ridiculous, how is there not a soul in the area?"

"These bastards have Alex. I'll rip them to shreds."

The two of them made their way down South Street. Reaching the main road, they spotted a line of men. Each was equipped with a variety of weapons. For every ten soldiers, a female stood in front. The women's murans were different shades of blue. Some of them even had different markings with several other colors. *I suppose these are all the commanders.* One of the women had her hair in a ponytail. With a dark shade of blue, her veil had purple stripes across it. *Royalty.* Eric caught sight of the same female, examining her. A light bulb suddenly lit up.

"That was the woman at Flores!" Hearing his excitement, her head whipped in their direction.

She erupted into a cackle. "Interesting meeting again in my

hometown."

"Where *is* Alex?" demanded Eric.

"That information is classified and I am the only lucky one to know."

Before Eric could lose his temper, Phoenix stepped in. "Gauri, I believe is your name? My name's Phoenix. Phoenix Reinhard. Who are you?"

"Do not bother appeasing me, boy; I do not mess with your kind. I am aware of your identity. I am familiar with your entire group. Random children with too much hubris and testosterone trying to play hero."

"*Tell* me where my son is!"

"What do you want?"

She shook her head. "Simple minded men. I will play this game. Your friends will be released if you pass along the emeralds that you rudely swept from under my nose."

The boys both looked puzzled. "They're in our rooms at the hotel."

"We crossed no emeralds. Do not lie! Unless your wish is to lose your worthless, filthy lives!"

"Watch your tongue, witch!" snapped Eric.

Gauri hissed. "If you are not going to obey, I will just scavenge them from your dead bodies! Men, obliterate them!"

The line of thirty men charged toward Phoenix and Eric. Their weapons went waving in the air as they rushed forward. Swords, spears, whips, knives; the variety was endless. Phoenix unhitched his White Dragon, steadying himself for the onslaught. Eric watched the crowd with thirst, balling his fists, remaining defenseless.

Eric went berserk, swinging his fists at the nearest soldier. He successfully landed blow after blow upon their torsos. The sound of impact was music to his ears. Trying to stay focused, he was able to slide his body away from the blades. But the moment he heard the crack of bone and watched the blood leak from the men's noses, instincts assumed control. He released a powerful jab, fracturing a man's ribs. He pulled back his elbow and knocked another soldier in the gut. After bashing a face against the ground, he stole a knife from the sand.

As Phoenix fought his wave of enemies, he sensed Eric's aura. The connection they had made earlier created a channel of communication between them. He felt his rage. Aggression. Sadness. Loss of control. He somehow was able to manage and separate these extra emotions in his body from warping his own mind.

Despite being in the middle of bloodshed, Phoenix felt elated. This was the first time he had the chance to put his blade into practice. And he loved it. The White Dragon glided swiftly through the air, striking the resistance in half. He was astounded by the sharpness of the blade. His weapon was treating each man like a pond of water, surfing right through the surface.

Gauri watched as her men littered the battlefield. The corpses bled as the outsiders remained standing and unscathed. The other commanding ladies readied their weapons, preparing for battle, but stopped as Gauri wielded her weapon high. They stood down as Eric caught sight of the nonverbal battle cry.

Instinct driven, his feet rapidly hit the ground. Taking the first strike, his knife aimed directly for her chest. Gauri carelessly deflected the blow, backhanding him with her sword. The wound was deep, but none of his concern. Taking a step back, she charged at him like a wild boar. Every swing created a hum that vibrated through the air. Phoenix practically felt the impact of her sword on Eric's knife. Or bone, depending on where she landed. Gauri relentlessly attacked Eric, hammering away at his defense.

Eric moved away from his target to recover and breathe. His berserk mode began to vanish, leaving behind the drained, in-over-his-head host. But nonetheless, he mustered up a second wind. This time a weird phenomenon happened: when his weapon came in range, her sword began to glow a bright white. The blade of her weapon stretched, going limp at the end. With a mind of its own, it curled itself around his knife and forearm like a chain. With a strong ferocity, she ripped the metal from his possession. Bringing most of his skin along with it. Before he could *really* comprehend the intense pain rendering his arm useless, her weapon glowed once more to retake its original form. Completely stunned by this magic, Eric didn't budge as the weapon was plunged into his lower abdomen. He bellowed as it was pulled out to only change back into its rubbery form. It was swiftly wrapped around his throat, forcing him to be silent.

Phoenix raised his Dragon at her, but his intimidation failed. "One false move and monkey boy gets it." Seeing no good avenue, he angrily placed the sword back into its sheath. "Good. Now that you laid waste to my troops, we are going to reunite the two of you with the others. Follow me, but *watch* yourself. My women will be vigilant and the only thing stopping me from slicing this boy's neck open is the boss. It might look like rubber, but it's still a hundred percent blade."

Phoenix unwillingly followed her through the town. He couldn't see Eric's face, but he knew his body was screaming in agony. He was leaving a trail of blood. *If he doesn't get medical attention soon . . . he might be seeing Brett sooner than he thought . . . How would he tell him about that kiss?* All of Zannala's citizens came out of hiding, watching them be led to their destination. Walk of shame had now been granted a new meaning. Gauri led them up South Street, straight into the palace yard. Finally, the parade stopped at the front entrance of the home of the ruler of Zannala. Phoenix soaked in the sand castle and was able to put the pieces together.

"A question before we enter?"

Gauri banged on the gate. "Is it necessary?"

"The Queen—she has been the person behind those attacks. The destruction of Luminar, Emerica, Flores—she ordered raids on the cities?"

She smiled showing her glistening teeth. "Him—and any mercenaries that signed on to the job." Before he could even react to her pronoun correction, his blood pressure skyrocketed. The excitement of cutting her in two became the only thing on his mind as they entered through the large doors. The entrance brought them straight into the throne room, which was filled with complete darkness.

"I have brought the last two, my Majesty."

Instantaneously, the lights flashed, illuminating all the corners. The throne room consisted of small decorations and pillars that reached the tall ceiling. A long, purple rug lay upon the sand to a step in the center. A total of twenty steps separated the royalty from the peasants. The King of Zannala's giant body rested comfortably in his cushioned seat. His eyelids opened, revealing yellow irises.

Standing, he easily reached a height above six feet. A thin layer of black hair covered his dark complexion. His broad shoulders showed the definition of his strong build. Wearing nothing besides a vinyl cape and beige pants, he puffed up his chiseled chest proudly. With black combat boots and a tamed beard, he made his departure downward, holding a giant, metallic staff. Firmly attached to the top was a blue emerald. Proceeding behind him were several male guards. Each one held on to their victims: Crystal, Alex, and Talon.

His deep, dark voice echoed throughout the chamber: "Thank you, Gauri. Please escort Sydney from the dungeon . . ." Gauri bowed, still holding Eric in her clutches. She transformed her sword back into a solid blade, allowing Eric to gasp freely. Rubbing his neck, he began breathing heavily.

"We know why we all stand in the same space," the King chuckled. "Hand me the two emeralds you stole from us and I will release your comrades . . . without harm."

Phoenix refused to take his eyes off the King. He clenched his jaw, forcing his teeth tightly together. He knew if he spoke, his execution would be imminent.

Eric, on the other hand, had no problem speaking his mind. "We don't have the emeralds, you monstrosity. How many times do we have to repeat ourselves?"

"My child, you stand in my home. Disrespect me and the penalty will be your life."

"Kill me then."

"Your Majesty, he is delusional! I swear!" protested Crystal.

"Silence!" shouted the King. "You," he pointed to Phoenix. "Speak. The emeralds, where may they be found?"

Phoenix bit his lip, but inevitably broke his silence and lost restraint. "You . . . *you* are the monster that murdered all those innocent people. You destroyed countless lives, burned down every sister city. And for what? Power? Control? These emeralds are too strong for you to even handle!"

"I sense hatred toward me? Tell me, what is it that I have done?"

"Luminar. It lies in ruins and the blood of those civilians stains the land. You claimed the lives of innocent people and contaminated the beauty of that city!"

"And . . . I enjoyed *every* second of that night," a mischievous smirk crossed his face, making Phoenix's skin crawl.

"I will avenge each one of them!"

The archers took aim, all sights on Phoenix's chest.

"Enough! My patience has reached its limits. It wears rather thin after all these years." He tilted his staff, pointing the emerald toward Eric and Phoenix.

"What are you doing?" shouted Eric.

"The emeralds have amazing abilities, I've read. For starters, they sense when another emerald is near." He narrowed his eyes at the two convicts. His emerald began shimmering brightly. Nothing happened.

"We told you we don't have those—" Eric stopped mid-sentence, noticing a light being emitted from his crotch area. Two beams reached for the staff, connecting to the blue emerald. Confused, the whole audience watched as the Flores and Emerica emeralds floated from the pockets in his pants. Phoenix also felt some of the demonic aura leaving Eric. As the emeralds drifted toward the King, he could sense the darkness following them.

Grabbing them from midair, the King slammed down his staff, vibrating the entire room. "Tricking a King? How foolish." Eric's eyes drifted between his companions, beyond frazzled. "Such insolence will not go unpunished, but the question is how?" There was a slight pause. "Guards, strip them of their equipment and stash it in the storage room. Lock Phoenix, Eric, and Talon in our dungeon. Bring Crystal and Alexander along for the ride."

"H-how d-do you know our names?" cried Crystal.

The King's eerie smirk showed again. "The emeralds have spoken."

At once the guards were in motion. As they pulled Alex and Crystal away from the group, the two of them cried for help. Phoenix and Eric wanted to fight their way to them, but there was no hope. They were outnumbered, injured, and weaponless. The guards brought the three men down to the prisons, taking the rest of their possessions.

Locked away beneath stone and sand, the men sat in their respective corners. Defeated. Desperation clawed at their throats making it difficult to breath. Failure suffocated the room, creating an imaginary fog no one wanted to inhale. No one knew what to say. Or how to say it. The one question they were all thinking: *how does one admit defeat?* Seeing the uselessness of soaking in their own pity, Talon came to Eric's side, attempting to treat his wounds. He tried to humor them about how the emeralds have an ability to talk to psychos, but no one responded. Their spirits were broken.

"Does anyone else find it odd that their leader is a king and not a queen? This city has been ran by women since the time of the Protectors . . ."

"This is not the right time to debate the King's gender." Phoenix watched as Talon used
his shirt to apply pressure against the abrasion.

"The mood is a tad bit miserable down here is all . . ."

"Eric . . . please fill in the gaps. Why did you have the emeralds? Have you been in contact with them this whole time?"

He kept his eyes away, as would a child that knows he had done wrong. "Back at the City of Assassins . . . after that shit went down . . . I felt as if there was a presence in the carriage with me. Calling my name. Offering the release I needed. I-I know I shouldn't have—especially after everything they did to you, but I reached out to them, searching for comfort. Must have had other motives. Eventually . . . I no longer had control."

"Nightmares . . ." Phoenix watched Eric's shocked expression. "Did you have nightmares?"

"Every night."

"Hold up, I am lost. They are holding Crystal and Alex hostage, and you two are worried about the emeralds we don't have anymore?"

"We lost." The phrase caught Talon and Phoenix off guard. "I'm sure they are marching to Cosarave as we speak. Without transportation . . . we would never be able to save them."

"That's the spirit . . ."

"We haven't lost yet." The others glanced up at Phoenix who stood, staring through the cell bars. "I'm still standing. The two of you, you're both breathing. This is not finished until I say." He faced his companions, his friends. A glimmer of hope flashed through their eyes. "Each one of us has gotten through a lifetime of days where we thought there was no way to continue or move on . . . but here we are. Our worse days—days we thought it would be easier to die—are now in the past because we survived. Neither of you can look me in the eye and say this is where we give up. There is *still* something to fight for."

Kneeling beside Eric still, Talon remained fixated on Phoenix. Emotions of nostalgia rang through his body as he rose to his feet. "A wise youth once told me a wolf is unable to live without his pack. I told him he's never come across a true alpha before. It took me some time and few kicks in the ass to realize that . . . I had not either." Talon offered his palm to Eric. "Pretty boy, there is a son to save and a spouse to make proud. I suggest you join us up here."

Happily accepting the gesture, Eric stood upon his feet holding his wounds. "As Brett would say, there's no time like the present. Or, thank the Protectors. Either works."

Phoenix stood before the two men, renewed. Refreshed. "I have an idea."

"Last time I heard that phrase I was harassed . . ."

"This should be good," replied Talon.

Several hours passed before a crew of guards strolled by for a check-in. Mustering his energy, Phoenix shouted at the guards.

"Sir! How dare you place a female into this *dreadful* dungeon?" he accused, pointing to Talon who undergone a complete wardrobe change. His bandana was wrapped around his hair, covering most of his face. His shirt was wrapped up and tucked inside itself. He stayed back in the corner, hoping the shadows would hide his masculine features.

The guard peered inward, squinting. Examining Talon, he leaned in farther. "That is one ugly lady!"

Talon, with his best voice impression exclaimed, "I resent that!"

"Well ugly or not, we have a special holding chamber for women," stated another guard, unlocking the gate.

The first guard grabbed his arm. "Our men know better than to place a woman below sand. Don't be stupid."

"All of you are *incredibly* rude!" exclaimed Talon who continued to mimic a higher tone. "I'm like your King!"

The guards raised their eyebrows. "How do you figure . . . missy?"

"I was mistaken for a man just because I look like one! I'm a female on the inside. Please release me from these terrible chambers."

The guard went back to unhitching the lock. "I could

understand the confusion. The King went through the same transformation."

"Fine, go retrieve the woman. I'll watch the other fellow."

The moment they entered through the gate, Eric came pouncing out of the shadows. He beat the guard senseless and pilfered his weapon, an iron whip. "You're terrible excuses for soldiers." Before the other one had a chance to retaliate, Phoenix and Talon lashed out. Taking their equipment and locking them behind bars, they regrouped.

"Thankfully *my* pride was not cut down this time . . ."

"What were you saying about the King? How did you know to say that?" asked Phoenix.

"During the After Creator period, or AC, people felt as if they were not the sex they were assigned. Majority of them claimed they were the opposite gender, some even declaring they were neither."

"I don't . . . quite understand?"

"It can be pretty confusing for some, but in layman's terms, they felt as if they were born in the wrong body. Back then, they were referred to as the lost ones."

"And this led you to believe that the King of Zannala is a lost one?" questioned Phoenix.

"I find it highly improbable that men in a matriarchal society could rise to such a status without having been known as a woman first."

Eric shook his head in confusion. "Back to the task at hand. We still have no way to reach Cosarave."

"Wait, before we make drastic decisions, let's pull together the facts. Phoenix, you mentioned before that you had no inclination of how to rid the world of these terrible creations. This King clearly has been doing some research if he knew they had the ability to sense a brother emerald. I say we snoop around his study. Maybe we can learn a few helpful hints." With no other useful suggestions or ideas, the trio made their way back into the castle.

Blindly running through halls and up and down staircases, they made no headway. Making their way back to the throne room, they encountered another squadron of guards. Using their new substitute weapons, the enemies were quickly defeated. Eric was forced to stay away from the fighting—his arm was still throbbing.

Wrapping them up with their own whips, the bodies were hidden in a secluded area nearby. Only one guard was left conscious who they forced to take them to the King's chamber. Once there, their capture was detained. Talon picked several locks without breaking a sweat. The door opened, taking them further into the King's private quarters.

"In a castle such as this, I would expect to find more soldiers stationed in the halls. Not that I am complaining."

"They are probably marching to Cosarave as we speak. This is their final assault on a city."

Without a word, they split to begin searching the sleeping chambers. Breaking into drawers, rummaging through chests, and flipping through papers, they came across nothing. Phoenix made his way to a bookcase, pulling a book, reading it, and then tossing it to the floor. As he slid a purple book from the shelf, it became stuck. On command, the bookshelf began moving downward beneath the floor.

"A secret entrance? Is he *serious* right now? Creativity is dead," scoffed Talon, examining the wide corridor.

Phoenix peeked into the new hallway. "I have a feeling what we are searching for will be found down there."

"Wait," paused Eric, turning away. "We need our supplies. Go ahead, I'll find our equipment."

"This is an extraordinary building; to find the correct room could take hours."

"That may be, but there are not many guards stopping me from busting into every one."

Talon and Phoenix entered the secret entrance. Talon yelled a few words that echoed throughout the passageway. He started laughing at his own comedy as his words bounced back at him. Stepping free from the dimness of the hallway, their pupils had to take a minute to adjust. They found themselves in a humongous chasm. They stood upon a semi-circle platform that was connected to a center island by a bridge. A rickety, ancient bridge that had not seen any maintenance. Candles were attached to the walls of the chamber, but all of their light combined seemed dimmed compared to the intensely glowing object held in the center of the sphere. Taking a closer examination, both of their jaws dropped, coming across Zannala's yellow emerald in all its glory.

Baffled, Talon questioned the sight: "Why is this emerald still here?"

Steering clear of the manifestation of darkness, Phoenix headed toward a clutter of books and paperwork located by the entrance. Most of the pages were torn and scuffed. Some of the articles were even written in the Forgotten Language. Talon came to decipher the text, but was dumbfounded by the writing. Time and moisture had caused the words to begin to fade away. In fact, all the books appeared to be suffering from thousands of years of torment induced by time.

Flipping through a few texts, Phoenix found one that seemed to be published within the last three hundred years. It was titled "The Protectors' Finest Jewelry." He flipped to the chapter that read "Gem Hidden in the Sand." Scanning the page, he found it was written in the Forgotten Language as well, but certain parts were highlighted with descriptions beside the sentences.

"The yellow gem is not one of the same, compared to the others in this novel. This gem is permanently stuck in place, hidden away in the lost castle of the desert. To release the emerald, the other four remaining must be gathered together. Once they are in close range, their combined energy force will trigger the release of this emerald's holding cell. A flash will blind the room as their power mixes and the charm keeping it secure will be lifted. The five of them do not have to be in the same room, but in an approximately close radius of one another. It will then be able to be removed from its resting spot. Note: do not touch with bare hands.'"

"Then we wait for Cosarave's destruction?"

Phoenix had no answer. He placed the book down only to pick up some handwritten notes. He skimmed through them, reading the words intently. "Talon, here . . . look at these."

"He . . . takes detailed observations." Talon took a moment to gaze around. "This man . . . must have dedicated his whole life to this legend. I wonder what would have happened if it was just stories and folklore . . ."

Phoenix paged through more and more details. With each sentence, his excitement increased. "Imagine! If we had this information from the start, this journey would have been easier. There are notes on each individual emerald and their locations. Specifically where in the city it's being held and how to reach it . . . Clearly skipped his own notes stating the peaceful ways . . ."

Talon began reading through the research that lay before him. One topic struck him very uneasily. As Phoenix ranted away, Talon strained his eyes looking at the new-found information.

"Uh . . . Phoenix . . . did you know about this?" Phoenix peered around his shoulder, reading the sentences above Talon's finger. "Eric said he had an extended exposure with the emeralds?"

"I did as well. What's this trying to say?"

"From what he wrote . . . it appears . . . both of you are a *part* of the emerald now."

"I'm . . . connected to them? Like an *X-creature*?"

"Remember how the surrounding area the emerald was resting in soaked up an intense quantity of energy, thus creating those monsters? It states, once removed, it continually emits the darkness and desires to latch on to new victims. The emeralds have a mind of their own . . . I knew there was something special about you."

"Those emeralds must be destroyed and I do not want to be considered one of those monsters!" Phoenix felt his temperature rising. "How do we rid us of its . . . taint?"

Talon scanned the paper. "He has nothing written down. Check the rest of the literature."

The two of them rummaged through the seemingly endless pile of books and papers. By the end of their readings, they had composed a number of their own notes. Organizing their mess, they heard clacking sounds echo through the hallway. Their senses heightened, getting ready for an altercation. Ready to strike the person who entered the chasm, they were relieved to find Eric stumbling along. His face expressed songs of amazement as he gawked at the interior of the room. Before he could say anything about the emerald floating just at an arm's length away, the others said they would explain later.

"There was too much to grab." He handed Phoenix the White Dragon, several daggers to Talon, and some food. "I searched for Crystal's rings . . . She's going to be upset if they have been misplaced." Eric took a moment to look at their faces, seeing signs of distress. "Hope we learned something positive."

"For starters . . . to destroy the emeralds we must bring them to an assigned shrine. The location of the shine is not listed, but all five of the emeralds are necessary to begin the ceremony."

"Another surprise: that is the exact method on how to harness their power as well," added Talon.

"Meaning," explained Phoenix, "by bringing the emeralds there, we are also helping the King prepare for his ritual. It reads: once all the emeralds are in position, stand in the center of the altar. At this pivotal moment, the selected person may either harness their strength, unleash them, or by having an item with the emerald's taint, the person may rebound the energy, thus charging the emeralds. This will eventually cause them to shatter."

"The King needs to be removed first before we move forward. It is only another accomplishment we may add to our resume of treason to this country. Any information on why someone would desire this corruption?"

"Power is the easy answer," answered Talon. "Maybe to try

and make a fortune? Plenty of people would pay a large tariff to be saved from an onslaught of attacks. Which in return would bring Zannala from the depths of poverty."

Eric sighed. "All for this one city he is willing to risk the lives of every Teague citizen. It's similar to a form of corrupt nationalism, but for Zannala. Killing the King can't be difficult . . . and obviously we will continue with the plan of destroying the artifacts. May someone explain what it means by their own taint though? Do we need to capture an X-creature?"

"Talon . . . what's a delicate way to explain this . . .?"

"You *are* an X-creature!"

CHAPTER 25

Crystal kept Alex close by her side as they marched to the perimeter of Cosarave. Sirens began blaring as an all-out manslaughter occurred at the entrance to the barricade. The mercenaries tried to keep their ground, but the battle was clearly not in their favor. Most of the front men were annihilated. The captains sent their runners on their way, praying to the Protectors that their message would arrive on time. Zannala's King ordered his best marksman to climb the barricade and hunt down their game. Their prey barely reached half a mile before they were struck down.

Explosives were carefully placed against the base of the wall. The soldiers took cover, waiting for the roadblock to come tumbling down. The sound of rubble colliding together signaled the clearing of their path. Walking by crumbled rocks and corpses, Alex shielded his eyes from the scene. Crystal also tried to avert her gaze, but the horrific sight glued her attention forward. *Pointless deaths . . . why? All for these emeralds!* Her feelings began transitioning from depressed longing to an uncontrollable resentment. As their march continued, they came across the messengers who had attempted to escape lying upon pink snow. She fixed her attention on the two females leading the army. *Sydney. Gauri. I won't forgive this.*

Cosarave castle was breathtaking. The crystalized structure acted as a mansion. With sturdy walls surrounding the entire premises, the ice castle glistened intensely beneath the rays of the suns. More explosives bombed the side of the structure. The moment the wall collapsed, Zannala's soldiers were ready to raid. They stampeded through their newly created entrance, shouting and causing a scene. But to their surprise, an army was awaiting their arrival. Rows and columns of Icilic Crusaders stood before them adorned in their traditional igloo armor, mimicking the design of samurais—items crafted from a similar crystalized structure of a glacier.

One of the Crusaders stepped forward speaking with a thick accent that sounded like his nose was clogged: "As one of the last great cities remaining, the men and women *refuse* to lay down and freeze. This battle marks the end of your terror on Teague. Citizens! Charge!"

With those last words, the war began.

The King split a section of his army, trying to avoid the unnecessary conflict. Bringing his right hand females and the prisoners, they traveled an alternate path to the castle, which lead them through back roads in a development. The immensely cold environment caused Crystal's hair to stand on end. Shivering endlessly, she thought to herself, *Wish I could have taken the jacket Talon bought.* She rubbed Alex's arm, generating some heat for them to not die from hypothermia.

The streets were oddly quiet besides the disturbing clanging of weapons a few blocks over. *The citizens must be hiding . . . or fighting. Protectors' bless them.* Two civilians crossed their path. Unarmed, one being a child, they scrambled to escape from the warzone that was disrupting their life. Their home. Zannala's soldiers wanted no survivors, especially after one had grown up and become a thorn in their side. The two were hunted down. And murdered. Crystal was unable to stomach what she witnessed.

Reaching the castle, they re-entered the midst of the fighting. The Icilic Crusaders defended their home with more success than anyone would have believed. Wielding maces, clubs, and morning stars, the men fought close and personal with their intruders. The women held scythes, keeping their distance from the enemies' weapons. Alex spotted a few household items amongst the mayhem such as brooms and rolling pins. A few pans here and there.

The Zannala soldiers set up enough dynamite to blow up a miniscule mountain. The Ice Fortress doors shattered apart. The explosion made the entire palace tremble, forcing icicles from the ceiling to come crashing down, causing many casualties. The temperature inside the Ice Fortress dropped almost in half. Neither Alex nor Crystal could stop their teeth from clacking against one another.

The Royal Crusader's resistance was immediately crushed inside the castle. With Zannala's surprise advantage and sheer number of soldiers, the Crusaders stood no match and were melted underneath the weight of the sand. The King traveled through the room unopposed. As more guards were quickly disposed of, he was able to maneuver his way to a solid, ice staircase without a reason to hesitate. Leading them to the highest point of the Fortress, a singular door blocked his path. With no word of warning, his group of soldiers aggressively entered. Standing in the throne room, Cosarave's King and Prince drew their swords. Only four Royal Crusaders stood at their side, ready to sacrifice their lives for their royalty.

Cosarave's King's face tightened with dismay. "Scorpio . . . Plea-please tell me they have taken you hostage!"

Zannala's King released his bone chilling laughter. "I am not one to lie."

"I-I . . . Why would you commit such treason? Destroying our sister cities . . . What motivates you?"

"Pa, there is no reasoning with him," pleaded the Prince. "He's not the man you remember. Regardless of his reasons, his hands are soaked in blood. Osiren citizens' blood. Cosarave's blood. And now he is here for ours."

"I'm pleased that I could lighten your minds by revealing who has been behind this since Luminar, but that will not make your death any less painful. Sydney, Gauri, please show them the true coldness that death brings."

The Zannala troops were being fended off by the Royal Crusaders, giving the ladies a free route to the royalty. Neither of them gave a single thought as they began swinging for blood. The King's agility surprised them for his age. He kept up with Gauri's strikes that never ceased to stop. Deflecting blow by blow, his strength began to fail him. He never had the chance to gain the upper hand. Her magic weapon performed its routine trick, swirling around the Cosarave King's neck. With a quick whip of her wrist, he was decapitated.

The Prince jabbed his spear repetitively at Sydney. She swerved around each one, waiting for her own chance to strike. Spinning around another swing of the spear, she swiftly ducked underneath to rise up with her blade out. The tip just skimmed his torso as he rolled away from her. Bouncing back into action, he twirled the tip of his weapon in hopes of disarming her. It was no use; his abilities were no match to hers. His weapon slid away as he was forced into a corner. Seeing his personal bodyguards down for the count and his father's corpse, his feet got cold. Fleeing from the area, his pursers began to chase him down until Scorpio shouted a command.

"Leave him be."

"Your Majesty!"

"His tongue will not slip, and if it does, no one will believe his tall tales. Let's proceed to the reason why we are here freezing in this unnatural hell."

Crystal's stomach was doing somersaults. A knot formed in her throat as she peered upon the King. Tears formed in her eyes. *This needs to stop! I can't just keep watching from the sidelines like a damsel in distress.* Her attention was brought to the weapon lying beside the body. *Nothing about this is okay.*

Scorpio stepped over the headless corpse toward the throne. Nothing was in his way now. Melting down the royal seat, a secret lever was revealed behind the smoke and liquid. Pulling the lever triggered the entire wall on the side of the room to melt. As the water rushed by only to refreeze in minutes, a hidden staircase was revealed. The spiraling steps led to an even higher point in the fortress. As the remainders of the legion of mercenaries and soldiers stepped onto the stairwell, Crystal struggled to keep her tongue silent.

"You will *not* get away with this! Phoenix will break free!"

The King chuckled. "My dear, he does not have to break free! Once this city melts away, we will be returning to him. His release is guaranteed . . . Only to allow him to be slaughtered by my own hands. If you are to behave, I will allow you to watch."

She kept her attention on Alex. The fear across his face expressed how scared he was. How scared they both were. When they reached their destination, she was in awe. The entire area was covered in what looked like fresh snow with glaciers peeking through from below. The sharp points were scattered around the frozen sanctuary, mostly hidden beneath a layer of white. In the center of the chamber, completely encased in ice, was Cosarave's pure, white emerald. Scorpio motioned his soldiers to halt, having only Sydney and Gauri follow him.

"Ah . . . at last! My life's conquest . . . The last emerald . . . All these years have passed and now it is finally in my grasp."

"I will not let that happen!" yelled Crystal, sliding her way between them and the emerald. She held her back straight, holding the sword she had swept away from the battle before her.

"How did you manage to hide that?" growled Gauri, angry at her own ignorance.

"Stupid girl! Do you realize you will die?"

"This emerald will not fall into your hands!"

"Sydney, make her regret standing between my love and I."

"Yes, Majesty."

Sydney waltzed up to her, pulling her sword from its sheath. Straight away she swung, and Crystal rolled through the snow. Hopping onto her feet, she lunged forward, scattering white flakes around her boots. Sydney attempted to intercept the swing, but she slipped and lost her balance. The terrain gave Crystal the advantage to leave an incredibly deep laceration across Sydney's chest. Watching the blood drip from her blade sent an electrifying signal to her brain. She couldn't even imagine, let alone act, on an instinct to harm another person. But here she was, standing before her opponent with their blood on her weapon. Like a real warrior. Though the sight of blood sent an uneasy tingling sensation through her lower extremities. Or she was getting frostbite.

Sydney, infuriated, hastily retaliated. Her blade struck wildly in the air, blasting whooshing sounds around the room. The weapon crushed Crystal's defense fast, leaving slits all along her arms. Her annoyance was turning into frustration, causing her swings to be less precise.

Crystal saw her opportunity as the steel came toward her once more. Sliding on the frozen ground, Crystal glided beneath the swing. She rounded to Sydney's flank and tackled her. Her face plummeted into a puff of white. The powder sprinkled upon her blonde hair as she struggled to keep Sydney down. Crystal was unable to stay upon her for long as she was thrown onto her back. Steadying herself onto her soles, she squared off against Sydney once again.

Right as Sydney stepped forward with her weapon raised, she lost her balance. As she failed to steady herself, Crystal moved in for another physical takedown. As she slammed against her, Sydney remained standing, trying to keep herself from moving.

Crystal continued pushing until the resistance had fallen. She was able to thrust her opponent back. She exhaled in relief watching Sydney stumble backward and get caught by the tip of an iceberg. She watched as her face cringed and she whined in agony. This was her golden chance. Taking a deep inhale through her nose, she lowered her lids. Blindly, she jetted forward implanting the weapon through her abdomen, hearing the ice crack on the other side. The snow slushed around as the body fell to its knees. She watched the body twitch as it leaned gracefully back against the glacier.

Practically in the process of gagging, she turned to Gauri. "You're . . . you're next."

Starting with a dash, Gauri furiously rushed into the fight. Crystal deflected Gauri's first strike, almost cracking under her strength. She shielded Gauri's weapon several more times. The sound of metal clashing against one another voided the room of silence.

Crystal was eventually able to dodge, coming at her with a twirl. She missed. Gauri saw her chance and seized it. Before Crystal fully recovered from the strike, Gauri rammed her body against hers—sword first. The impact forced her onto her back, knocking the weapon from her grasp. With the magical transformation, Gauri whipped her weapon back, gearing up for the final strike. Suddenly Scorpio ordered Gauri to halt, but the attack was already set into motion. She only had enough time to curve the elastic weapon, leaving a gaping gash across Crystal's chest.

"We need her alive."

"She killed Sydney!"

"A tragedy indeed," the King's tone was low and stoic.

"How could she be of use?"

"The emerald's say she will come in handy. She could be used to our advantage."

Gauri looked down at Crystal, who desperately tried to apply pressure to her wound. When their eyes locked, Gauri's wrath forced her to spit in disgust. The throbbing pain was too much for Crystal to speak. Gauri stomped by the wounded woman, grabbing the emerald from its resting place. She admired the pure white jewel in her dirty, blood-drawn hands.

The King smirked. "Shall we release Zannala's emerald from its prison? Hold up Cosarave's jewel!" Gauri raised their prize into the air, stepping closer to the King. Scorpio, in return, raised his staff, lifting Luminar's emerald into the air, while the other two were aligned with his free hand. Once they were in close enough range, the four artifacts began glowing. Their lights swirled together. Forming a colorful mass in the air, it projected a beam into the sky that bypassed all physical objects.

Crystal, wincing with each breath, watched in awe. As the divine relics released their massive power, she finally could see it. The craziness Phoenix had spoken about was now as visible as day. A layer of chaos that pulsed intensely consumed each emerald. Tendrils of evil reached out of each one, slithering around the arm of their holder. The origin of the X-creatures. Ignoring her wound, she reminded herself of what had to be done. As Scorpio and Gauri were preoccupied, Crystal reached into the pocket of her vest. Her fingers dived into the warm liquid that soaked into her sweater as she searched the inside pockets. Holding onto the last souvenir from Luminar, she released the seal and poured it upon her sword.

With all the willpower she had stored, she dragged herself to the miniature iceberg the emerald had been resting upon for centuries. Her last moment of consciousness fading, she plunged the blade as deep into the ice as she could manage. A blaring rumble shook the ground she lay upon as glowing lights were released from the crack and shot into the air. Within seconds of contact, it exploded. The force flung Crystal to the opposite end into a collection of snow.

CHAPTER 26

"What I am hearing is that I'm a twisted monster!" Eric hysterically exclaimed.

"That has always been a true statement, pretty boy," smiled Talon.

"Damn the Protectors...what do they have in store for me next?"

"When the emeralds fed from our misery, they intertwined with our beings."

"Which means one of us is responsible for saving Teague?"

"Correct."

"Well, Phoenix, I'm not made to be a hero. The honor is yours."

"I'll say," remarked Talon.

"Have we found the location of the altar yet?" asked Eric.

The two of them shook their heads. "There is only a single place mentioned in all of his notes. Pleasant Valley Groove."

"The legend states that the destruction began there."

"The ending of this madness has us traveling back to its beginning," replied Talon.

As he finished his sentence, the three of them were suddenly startled. A beam of light dropped down from the sky into the chasm. Making direct contact with the emerald, the force caused the whole room to quake. The emerald's tint began illuminating vibrantly. The brilliant, yellow shine continued to grow stronger until the darkest corners were revealed. As it settled, the three men gaped at one another.

"What was that?"

"Obviously some kind of explosion."

"Talon, I swear on Brett's grave I'm going to—"

Phoenix intervened, "I think . . . the emerald was released from its hold."

"Which also means Cosarave . . . has fallen," announced Talon lowering his head making contact between his palm, fist, and forehead.

"It is now or never. Who knows how long it will take for them to return."

"I-I honestly don't know. I have not thought this far ahead. Everything happened too fast, this moment has blindsided me."

Eric and Talon observed him in astonishment.

"We better create a plan fast."

Being too weak to walk, Crystal was carried back on a stretcher. After what felt like weeks, they finally returned to Zannala's desert climate. Scorpio stomped into the castle and began casting orders to his nearby henchman: "Gather all available troops! Pack supplies! Prepare the horses! I want all preparations finished within the hour!"

"You," demanded Scorpio pointing at a trooper. "Take these two prisoners to the dungeon. Make sure she receives medical attention. Then bring Phoenix before me. And you! Retrieve Zannala's emerald from my secret chamber. Be careful or I shall have your head."

Dismissed, the guards immediately went about their assigned tasks.

"Gauri meet me in the war room. There are plans to be made."

The guard swiftly led Crystal and Alex down into the dungeon. Bearing the pain with each step, Crystal flinched as she placed her foot on the next level. She was in no condition to resist, but this was not a moment to be injured and docile. Her gaze fell upon Alex who held a face of determination. He caught her eyes and without a word, she understood their feelings were mutual. She watched as his focus fell forward to the jingling of their leader.

The guard shoved them into the cell and began defending himself. "Women do not belong here, but this is an unusual situation. I apologize, miss." As the cell door slammed shut, he listened for the click of the lock. He turned to the other line of cells, peering into their depths.

"Phoenix, my Majesty wishes to have your presence. Come forth to the gate." Only drips of water responded.

"Ridiculous," he mumbled approaching the lock. He patted his pockets, searching for his keys. "Where did they get to this time?" The guard stopped in mid-search once he heard the familiar clang of metal. Turning slowly, he found the young child standing before him, dangling the keys from his fingers as if they were a treat for a dog.

Before he had a moment to react, Crystal mustered her strength. She pounced onto the guard, beating him senseless. *If I don't take him down . . . it was all for nothing.* As she finished clobbering the poor fellow, she breathed in a sigh of relief. But the pain resurfaced instantly. Before they locked him away, she confiscated his spear. *Any weapon is good right about now.*

"What do we do now?" innocently asked Alex.

"It is no shock that Phoenix escaped . . . and knowing him, I doubt they left the castle. We will head upstairs. Phoenix and the others will appear wherever there is chaos."

"But Crystal, your wound!"

She peered down at her chest, watching the blood seep through her cotton top. *Now I know how Phoenix feels.* "I-I'll be fine. We just need to find a safe place to hide. And rest."

Gingerly taking Alex's hand, they quietly tiptoed up the stairs.

The second guard made his way to the King's personal study,

puzzled to find the secret entrance already revealed. He brushed away his sense of danger and excused his Majesty's forgetfulness. He paced down the corridor at a slow speed, cautiously watching the shadows. When he reached the opening, he laid eyes upon the golden beauty.

A sinister smile crossed his face as he stepped toward the jewel of the desert. His fingers cradled the bottom, allowing the freezing warmth to numb his senses. A rustling from behind snapped him from his trance. With a curious eye, he cautiously made his way across the bridge to the scattered novels. His eyes darted around, but he found nothing out of the ordinary. As he sheathed his weapon, one of the novels fell from a pile. A scorpion crawled onto its page facing the towering giant. In awe, he bent over to greet the small fellow.

Silently, Talon struck. He twisted the guard around and plowed his fist into the man's stomach. He keeled forward, giving Talon a perfect angle to grasp his throat, digging his nails into his jugular. The man squealed, kicking his feet and scratching at Talon's hold. In return, Talon grunted as he slammed the body against the bookshelf, causing books to fall from their places.

"What is it that you want?" he whispered with breathless words.

Talon clobbered his face, "We ask the questions!"

Phoenix and Eric appeared on each side of Talon's shoulders. Eric was cracking his knuckles, while Phoenix kept his arms crossed. Eric threatened, "Answer each question fast and honestly, and you will live to take the emerald to your King. But, a single little lie, and I will personally dispose of your corpse by rolling it off that cliff. Do you understand?"

The guard whimpered, nodding his head.

"Good. Phoenix, begin."

Phoenix raised his sword, holding it at the guard's eye level. "Is Cosarave destroyed in the same fashion as its sister cities?" He nodded. Resentment slithered into his chest. "How did you reach Cosarave and return in a timely manner? How do you plan on traveling to the ritual ground with the emeralds?"

"With . . . camels and horses. My Majesty has his own personal automobile."

Eric spoke: "Where's Alex? How does he fare?"

"Him and the girl . . . in the dungeon. The girl's wounded . . . badly."

"Where is the ritual being held?"

The guard smirked through his struggle, "I bet you would . . . like to know."

"We would, hence the question we asked?!"

"I am not-not committing treason."

Talon's grip clamped tighter.

"You already have!" Eric felt his pulse thud. "Scum. Petty, worthless scum."

"Fine." With a steady hand, Phoenix used the tip of his Dragon to carve a line on the man's skin. He screamed and hollered as Phoenix drew across the bridge of his nose. Almost getting lost in his carving, he threatened, "Nothing is stopping me from slicing deeper. I advise you to speak if you value living."

"Pleasant Valley Groove! Sou-south of Zannala!" Talon relaxed his grip. "There's a secret altar that the people originally used to trap the Protectors' curse into the emeralds. It's in the same location where the tornado first touched down! Please—I have children!"

"I was right!" exclaimed Talon, retracting his hand. The guard held his neck, gasping for breath.

"We need to save Alex and Crystal from the dungeon," commanded Eric. He lunged forward only to stop and turn around. "But what are we to do about him? We can't allow him snooping around."

"Leave him be. We assured him he may return to his duties."

"Sorry. A threat is a threat, and holding him over that ledge is tempting."

"Do it, and he will not be the only thing that goes

overboard."

Eric grumbled, "Fine, Phoenix. You win." He approached the defeated soldier who was still rubbing his neck. As Eric's shadow covered him, he waited for their eyes to meet. With two quick jabs, his nose cracked and his head dropped to the stone.

Phoenix glared at Eric.

"What? He's not dead and will eventually be able to return to his King."

"Talon, please grab the emerald."

"Hell no, I'm staying away from that contaminated thing."

"I'll get it . . . but you are the single owner of Bright Light. I need you to—"

"Understood."

Talon swiped the sword from the beaten man and went to eradicate the essence of the gem from its surroundings. The mineral sparkled before the rotten pedestal, erupting on contact. The familiar light show took place, sending waves of purification through the chasm.

Talon turned to the men, "Time to save Alex and Cupcake."

Crystal and Alex crept into the main lobby, trying to stay hidden from view. They needed a safe location to regroup. Guards frantically hurried through the corridors of the castle. *Probably hustling to carry out Scorpio's demands.* She held Alex behind her, hoping no one caught on to their stalking. After patiently waiting for more soldiers to filter through the room, they began making their way forward until they spotted their friends enter the room from the opposite end. With a burst of joy, she alerted Alex who shared her excitement. Suddenly feeling invincible, Alex beelined straight to his father while calling his name.

The ruckus alerted the soldiers in the proximity. The five of them were discovered immediately. Protecting Alex from harm, Crystal threw him behind her. Despite her agonizing ache, she had to take lead on keeping the enemies at bay.

The men had their own crowd swarming them. They watched from afar as Crystal began defending herself. Her fighting style was weak and sloppy. She could barely stand upon her feet. Her resistance was not going to last much longer. On instinct, Phoenix leapt to aid her, but Talon caught his arm. His insensitive action was balanced with his intellectual stare, which calmed his rage.

"I know you ache to rescue her, but that is not what is important. The two of you need to get to the groove before Scorpio. You will need as much time to prepare as I can grant you."

"I refuse to leave my son behind."

"She needs my help!" exclaimed Phoenix.

"Teague needs your help." The cold reality of Talon's words washed Phoenix like a cold bath. "I will stay and fight. And protect Alex. The two of you have a deadline."

Wanting to disobey, and knowing that nothing could stop him from doing so, Phoenix bit his lip. He nodded. Talon's argument stood true. With Eric by his side reluctantly leaving, the two of them exited the chamber.

Busting into Zannala's forbidden heat, they searched the grounds for any sign of animals. Circling around the castle, they discovered the horse stalls. Zannala men were prepping the mounts for the trip. They were each knocked unconscious as Phoenix and Eric boarded their transportations that were already equipped for the journey and specially geared with armor that helped them through the sand. The horses roared as they began galloping into the swirling stones, and they never looked back.

CHAPTER 27

Talon flanked the battle and slaughtered three guards before they had realized he arrived. To his advantage, none of the soldiers wore armor, making the entire torso fair game. Crystal had no intentions of winning this round; she was only trying to avoid getting struck. Luckily, her plan was working in her favor. She twirled her spear, lodging it in a man's sternum. Talon and Crystal met up in the middle as she yanked her spear free. After Talon finished the final guard, he caught Crystal in her arms. She latched on to him for dear life.

"What happened to you?"

"You are the one *bleeding*!"

"I fought back as well as I could, but I failed."

"Nonetheless, it's impressive enough that you withstood this onslaught."

"Skilled teachers have taught me."

Alex popped out, "Where's my father?"

"He . . . and Phoenix have already gone. They are traveling to Pleasant Valley Groove. That is our destination as well."

"The one spoken in the legend? That's real?" marveled Crystal.

"Experiencing all that we have, this is what shocks you? I figured talking with a dead spirit is as abnormal as life could become."

Crystal shrugged. "I will lead us to his horses." As the three were about to make their dash to the cavalry, an adrenaline pumping noise paralyzed them. A booming laughter surged through the hall, keeping them motionless. Their escape would have to wait.

Phoenix and Eric rode through the desert listening to the beat of hooves galloping. Sand twirled around them, sneaking into their eyes and scratching their bare skin. As the heat pounded on their backs, Phoenix tried to remain focused. His thoughts found themselves traveling to Crystal and her well-being. He glanced at Eric, who was having the same issue about Alex. Neither of them spoke, not until they could escape from the awful climate.

They continued riding until they crossed a lake. Their goal was to reach the groove in as little time as possible, but the horses' neighs meant the decision was not theirs to make. Which both men were fine with since their throats were dry and parched as well. Sitting beneath the shade from a cluster of trees, they watched the horses quench their thirst. Eric randomly began giggling.

"I fail to find the humor in this."

"I would have believed . . . none of this. If it was told to me a year ago that I would find myself standing amidst this huge chaotic, underground war to decipher between right and wrong . . . while Teague hovers over the brink of destruction and I would be cursed with the responsibility of putting an end to this crazy, power-hungry King from ruining Osiren . . . I would have delivered them to a psych ward or killed them . . . They could foresee my destiny of being widowed, traveling the country, and finding mythical objects . . . I would have called them fools with lunatic delusions. Yet, here I sit. Far from Holick, miles away from Zannala . . ."

"This stands for me as well. As a boy, school and homework were my hobbies . . . My beloved sister and the Luminary Lake were how I spent my free time. Even with the imagination I had, this is a future I could never have created. None of this. These types of stories were just tales to scare children into believing the Protectors exist. To think Luminar would be erased from maps in the years to come seemed unfathomable."

"School work? Never a real hobby or friends?"

"My shyness kept me at bay. To approach a person took a man with real courage. I was only a timid boy. Friends I made eventually left for someone—or *something* more exciting. My entertainment revolved solely around my sister. That is, if she had nothing planned, which was not often."

Eric kept silent for a little, allowing the conversation to die. He spoke a few minutes later, "We should discuss the elephant in the room . . . I apologize for what I pulled . . ."

Phoenix had no need for clarification. "Do not fret, Eric. This was the emeralds' doing, not your own."

"They are not entirely to blame . . . even though that would be the easiest to do. The emeralds may have controlled my actions to act upon my thoughts, but I was aware and present. Almost like watching a play from inside my head. As it occurred, I did not attempt to stop. Not that the outcome was upsetting to me."

"What are you trying to say?"

Eric grew sheepish, "The words I spoke still came from me."

Staying quiet, Phoenix searched for a response. "Eric . . . I never had the pleasure to have a brother. I could only imagine what I feel for you is similar to the love I would hold for him. I'm . . . flattered you harbor these passionate emotions toward me, and our moment of intimacy is not to be regretted. But the feelings are not shared for the same sex. My heart also lies with another . . ."

Eric smiled ear to ear, "Never had a doubt in my mind. It's time to express that to her."

Phoenix inspected the three suns, watching as they took their time creeping across the blue ocean above them. Seeing the horses raring to go, they mutually agreed to continue on with their journey. They mounted their stallions, cantering to their destination.

CHAPTER 28

Scorpio rested in his luxurious chair made with the finest cloth. Gauri sat beside him on a bench built into the carriage. Several horses pulled them along with women saddled up, steering them forward. The entire Zannala army marched beside their King's compartment. Hundreds of men kept pace in rows, while female officers were scattered throughout the ranks, either riding on their assigned mounts or striding along their fellow men. Behind the wagon was another, being drawn by camels. Rocking back and forth, the prison held their captives. They were tied down and stripped of their weapons. Talon's goggles were even confiscated.

"I pray they arrived on time," whimpered Crystal.

"They must be prepared. The matters now lay in their hands. We are utterly useless . . ."

The camels fell behind the rest of the army. The prisoners were able to watch the land scroll by, as they remained practically motionless. The clippity-clop of the hooves and the freeze-frame scenery made them stir crazy. Their skin crawled thinking of the eternity that had passed since they were loaded onboard. The wagon finally slowed to a halt. Peering through the barred windows, the area took them by surprise. Nature was flourishing across the land with beautiful flowers scattered throughout the field. *Must be why it's called Pleasant Valley.*

None of them minded the aggressive manhandling while

exiting their cart. The movement was welcomed. They continued to observe the magnificently wonderful nature around them while inhaling the fresh breeze. The grass grew a vibrant green as leaves danced through the wind. Trees stood strong and proud with trunks of ancient proportions. The hues that surrounded them provided such a serene calm. Until tremendously healthy growth reached a certain line. From that point all the way to the opposite side of the valley was a barren wasteland. Not a single plant was blossoming between those boundaries; the ground itself was tainted from the evil.

"Those stories father told me . . . they were true," gawked Alex in despair.

The guards rudely shoved the three of them down the hill. Almost tripping over her own feet, Crystal regained control as the ground evened out. The terrain around her was tinted gray with very little evidence that life had ever existed there. The dirt appeared dry and lacked nutrients. The horses and carriages stayed at the top of the hill, the descent being too steep for their travel. There were several miles spanning across the valley with the ancient altar centered in the middle, towering above their heads. One hundred steps high, circular in shape; it was a monstrous sight.

"This . . . This is *where* it all began," marveled Scorpio in wonder. "The scenery, breathtaking. The wildlife, astounding. Better find comfort in these surroundings. Once my power is claimed, all of Osiren will succumb to this state."

"A necromancer has more heart and purity," growled Crystal.

"Bite your tongue, you worthless wench!" snapped Gauri.

"I will be freed in due time and I will find you. Don't underestimate me. We're not through."

"How quick to forget how smoothly the last match went in my favor. I have no quarrel with silencing that—"

"Enough bickering! Bring me the satchel containing the emeralds."

"I apologize, my Lord." Gauri snapped her fingers, cueing a guard to approach. She transferred the sack from the servant to the

King. "My Lord, as requested."

"Excellent," smiled Scorpio.

The King and his men approached the steps. *They . . . failed.* Talon's head drooped and his shoulders sagged.

"I have been waiting my *entire* life for this moment!"

"An entire life wasted, to be defeated on the eve of your success!" bellowed a voice from atop the altar.

"Phoenix!" the two of them cried in unison.

"Skull should have murdered you as a child. You cannot stop an army, my lad!"

"Those odds never stopped me before!" He unhitched his White Dragon, wielding it for all eyes to witness it glisten.

"I want his blood dripping down every side of this altar!"

Every guard, male and female, charged toward him. Flooding the stairwell, they swarmed Phoenix. He was utterly outnumbered, but had a height advantage on his side. Protecting his position, he warded away the threats they posed. His Dragon slipped through the endless line of footmen like butter. The soldiers were repelled, tumbling back down the steps, but with each defeated soldier, another would replace them. Another just as eager as before.

As the commotion continued, Eric crept around their flank. All the attention was focused on Phoenix, providing Eric the necessary stealth. With his iron whip in hand, he tried cutting the rope discreetly. Once his companions were no longer restrained, they all rejoiced. Alex wrapped himself around his father.

"Alexander, find safety. Hide on the hill—anywhere is fine; just stay away from the fighting. And *stay* safe." Obeying, Alex began climbing the tremendous hill in the opposite direction of the battle. With a final glance, he was gone from sight.

Eric offered his whip to Crystal. "Take this. Talon and I can fight without." She nodded, accepting the weapon.

"What's the plan, pretty boy?" asked Talon.

"You see it. Fight. Fight until we are the last ones standing."

"That is the dumb—"

"What do you suggest, genius? Shut your trap and let's help Phoenix." The abrupt, aggressiveness left Talon stunned. But Eric was correct. There was no alternative to be found and being fussy would not help.

The trio traveled toward the war, until Crystal saw the King's sidekick. "Go ahead; there is a score that needs to be settled." She quickly snapped her head at Gauri, who watched with hunger.

"Insinuating a duel?"

Crystal unraveled some of her whip. "I'm insinuating that this will hurt. Badly."

Crystal whirled her weapon above her head and took a swing at Gauri without any thought. She evaded each attempt unscathed. By Crystal's fifth round, she was tired. Gauri smelled her weakness and thrived from it. As the whip came toward her once more, she blocked the wire. The whip wrapped around the sword, just as Gauri planned. Her sword began to glow and their weapons formed a knot.

Crystal tried to rip the blade from her, but it was no use. She lacked the strength. Gauri, on the other hand, had no issue knocking her over. Sliding forward, the dirt scratched her face. Gauri's sword returned to its original form, releasing Crystal. As she tried picking herself up, Crystal realized this fight was not siding in her favor. The end was going to be the same result. With an act of desperation, she moved.

Phoenix attempted to carve a path to his companions, but there were too many people. They were replenishing their numbers at a rapid pace. Talon rapidly beat his fists against his targets, leaving bruises across their faces and chests. While grappling with a soldier and placing him into submission, another enemy came from behind. He struck, leaving a long gash up Talon's leg. The sudden rush of pain forced him to his knees just as a weapon came charging at him, aimed for his neck. The tip of the blade struck, but Eric slid between them. Blood splattered around his body; a few droplets bounced against Talon's forehead. Phoenix came around back, clearing their rear guard.

Despite their wounds and injuries, they continued fighting valiantly. Phoenix searched the chaos for Crystal, who was struggling to push herself from the ground.

Gauri started walking to her, holding her sword to her side, which appeared sharper than ever. Crystal made a sudden snap of her wrist and the whip shredded the bag of emeralds the King held. Scorpio cried a terrible bellow as the emeralds bounced away from him. She attempted to retrieve her whip, but there was no time. Gauri released a forceful kick to her side, rolling her back to the dirt.

Phoenix read Gauri's lips, almost hearing the sentence clearly through the mayhem: "Any last words?"

Like a trigger pulled, he felt his anger fermenting inside. It began bubbling, flying through the roof. A warmth radiated from his core as his eyes narrowed. Talon and Eric could feel the electricity spark the air around them. One of the soldiers, out of fear, swung his sword. Making a direct hit, the blade shattered. Leaving no wound. *What's happening? I'm unable to control my body . . . going dark. I'm blind . . . Crystal.* Within seconds, his analytical brain transformed into the mind of a starving animal. He was utterly consumed by rage.

The berserker traveled to the scene like a torpedo. All that crossed his path was immediately disposed of, their blood decorating the landscape. His blade spilled more gore within a few minutes than the whole battle had. Despite the weapons that collided against him, his skin received no damage. The assaults just fueled his aggression more.

Crystal was speechless—clueless and petrified as she watched Gauri take her place above her. The magical sword was practically calling her name, ready to finally finish her. Crystal took a deep breath, preparing herself for the dark embrace that would proceed afterward. Her lids closed, accepting that she would be by the Protectors' side soon. When the final blow was never delivered, she peered up, confused.

Gauri was distracted. Her attention was focused on something else. Someone else. The grip on her sword grew tighter. It shook in her hands. Crystal tilted her head to see Phoenix in all his might dash toward them.

Thinking fast, Crystal kicked out Gauri's legs. With all her might, she rolled backward onto her feet and lashed her whip. It snapped at Gauri's arm, blistering the skin. A second strike was shot, breaking skin at her wrist, thus creating distance between her and her weapon. With a smile of satisfaction, Crystal raised her arm ready to wipe the look of disgust and puzzlement from the woman's face.

Scorpio grasped Crystal's arm, holding her still. He lifted her from the ground, gripping her arm as tight as possible. She screamed as he dragged her across the dirt. This gave enough time for Gauri to stand, regaining her composure. Scorpio turned in time to find the White Dragon pierce the space by his chest. He swiftly hopped back escaping the strike and releasing Crystal.

"It comes down between us two."

"Prying your head from your body will never equal all the pain you caused me."

"What cause of this pain falls onto my shoulders? Skull burned down your home, murdered your family, and the people you idolized. Besides, Phoenix, my lad, you had no life. No friends. Without family, what did you live for?" Phoenix blatantly stared. "Tell me, is that really considered living? But now, examine all the good I have done for you: friends, courage, physique, and a lover!" Scorpio pointed his staff at Crystal who struggled toward the emeralds. "You even traveled the country, my lad! If the order to raid the city was never given, that whiny little boy would still exist."

Talon watched the standoff as they struggled to retain their position. The ratio of men to women was decreasing as more women replaced the death of the soldiers. Their abilities caused more of a challenge, forcing them to be swifter on their feet. Talon shouted to Eric, telling him to assist Phoenix. Eric nodded and made his way down the stairs.

"Join my side, Phoenix, together we will rule this land. I shall even spare the lives of your friends."

"No, Phoenix!" yelled Eric, racing to his side. "That is not what we fight for!"

"That is not the same tale I heard from the emeralds. They have stories of you, Phoenix; you would do well to embrace the curse."

The emeralds want me? They chose me . . . to become one of them. My thirst for vengeance was stronger than my vow to collect the emeralds. One of his earlier nightmares replayed before him. The powerful voice echoing over his shoulder spouting his venom: "Your heart is filled with darkness. Allow it to consume you." He remembered holding the bloodied sword as it had just been removed from Eric's cranium. His palms covered in the blood of those he slaughtered . . . those he did not consider innocent. Mercenaries who were doing what they thought was best for their families' futures. Maybe they are not wrong . . . Joining Scorpio is the best decision. After all, he wasn't the one who burned down Luminar . . .

Scorpio continued: "This power; this strength! That feeling surging through your veins. Hubris. Invincibility. All of this and more will be yours to control!"

Phoenix stared at Scorpio, his mind searching for a response. An answer. Zoning in and out of reality, his vision became hazy as he succumbed to a phantasmagoric state. Reminders of the demon's words crawled through his brain once more. *"Your heart screams differently. It desires to watch flames dance. Watch them burn. You want others to suffer, just as you have."* The dangling bodies circled around him once again, hanging by a noose tied to their necks. The emeralds were preparing to be utilized, by *him*. Their colors danced before him, taunting him. Blood colored his vision as the demon spoke: *"A demon lingers deep inside that growls to be released. You will succumb to this image once we rule."* The emeralds lined up before him. *"These are your weapons of mass destruction; the tools that will grant ultimate power."*

"Crystal, no!" cried Eric.

The distress in his voice caught Phoenix's attention. His gaze wandered to where Gauri was pointing her weapon at Crystal.

Instantaneously, he was enraged again. His visions vanished as he remembered who was important to him. Completely ignoring the King, he sped past the overgrown man making his way toward his next victim. With one quick shove, the sword disappeared into her back. Crystal listened to the sound of sword entering body and then sliding out. She turned her head to watch Phoenix's hand slither around Gauri's neck, chucking her aside.

Laying his eyes upon Crystal, his senses relaxed. His pupils returned to normal and his pulse slowed. Calming down, he dropped to her level. He threw himself onto her. Though she was terrified, she hugged back. She was astounded to feel tears drip onto her skin. The anger that stole his body dispersed, being replaced by another, just as powerful emotion.

"Crystal, I will *never* allow anything to happen to you. Back at the city . . . you were right. I'm scared . . . scared to allow someone become close to me. I'm afraid I won't be strong enough to protect them," he shook his head, shaking drops from his face. "It's better to be the weakest man on Teague than to have no one. I wish to have you be my weakness and the source of my strength. My heart swells when you are near; I love you."

The moment was ruined by Scorpio: "Adorable. Simply vomit inducing. Glad to hear you confess the love you have for this woman. There will never be another chance." He lowered his staff to Phoenix's line of sight. "I am offering a one-on-one duel. If you deny, I have reserved the right to strike you unannounced. Raise your weapon, lad."

As Phoenix started to rise, Eric spoke. "Phoenix, the emeralds!"

"There is a little situation I'm dealing with. The rest of this hangs onto you, my friend." Phoenix wielded his precious White Dragon by his side.

Phoenix had no more time for words or arguments. He dashed to his opponent. The two weapons collided against one another, brawn against brawn.

Gathering the emeralds, Eric watched as the King spun the staff, slamming it against Phoenix's block. The force slid him back a few feet. He balanced himself, retaliating with an equal amount of strength.

Sparks flew with every strike. They raged against each other as Eric ran toward the stairs. Phoenix went wild swinging his sword, placing a barrage of slices into action. The harsh blows vibrated the ground. Scorpio swiped his staff toward Phoenix's feet. With great agility, Phoenix dove out of the way. Standing up erectly, he drove the White Dragon straight into Scorpio's flesh. The sensation of pain compelled Scorpio to strike his inflictor. With a loud crack, Phoenix tumbled across the valley, holding his forehead.

Eric tried not to pay attention to the soldiers calling after him. He ignored all the fallen warriors, until he saw Talon barely fending off his opposition. Talon's eyes carefully scanned the battlefield trying to plan his next moves as his opponents attacked. Eric watched his eyes swerve from soldier to soldier, the whole time drawing blood. Eric slowed down his pace, coming at an even level with Talon.

Talon carefully maneuvered around the field trying to get ahead. He quickly caught a glimpse of Eric when a woman was sneaking from behind. Without thinking, he flung his stolen spear, making direct contact into her chest. Eric was in shock and unable to move. Talon attempted to make his way over, but guards surrounded him like vultures. Eric tried to come to the aide of his companion.

"Destroy the emeralds!"

"You won't survive—"

"Don't worry your pretty little head about me. End this."

In silent agreement, he left Talon alone. The sound of weapons clanking against the steps around him and cries of the fallen made each occasional breeze much colder than expected. Archers aimed their arrows as Eric climbed closer to the top of the altar. The projectiles lodged themselves into his back and legs, but he persevered. Before reaching the highest point, a few of Zannala's members were able to block his path. Eric fought the battle valiantly, staining his weapon in crimson. Releasing the last man from his body and into the essence of Teague, a familiar cry caught his attention. *Talon?* A pulsating fear flooded his mind. He turned back around to scan the crowd for his friend, but there was no sight of that purple hair.

Eric tore himself from the mob climbing the steps behind him. He stepped onto the altar and was awestruck. An ancient, cement railing fenced in the ritual area. Within the middle, five pedestals were stationed along the sides of the boundary line. Each pedestal was coated a certain color. Seeing the correspondence between the color and the emeralds, he gently placed each jewel in their assigned slots. Once they were in place, they began shimmering intensely. *Now . . . what do I have to do? Scorpio said . . . Ah! I don't remember! I think I have to stand in the middle . . .* He stepped back, positioning himself in the center and instantly, a reaction occurred. Streams of pink, blue, yellow, white, and green shot toward the sky. The hues began to outshine the suns as they caught everyone's attention in the area, momentarily stopping the war.

Seeing the rainbow paint the atmosphere, Scorpio produced an angry snarl even though he was overwhelmed by excitement as well. "The research described it perfectly. Marvelous." He swung his staff, the blow causing Phoenix to falter back and collapse to his knees. With another swing, Phoenix was pummeled against the dirt. Scorpio stampeded to the emeralds with lightning speed.

The beams of light dazzled Eric. He was taken from his stupor as Scorpio hollered, accompanied by the pounding of hundreds of feet. Eric remained stationary, thinking hard about what was to be done next. He couldn't rack his brain for the next task, until the thought of Brett came to mind. With his fist underneath his palm, he tilted his head forward touching his knuckles. Nothing happened—until a surge of energy traveled through him. He let go of his stance clutching his stomach in pain. Squinting, he watched as the beams slowly retracted back into the emeralds.

The pain continually increased as he fell into a dazed state. He examined each emerald individually. The ones they held with them, Flores and Emerica, began playing memories absorbed during the travels with the group. He watched the trials back in Flores and witnessed the death of a woman on a boat. They projected the death of Brett. As Scorpio's stomps became louder, the emeralds' colors increased intensely. Without a warning, each emerald blasted a similar energy at Eric.

When the rays came into contact with his torso, he could feel his darkness come to life. Suffocating him. The energy in the beams was powerful, almost knocking him clean off his feet. The ceremony was all too much for him to manage. He fell, catching himself with his palms. He cried, screaming for help. He felt the fingers of the emeralds slowly wrapping themselves around him, finding orifices in his body. The monstrous things that were intangible became tangible. His sadness and despair became real. He knew it would not be long before he would experience how it would feel to physically drown in his own misery.

Scorpio reached the altar finding Eric upon the floor. Furiously, he hurried toward him, ready to kill, but was flung back by a mystical force. Baffled, he cautiously extended his hand. Slowly approaching the area, he eventually felt the invisible field. All his followers reenacted his failure, also being tossed back.

"You damn fool! This power will destroy you!"

Eric was unable to respond. He could feel no emotions. *I'm losing . . . It's engulfing me.* His quivering stopped as he felt a hand on his shoulder. Slowly tilting his head, he was startled. His strength was suddenly restored, and he struggled to stand back on his feet. He wrapped his arms around himself and thought aloud:

"Yo-you're here. Here to help me—Brett . . ." Brett merely smiled, removing his hand from Eric's shoulder. "I love you," he whispered as his partner evaporated.

"What in all of Teague was that?" yelled Scorpio.

"The beginning to your end," announced Phoenix, appearing

beside him. The two of them gawked as Eric absorbed all that the emeralds offered.

Eric began showing an array of colors swirl across his skin. Turning into a human rainbow, he accepted the energy flowing toward him until each of the jewels went dry, turning gray. He lowered his arms to his sides examining the multiple hues being discharged from his body.

His skin was vibrating right off his muscles. It raced around his body like a speed track, and felt as if he crashed on to a rubber mat. Eric's mind, though, felt as it was floating amongst the three suns of Teague. He was weightless, swaying with each breeze that rolled across the altar. The tips of his fingertips tingled as he looked beyond his shoulder to his audience and gave a sly wink. Then with a deafening grunt, he pushed the darkness from his soul.

The vibration came to an immediate halt, turning the energy into extra baggage. It was as if gravity came plummeting down upon him. The tingling shot from his fingers to his chest, spiking his heart rate. The jolt spread gradually across his torso, followed by his legs to his feet. The entire experience simulated drowning in the ocean. The sounds around him dampened. Breathing became impossible as he choked upon his own exhale. Pressure began building in his temples, pounding on his forehead and eardrums.

He reached for the sides of his skull, hoping to ease the frustration and pain. The intense feeling continued to grow, hampering his internal thoughts. Straining all of his muscles at once, the dark water around him vanished. Instant pressure relief. Recovering from his state, the last vision he saw was of an unfamiliar man standing before him. Then, unconsciousness struck him.

The release sent airwaves rippling through the valley, creating a miniature earthquake. The shock of the blast caused Scorpio and Phoenix to fall down the stairway. They tumbled backward, colliding with corpses and other Zannala soldiers who couldn't remain balanced. The explosion hit the entire valley, rocking it back and forth. The altar itself crumbled beneath Eric's outburst.

The same beams of light left Eric's body, returning to their original emerald. The blast of each stream hitting the emeralds caused them to tremor in place as they tried to reabsorb what was lost. The intensity of the returned energy overwhelmed and exceeded the capacity they could handle. Eventually, after forcing more power into them than they could maintain, cracks emerged.

Phoenix rolled onto his back, recovering from the collision down the staircase. The steps of the altar began separating and falling inward. He staggered between his feet as the ground beneath him shifted. Attempting to make his way off the structure, he hurriedly limped away. A humongous explosion propelled him off his feet.

Each emerald shattered into a million pieces, floating with the wind. The sound, almost cry-like, was ear-piercing and swallowed the entire valley. The shards sparkled in the air, painting a miraculous picture across the barren wasteland. The entire altar collapsed beneath its display. Eric came back around as the structure began trembling. He struggled to rise to his feet as the ceremony circle became unstable. He fell onto the railing as his side of the ground began crumbling. He threw himself forward and took a giant leap, reaching for the other side. Though as he landed, the new platform shifted and dropped. He was taken down with the destruction.

Phoenix landed in a pile of rubble. Cradling his sensitive body, he squinted to see through the rising mist of dirt. Through the cloud of demolition, he was in awe the jewels that had embodied evil could create a display this spectacular. Full of wonder, he felt his wrist pulse. A throbbing. The same ache he felt in Luminar—

Phoenix was ripped from his fantasy by a sudden pain that felt like a blow to the stomach. His pupils went black as the hair on his neck rose. He started fading, watching the shards hover around. Suddenly, all the pieces reconnected forming the five emeralds again as whole gems. Each one floated away until they instantly disappeared. Along with his consciousness.

Crystal was in shock. Once the dust settled, she crawled out of hiding. The entire area was different, as if they were transported to a new valley. The taint in Teague had been expelled and replaced with rich grass and vibrant flowers. She looked around for any sign of her comrades. Or enemies, for that matter. Among the new, freshly sprouted nature, no one was to be found. All the corpses that were strewn between the hills were gone. Only weapons and armor remained. Even Scorpio and Gauri were nowhere to be found. But none of that mattered once she came across Phoenix.

She crawled to him. He was lying still—limp, barely breathing. Crystal did her best to wake him, but he did not stir. She began yelling his name, shaking him aggressively. A sudden bang from behind startled her. She spun around to spot Eric shoving rubble off himself. Covered in cuts, bruises, and blood splatters, she was surprised to find him alive. He heaved another giant mass to the side.

Eric dragged his foot along, but stopped when he heard a peculiar sound. Listening in, he identified hoarse breathing. Out of the corner of his eye he saw Talon holding up his hand from underneath a mountain of wreckage. He dug Talon free of his premature grave. Even though he was just as impaired, he slung Talon's arm around his neck and assisted in his walking.

Many feelings emerged as the crew came together. A giant group hug was put in place, with a horde of tears coming from Crystal. "Eric, you did it! You saved everyone! You saved all of Osiren! And Teague!" He gave a sheepish smile.

Talon coughed, "Since the darkness was released, you should be all clean now, pretty boy."

Phoenix started moaning as Eric answered, "I'm an X-demon no more!"

"Phoenix!" exclaimed Crystal wrapping her arms around him.

He grunted as she applied pressure to his sensitive body. His eyes lazily lay over her, almost looking through her existence. "I'm glad to see everyone . . . How does it feel to be the hero?"

Talon cut in, "What happened to all that matter of energy? Once the emeralds were destroyed, where did it go?"

"The darkness must have split between each emerald shard," replied Phoenix.

"If it remains inside each piece . . . would it be possible to put it back together?" asked Crystal.

"Like a puzzle? Possibly, but it'd be impractical. I'm sure the wind will scatter them."

"Besides, no one has time for puzzles," laughed Eric.

Talon observed the flowers at his feet. "Where did the King retreat to? And Gauri?"

"Gauri's corpse should be around here somewhere . . ." answered Phoenix.

"Their bodies are not here; I assume they escaped . . . Actually, no bodies are here. Where are all the corpses? It's like nothing ever happened . . ." Eric dishearteningly stomped on the ground.

Crystal giggled. "Not much of a hero if he leaves no legacy, huh?"

"If my knowledge on the Protectors is correct, then maybe the force that surged through the entire valley sent the spirits that were casted from their bodies into the planet, creating new life for this place to regain the beauty it once had."

"Scorpio was not among the deceased . . . Shouldn't we search for him?" questioned Crystal.

"Why? His lifelong goal, his dream, will never come to fruition. All he lived for is now mere particles. There is nothing left; he's finished."

"Do you think he will resume his role as King of Zannala?"

"Not possible," stated Eric. "His crimes will be discovered. He will most likely be executed for treason."

"No one knows he's behind this entire travesty . . . His wrong-doings may never come to light. We will continue to be blamed."

"I still think we should be certain he will not cause an issue later in life . . ."

"Crystal, we must celebrate the victories we accomplish, as we may never celebrate another. A wise woman taught me that," Phoenix grinned. "And saving the entirety of Teague falls under the category as a win . . . a big win."

The four stayed silent for a bit, experiencing the brand new scenery with fresh eyes. They watched the flowers sway in the breeze. The smell of fresh air sent a relief to the beaten up heroes. Without the idea of destruction or chaos or collecting emeralds, all of them could finally enjoy what existed around them. No one broke the silence until a high-pitch cry shattered their new tranquility.

"Dad!" screamed Alexander as he shuffled down the hillside.

"That's my boy." Eric greeted him halfway, lifting him from his feet and swinging him around. "Thank the Protectors you are unharmed."

Tears brimmed along Alex's lids, "I heard the explosion and-and—"

"I'm okay. *We* are all safe now."

Eric walked his son back toward the group as Crystal said, "Skull's dead, the emeralds are destroyed, and our homes are gone. What happens now?"

"Appears your dreams of moving to Cosarave are over . . ."

"Way to point out the obvious, pretty boy. Do not fret, cupcake, we shall come up with an idea."

Phoenix commented, "We are outlaws in Osiren. We're not welcomed any longer."

"But we are heroes!" exclaimed Eric. "Our crimes should be lifted! Expunged!"

"The citizens never realized they were teetering close to the end of days. Not a soul would believe us," answered Talon.

"Then where shall we go?" Distress was prominent in Crystal's tone.

Phoenix gazed at the horizon of Pleasant Valley Groove. The smell of death and blood lingered in his nose, giving him a calmness he immediately felt nauseous about. "We leave. Bancouver is still likely in chaos from their tyrants; our only choice left is to migrate to Ventaceny. The city of Reshadeo would welcome us until we are stable. Or clear our names."

"After all this . . . I'm still the bad guy who has to flee another country because I'm a fugitive. Will I ever be able to bring the Zaccaro name from the depths of its defamation?"

"Whether or not this was planned, the five of us are officially family," declared Eric, looking at Phoenix. "I may have had my issues at first, but now . . . Phoenix, I'm with you until the end." He offered his hand to help him up. Accepting the offer, he was lifted and greeted with a nod.

"My plans of retirement will have to wait," Talon sighed. "Any hopes of me leaving now are gone. Just like pretty boy here, you are stuck with me like a thorn in your side."

Crystal hugged him by the waist. "I will always be here."

Standing before his family, Phoenix felt his head pound. He collapsed to his bum, chuckling at his own fatigued state. "Perhaps we shall wait until we are in better condition."

Their wounds were much worse than they believed, all agreeing to wait a bit before they decided to move. Phoenix stared up at the smiles before him. He looked beyond them to the sunset filling the sky with its pallet of colors and the remainder of emerald pieces littering the horizon. *Beth, Mother, John, Father— those who lost their lives to the emeralds, I hope I avenged your deaths and you may rest easy beside the Protectors. I will live a life worthy enough for all that cannot.*

Listening to his comrades' banter, Phoenix's attention dropped down to his arm. Then slowly to his wrist. Horror filled his chest. Spider-like webs spread around his hand, stretching for his palm. Eyes flushed with fear, he swiftly shoved it behind his back. With a nervous smile, he locked onto the emerald particles. *This is not the end, is it?*

ABOUT THE AUTHOR

Brandon Hoy was born in the suburbs of Philadelphia. Raised in a more untraditional family in a typical trailer park, he always sought for a means to escape. He began writing at a very young age, starting with his story of receiving his first dog on scrap paper. His passion and interest never ceased as he grew older. Around sixteen, he began a short story. After receiving praise from his friends, he continued working on his piece and turning it into his first published novel, Emerald X. Creating a new immersive world, Brandon hopes another generation will become fascinated in this adventure. He plans to represent every type of a reader throughout his novels. Readers of all ages will be able to connect to and fall in love with the characters, following their growth in a thrilling story from beginning to end.

Brandon has been in the hospitality management and food industry since he was fourteen. Currently working as a restaurant manager and as a part time server, he enjoys being around people. He believes there is something to learn from everyone. Graduating from Methacton High School, he also received his Associates Degree in Liberal Arts from Montgomery County Community College.

Made in the USA
Columbia, SC
15 February 2020